Theodore Brun studied Dark Age archaeology at Cambridge. In 2010, he quit his job as an arbitration lawyer in Hong Kong and cycled 10,000 miles across Asia and Europe to his home in Norfolk. *A Savage Moon* is his fourth novel.

Also by Theodore Brun

A Mighty Dawn
A Sacred Storm
A Burning Sea

A SAVAGE MOON

Theodore Brun

CORVUS

Published in trade paperback in Great Britain in 2023 by Corvus,
an imprint of Atlantic Books Ltd.

10 9 8 7 6 5 4 3 2 1

A CIP catalogue record for this book is available from the British Library.

Trade Paperback ISBN: 978 1 78649 612 6
E-book ISBN: 978 1 78649 614 0

Printed in Great Britain by TJ Books Limited, Padstow, Cornwall

Corvus
An imprint of Atlantic Books Ltd
Ormond House
26–27 Boswell Street
London
WC1N 3JZ

www.atlantic-books.co.uk

MIX
Paper from
responsible sources
FSC® C013056

For my old friend Will.

The light shines in the darkness. And you were first to point me towards it.

Thence come the maidens mighty in wisdom,
Three from the dwelling down 'neath the tree;
Urth is one named, Verthandi the next, –
On the wood they scored, – and Skuld the third.
Laws they made there, and life allotted
To the sons of men, and set their fates.

From 'Völuspá', Stanza 20.

CAST OF CHARACTERS

IN THE CITY OF BYZANTIUM:

Erlan Aurvandil – the 'Shining Wanderer', a crippled warrior of the north, lately in service to the Byzantine Emperor.

Lilla Sviggarsdottír – the exiled Queen of the Twin Kingdoms, a Sveär by blood, and only surviving kin of Sviggar Ívarsson, the murdered King of Sveäland.

Emperor Leo III, the Isaurian – Basileus of the Byzantines and victor of the Great Arab Siege of Byzantium.

General Arbasdos – *Strategos* of the Armeniac Theme and *kouropalatēs*, the second most powerful man in the empire and Leo's personal ally, who once held the Wanderer as a slave.

Princess Anna – the Basilopoúla, oldest child of Emperor Leo, and young wife of General Arbasdos.

Einar the Fat-Bellied – Erlan's comrade in arms, a Sveär still loyal to the kin of Sviggar the Bastard.

Orīana – an actress and star of the Hippodrome, and Einar's lover.

Marta – her daughter, a novice nun.

THE REMNANT CREW OF THE *FASOLT*:

Demetrios – a Greek helmsman, who joined them in Varna.

Mikkel Crow – an Estlander river-man.

Snodin – de facto skipper during the Arab siege, also an
  Estlander.

Ran – a Gotlander.

Black Svali – an Estlander shipwright.

Vili, known as 'Bull' – the youngest and biggest of the
  Estlanders.

Dreng, Krok & Kunrith – their crew mates

IN THE CITY OF ROME:

Katāros – the disgraced High Chamberlain of the Imperial
  Palace or *parakoimōmenos*. A eunuch of northern origin
  and traitor to the empire.

Dom Vittorio Massimo – a judge of the city.

Antoninus – Dom Massimo's personal secretary.

Justus – steward of the Palazzo Massimo.

Emilius – a merchant.

Peter, Duke of Rome – the chief administrator of the city.

Brother Narduin – a Frankish pilgrim.

IN THE KINGDOM OF THE FRANKS:

Karil Martel – Duke (dux) of Austrasia, eldest surviving son
  of Pepin of Herstal and leader of the Austrasian nobles
  against the Merovingian king, Chilperic. Later known
  as 'the Hammer'.

Childebrand – a Frankish nobleman, illegitimate son of
  Pepin of Herstal and brother of Duke Karil.

Wynfred of Nursling – an Anglo-Saxon missionary. Known as 'Wyn'.

Berengar, son of Berulf – a Frankish trapper.

Alvarik the One Eyed – a shaman and leader of the cult of *Báleygr* – 'the Flaming Eye'.

Fenna – a Frisian girl.

A Savage Moon

FRISI

Dort

AUSTRASIA •K

Two-Rivers

•Mettis

NEUSTRIA

IMMERWALD

INNER SEA

VOYAGE OF THE FASOLT

0   200   400 miles

0   250   500 km

PART ONE

Urðr

The Threads of What Was

CHAPTER ONE

She smells pine needles, and death.

The sweet, damp scent of the forest litter. A scent so unmistakably of the north that she knows she must be dreaming. She feels the warm earth beneath her feet, its touch familiar to her as her father's embrace. Even in the dream, her heart aches with a sudden pang of longing.

For home.

So far away. And yet, in the dream, near as her hands and feet.

There has been rain not long past. And now she sees the pines around her, their branches close enough to reach up and touch. Droplets of water still cling to the tip of each needle. She brushes them, her fingertips scattering tiny jewels of light to the ground. There is no hurry. She is at peace. As she always has been in the Kingswood, close to her father's hall.

The hall that was torn from my grasp.

This thought enters her mind like a splinter. But the forest air is still. Her footsteps tread softly in the earth. The light is dim, though she cannot tell whether it's the gloaming of dusk or else the grey before the dawn. She glances up again and the tops of the trees now seem far away. Far as the great vaulted dome of the Holy Wisdom. Far as the heavens. Yet dark as them, too.

No light penetrates their branches, only shadows seeping through like a mist, filtering down to her from on high.

Now that other smell grows stronger. Sickly sweet, like rancid meat.

She is following a trail through bracken. A deer trail, maybe. There were often deer in the Kingswood. Some animal has been this way, anyway. She knows this place, knows where it leads. To the Great Ash. To *her* ash. The one tree in all her father's kingdom which, as a girl, she could make believe might be Yggdrasil itself – the ancient World-Ash and the bridge between the world of men and many others. Later, when a woman grown, she went there to breathe in the smoke of Urtha's Weed, thinking herself wise, and skilled enough to journey between them, like a *vala* of the Old Times. Now she knows better. Now she is wise enough only to know her own ignorance.

The smell of death becomes a stench. She covers her mouth. A low hum invades the silence, dull at first but growing louder, and louder still, till the sound fills her ears. Fills her skull. Flies buzzing. Hundreds of them, thousands. All come for a feast, swirling about her head like the sands of some desert storm in a spice-merchant's tale.

Then she sees it – a great hulking shadow in the dismal gloom. A monstrous beast, its outline blurred in the hungering dark, a huge muscular back, spiked with hair stiff as thorns, head bent low to some busy work. A boar, she now sees, and over the buzzing of the flies she hears a repulsive, eager gulping as the boar scarfs down... something.

She cannot make out what.

She circles the clearing until, through the swarming flies, she is able to spy what the boar feasts upon. Another creature of the forest. A large grey wolf stretched out under the boar, its lifeless limbs jerking with each thrust of the brutish snout as the boar burrows hungrily into its innards.

She halts, revolted, yet gripped by the weirdness of the scene. She wants to turn away but cannot. And as she looks, the vision becomes stranger still. The shape of the wolf corpse begins to change, like a long, lean sculpture of wax, melting away, resolving into something new. Now she could not have torn away her gaze though her life were the forfeit.

For where before she saw a wolf lies now the wasted body of a man. Naked, limbs withered, face gaunt. And worse, a face she knows. The long black and grey hair, the blunt edge of the jaw, the strong crooked nose.

Father.

The word ghosts over her lips as the boar gives the corpse another shunt. His head flops over, his dead eyes fix on her. Calling to her. Accusing her...

Where are you, my daughter?

She recoils, her belly filling with horror. A stick snaps underfoot. The boar lifts its head. For a long moment, they regard one another – woman and beast – the air between them filled with the boar's grating pants, the coarse bristles of its snout glistening with her father's blood. And as she looks, the animal's long, thin lips curl into a sneer, moving as though in human speech, a whisper in her ear:

Whatever you have, I will take from you…

Queen Lilla Sviggarsdottír sat up suddenly, pulse thudding in her temple. Her long hair hung like a funeral veil over her eyes, dishevelled and clammy with sweat.

For a few seconds she stared wildly through the tangle of honey-gold strands, panting as if she'd run a league, forcing herself to take in the pale cream curtains, the thick marble pillars flanking the muslin drape across the doorway, its folds riffling with the breeze off the Bosporus. She smelled cedarwood and cinnamon. And the scent of the man beside her.

'Are you all right, my love?' His voice cracked the darkness, his breath close to her cheek.

Erlan.

It didn't seem long since that had been her question to ask of him – when the fever had had him in its grip. *Are you all right?* Which really meant: *Are you still alive?*

Too often, she had feared he was not.

She nodded at his shadow, unable to do more as the terror of her dream leached from her mind. This was her present, she told herself. This was her now. And yet she heard the echo of those words:

Whatever you have, I will take from you…

Words from her past. Words that the man who usurped her kingdom had hissed in her ear as he thrust her face down into the fresh earth of her husband's grave.

She brushed aside her hair, sank back into the goose-down pillows and expelled a long sigh. 'I'm... I'm fine.'

'You were dreaming again.' Erlan was propped on one elbow beside her, his dark eyes still luminous in the shadows of night, even though the sickness had stolen much of their lustre. He reached out and chased a last lock of hair from her face. 'Was it the same?'

'Yes. The boar... and my father.'

'I'm sorry... that it troubles you so.'

'Of course it troubles me,' she answered quickly. 'It's four months since you told me it was time to go home.' She sat up, drawing her knees to her chin under the silk coverlet. 'Yet here we still are.' She knew she sounded cold. She couldn't help it. The well of her sympathy was deep. But even the deepest well could run dry.

'I can't help that I was sick—'

'You know I don't mean that.' Still her tone was sharper than she intended. After all, Erlan had come within a blade's edge of death. The wounds he had taken on that night of fire had festered. It had needed all the skill of the emperor's best physicians to keep his feet from the Hel-road. Looking at his sunken eyes, his hollow cheeks, it was doubtful whether even now he was quite well. 'I'm not blaming you. I just...' She shook her head. '*We* must go back. I owe it to my father's memory. And to the oath I swore to my husband.'

'Your father's memory has waited this long. Wherever he is, he can wait a little longer,' he said, his voice a croak. 'As for Ringast, you owe him nothing.'

She stared at him in the dark. 'How can you – of all people

– think so little of an oath?' *Gods, hadn't he made her suffer for his own?*

Erlan jerked upright, fully awake now. He reached across her to a cup and the pitcher of watered wine on the stand beside the bed. He poured it out, gulped down a couple of mouthfuls. 'Oath or none, you heard what the emperor said. He has nothing to spare you. No gold, no men.'

The disappointment of her last audience with Emperor Leo still lingered, sour as rancid milk. Leo the Isaurian, third of his name, now hailed the Great Lion of the City. Saviour of the Faith, the Anointed of God. She frowned, remembering how her appeal had fallen on deaf ears. *It is a time to rebuild,* Leo had said. *For the city to breathe. And you, too, my lady. Wait till the spring… then we will talk again.*

'We still have the crew,' she said, fumbling for some thread that would still hold. 'And the *Fasolt*, thank the gods.' Although the last time she'd seen him, her helmsman Demetrios had said the ship was in need of some upkeep if they were to make any voyage north again. As usual he was evasive on the details.

'It's not enough though, is it?' Erlan offered her the cup but she refused it with a flick of her hand. This argument was stale, each time they had it more frustrating than the last. 'Even if we made it back, what then?'

'The longer Thrand holds the Twin Kingdoms, the harder it will be to take them from him. He's destroying Sveäland. The dream—'

'You don't know that for certain,' he said, his voice clipped with impatience. 'Dream or none.' He threw the rest of the wine down his throat and sagged back into the pillow. As if

8

even impatience was too heavy a burden for him to bear for long.

'I feel it. That's enough for me.'

Thrand was the last surviving son of King Harald Wartooth. Brother to her own dead husband, and the man who had taken from her the throne, her lands... *and worse*. Thrand hated her people as much as she loved them. She feared to think what he had done to her beloved homeland.

'You know I want to help you, Lilla. But we'd need an army to stand any chance against Thrand and his hirds. Not a dozen ale-sot river-men and a leaky boat.' He gave a snort of disgust. 'By the Hanged! Gerutha's dead. Einar's dead. Aska is dead...' His words trailed away, and for a moment it felt as if the ghosts of their friends – her murdered servant, his fallen comrade, even his wretched dog – filled the silence between them. When he spoke again, it was barely more than a whisper. 'Maybe it's time that—'

'What?' she snapped. 'Time that I give it up?'

'Yes,' he said, his voice as tender as it was insistent. 'Make peace that we are here and Thrand is there, and...'

'And what?'

'And that Sveäland is lost to you.'

'How can you say that? We agreed—'

'I know what we agreed.' He rubbed at his temples, squeezing his eyelids shut, as if he could crush all the thoughts racing behind them. 'I wanted to go back... Part of me still does. But... maybe I have to accept there's nothing left for me in the north either. Those ships were burned a long time ago.'

This was the voice of defeat. It sat ill on the tongue of Erlan Aurvandil, the 'Shining Wanderer'... *Shining no more,* she thought, feeling at once sorry and angry at him. *Like a sun that has dimmed.*

But she understood whence his reluctance came. She knew all of him now. He had held nothing back. In his shoes, would she want to return? Or would she hesitate, too?

She reached out, traced a fingertip down the scar on his cheek. His eyes opened, flicked up to hers. Those dark eyes that still saw right through her. 'I can't let it go, Erlan. I can't dream the same dream every night. This place is a gilded cage. I'll go mad if I stay here.'

'Then at least wait,' he said. 'It's too late in the year to leave now anyway. The land would be ice-locked before we reached halfway home. Who knows? By spring the emperor might feel more secure. He may help us like he said.'

'I saved his daughter. So did you. If Leo doesn't feel the weight of that debt now, he never will.'

'I'm telling you, have patience.'

Patience? She snorted. 'You don't want me to wait. You want me to give it up.'

'Well, is that so wrong?' he exclaimed. 'By the Hanged, don't you know how much I love you, Lilla? I don't want to lose you, not now I have you. I've lost everything else… *Everything.*' He raked his fingers through his hair. 'Besides… we'd be walking into a bear trap.'

'You don't know what the Weavers of Fate intend.'

'Nothing good,' he snarled. 'They never do. That much I know.'

'The fates of men are graven on the World Tree,' she murmured. 'I must return – even if it means death.'

'*Why* must you return…? So you have bad dreams.' He

10

tapped his own skull. 'You should try sleeping a night in my head.' A tear glinted in the corner of his eye like a jewel, then fell in a silver trail down his cheek. He knuckled his brow, squeezing his eyes shut again. 'These thoughts, so many terrible, mad thoughts. I see fire and blood and rage. Ringing steel... and death.'

'My love.' She reached out, put a soothing hand to his face. 'My love...'

'I don't need your sympathy.' He palmed away the tear. 'I just need you to give this up.'

'I can't. I will not—'

'I don't understand.' Suddenly he sat bolt upright, more alive than she'd seen him in weeks, seizing her hands. 'Why this urgency? Why this obsession with regaining what he took from you? Tell me! *Why*? I need to know.'

He squeezed her fingers so tight it hurt. As if physical pain could make her forget the wrong done to her. Could make her forgive.

'Because,' she hissed, her voice cold as the northern snows, '... he raped me. The boar in my dream is *Thrand*... He raped me.'

The words hung there between them, vomited up from inside her at last. And into the void left behind them rushed pain and shame and fury. Erlan did not move. She saw his dark eyes flash with incomprehension... and then fill with pity. Which stung her far worse.

'He raped me.' She could speak more calmly now. 'And I mean to make him pay for it. For that, my love, I will not wait.'

CHAPTER TWO

Gravel crunched uncertainly under Erlan's boot.

His mere presence in the imperial gardens felt like a stain on them as he limped like an intruder past rows of perfectly manicured spice-beds, low hedges with corners cut sharp as blocks of marble, spreading cedar trees, pergolas heaving under their winding vines. It was a place of peace. Of order, of design. And here he was, an alien. An agent of chaos. Of destruction and death.

Was that the inevitable course of a warrior? Each cut of the blade carrying him into a deeper sense of dissonance with the world around him. He had certainly come to feel it in this place.

Even so, he came here often. It was here that he had buried his dog. He had lain Aska's body in a hole under the shadow of the sea-wall with as much reverence as he would a fallen comrade, marking the spot with a bit of broken stone which any visitor to the garden might have thought fallen from the wall above.

Aska was his secret.

He knelt down in the earth before the stone and closed his eyes, the scent of the nearby laurel bushes filling his nostrils.

Funny, that a dog had come to mean so much to him. That the loss of him was as painful as any Erlan had endured. Sure, Aska had saved his life once and been a faithful companion to his end. But maybe it was more than the dog he'd lost. Maybe something of himself had died with Aska and lay here in the ground. Some part of him that bound him to the north. Here, too, he remembered Kai – his blood-brother whose laugh he could still hear if he closed his eyes. And the scar burned across his heart like a branding-mark when he thought of Inga. Sister. Lover. Mother of his child. All three and yet nothing but bones in the black earth of Vendlagard now. Even his blade, Wrathling, the famed ring-sword of his people – a hero's sword – which had served his forefathers so well. Served him no less. Lying on the sea-bed now, under the Bosporus's shifting currents. And there it would lie until the Ragnarok. Perhaps part of him would lie with it until the Final Fires too.

Aye, there were many things to remember.

Each death diminished him, stripping him limb by limb until he no longer knew who he was. Two lives. Two names. Erlan. Hakan. But which was he?

Who was he?

Perhaps neither now. Perhaps there was a third man buried deep inside him, under the caked blood of a hundred deaths, lost in the cacophony of a thousand screams, trying to find his way out.

His eyes closed, his fingers dug into the loamy soil of the

seed-bed, and he listened. Listened to the gentle rush of the wind through the crenellations of the sea-wall, to the trilling calls of the turtle-doves which fluttered among the tops of the ornamental trees, to the faint crunch of a gardener's footsteps elsewhere in the gardens as he toiled to keep all around them beautiful and serene.

Yet, behind it, softer still, he heard the ring of steel, the rending of shields, the dull sound of ripping flesh. It was always there. The skirling winds of Skogul's storm.

The truth was he was tired. Part of him still longed to return, to see his father again, to feel those strong arms pulling him close, to smell the familiar tang of salt and sweat fused into his woollen tunic. But another part – that unknown part – felt like he had already died.

Had he not earned his rest? What was glory or victory worth if it did not win a man the right to rest? To cease the slaughter. To lie down and breathe. If only for a while. Long enough for that third man to dig his way out.

That was all he wanted.

And yet now Lilla's burden had become his.

After the first rush of her anger, her tears had come. He had held her, listening to the grim details come pouring from her lips, feeling her rage infecting him like a fever, as if her blood was somehow coursing through his veins, filling his muscles and his limbs, until he had to thrust her away from him and get up and pace the room, so smothering was the violence he felt for Thrand.

It was too much for him to bear – too much for her – this weight of vengeance. A burden so great that it was bound to crush them both. To destroy their love…

14

Aye, he thought ruefully. *If love is what we have.* He wasn't so sure anymore.

Everything in him was a blunt edge. Every feeling, every thought. He was a blade that had seen one too many battles. Nicked and notched and dull. He wondered what it would take to become sharp again. To love with passion. To live with purpose. To stand up, to shout, to run—

Piss on it, he snorted to himself. He never had been much of a runner.

From somewhere behind him came the sound of footsteps on the gravel. Faint at first, but drawing closer, purposeful. A soldier's gait. He glanced over his shoulder towards the main path and saw two guards dressed in white cloaks with purple trim talking to the gardener. Excubitors – the so-called 'Sentinels' who guarded the imperial palace. He watched from the shadow of the wall as the gardener raised a grubby hand and pointed in his direction.

Discovered, then.

He sighed and turned back to Aska's grave, knowing time was short, staring down at the stone. And behind the tramp of the Sentinels' sandals, other words came into his mind, soft and unbidden. The words of the Vala, words that had haunted him since the night she spoke them:

You will bear much pain, you Chosen Son – but you will never break. You will fall and rise again.

Some men might take them as a curse. For him, they were a promise. Of life.

...In the end, life.

'My lord Aurvandil,' said a voice behind him, gruff and formal.

Erlan turned and acknowledged the two Sentinels with a nod. 'What is it?' he said in Greek, a tongue that was second nature to him now.

'His Holy Majesty, Emperor Leo, third of his name, commands that you attend him.'

'When?'

'At once, my lord.'

Erlan grunted. Of course. If an emperor wants to see you, could there be any other answer? 'Very well, kentarch. Give me a moment.'

The kentarch hesitated, perhaps deliberating for a second. Then he gave a curt nod of acquiescence and the pair withdrew a few paces to the main path. Erlan turned to bid Aska farewell.

'I will fall... and rise again,' he murmured to himself, laying his hand gently on the stone. 'Unlike you, old friend. Rest well.'

Aye. For Lilla's sake, he must rise again.

One day there might come a time for him to rest. *But not today.*

Erlan got to his feet, dusted off his knees.

Not yet.

CHAPTER THREE

Far above the eunuch, a panoply of stars glistened out of the black like a scattering of diamonds. Like the diamonds that should have been his. *Would* have been his, were it not for one man.

Erlan Aurvandil.

Katāros breathed the Northman's name to the pitiless night like a prayer. As if his hatred could become a physical thing and fly like an arrow-shaft through the heavens, searching the earth till it found its mark. But for *him*, the City would have fallen. But for him, Katāros's revenge would have been complete. But for him, glory and riches.

But for him…

The sea was calm now. A calm which, after the violence of the storms, seemed to mock at the eunuch's fate.

The Caliph's forces had finally withdrawn a year to the day after they had first laid siege to Byzantium. And Katāros had been forced to leave with them. After all, his betrayal of the emperor and the City was too widely known for him to stay; he had chosen his side, and chosen poorly. By then, the Arabs were a ragged, broken force, slinking away from Byzantium's unbreached walls like a whipped dog with its tail between its legs. Prince Maslama's armies had been starved and smashed. The Caliph's fleet bottled up and ground down to a husk of what it had been – the emperor's fire-runners had seen to that. Even so, when the Arab fleet quit Byzantium, it numbered nearly a hundred ships, the men aboard fleeing at least to fight another day.

What they hadn't known was that disaster was to be added to the shame of their defeat. The storm fell on them like the fist of God somewhere in the south Aegean. The fleet was scattered. Many were lost.

But somehow, not Katāros. He had been spared... at least so far.

And yet, he was helpless. Helpless and powerless, a pitiable creature under the great vault of God's sky, adrift now in the eastern Inner Sea. Its dark waters lapped against the piece of broken decking on which he lay, and had lain for two days. His sole comfort was that he would not have to lay there many days more. For there could be only two outcomes for him, and one of them would not be long in coming. Either thirst would drive him into madness and thence into the arms of death. Or else a passing ship must pluck him from this solitary fate. A fate as stark as it was simple.

No one else on that ship had survived, he was certain of that. The storms had been relentless, ceaseless... *unnatural*. Or maybe supernatural. For even a man as faithless as Katāros could discern in those whirling gales God's grim judgement against the heirs of the Prophet. Prince Maslama and his Arab host had boasted of so much, believed so much. They would win the whole world to the Prophet's cause! And yet what had they accomplished? Nothing, except the utter destruction of the mightiest combined force of land and sea that the world had ever known.

Failure. *Total* failure... and now Maslama and the rest of those peacocking fools had dragged him down with them. He, who had been the brightest star in the empire, whose beauty knew no rival, even among the finest courtesans of the City. He had made his choice. Thanks to the Northman, it was the wrong one. Providence had been unforgiving of his mistake.

A shiver rippled through Katāros's salt-raw limbs as he recalled the horrors of the storm. Weak, wounded, hungry men had been cast into the water. Ship had been flung against ship with brutal force, then swallowed up into the maw of the insatiable sea.

How had *he* survived?

Katāros could no more account for that than any other occurrence in this senseless world. Blessings and curses, favour and infamy – the shadow of these fell over a man like clouds skudding with the wind, whoever he was, whatever he did.

The Lord gives, and the Lord takes away, he thought bitterly. So prated the priests in every basilica of the City. What cringing fool would worship such a fickle god? But whether he longed for death or for life, this capricious Deity – the Great Equivocator in the heavens – gave to him neither.

Night turned to day again.

His throat was swollen, each breath sibilant as a cobra's hiss. The old wound between his legs, the great absence there, stung like a branding from the saltwater.

Hours passed. His ears rang. His listless body rose and fell with the swell of the sea. The sun coursed by like a great eye of judgement overhead.

And then...

...*Something else.*

Some other sound now, prodding at his callused senses. Faint as a whisper. Gentle as a promise.

His chest rumbled then with a mirthless laugh, too weak to escape his salt-swelled throat. He heard voices. The clunk of wood. Splashes in the water. And all he could think was: *I'm still here, you bastard... still alive.*

Though whether he addressed God or the Devil or only himself, he could not have said.

The first two days Katāros could do little but lay out on the fore-deck in the shade of a scrap of old hemp-cloth flapping in the breeze. It made for a contemptible shelter, but still it kept the worst of the sun off him. He lay with his eyes closed, listening to a gruff voice speaking now and then in a dialect he couldn't understand. Eventually, when he could bear to open his eyes a little he discovered he was aboard a small fishing boat, barely ten strides from bow to stern, hardly four gunwale to gunwale across its belly, and the voice belonged to its captain.

The man was wind-bronzed with a greying beard and a white head-cloth wound round his head against the sun.

He was often grunting orders at his two young crewmen. He looked to be Latin by blood, while the boys were darker-skinned and wore only simple tunics that stopped at the knee. It was they who took turns caring for Katāros when all he could do was lie there, helpless as a newborn. One of them was almost tender, resting Katāros's head in his lap, smoothing down his long hair, even caressing his cheek, as he murmured an old song of the sea and tried to coax stale water down his throat.

On the third morning, after a long and heavy sleep, Katāros was ready to speak.

He sat up, feeling at once a dizzy rush of blood from his head. He clutched his knees to steady himself and waited for his vision to clear.

'Ho-hoa! Look there, lads, our siren awakes!' cried the skipper, in a rough dialect of the Greek tongue.

Above Katāros, the wind rapped at the sail. He smelled the reek of unwashed tuna casks. 'Where… where are you taking me?' Each word scraped out of his throat.

'Pete's bones, don't worry your head about that! Least for now. Here.' The fisherman seized a skin and tossed it over, landing it in the eunuch's lap. 'Drink!'

Katāros stared stupidly down at the skin, his long black hair hanging like ropes about his face.

'Well, go on, woman, drink it,' urged the fisherman. 'It'll do you good.'

'I… I am no woman.' The pitch of his voice was still high, floating in that nowhere place between the sexes. But by God, his throat was raw, the sea air having scoured the smooth timbre of his voice to a rusty croak.

'No woman?' The fisherman frowned, doubtless taking in the fine bone structure of the eunuch's hairless jaw, his thin, straight nose, the salt-stiff cataracts of dark hair. Hard to disbelieve the evidence of your own eyes, and Katāros recognised in the man's gaze the barely veiled suspicion which he had seen in so many eyes before. 'You must forgive me, friend. Only, when the lads cleaned you up—'

'I am neither man nor woman,' Katāros cut him off, irked to be explaining himself to some lowly fisherman. 'I am... what I am.'

The other gave a decisive nod. 'Well, makes no odds with me, my friend... Still, no offence meant. Anyhow, drink up, drink up. You need to build up your strength.'

'My thanks to you. To all of you.' Katāros raised his creaking voice past the old man to the two youths lurking in the stern. Their eyes were riveted on him. 'I suppose I should be dead.'

'That you should! But seems the hand of providence scooped you up to some good purpose. God's will 'n all that.' The fisherman touched a little amulet hanging around his neck.

God's will? Katāros took a deep draught on the skin to conceal his scowl. The wine was heavily diluted – a sailor's drink to quench the thirst, not the rich, dark grape of the emperor's table he was used to.

'There's flatbread, too. And dried hake when you're ready.'

'In a while.' Katāros took another long pull. Mother of God, he could have drunk an ocean. And so he drank and drank, feeling the eyes of all three on him, until his stomach could take no more.

'Better?' grinned the old fellow.

'Some,' he gasped, licking dry his painfully sun-cracked lips. 'So then, friend. Where *are* we headed?'

'Isle of Malta. And with this wind, we should be in harbour by noon tomorrow.'

'Malta? Christ's blood!' The two boys crossed themselves at his blasphemy. The old man touched his damned amulet again. For once, Katāros might have done the same. Malta was six, maybe seven hundred miles west of where the storms had hit the Arab fleet. The aftermath winds and currents must have carried him past the island of Crete and onward for another five hundred miles or more as he clung like a barnacle to his scrap of decking.

'Was it far away your vessel foundered?'

Katāros hummed vaguely. 'Far indeed.' All three of them were leaned forward over their knees, wanting more. But he had no inclination to tell them more than was necessary. 'I'm afraid I'm no sailor so I couldn't tell you exactly. All I know is we were in the southern Aegean... Is Malta your final destination?' he said, deflecting from the subject.

'Aye, for now. Home harbour is Massala in the south-east. We'll be there ten days or so to refit, then we sail back east.'

'You wouldn't believe the mass of tunny-fish to be had west of Kithira late summer,' volunteered the older youth from his seat by the tiller.

'I've no doubt,' returned Katāros with a flicker of a smile and a flash of his dark brown eyes. Although he had no interest in the comings and goings of a few wretched fish.

He was thinking of Malta. That was still imperial territory. And although the chance that word of his treachery to the emperor had reached there was vanishingly small, he wanted to be certain of his anonymity. Recognition would be disastrous. The very idea evoked precise mental images for him – of sharp blades and severed noses; fingers or ears, or God knows which body parts falling to the floor. He of all people knew how the Byzantines were fond of such measures of correction.

Meanwhile, the fisherman's weather-lined eyes had narrowed at him. 'Where you from, friend? You don't look Greek. And you're surely no Arab.'

'Varna,' Katāros lied. It was a port on the western shore of the Euxine Sea. A place suitably far removed from the truth. 'You know it?'

'Heard of it.' The fisherman gave a low whistle. 'Pete's bones, you're a long way from there.'

With one lie told, others came more easily. 'I was agent to a Bulgar merchant who had trade in Crete. The storm caught us on the last leg into Heraklion. That was four days ago, I think... maybe longer.'

'Not without fresh water, wouldn't be. Or we'd have been pulling your corpse out the drink. You the only survivor?'

'I don't know.'

The fisherman grunted, scratching thoughtfully at the thick curls of his beard. At length, he seemed to make up his mind and thrust out a hand. 'The name's Elias. These here are my boys, Tomas and Andreas.' The boys nodded, the younger venturing a shy smile. 'And *you* are damned lucky – whoever you are, wherever you're from.'

24

So now he had their names. In return, no doubt they expected his. Katāros searched for something generic. Something forgettable. 'They call me Markos.'

'Well then, Markos. Can't promise you much when we make land. A change of clothes, maybe. Enough coin for a night or two at an inn. After that, your best bet is to find your way to Melita.'

'Melita?'

'The main town on the island.'

'Forget Melita,' piped up Tomas, the older son. 'With a ring like that one, you could buy passage at least as far as Byzantium. My guess is it'd see you all the way home to Varna.' The boy was staring greedily at Katāros's hand, where, on his middle finger, he still wore a thick gold ring. It was the official seal of the *parakoimōmenos* – the High Chamberlain of the Imperial Bedchamber, and one of the most powerful offices in the empire. An office, it need hardly be said, he held no longer.

Instinctively, he turned the seal inside his knuckle.

Seeing this, Elias snapped at his son, 'No one asked for your opinion, boy.'

'The lad means no harm.' Katāros smiled at the prying little weasel. 'Anyway, he's right. I must use what little I have to return home.'

Home...

There was another lie. The word had no meaning for him. Not now. Not ever.

'Let's see how things fall when we reach harbour,' said Elias. 'I'll ask around. Massala is only a small place but there may be more imperial ships stopping in the bay now the

25

siege of the Great City has lifted… O' course, you must know all about that.'

Katāros's eyes shifted between the father and his boys, a sudden instinct for survival pricking him to tread warily. 'Of course. We wouldn't have had clear passage through the straits if it had not.'

Elias grinned encouragingly. 'Go on! What more can you tell?'

'Oh, little enough. We stopped only briefly in Chalcedon to take on water and provisions. One of the port officials told me the Arab fleet had withdrawn not a week before. They took what was left of their army with them.'

'We heard it was the Bulgars that really did for 'em,' said Elias, mopping the sweat from his neck with a filthy rag. 'That true?'

'Did for them?' exclaimed Tomas excitedly. 'They butchered them to a man, is what we heard!' He was grinning from ear to ear, the blood-thirsty brat.

'Not quite to a man, as I understand it,' corrected Katāros. 'But I heard their mounted warriors were effective.' Indeed, he thought bitterly to himself, the Bulgar horde had proved quite the ally to Emperor Leo in the end, although Katāros was loath to admit it. Remembering that it was Erlan Aurvandil who had secured their alliance nettled him worst of all.

Perhaps it was his body's way of shutting out the unwelcome memory of it all, but he felt a wave of exhaustion wash over him, the wine suddenly filling his head. 'Listen, friends, I would be happy to share what else I know. But my head is throbbing, you see, and—'

26

'Say no more,' cut in Elias. 'And God forgive our damn fool questions! Only news is harder to come by than a shoal of swordfish in this line of work, see?'

'Nothing to forgive,' murmured Katāros. He lay back on the matting that served as his bed and stretched himself out under the little patch of shade.

Elias reached out and patted his knee. 'Rest good, my friend. Then eat your fill... you're safe now.'

Katāros closed his eyes.

Safe?

Alive, yes. But he would never be truly safe until he was well beyond the reach of the long arm of the emperor's justice. Drowning would be a mercy compared to what that Isaurian brute would mete out on him, should he ever fall into his hands.

And yet, even if he got clear, what dangers might await him beyond the empire's dominion – a penniless eunuch, weak in body, without a friend in the world, and only his wits to protect him?

Safe? No, indeed. He doubted that.

CHAPTER FOUR

Erlan found the emperor in his private quarters high up in the Daphne wing of the Great Palace, where the mid-morning sun was streaming into the chamber in golden cataracts of light. Leo the Isaurian, third of his name, was bent over his blue-grey desk of Tuscan marble like any imperial accountant, knuckles pressed white on its surface. Strewn before him was a mess of scrolls and parchments.

As he entered, Erlan couldn't help but mark how ordinary the man looked without his imperial raiment of purple robes and golden diadems. From where he stood, he could see the bald patch spreading from the crown of the Great Lion's head of dark curls. And when he looked up, how the grey around his temples had bloomed this last year. Like lichen on damp walls.

His eyes were still young, though. Young and thorough and commanding.

'Aurvandil. Come in.' The emperor indicated the silver pitcher and a couple of blue glass chalices rimmed with gold on a side-table against the far wall. 'Help yourself. And one for me. I've a thirst like a camel trader on me.'

Erlan obliged. 'Majesty.'

Leo looked up from his desk and took the chalice Erlan had proffered him. He took a sip. 'Mother of God, Northman! You're supposed to cut the stuff with water or I'll be drunk as a monk before noon.' He pointed at a little earthenware jug, also on the tray. 'There... Ah, no matter, no matter now! Here, sit.' He indicated a stone chair with no back placed before his desk.

Erlan took his seat, unable to prevent himself stealing a glance at the pillar to his right. That was where he had cradled this man's bleeding head in his lap, wondering whether he would live or die.

That was where I drank his blood, he remembered.

Strange where the Norns' weaving led a man.

Leo took another gulp of wine and settled back into his chair. 'How's the hip?'

'Better.'

'The most curious thing, how the smallest wounds can prove the most deadly.'

'Almost deadly,' Erlan corrected him.

'Indeed! Heaven be praised.' Leo shot a glance skyward.

The wound had only been the rake of an arrow-tip across his hip. Little more than a scratch. Yet the infection had swelled into a hideous bulging purple and black abscess, for weeks suppurating an oily yellow pus. He had been delirious for much of it, a fever from which, were it not for the skills of Leo's personal physician, and Lilla's constant vigilance, he might never have woken.

Leo nodded. 'You have suffered much for my cause. I'll not forget it. Nor have I forgotten the terms of your service.'

'The siege is long over. My vow to you fulfilled.'

'And now you serve your queen.' Leo sucked his teeth and stood, moving to the doorway that gave out over the Hippodrome and its myriad arches. The tallest of the obelisks that formed the spine of the great amphitheatre was just visible over its walls, the inlaid gold in the stone flashing in the sunlight. 'How is she, by the way?'

'She'll overcome her disappointment, if that's what you mean… With time.'

The emperor had grace enough to give an equivocal grunt. 'An unfortunate business – her being caught up in the eunuch's deception.' He took another swig on his wine. 'Pity he escaped.' He turned and looked Erlan in the eye. 'And a shame I can't help her… Of course, I would like to. But expedience binds my hand, you see.'

'A man in your position has to be practical.'

'Exactly! That's exactly it.'

'Queen Lilla understands your position.'

'Good, very good. I'm glad… Christ's blood! Is it such torment to remain here?' He threw out his hand at the honeycomb facade of the Hippodrome, looming over the palace with monstrous grandeur. 'Look out there. This is the centre of the world! The jewel in the empire's crown! Here, she has everything she could ever need. Let her stay, for the love of Christ, let her stay… we will treat her with every honour.'

Erlan knew well what honour Leo had in mind. Lilla had told him that Leo had as good as proposed marriage to her when he feared his own wife was dying. But the Empress

Maria had lived, and, more than that, had now borne a male heir for Leo. A cub for the Great Lion. That was a feat beyond Lilla.

'This city is a wonder,' Erlan admitted. 'But it's not her home.'

'Did she not come here to make an alliance?'

'In that, she accepts her failure.'

Leo looked at Erlan, his tongue running over his lips. 'As I said, I wish I could help her.' He lifted his chalice and jabbed it accusingly at Erlan. 'The irony is that *you* are the reason I cannot.'

'Me?'

'You've damn near beggared the empire with your wild promises to that Bulgar rogue.' Leo picked up a piece of vellum unfurled on his desk and flapped it at Erlan. 'Khan Tervel writes to remind me of what I owe him.' He shook his head. 'Three times the annual tribute for this year alone! Oh, and the small matter of the two additional years we failed to pay before I took up the purple. By the blood of all the martyrs, he means to have near a million solidi off us!' he cried. 'Did you have any idea what you were committing us to?'

The truth was Erlan would have promised the fat Khan – whose avarice was only matched by his gluttony – double if it meant the Bulgars would honour the treaty. 'The Bulgar horde came. The city stands. The Arabs are gone. That was surely worth any price.'

'Easily said, Aurvandil, easily said. But now we have to pay the singer for his song.'

'Can't you delay payment?'

'And risk turning an ally into an enemy?' Leo scratched

31

irritably at the thinning patch of hair on his crown. 'No. The siege may be over, but I can't afford a war on two fronts. The Caliph's remaining armies are still harrying our cities in the east.' He pulled out another scroll from the pile, this one a map. The ring of the imperial seal tapped on different places. 'Cappadocia, Cilicia, Phrygia. All these are still to be cleared. An aggrieved Bulgar is a vengeful one. As like to stick a knife in your back as smile at you. No. Better to pay them now, even if it means a lean couple of years for all of us.'

Erlan glanced around the room. At the tapestries gleaming with golden thread, the silver candlesticks, the silk cushions. He doubted it would be the emperor suffering privation for want of a little gold.

Leo gave a last decisive rap of his ring upon the marble. 'Which brings me to the reason I summoned you here.'

'Majesty?'

'The tribute mission leaves in seven days under General Arbasdos's command. I would like you to go with them.'

'Me?'

'Oh, I know you do not owe me this. But I ask you, as a friend. The Khan knows you.' He gave an exasperated chuckle. 'Mother of God, you're the only one of my courtiers whom the Khan has ever met – and lived!'

Erlan remembered the last time he had visited Khan Tervel in his capital. Pliska was little more than a glorified horse pasture, strewn with animal shit, hole-houses and dangerously capricious savages. They had thrown him in a pit of wolves and the fat Khan had laughed heartily at the fun of it. It was no thanks to him that Erlan had come out of that alive. 'He knows me, certainly, but—'

'And he trusts you. If he didn't, he wouldn't have let his son ride to our aid with his entire strength.' Leo leaned forward, knuckles on his desk, the military accountant. 'You must see how valuable you are personally to preserving this alliance?'

Though he was loath to admit it, Erlan could see reason in the emperor's request. But he felt like a boar being driven into a pit and didn't like it. Besides which, the prospect of spending even an hour in the company of General Arbasdos was hardly something he relished. 'Do you want an answer now, Majesty?'

The emperor eased himself further back into his chair and threaded his fingers on his chest. 'Many would consider the wish of an emperor tantamount to a binding command, Aurvandil.' He regarded Erlan with that unflinching eye. 'But if you need time... I'll have your answer tomorrow morning.' With an abrupt snap of his wrist, he snatched up another parchment from the top of the pile and threw it down before him. 'That is all.'

Erlan set down his cup. 'Majesty.' He gave a curt bow and went to the door. Was almost through it when the emperor called after him, 'Oh, when you do think on it, Aurvandil... Consider the goodwill you have won among us.' He peered up at Erlan. 'It would be a shame to jeopardise that, would it not?'

'I will think on it with care, Majesty,' Erlan assured him, and closed the door behind him.

But he already knew his answer. Goodwill or none, the fate of Byzantium was no longer his concern.

CHAPTER FIVE

Lilla's hand went to the cross nestled in the crucible of her neck as she swept along the corridor, feeling grateful for the cool air of the palace interior after the blistering heat of the day.

The pendant was solid gold, dull with the patina of age, and marked with symbols in the Greek tongue. Lilla knew not what they signified exactly. Something about Christ the Saviour, as the citizens of Byzantium called him. Or simply the Lord Jesus, as Gerutha had known him. *Sweet Grusha…* They had found the ornament clutched in her lifeless hand, covered with her own blood.

That terrible night of fire…

Grusha had found comfort in this foreign deity, so different from the gods of the north. Her body was ashes now. Part of Lilla felt the pendant should have burned with Gerutha on her funeral pyre since it had meant so much to her. But in spite of that, she had kept the cross for herself. A memory of her friend, a whisper of her spirit, that would always be close.

Lilla felt a sudden pang of anger. Grusha had deserved a better end than the cheap betrayal which the servant-girl Yana and the eunuch Katāros had wrought between them. But the threads of fate had bound her, as they bound every soul. And so it was...

Lilla came to the large studded door to her chambers. Lifting the latch, she wondered what Grusha would counsel her now. Her trip to Chalcedon had wasted an entire day. Demetrios had nothing remotely useful to tell her. Indeed, it was worse than that. There now seemed to be some mischief brewing amongst the crew. *Nothing he couldn't handle*, Demetrios assured her. 'They're just bored,' he said. 'They feel stuck here and some of them feel cheated.'

Aye, she thought. *Them and her both.*

Inside the chamber, it was already dark. An oil lamp was burning in the corner, its orange flame affording the room no more than a sepulchral glow.

Her feet were sore. She slipped off her shoes and stood for a moment savouring the kiss of cool marble on her weary soles. But it was no balm to the irritation in her heart.

According to Demetrios, it was *she* whom the crew held responsible for their predicament. *She* had lost half their number. *She* had got them stranded on the far side of the world. As if she held sway over the tide of war that had engulfed them all in its flood.

She sighed, trying and failing not to count up the improbabilities weighed against her. A half-mutinous crew, a ship in need of repair. Even Erlan, her closest ally, seemed hardly the man he had once been.

In spite of the day's frustrations, she didn't want to go to bed at once. Instead she was drawn towards the beams of moonlight lancing in through the quavering drapes. She scooped up a cup of wine left out by her servant and went onto the balcony to gaze out over the shimmering waters of the Straits.

The moon was still rising, bathing everything in its wan light – the roofs of the city, the sea-walls, even the distant hills of Asia strangely illumined as if gilt with silver. The air still smelled of the dust and heat of the day, the scents of the spice district drifting over the city.

Patience. Is that the lesson Gerutha would want to teach her?

To wait, to bide her time, to be content in this gilded cage – just as Erlan had counselled her. By all the gods, how she wished she could be content. For the old Lilla, the young woman she used to be, that might have been enough. But now… now she was hard inside, like a blade tempered in fire, and something deeper and altogether darker hid within her heart that would not let her rest.

A noise sounded faintly from within the chamber. When silence followed, she thought it must have been a trick of her mind, or perhaps Erlan stirring in his sleep. Instead, she took a long draw on her spiced wine, relishing the mellow mix of Cretan grape and spikenard.

The first she knew of him was a hand coiling round her waist, then the warmth of his hard body as he drew her back against him.

'You're late.' Erlan's lips brushed over the crook of her neck, light as silk. 'I thought you must have drowned.'

'I might as well have for all the good the trip did us. There's trouble with the crew.'

'What... kind... of... trouble?' Between each word, he shed a kiss on her nape, sending rivers of pleasure down her spine.

'The crew despise me. So Demetrios says.'

'Honey-coating it, is he?'

'I don't blame them. They've been too long in this place. Like us...' She pulled the pin from her carefully constructed coiffure and shook out her mane of blonde hair. 'Dear gods, what I would not give to leave this city?'

Erlan blew out a long sigh. The kind before a man makes a confession. 'Well... seems the emperor has given me a chance to do just that.'

'What?' She spun around. 'How?'

'He's sending a tribute mission to the Bulgars. He wants me to accompany them as envoy. Says because I've met the Khan before, I'm key to its success. I have my doubts. He's given me till tomorrow to accept.'

'And will you?'

He smiled and squeezed her arms. 'Lilla... I'm not leaving you again.' He pulled her close to him.

She lay her head against his chest, listening to the beat of his heart, thoughts stirring in her head. 'A tribute mission?' she said at length. 'What kind of tribute?'

'Gold – what else? Near a million solidi, Leo told me.'

'A million?' Lilla gaped in astonishment. And all at once she felt a crack in the crushing walls of her frustration.

'Although what in the Nine Worlds a puffed-up horse-herder like Tervel will do with a million solidi—'

'Erlan, don't you see! This is our way out.'

'What is?'

She laughed suddenly. 'By the stars, elskling, your eyes are far too honest! Can't you see what's under your nose?'

'What are you talking about?'

'How many spears would that much gold buy in Sveäland? How many sell-swords? How many lords and their hirds come to that?'

'A fair number, true, but—'

'Five thousand… no, ten thousand!'

'Perhaps more, but… wait, you're not suggesting—'

'We steal it!'

'Steal it? You've lost your wits.'

'I don't know,' she laughed. 'Maybe I have.' Yet for the first time in an age, she felt a tiny ember of joy glow in her heart. 'When does the mission leave?'

'Seven days, he said.'

'Only seven? By land or sea?'

'That much gold, by sea, I suppose. But—'

'So much the better.' She clapped her hands in delight. 'We intercept them. Steal the gold. *And* be on our way. They'll never catch us. Not once *Fasolt* finds her wings.' She felt giddy with excitement.

'Wait, slow down, woman. Quite apart from the question of how we're supposed to separate forty thousand-odd marks of gold from its escort… think what would happen if we succeeded.'

'What do you mean?'

'You realise the position it would leave the emperor in?'

'Hel take Leo! And Hel take his empire!' she snarled, her anger flaring even quicker than her mirth. 'I owe them nothing. Not after what they did to me.'

'Aye, but…' He shook his head. 'By the Hanged, Lilla! It wasn't but a few months ago I was bleeding to save the fucking empire. And now you want to pull all that down? This really is madness,' he hissed. 'Not to mention treasonous.'

She smiled, letting a few more of his angered heartbeats pass. 'But you no longer serve the emperor, do you?' she said, sliding her voice into beguilement. 'The siege is lifted. That was the arrangement.' She moved closer, slipping a hand inside his robe and tracing a fingertip down the contours of his stomach. 'You serve me now.' She looked up at him, the tip of her tongue skating over her lips. 'No?'

'Hel's teeth, woman, you'll be the end of me.'

'Oh,' she breathed, 'in so many ways.' Slowly, she pulled his head down, his mouth to hers, her tongue questing between his lips. A small moan of desire escaped her throat as her hand glided lower, down through the coarse hair of his belly until her fingers slid round his manhood.

'Accept this… *honour*,' she murmured. 'Be his envoy if that's what he wants. Find out all you can.' Erlan's breathing grew deeper, slower, as her hand found its rhythm. She felt new strength growing inside her with each stroke, like wind filling her sails. Here was a way out. She would not let the chance slip away.

'Damn it,' he growled. 'I like the man. He's done me no wrong. This betrayal would be—'

'Yes? Tell me, what would it be?'

Suddenly he seized her wrist. In the darkness, his eyes stabbed hers like arrow-shafts. '*Monstrous.*'

She scowled and flicked away her hand, slapping his swollen member against his belly. He let her go.

She recovered her wine and went to the balustrade. Took a long, cooling sip. 'I ceased to care what good I owed to Leo when he locked me in a fucking cell.'

'That was Katāros.'

'Oh, you were there, were you?'

'No,' he said carefully. 'But I know how you suffered.'

'No. You *don't*.' She took another gulp of wine, enjoying the feeling of recklessness coming over her. 'I came here for you. Now I have you. But I also came here to raise an army. And if there is a chance, however small, I'm not leaving here without that gold.'

'Lilla—'

'This is who you serve, my love.' She turned to face him. Shrugged her robe off one shoulder. The silk folds and the brooch that fastened them fell away, revealing the soft curve of her breast to the moonlight. 'This. And no other.'

'By the Hanged, you... *Lilla*.' His voice was guttural as a wolf's growl. In two strides he'd crossed the gap between them. He lifted her by her waist, wine cup and all, carrying her across the balcony, kissing her mouth, her cheek, her neck, until her spine butted against the pillar. She caught her own weight on the tip of her toes as he moved lower, kissing her breasts, her stomach, sinking down to his knees.

She felt the cool night air spill over her thighs as he pushed aside her skirts, eager to burrow under them as a dwarf mining for gold. But, tempting as it was to surrender to his caresses, instead she caught his chin, twisted his face up to hers. 'Will you do it?'

His eyes glinted up at her. 'I will... For you, I'll do anything.'

She let him go then, and smiled up at the night, the feeling of victory mingling inside her with the sweet flood of desire. A moment later the heat of his tongue sent a chime of pleasure through her loins. She moaned, letting the cup slip from her grasp. It hit the floor and clattered away. She watched the spill of wine race across the white marble.

Strange, she thought, before she gave herself to him completely. How, in the pale light of the moon, the wine looked like a river of blood.

CHAPTER SIX

Katāros drifted in and out of consciousness, but this time it was the pleasant yaw and roll of the fishing boat that accompanied his thoughts as they ran west with the wind and the waves.

His belly was warm with food, his monstrous thirst slaked at last. And in his wakeful moments, he reflected that Malta was not such a bad place to recover himself. There, fed and watered and properly clothed, he could assess his position, decide on his next move. One thing was certain: he would not be returning east as the boy Tomas had suggested. Maybe Melita *was* his best chance. He knew it was a fair-sized town, from which a smattering of obscure officials administered the island. Provincial, of course, and therefore unlikely to have gotten word of his betrayal of the empire. Or so he hoped.

But after that?

Continue west, to Tunis? That was part of the Caliphate now. Would the Arabs give him a welcome reception? His name was hardly burnished with glory, even among those who knew him, and there were few enough of them still alive. He had sold out his city and his emperor and all for nothing, his plan unravelling like a piece of old twine. Neither the new Caliph Umar, nor his people, would thank him for the mere attempt. Failure was failure.

Besides, he thought, all that sand and heat and sun-blasted rock. He hadn't the stomach for it.

North, then. To Syracusa on Sicily? Why not to Rome or even the imperial city of Ravenna? Far to the north where he could lie low for a time. Perhaps he could find a position in the household of some fat patrician drifting along the edge of the court there, at least until he was able to find out just how black his name had been tarred.

As he lay turning over the choices before him, his fingertips traced the scar forming on his side. The wound had been the doing of Lilla Sviggarsdottír, Queen of Sveäland.

The honey-haired whore.

That bitch was as responsible as Erlan for his downfall – and just when all had been within his grasp. Victory. Riches. Revenge.

At least the wound was improving now. The saltwater had helped its healing, but too much had also weakened the flesh. He feared it could re-open if he moved too fast. He must take care. And he would not forget the whore's gift. One day, if fate was kind, he would repay it.

Elias and his boys were hard at work. The afternoon had seen their nets fill with a heartening catch of tunny-fish. Katāros watched the boys, stripped to their waist, hauling in the nets under their father's direction. The wind riffling their salt-flecked hair, the sun making shadows off the muscles working in their arms as they dragged the tuna onboard and set to gutting them and packing them in salt casks for the voyage home. Fishermen had been doing this for a thousand years, since the Age of Heroes. Ancient ways of working, a dance between man and wind, sea and sail. Only he was the anomaly here. The abomination.

The older boy, Tomas, reminded him very much of another from his past. Anastasios had been perhaps his only true friend in the Great City, when Katāros was himself a youth of twelve or thirteen – before cynicism had entirely swallowed up his heart. Stasi had been a fishing boy, too. Had taken him out in his boat on the Marmara for hours on end, where he had wanted nothing from him but his company. Katāros recalled the way Stasi would shade his eyes against the late afternoon sun, slants of gold glinting off the waves. There was an impossible sweetness to that memory. Those hours out on the water, Stasi always talking, talking – of life and what he meant to make of it. But time overtook it all. One day Stasi told him that he had been drafted into the Opsikion Theme as a marine. He was sent south to defend the southern islands against the Arab advance. That was the last Katāros ever heard of him…

The day was drawing on, the bright blue sky bruising at its eastern rim to a bloody purple, when a yell startled him from his thoughts.

'A sail, Father! Look there!' Tomas was pointing excitedly to the north-east.

Over the next hour, it drew closer and closer. The vessel was much swifter than their smaller craft, and shortly before the light began to fail, Elias declared that it must be an imperial ship. 'See the red sail and black sigil? Could be a dromon. A small one, anyways.'

He happened to be right about that.

It was a dromon of the Naval Theme, a fighting ship, and one which was taking a good deal too much interest in them for Katāros's liking. By the time night was closing over them completely, the ship had gained on them enough that they could call from crew to crew. An officer holding a flaming torch came to the bulwark and hailed them, a *drougarios* of the marines, judging from the ostrich feather in the spike of his helm.

'You're fair flying along there, captain,' Elias called back to him.

'Fine wind up,' returned the *drougarios*. 'Pray God it holds another day and a night.'

'Where're you headed?'

'Panormos.'

'Be lucky to make that end of Sicily in a day and a night.'

'We cannot delay. We carry reinforcements against the rebel uprising there.'

'Rebels? In Sicily?'

'Have you not heard? Seems the governor was betting on an Arab victory.' *He wasn't the only one*, thought Katāros, hiding a scowl. 'He's turned the garrison forces around Catania against the emperor and appointed a rival to his throne,' continued the *drougarios*. 'Only the magister at Panormos has remained loyal to the purple.'

'Then he'll be pleased to see you, no doubt!'

'Ha! No question. But he'll be over the bloody moon when he hears the latest news from back east.'

'You mean the end of the siege?' Elias laughed. 'Why, that news is old, sir.'

'Nay, that's not the best of it. The Saracens aren't just gone, man – they're scattered! Smitten by the very hand of God!'

'Eh? How so?'

The *drougarios* explained that once the Arab fleet had withdrawn, somewhere in the south Aegean they had sailed straight into a storm that blew for three days full. 'What ships they had left were buried under the fury of it.'

'And the enemy?'

'Perished to a man! There's bodies been washing up on Naxos, Crete, Kithira. Christ's blood – over half the damn Peloponnese! We must have passed four or five dozen ourselves, all bloated and torn by the sharks.'

'We just came from the east. We saw none of that ourselves.'

'Nor would you, friend, you're ahead of it all. This news is fresh, I tell you! Not five days old.'

Elias nodded. Katāros was watching him carefully. The ratchets in the old man's mind were turning, that was all too clear. 'Five days, you say? And no survivors?' Katāros could not fail to catch the glance in his direction, though the old fisherman tried to conceal it. The breath in the eunuch's throat froze. He waited with awful anticipation for old Elias to denounce his passenger there and then.

And yet... still those ratchets were turning.

Perhaps the salty old bastard was one of those men afflicted with a soft heart. Or else, a greedy one. Katāros would find out which soon enough.

Before long, the dromon was on its way, its bulging red sail bearing westward into the thickening night, leaving the fishing boat to wallow on through the swell.

Elias, normally talkative with his lads at this time of evening, gave them only a few terse instructions and instead sat chewing over his thoughts like a piece of old dried hake.

Katāros saw the change in him and breathed a weary sigh within. It was a pity after their kindness. Because he knew now what it meant for all of them. He knew now he had no choice.

Katāros slept. And he dreamed… of dark forests, of the scent of the damp, loamy earth, of a bright moon pouring silver over the land. It was the north. It was his blood calling to him, as it had now and then through his life. But the longing this time was different. Soft and insistent as a siren's song.

Still, when the prod came, he was expecting it.

'Wake up, friend.' Elias's voice was gruff and hard. 'Wake up, I said.' Yet hidden within it, a tremor of fear.

'What is it?' Katāros murmured, seeing the knife in his hand.

'I know who you are.' Elias blew out a sigh, full of regret. 'That's to say, I know *what* you are.'

'Do you?' Katāros felt strangely calm. He sat up.

'Stay where you are.' The tip of Elias's blade, sharp enough to gut tunny-fish, was quavering only inches from Katāros's chest. 'You're no merchant's agent, are you? You're… you're—'

'Say it, old man.'

47

'A damn fugitive. An enemy of the empire, and every honest citizen.' He was speaking fast, nerves tripping him along. 'And I'm sorry for it, sorry for this.' He gestured at the knife. 'Won't use it 'less I have to. But if I do, I will, mind,' he said, with an eager nod.

'Poor, foolish Elias,' Katāros sang softly. 'You think you know *me*?'

Elias steadied himself, edging back an inch. 'I... I knows enough. Plenty enough for—'

'No one knows me,' snarled Katāros, and before the frown had even creased the old man's brow, Katāros's hand sprang from his cloak like a cobra, seizing Elias's wrist, twisting and bending his arm backward while pulling his body forward. The blade slipped neatly into the fisherman's heart like a dagger returning to its sheath.

It happened so quick, the shock on Elias's craggy face was instant, almost sublime. A soft grunt escaped his lips, nothing more. Then he fell like a sack of spilled grain to the deck.

Katāros stooped over him, drew the knife from his blood-soaked chest while his aged body still kicked and scraped at the strakes, the iron smell of blood rising sharp on the sea air.

A wail of horror rose from the stern. Tomas was first to his feet, snatching up a long boat-hook and lurching towards Katāros. Katāros watched the spike drop level with his belly. But the boy was too headstrong, too filled with rage and fear. It was a simple thing to step outside its point, to arc the blooded blade over the boy's shoulder and drive it hard into his back. The point entered through his kidney, angled upwards towards his heart. Katāros twisted the haft, feeling viscera and organs tear, and the blade-edge grate along the boy's bottom rib. Tomas gasped, his mouth yawning absurdly wide as his back arched, their faces so close Katāros could smell the olive oil on his breath.

The boy fell dead at his feet.

Katāros turned to the last of them.

Andreas had not moved. He sat by the tiller, his face calm, betraying no fear, while Katāros ducked under the sail, fingers sticky with Tomas's blood.

Two paces off, the boy rose to his feet. His eyes were clear and dark. Like sapphires glinting in the night. 'You don't have to do this.' His voice was soft, as it had been in the songs he had sung during Katāros's delirium.

'I'm sorry.' The eunuch smiled sadly, his fingers squeezing the bloody knife-haft till his knuckles burned. 'I have no choice.'

CHAPTER SEVEN

By noon the next day, Erlan stood on a different balcony, waiting. The sun blazed down onto the square space beneath him, making the pale pink paving-stones shimmer with heat, and the shadows of the surrounding colonnade so dark they seemed impenetrable. At the corners of the courtyard, four statues of half-naked nymphs stood sentinel, their coquettish smiles a throwback to an earlier age.

His presence had been announced some while ago, but it seemed General Arbasdos was happy to take his time attending to his guest. No matter that Erlan had come directly from an audience with the emperor with orders of his commission.

Erlan guessed this was all quite deliberate. There was no love lost between him and the general. Indeed, there was no man in the city for whom Erlan had greater loathing.

Arbasdos, *kouropalatēs*, stragegos of the Armeniac Theme, *comēs* of the imperial navies, and, some said, blood-brother to Emperor Leo himself. Whatever oaths they may or may not have sworn, Arbasdos was certainly Leo's son-in-law, married to his beloved daughter, Anna. A connection even the loftiest patrician in the city must envy.

Besides these more elevated titles, Arbasdos had once been Erlan's owner, and he the general's slave. Something neither man was likely to forget. Aye, and Erlan had still darker reasons for hating the man... But he had buried that grievance deep since he reckoned no good would come from airing it.

Instead he took a swig of the wine that the steward had at least had the courtesy to serve him, and leaned back against the pillar of black marble, peering down into the courtyard. That was the very spot where Arbasdos had had him flogged. The memory sent an involuntary shiver down his spine, as if his muscles recalled the savage bite of leather and bone just as well.

'It seems we meet as equals now, Northman,' said a voice behind him.

He turned. General Arbasdos stood in the doorway to his airy chamber, Erlan's letter of commission clutched in one hand. He looked ten years older than the man he'd been that night of fire, with his artful curls and fastidious beard, always clothed in silks and short tunics, boyishly vain of his fine muscular legs. Now his sad, docile eyes looked half-dead, his hair had grown long and lustreless, an ebony walking stick propped up his stooped frame. Erlan noticed, too, the longer breeches of the common footsoldiery he wore, and wondered what scars they must conceal.

'I'm hardly your equal, Lord Arbasdos.'

'You're right. If anything my limp is worse than yours now.'

'That's... not exactly what I meant.'

Arbasdos gave a bitter chuckle, threw down the letter, then beckoned Erlan in from the balcony. Erlan followed as the general hobbled to a large table of polished porphyry, the silver tip of his cane clicking with each laboured step. He took up a chalice and poured himself a cup of wine. This must have been how he had poured out wine for Lilla, thought Erlan, when she had come to him.

'Care for more?'

'Thank you.' Maybe more wine would sweeten the bitterness of that thought.

'Not too proud to drink with me, then? You surprise me.'

'Whatever bad blood existed between us burnt away that night. Along with everything else.'

Arbasdos grunted, seeming irritated at the reference to the debt he owed Erlan so soon in the conversation.

'Such things are not so easily forgotten. Nor forgiven.'

'I came here on the emperor's business, not my own.' Erlan gestured to the vellum on the table, which bore his new credentials, and the broken imperial seal.

The general sighed, allowing his escape for now. 'Indeed. You've risen high, Aurvandil.' His sad eyes hardened. 'Perhaps you mean to rise higher still.'

'It's no secret Queen Lilla is eager to return to the north. I go with her. I've no ambitions here.'

'Yet here you are.' He prodded the vellum gingerly. 'Principal envoy to "our brother Prince, Tervel the Magnificent" no less. "Personal Ambassador of the Emperor Leo, Third of his Name," it says there.'

'The title matters little enough. The bones of it is I've convinced the Khan once before. Leo hopes I will do so again.'

'You're too modest, Northman.' Arbasdos eased himself onto a couch with an involuntary growl of discomfort, then dragged his ruined leg up onto a cushion. 'I have difficulty trusting a modest man... Hard to trust a man you don't understand.'

'Even one who saved your life?'

'Huh. Oh, you saved it, to be sure, but for no good of mine. You were merely following orders. So I hear.'

Erlan wondered how he had heard that. Whether he also knew the other half of the emperor's last command: that if Arbasdos proved traitor, Erlan was to slit his throat. 'Very well, general. I propose a clean slate then. No debts owed, no trust given... But we still have this duty to discharge.'

'I need no reminding of my duty, Northman.' For a moment, the two men glared at one another, mutual dislike simmering between them. 'Speaking of which, I am rather busy. So would you mind explaining what you're doing here?'

Erlan bridled his goaded pride. After all, being patronised was a cheap price to pay for the information he needed. 'I came to find out the arrangements for this mission.'

'Arrangements?'

'Timings, provisioning, armaments, itinerary. That sort of thing.'

Arbasdos affected a yawn. 'Mother of God, how dull you are! You're a passenger, Northman, nothing more. Present yourself at the Prosphorion Harbour before dawn in six days' time. That's all you need to know. I'll deal with the rest.'

'At least tell me how many ships in our convoy?'

'Really?' Arbasdos expelled an exasperated sigh. 'There happen to be three—'

'Which ones?'

'Dammit, I already told you. Everything is under my control.'

'So the gold will be split?' Erlan persevered.

'How the gold is distributed is my business. Leo has charged me with delivering the gold – and *you* – to that fat Bulgar leech. What you say when you get there is up to you. Till then, I don't answer to you.'

Erlan pulled back, aware his questions were too clumsy and could betray some other intent. 'It's a long voyage to Varna. I simply want to know we're going to get there—'

'God's blood, you sound like an old woman! I've said you and the gold will get there, and so you will.'

Erlan saw there was no gain in probing further. What had he hoped for coming here anyway? Some great revelation? Some hidden key to what they intended? He felt a sudden flash of anger. By all the gods, wasn't it obvious enough? Each ship would be bristling with armed marines, bolstered by at least three fire-syphons apiece, and the gold plumb in the middle of them all. *Divided or not, what does it matter?* They might as well talk of stealing the moon as getting their hands on the Khan's gold. They barely had a sea-worthy ship, let alone a willing crew. And there were only six days left before the convoy sailed. The idea of stealing it was absurd. The sooner Lilla was dispelled of the notion, the better. Suddenly he wanted to be far away from this place. From this man.

He set down his cup. 'My thanks for the wine.'

'Of course.' The general leaned back on his cushion, a complacent smile sliding over his sad mouth. 'Oh, you must remember me to your queen.'

Leave now, Erlan told himself. *Better to leave before—*

'You know how we have a special bond, she and I,' Arbasdos added, no attempt to conceal the libidinous look in his eye.

'Queen Lilla assures me there was little enough of you to remember.' Erlan leaned in and lowered his voice. 'No doubt there's many a whore in the city could attest the same.'

Arbasdos's smirk died. 'The fact remains, Northman, that I fucked your precious queen.'

'Aye. A price she chose to pay for my freedom. But you, General... you've yet to pay the true price for what you took.'

'Is that a threat?'

Erlan smiled. 'Like I said, while we have this duty to perform, I'm happy to deal with you on the level.'

'Hm... "No debts owed, no trust given."' Arbasdos took another gulp of wine and turned his gaze out the window. 'You mean to wage war when you return to your homeland, do you not?'

'To restore Queen Lilla as rightful ruler over her people, yes.'

Arbasdos gave a cynical snort. 'And you as their king, I suppose?'

'King?' Erlan shook his head, nonplussed. 'No. I... I've not thought of that.' Yet now he did, it seemed so blindingly obvious he marvelled it had never occurred to him. He, Erlan, a king?

Arbasdos saw his confusion and a laugh burst from his lips. 'By heaven, look at you! Shall I tell you your trouble, Northman?' he snarled. 'You're a man with no vision. You're nothing but a grunt, a stooge. A boy who follows orders, that's all you are. When all's said and done, you *are* no better than a slave.' He shook his head, his grin souring to a sneer. 'You were right. We are no equals, you and I. For I am already a great man but you...' He sat up, leaned forward, disdain etched on his face. 'Oh, laugh about me with your frigid queen all you like. She knows how it was between us. But even if I had the smallest cock in the empire, by God, I'd still be a bigger man than you. Because you,' he tapped the side of his head, 'you are small in *here*. And what's more, you always will be.' Slowly, painfully, the general dragged himself to his feet. 'Now if you don't mind, Erlan Aurvandil, I have real business to attend to. So kindly get the fuck out of my house.'

CHAPTER EIGHT

Erlan hobbled weakly uphill from the House of Arbasdos, anger burning in him. Because the truth does burn. Arbasdos was right; for as long as he could remember, he had been hiding. Gods, hadn't his father always told him he was born to lead? Yet how much time had he wasted by now? Hiding from his destiny. Ducking his duty.

It was already long past time that he stepped up and took hold of the fate the Norns had chosen for him. He thought of those old crones spinning and weaving away, there in the dank darkness at the foot of the World Tree.

Aye, the time for serving is over.

It was time for him to lead.

Even as he thought it, he felt his gait strengthen, his uneven stride lengthen over the cobblestones. As if with this realisation, resolve suddenly came pouring into his limbs, stiffening his sinews with purpose. He felt his back straighten, his head come up, as though a heavy weight had fallen from his shoulders, like a sodden cloak shrugged off at last.

Time to lead. Aye.

Even so, though this change had come over him, it didn't alter the nature of the problem. As he walked on, quicker now, his anger settled into deeper thought, his mind picking and pulling at the riddle of the gold like Fenrir Wolf brooding over his unbreakable fetter.

How could it be done?

He became so preoccupied he hardly noticed the carters rattling by over the cobbles, laden with bolts of Egyptian cotton and linen from the Indus, on their way down to the clothier's quarters; or the dull ring of hammer blows as the coppersmiths put the final touches to their pots and kettles in readiness for their market on the morrow. He paid no heed to the great monument of stone that rose on his left with red majesty. The vast basilica of the Holy Wisdom with its great bulging dome – in which he had not dared set foot since those mad visions of blood and fire on the Day of Repentance, when the City had teetered on the brink of disaster, the Caliph's teeming hordes hammering at her gates.

How shall it be done? was all he thought.

He had no answer. Only that it must be done. And in six days.

Six days, by all the gods!

The afternoon was dry and sultry, like every other in this long, long summer. By the time he had reached the crest of the hill and was passing under the high stone archway that led into the Augustaion, the central square of the City, he was streaming with sweat under his cloak and tunic. He wondered what he should tell Lilla. He had gained nothing of real use from his interview with Arbasdos. A direct attack on the convoy seemed out of the question. That would do little more than expose the *Fasolt* to the punishing jets of fire that any imperial ship – whether dromon or chelandion – could spew out in less time than it took a man to fart. No. There had to be some trick to it. Though for now, he could not see it.

But one thing at least he had gained from his visit. This steel resolve. He was determined to do it now, determined that Arbasdos should suffer. And if he knew Arbasdos at all, the worst kind of suffering would be to lose face before his ally, Emperor Leo. The general's humiliation would be sweet recompense for what that son of a whore had taken from Lilla.

The Augustaion was a meeting place, a crossroads, a market square, a sacral space of ceremony and ritual. It was all these things, and most days contained the necessary players to fulfil its divers uses. Patricians strolling to the senate, pedlars of foodstuffs and trinkets, soldiers, shop-keepers, priests and slaves, even stray dogs, all crossed each other's paths as they went about their business.

Erlan weaved his path between them all towards the towering archway of the Chalke Gate and the palace beyond it. But as he passed by the Column of Justinian which dominated the square, a figure stepped out from behind its plinth. He might have walked straight on, but for one detail: a splash of scarlet that caught his eye long enough to turn his head. He found that it belonged to a woman, dressed in stylish but not extravagant clothes, a quantity of bright scarlet hair tucked loosely under her headscarf. She was looking directly at him and seemed now to have placed herself in his path. Surmising what was her business, he made to walk on, muttering that he wasn't looking for that right now. But before he could pass her, she reached out and held his arm. 'Erlan Aurvandil.' It was not a question.

Hearing his own name surprised him, and now that he really looked at her, he saw the woman was strikingly beautiful – not a face to forget – and yet still he could not place her. 'Do I know you, sister?'

'Maybe. I know you. You are the friend of Einar.'

The mention of that name was a slap in the face. But it jolted something in his memory. 'Orīana?'

She nodded. This was Einar's woman.

Poor bloody Einar...

He opened his mouth to say something sympathetic, but instead found a lump choking back his words. The thought of Einar, his friend... That last cry as he went over the gunwale into the broiling sea, body wreathed in flames...

She took his hand. 'Come with me.'

'Where are we going?'

'Just come, you silly *malakas*!' she cried, already pulling him on with a wild laugh. 'Don't you trust me? Come!'

The staircase groaned with every step, each tread bowed and dusty from the tramp of many sandals. The landlord of the insula was either too poor or too mean to invest much in its upkeep, its run-down appearance at odds with the easy beauty of the woman he was following up the stairs. A faint smell of urine pervaded the place. Slitted windows blocked all but a few rays of light. At length, they came to the fourth floor. There were only two more above it, which meant Orīana was not the poorest resident in the block, though not far from it. An old man was seated on a small stool staring blankly into the gloom. Orīana murmured a greeting to him; he croaked one back. As Erlan passed, he saw a pair of glassy eyes, milk-white with blindness.

He still could not believe what she had told him as she dragged him across the city. Would not believe it until he had seen it with his own eyes.

But if it was true... Already his mind was making calculations, seeing the possibilities opening up before him. Seeing the odds shift in his favour.

If it was true...

He followed Orīana to the end of the corridor where she stopped before a door, put her hand to the handle. 'Ready?'

He nodded.

'I told you. He's not—'

'I'm ready,' Erlan insisted.

'Very well.' She opened the door and he followed her inside.

The apartment was surprisingly airy after the dinginess of the staircase and landing. The walls were red ochre and the floor covered with a long, narrow carpet – perhaps from Armenia or even further east along the Silk Road. The scent of sandalwood mingled with Orīana's heavy oudh perfume.

She led him into a living area, sparsely furnished with a table, two stools, a wash basin, a few urns on shelves. He noticed a large pitcher of wine on the table.

Orīana followed his gaze. 'Thirsty?'

'Let's get on with it.'

'Huh. He always said you were blunt.' She gestured at a doorway into an inner chamber. 'In there.' A drape hung limp and ragged, pulled half across the opening.

Erlan hesitated. There was something uncanny, almost sepulchral about the shadows within.

'Well?' She shrugged a shapely shoulder. 'See for yourself. That's what you wanted, isn't it?'

He went inside. The room was cool and dim, the only light a tiny red glow from an incense burner in one corner. In the gloom, he could discern the outline of a large bed. His periphery took in the rest of the room, the usual things one might expect in a woman's bedchamber: a table, a casual scattering of small pots and combs and pieces of jewellery, a mirror, a washstand.

But his attention was fixed on the unmoving heap of blankets on the bed. He could hear the rhythmic rasp and sigh of a man sleeping deeply.

He swallowed hard. 'Einar?... *Einar?*'

'He's still weak,' murmured Orīana from the doorway behind him. 'Go to him.'

Just then the great pile of blankets shifted and gave vent to a thunderous fart. That certainly sounded like Einar, no question.

'I've a thirst, woman,' croaked the blankets in Greek. A breath and then a bellow. 'Orīana! I need wine, dammit!'

'Fetch it yourself, you lazy whoreson,' Erlan said in Norse.

The heap suddenly sprang upright. Erlan advanced with a grin as wide as a wolf, ready to throw his arms round his old friend. But the sight that greeted him stopped him dead.

No beard, no braids, just a raw and mottled patchwork of skin.

'Erlan! By the sweet teats of Freya! I must be bloody dreaming!' The voice was Einar's, but that face... one half of it a monstrous whorl of mangled flesh. 'I reckoned you well dead, lad!'

'No more 'n you, old friend.'

'Gods, don't you say that. You might bloody wish you *were* dead if tha' were true.'

Erlan forced himself beyond his shock. 'Here, let me get a hold of you then, fat man!' He went to the bedside and threw his arms around his friend, despite that the face he knew was gone. 'By the Hanged, there's not much left of you.'

Einar sucked his teeth in pain. 'All right, no need to crush me, lad. The damned fire took half my back.'

Erlan laid him gently back on the pillow.

'Well,' said Einar.

'Well,' said Erlan, looking at him. He was surprised when a sudden wave of emotion overtook him. Not sorrow exactly, not relief, not joy. Not anything specifically, and yet all of them at once. Tears welled in his eyes. 'You know, Einar... I mourned you. I—'

'Oh, come now, you miserable sod,' Einar cut in. 'I'll have none of your mooning now. We're both alive. May not deserve it but here we are.'

Erlan chuckled and wiped away his tears. 'You look like Hel.'

'Worse than her, brother,' Einar croaked. 'At least Hel's got half a face worth looking on.'

'It's good to see you all the same. No – better than good. The priests would call it a miracle!'

'Nay, the true miracle's that one.' Einar nodded at Orīana who was leaning against the doorframe, looking on with something like wry amusement.

'Do you know who this is, woman?' Einar cried in Greek.

'Imbecile!' she laughed. 'Was it not I who brought him here?'

'Well then, why are you standing there idle? Fetch wine! We must drink! Mother of God, my tongue's as dry as dust!'

'Bah! And there's nothing new,' cried Orīana, with a wink at Erlan. 'This one has a thirst would drain the Bosporus.'

'He's famous for it,' agreed Erlan.

Orīana disappeared into the other room and soon returned with the pitcher of wine and cups for all of them.

'So then.' Einar raised his cup. 'Here's to living!'

They all drank and raised toasts and talked a while, Einar insisting Erlan tell his story first. So Erlan obliged, beginning with the moment they had lost sight of each other in that hellish firestorm. Of his rescuing Arbasdos, of the deserters bringing them back to the city. Of his discovering Gerutha, of the frantic pursuit of Lilla and the princess through tunnels of shit. And last, of how it ended... 'We found Grusha where I'd left her. She was gone. Bled out. There was nothing anybody could have done.'

Einar said nothing, his only response strange nervous ripples passing over the ruin of his face. At length he muttered: 'There you are then. Always said you can't trust a man with no cock. No telling what he might do. Or why.'

'Well, he's gone now too. Dead or fled, it doesn't matter much which.'

'Still. Bloody shame about Gerutha. I always liked the lass.'

Erlan nodded, let the memory of Grusha settle for a moment, then jabbed his wine cup at Einar. 'So then, what about you?'

'I'm buggered if I can remember much of it,' he shrugged. 'No idea how I was fished out the straits. No clue who helped me.' He nodded at Oriana. 'First thing I knew I was up here in this bed.'

'Huh! Not a bad place to wake up from the nightmare,' observed Erlan.

'You said it.'

'I went looking for him,' volunteered Oriana. 'I don't know why. I knew it was futile if he was already dead. But I had to know. I couldn't just wait... and then nothing.' She explained how shocked she was when, against all hope, she found him laid out naked among the dead and dying. And yet she had seen some ember of life still glowing in him, had paid a carter to bring him back here. 'The next weeks I nearly beggared myself buying ointments and balms to soothe his wounds. And there were moments it looked like it was all for nothing.' She reached out and Einar lifted his paw to take her hand. 'But he lived.' She smiled at him. 'He lived.'

Seeing the look of affection between them, Erlan realised this wasn't going to be as straightforward as he'd hoped. After all, who could have foreseen this? The fat man up to his beardless chin in love.

'Why didn't you send word to the palace?' he asked, breaking their moment.

65

'I thought you were dead,' returned Einar. 'Same as you did me. I figured no one could have survived that mess. I told Orīana the same.'

'What about Lilla? You could have found her.'

This time the glances they exchanged were far less certain. At length the fat man blew out a long sigh. 'The truth is... I didn't want to be found.' He looked up, fixed Erlan in the eye. 'I'm done, lad. I'm just so bloody tired... By my reckoning, it were far better Lilla thought me dead.'

'You know I'll have to tell her,' returned Erlan. 'She'll want to see you.'

'No. No!' Einar repeated, shaking his hairless brows. 'I can't go back, lad. I won't.' He seized Orīana's hand again and pressed her knuckles to his lips. 'Too much to lose now.'

Erlan looked at them. They seemed... happy. And here was he, about to piss all over the little joy his friend had found in this world. But he had to. He could see no other way.

'Listen to me very carefully, my friend. In six days, close to a million golden solidi are sailing for Varna. We intend to steal it. And we need you to help us.'

Einar's pink brow furrowed, his mouth fell open, but since nothing came out, Erlan took his chance to explain it all: the tribute debt, his appointment as Leo's envoy, Lilla's plan to raise an army. As Einar listened, Erlan watched his expression change from bewilderment to disbelief, and finally anger.

'You've lost your fucking minds, the pair of you!' he snarled. 'You bled for that treaty, Aurvandil, remember? I watched you do it. And now you want to piss all that to the wind?'

66

'For that much gold, aye!' Erlan felt the nerve twinge in his ankle. Or was that his conscience? 'The Empire can look out for itself. We owe them nothing.'

'That's Lilla talking, not you. What do *you* think?'

Erlan felt honour trying to claw its way up out of the depths of his soul but he shoved it back down again. There was too much to gain. And he was determined to see it done. 'The fact is we need the gold to buy ourselves an army. Without it, what hope do we stand when we return north?'

'Suddenly you're the voice of expedience, are you? You – the prince of honour and oaths! Pah!'

'These aren't our people.'

'They certainly won't be after you've pissed off with their gold.' Einar shook his head in disgust. 'Hel, do you even have a plan?'

Erlan licked his lips slowly. 'Look, we only learned of the gold yesterday. Tomorrow we're crossing to Chalcedon to speak with the crew—'

'You still haven't even got the crew on side? By the Thunder!' Einar cried. 'You really are fucking mad as a birch-brush!'

'They will be on side,' insisted Erlan. 'Once they hear what's in it for them.'

'Did your brain turn to swine-shit since I last saw you, kid? Have you even met the fuckers?'

'Well… not yet,' Erlan admitted.

'Aye. Well, when you do, you'll find they're the most stubborn bunch of whoresons ever gathered under a sail. And they've no love for Lilla, that's for bloody sure.'

'They don't need to love her. They're still oath-bound to serve her now their skipper is dead.'

'Oath-bound? Odin's eye, did she not tell you?'

'What?'

'They blame her for getting half of 'em killed on the Dnipar portage. And to be frank, that ain't so far from the truth.'

'No.' Erlan's face darkened. 'No. She didn't tell me that.'

'Funny that,' sneered Einar. 'I doubt there's a one of them would stick his neck out for her. No, nor for a man they've never met. Not even the high and bloody mighty Aurvandil!'

Erlan peered into the dregs of his wine cup. He felt doubt stealing up like a thief on his newly found resolve. He cursed.

'Aye, that's about the sum of it.' Einar shook his head and took a pull on his own wine. 'The threads of the past, eh? They bind all of us tight as Fenrir Wolf.'

Erlan looked up sharply. 'You've a past with them too, though, eh? They'd listen to you, wouldn't they? By the Hanged, you could persuade a man to boil his own bollocks if you'd a mind to! You've the silken tongue of Loki himself.'

'Now hold on—'

'We need you, Einar,' said Erlan, a note of desperation entering his voice. 'Without you, we're stuck here. Lilla will go mad, I'll go mad. Hel, we all will.'

Einar sniffed and looked up into Orīana's warm green eyes. She'd said nothing while the two men had been speaking fast and in Norse. Erlan wondered whether she had any notion that he was trying to steal her man away from her, that he'd been planning to do that from the moment he walked in the door. 'I don't know, Aurvandil,' croaked Fat-Belly. 'From where I'm sat, life looks pretty bloody sane.'

Seeing he wasn't to be persuaded now, Erlan got to his feet. 'Look, I'm crossing to Chalcedon tomorrow. If you change your mind, I'll be at the Julian Harbour two hours before sundown.'

'I'm not coming, Aurvandil.'

'I know, I know.' He put down his cup. 'Just think about it... We need you.' He went to the door, looked back at the wreckage of a once-fine warrior. 'I need you.'

CHAPTER NINE

'Oh, Lilla, why ever can we not see more of each other?' Anna's welcome was effusive, as always. The *Basilopoúla* – the official title of the emperor's daughter – had changed little since their joint ordeal at the hands of the eunuch Katāros and his Arab overlord, brief though it had been. She still behaved as a girl in a woman's world, though she was now almost eighteen. 'Have you been hiding away from me?' she pouted, her dark eyes twinkling with youthful good humour.

The truth was, Lilla had. For the good reason that Lilla had found Anna's honey-sweet company increasingly hard to stomach. And besides this, Anna was married to General Arbasdos, whom Lilla had no desire to be anywhere near.

'It's this heat, Anna. My northern constitution cannot suffer so much of it.' Lilla laughed. 'I'm afraid I have been rather cowering in the shade these last weeks.'

'But we have shade here! You must come and cower with me,' said Anna gaily. 'Besides, the worst of the summer is over now and it will soon start to cool.' She signalled impatiently for her servant to hurry up with the refreshments – a glass jug of lemon-water and cinnamon sweetmeats – as they took shelter from the sun under a vine-draped trellis which covered one corner of her mansion gardens.

They did not have the scale of the palace gardens, but were far more elegant. Either Arbasdos or Anna had exquisite taste; Lilla rather suspected it was the former. As the two young women took their seats on the little stone bench, a perfect harmony of peace and serenity surrounded them, of meticulously manicured orange trees, brilliant white cascades of jasmine still in flower, dwarf laurels in the most enormous ornamental pots Lilla had ever seen, and beds of lavender in full purple bloom, filling the air with their relentless fragrance.

In fact, Lilla rather disliked the smell. She found it sickly and oppressive, preferring the subtler tones of cinnamon or eaglewood. But she was willing to suffer it for a while. She had taken the trouble to ensure that Arbasdos would not be at home before she had come. His presence would not only be distasteful to her, given their past interaction, but she feared it would also stifle Anna's natural loquacity. And this, she was counting on.

She and Erlan had argued again that morning. She had chided him too harshly for failing to glean anything useful from his meeting with Arbasdos, she saw that now. And that had sent him into a spiral of doubt. About the gold, about their return to the north, about galvanising the crew – with or without Einar, whose return from the dead had come as a strange but welcome shock to her. To smooth things over, she had backed down, even apologised. But she knew they

71

still needed to know more. The way Erlan was looking at it, stealing the gold did look like an insoluble riddle. But she refused to accept that it was impossible. They lacked only a key to fit the lock, that was all. And she was sure that, inadvertently, Anna could provide it.

So here she was, listening to Anna chatter on about her mother and the new baby, Konstantinos – Anna's brother and the heir to the imperial throne – whose baptism had taken place to great fanfare two weeks before.

'Did you hear, my dear, that he actually defecated in the baptismal font? Can you imagine it?' Anna squealed with delight. 'Of course, I shouldn't laugh. Patriarch Germanus is taking it very seriously. He says it is a terrible omen for little Konstantinos. *And* for the rest of us in times to come.'

'I would think starting life swimming in scat was admirable preparation for life as a future emperor.'

'Oh, you are scandalous, Lilla! And speaking of scandal, they say the stall-keepers on the Mese are already calling the poor little thing Konstantinos Kopronymos.' More peels of girlish laughter. 'Kopronymos' meant 'Dung-Named'. Recalling how bynames in her own culture could determine the course of a man's life, Lilla didn't rate this boy's chances. Perhaps the old Patriarch was right.

'And you, my sweet Anna,' she said. 'Are things better between you and your husband?'

'I admit it has not always been easy. He can be *so* secretive. And he spends much time away from here.' It was common knowledge that Arbasdos had a taste for the finest whores in the city. Seemed the only one who didn't know this was his wife.

'He is an important man. There is much demand on his time.'

'Yes, and how he makes sure I know that,' said Anna with a sarcastic flick of her eyebrow. 'But –' her face brightened and she leaned forward and seized Lilla's hand – 'I have news, Lilla, such happy news.' She dropped her voice to a whisper. 'I am carrying his child,' she said, releasing Lilla's hand and laying her own on her belly, though it still looked flat with youth.

Lilla smiled. 'Why, Anna, that is wonderful to hear.'

'Isn't it? Of course, it's early, I know. The nurse says I should not tell anyone. But I can tell you, can't I? Why shouldn't I?'

Lilla thought back to her own disappointment after the terrible carnage of the Battle of Bravellír, that bleak awakening with Gerutha leaning over her. Of her hope for the new life inside of her leaching away into the soil. She smiled. 'It's a delicate business. But better to be hopeful. Don't let anyone steal that from you.'

'I knew you would agree. That horrid nurse. I shall have to find another.'

'And Lord Arbasdos? Is he pleased?'

'He is overjoyed!' cried Anna, clapping her hands. She really was a perfect child. 'He says he is so proud of me. He has already chosen a name. Nikephoros.'

'A good strong name.'

'Isn't it?'

'For a boy.'

'Oh, it will be a boy. I've prayed about it so much that the Virgin Mother is sure to give one to me just to stopper my mouth.'

Lilla might have had some sympathy with the Virgin Mother. But she also had to admire the girl's hermetic certainty of her own good fortune. Then again, Anna was the beloved daughter of an emperor whose luck seemed destined to continue. Why shouldn't she believe that fate was on her side? 'I suppose you will miss him.'

'Who?'

'Your husband, of course!' laughed Lilla breezily. 'He is called away on this mission to... to Varna, or wherever it is? My Erlan is the same.'

'Oh that! Yes.' Anna sighed. 'It is completely tiresome! He talks of nothing else. Or *complains* of nothing else, I should say.'

'They leave in five days?'

'I believe that's right.' She started to count out on her fingers and then immediately gave up. 'Anyway, I'm half dreading it and half relieved.' She suddenly covered her eyes. 'Is that awful? God forgive me!'

'What's the matter?'

'I don't know. I just feel so full of emotions, Lilla. Like a ship thrown about on a storm. I'm sure it will pass.'

'He is kind to you, though?'

'Mm. It is kindness of a sort. When he sees me. Sometimes I hardly seem to draw his notice. He has been very gloomy since he took his wounds in that dreadful battle.'

'My dear, that is the way of war. You can't expect them not to be affected. Erlan was sick for weeks.'

'I know, I know.' Anna forced herself to a brighter mood. 'At least it is good that he is more open with me of late. He seems to trust me more now that I will provide him with an heir.' She shook her head and smiled. 'Really, he is so clever. Do you know how he means to safeguard the gold from possible attack?'

'Gold?' Lilla repeated, being deliberately obtuse. 'Oh, you mean the gold they carry to Varna?'

'Of course, that gold, Lilla! What other would I mean?'

'But surely no one would try to steal it? Now the Arabs are beaten, who else could pose any serious threat to an imperial convoy?'

'Oh, it's not that Arbasdos is really worried,' said Anna reassuringly, seeming happy to condescend her older friend for once. 'But he has taken precautions all the same.'

'Precautions?'

'Well, I'm not really supposed to tell you...'

'Ah.' Lilla gave an understanding smile. 'Then I shall not press you. I should hate for you to get in trouble.' She waited.

And as she had expected, after only a few heartbeats, Anna's mouth burst gleefully open. 'Oh, Lilla, I suppose I can tell you. It's terribly clever.'

Lilla took a nonchalant sip of her lemon-water. 'Really? I can only imagine.'

Anna leaned in again. 'He's forming a convoy of three imperial... Oh, what are they called again? Those bigger ships?'

'Dromons?'

'No, not the dromons... ah, chelandions! That's it. The *Theodora*, the *Stilico* and the *Aspar*,' she said, like a child reciting its lessons. 'He means to load each of them with identical stacks of cargo the evening before they depart, so that it looks to anyone watching as though the gold has been divided equally between the three. But in fact,' Anna dropped her voice still lower, 'two of the cargos will be decoys! Only one of the ships will contain the actual gold... all of it!'

Lilla's blood was fizzing with excitement. But she forced herself to say nothing, to look only half-interested, knowing Anna, and that the answer must soon come.

'The *Stilico*,' Anna whispered, then comically clamped her lips shut after the word had escaped. Mischievous triumph shone in her eyes. 'He says if they are attacked, the three ships will scatter and the enemy won't know which of them to follow. Don't you think that's clever?'

'Impossibly so,' said Lilla.

'I'm so glad you think so. He is brilliant, my husband.' Anna sighed, folded her hands and leaned back against the wall. 'I do so hope the expedition does not take him away from me for too long. I should hate to get melancholy, left here all alone.' Alone, with at least a hundred servants, Lilla thought drily. Anna suddenly clapped her hands. 'Oh, but you will be here of course! You *must* come every day. No more hiding. After all, who else will I have to tell about everything that's happening with the baby?'

Who else indeed?

Lilla reached out and squeezed Anna's hand. She could think of little worse.

'But you will come, won't you?'

Lilla smiled. '*Every* day.'

'Is that a promise?'

'Of course it is,' said Lilla. A promise which she already knew she would break.

CHAPTER TEN

The journey from Portus was a long, weary day of jarring jolts and sweltering humidity following the Via Campana.

Katāros lay sweating in a cart, enduring every rut in the road, along with a clutch of fellow travellers. He was unrecognisable from the sun-baked, salt-raw corpse Elias had fished from the sea. His hair was cut short into jagged black clumps. He wore a coarse woollen tunic and hose. On his feet, a pair of well-stitched sandals. In place of his golden ring of office and the boat he had stolen, a reassuringly plump purse of coins hung at his belt next to a battered but wicked-sharp dagger he'd bought in the Portus market. To all appearances, just another soul on his way to the *Urbs Æterna*.

To Rome.

The Via Campana followed the northern bank of the Tiber, trundling north-east. Over shallow hills, through olive groves, across sluggish and stinking marshland where foul vapours rose like wraiths of the damned. No wonder the nobility retreated to the hills in the summer months if this was what they had to suffer. Katāros could feel the fester of fever permeating the landscape, and he was glad when they left the marshes behind them and climbed into more undulating farmland on the slopes north of the river.

The other travellers stank almost as bad as the marshes, and there were far too many of them crammed onto the little cart. But far better to be wedged among these unwashed mercantiles than on foot where he would have been prey to the robbers and brigands for which the road to Rome was infamous. In any case, he found his desire to reach the old city far outweighed any discomfort he felt.

Rome – hearth-stone of the old Empire, which once had shone bright as a beacon fire. Rome – pinnacle of man, pride of the Caesars. Rome – light of the civilised world. But like the ancient Morning Star, how far she had fallen.

Where once had reigned the Caesars, the heir of Saint Peter now ruled. Pope Gregory – second of his name – sat on the Apostle's throne. Legally, the city remained under the protection of the empire – a detail that no doubt irked Gregory, and several popes before him – but the alternative was exposure to the Lombard threat, and that was all but unthinkable.

This was why Katāros had chosen Rome. She might be a mere spectre of her former self, but Rome was still a sizeable city. And being under imperial protection afforded her citizens a certain security. Yet Rome was still remote enough from the overbearing eye of Byzantium to ensure that the chances of Katāros being recognised were, he judged, acceptably small. He knew no one in Rome and no one knew him.

That suited him well.

Just then the carter announced they would have their first glimpse of the city at the crest of the next rise. Several of the passengers, Katāros included, craned their heads forward in their eagerness to sate their curiosity.

'First time, eh?' drawled a man slouched across from him. He addressed Katāros in Latin, which was the common tongue in these parts. Katāros knew it as well as half a dozen others. The man winked. 'You can always tell.'

'And you? A citizen of Rome?' Katāros lowered the pitch of his voice as best he could. Eunuchs were a rarity in the west and he had no wish to be remembered.

'Yep. Garum merchant by trade, me. Like my father and his before him.' Garum was the strong sauce made from fermented fish in which Romans drowned nearly every dish. Katāros had always detested the stuff. 'What brings you to Rome?'

'Work,' replied Katāros. 'At least, the seeking of it.'

'What kind?'

'I'm a steward. Or was.'

'Makes sense.'

'Does it?'

'The hands.'

Katāros glanced down. His hands were couched in his lap, pale and slender, not a dark hair on them. 'I see.'

'Oh, I meant no offence, lad,' the other pressed on. 'We've all got to make our way, ha'n't we? Steward, you said? Happens I know the head steward of the Familia Massimo. In fact, I'm his best supplier!'

'Massimo? I've not heard of them.'

'Go on! They're only the wealthiest family in the whole damned city. Listen, this fellow owes me a favour.'

'So – what are you suggesting?'

'Well, what d'you think, lad?' The merchant's eyes grew wide with enthusiasm. 'You're looking for work. A word from me to Justus – that's the fellow's name – and at least you'd get a hearing.'

'Why would you do that?'

People didn't just help one another; there was always an angle.

'Lord, it's no trouble. I need to see him anyway. Tag along.' Seeing Katāros's bristled expression, the older man shrugged. 'Or don't. It's up to you.'

Katāros considered his offer. Perhaps there was no harm in playing the grateful innocent. There might even be some advantage in it.

'Name's Emilius, by the way,' said the merchant.

'Amadeus,' Katāros said, saying the first Latin name that popped into his head.

'Well then, young Amadeus,' Emilius smiled. 'While you make up your mind, you might want to take a look behind you.'

Katāros turned to where the merchant's gnarled finger was pointing and for a moment the breath caught in his throat.

'Behold, the glory of Rome!'

And there, spread out below him, lay the Eternal City.

Katāros's eyes danced over the crumpled undulations of land beyond the Tiber, his gaze snapping hungrily at ancient ruins, shattered temple facades, the broken-down rubble of a once-invincible empire. Among these, he saw newer, sturdier towers of stone, of whose purpose he had no idea. There, the great eye of the Colosseum. Everywhere, churches, rising above the low-rise dwellings of the common citizenry. Beside him, Emilius was gabbing away, pointing out the belfries of the biggest basilicas, whose complicated names Katāros forgot as soon as he heard them.

'That there's the Basilica of Saint Paul.' Emilius directed his gaze to a sprawling rectangle of white marble on the other side of the river, just outside the walls of the city. Even at that distance Katāros could make out a gigantic facade adorned with bright frescoes and enclosed by a massive courtyard of monumental pillars. 'He's buried there, you know. Less his head, o' course. Poor bugger lost it not far from that spot. So they say.'

Good riddance, thought Katāros. No man, save Christ himself, had brought more trouble to the world. Although just then he almost envied the wild-eyed preacher the zeal of his mission. Paul had known his purpose, even if Katāros believed he was misguided.

What now was to be his own?

He was adrift, mere flotsam on the seas of Empire. Like Rome, he had fallen from a great height. But like Rome, he refused to die.

Was this a second chance?

For rebirth. For resurrection.

Was this why he'd been spared?

Perhaps, he thought, as the cart trundled downhill towards the bridge on the bend in the river. *Perhaps...*

*

'You *can* write, I take it.' The steward threw open a box on his desk and fished out a stylus, an ink-pot and a scrap of parchment.

'With hands like those, who could doubt it?' Emilius nodded eagerly.

'Still.' The steward Justus pushed the writing implements across the table to Katāros. Justus was an altogether different breed to the merchant. Humourless and cold, he wore a long robe of dark blue with large sleeves that he kept pushing up his arms and which, with ever more grating inevitability, kept slipping down again.

They were in his office, adjacent to the main kitchen under the Palazzo Massimo. From the outside, the palazzo was a monumental affair, standing proudly atop the Caelian Hill, looking west over the melancholic grandeur of the ruined Circus Maximus and Forum Romanum. Inside, the only rooms Katāros had seen as he was brought into the serving quarters at ground level were spacious, austere and, to his mind, rather gloomy.

Katāros picked up the stylus and smoothed out the parchment. 'What should I write?'

'Whatever you wish.'

Through the window beyond the steward's shoulder, he could see a little grove of orange trees in the courtyard with a babbling fountain at its centre. He began to write: '*Si hortum et bibliotechum habeas, omnia tibi necessaria sunt.*'

The steward peered down at his pen. 'Cicero.' He made a little grunt of satisfaction. 'I see you are educated then... And in Greek?'

Katāros obliged him, then continued writing, translating the phrase into Arabic, Gothic and finally Armenian script.

Justus watched in silence till the nib finished scratching. 'This last is...?'

'Armenian.'

'Mm. Where were you educated?'

'Cyrene. I was a slave there.'

'North Africa? Then how came you here?'

Katāros shrugged. 'I waited for my opportunity. When it came, I took it.'

'They castrated you?'

'They did.'

'Hm.'

'Is that a problem?'

'Problem? By heaven, no. If anything, an advantage.' For a moment, a trace of humour troubled his lips. 'Dom Vittorio's last notary had a regrettable taste for the – ah – *lower* diversions of the city.'

Emilius smirked. 'Died of the pox, did he?'

'I'm here to work,' said Katāros curtly. 'I'm not interested in diversions.'

'Just as well,' said Justus. 'Do you know figures, too?'

'Of course.'

'And anything of the *Leges Romanae*?'

'More than I'd care to. More, I'm guessing, than Dom Vittorio would need.'

'The master is a Judge of the City. Most of your work would involve the law.'

Katāros's heart sank. There was little he found more tedious than legal matters. But beggars had not the luxury of choosing their succour. 'I'm willing to serve the master in whatever capacity he needs.'

'The lad's most convincing, if you ask me,' said Emilius. 'Reckon I've done you a favour.'

'So it seems.' Justus gave Katāros a final appraising look. 'Very well. The position of head notary is yours. If you want it.'

Emilius slapped Katāros on the back. 'Well, that'll do for you, eh, my friend?'

And even Katāros could not withstand the man's infectious enthusiasm. For the first time in a long while, he smiled. 'Yes. I believe it will.'

Dom Vittorio was far younger than Katāros had imagined. A man of perhaps thirty years, he was an unusual mix of cool reticence, measured speech, and a deep-rooted, almost fierce vanity. He was intelligent, far more than most administrators whom Katāros had met over the course of his career, and diligent, too. He took his role of judge seriously. Every week he reported to the Duke of Rome – the secular ruler of the city – and every day would go to the old Roman Forum to carry out his legal duties, as well as seeing to his own personal matters of business.

All this, Katāros knew. But at first his own interaction with the judge was minimal.

Justus had given him a modest solar, simply furnished, in the draughty northern wing of the Palazzo Massimo. It was comfortable enough, with a small high window in the outside wall, a wooden pallet and well-made straw mattress for sleeping, a chair, a table. In truth, it was a little humble for his tastes and depressingly devoid of sunlight. But he didn't care. He had found a base and that was what mattered. For now.

If this was to be a new start, for a while at least, he could stomach almost anything. Even Justus, a cold sort of presence around the household, was not unpleasant to him. And provided Katāros fulfilled his duties as notary to the Dom, the steward more or less left him to his own devices.

If his goal had been anonymity, he had succeeded beyond even his most sanguine hopes. He functioned. He served. And no one paid him the slightest heed. He was given ample food. He was given money to buy new clothes. He restored himself to something of his old appearance. Though of course it was not to compare to the finery he had enjoyed in the emperor's service. Nor was it the custom for men to paint their faces in the west, nor to adorn themselves with jewellery and silken robes as once he had as the highest-ranking eunuch of the imperial court.

Instead, he learned a new sensation. That of being ignored. Of course, that had been his intention. To lay low. But even so, slowly, inexorably, this unwelcome feeling began to eat away at his heart.

In fact, there was only one man who seemed to have any use for him at all. That was Dom Vittorio's private secretary, a Latin from Naples by the name of Antoninus. And with equal inexorability, Katāros came to loathe this man who so enjoyed lording it over him. When the chance came to score a hit against him in return, it was too tempting to resist.

*

It was one of those rare occurrences when he'd been required to accompany the judge and his secretary to the old Roman forum. They arrived early, in the heat of the morning. The ancient pavings were covered in a layer of red dust, carried north from Africa on the late summer winds. Katāros still hadn't adjusted to the different smells of the city. Incense was the only passably tolerable scent on the air, emanating from the great basilicas and smaller churches around the centre of the city. Though it was a thin layer of modesty to cover the stench of the sewers and the unwashed pop-ulation. The epoch of aqueducts and municipal baths was long passed. Now the carcasses of fountains, their bowls broken, clogged with dust and debris, sat idle and abandoned in the piazzas.

The people were still there, at least some of them, although the great seas of the *populus romanus* who had occupied the city in centuries past were mere phantoms now. The edifices of empire lay cracked and crumbling, while a new kind of life had grown up among them. The churches. Saints like Cosma and Damiano were honoured at one end of the Forum, the soldier saints of Sergius and Bacchus at the other. The temples of the old pagan gods reborn into sacred sites of the newer Christian faith, holy martyrs and their strange histories sprouting like mushrooms among the ruins of faded glory.

Katāros was attending his master in the office of scribe, his duty to keep record of the administrative and legal matters Dom Vittorio decided upon through the course of the morning. It was tedious work. Meanwhile, Antoninus stood by, brandishing a pair of enormous codices which contained the entire *Leges Romanae*, though they were consulted only rarely.

As the morning progressed, callers would come – some clergy, some secular officers or administrators of the city – seeking the judge's opinion on this or that legal matter. Some interactions were more interesting to him than others. And none more so than the first time the Duke of Rome came calling.

Duke Peter had a convivial temperament yet a sharp, acerbic appearance: thin, sinewy and mostly bald. Very different to the languid affectations of Dom Vittorio.

Katāros had already decided that his master was a very different man on the inside to that which he appeared on the outside. His elegant sweep of copper hair, the glimmering, rather lazy eyes, the richness of his clothing – all these suggested a sort of limp and degenerate affluence which generations of privilege and entitlement had conferred upon him. But Katāros had already seen evidence of a mind as sharp as a leather-cutter's blade, at least in a legal sense, with an expansive memory and a quick intellect. In short, the man was impressive.

Nor was the eunuch surprised at the easy rapport between Duke Peter and Dom Vittorio. There was a respect and understanding there, to be expected between two intelligent men of the patrician classes. Their conversation, at first, centred around the young king of the Lombards, Liutprand, whose realm lay not a hundred miles to the north of Rome.

'He's a lion,' drawled Vittorio. 'And lions are always on the prowl for something to devour.'

'Agreed.' The Duke's voice was high and nasal. 'But there must be easier prey than Rome. Even if his strength is formidable.'

'He is young. The mantle of power is still a novelty to him. All we can do is watch and wait to see which way he moves.'

'Rome would be all but indigestible to the Long-Beards. They are barbarians, after all.'

'Ah, the eternal paradox of our city,' sighed Vittorio. 'We are bait that cannot be swallowed.' Both noblemen chuckled knowingly.

'What of Alaric, my lord?' Katāros couldn't have said why he should have bothered to correct their remark. 'And Genseric the Vandal? And Totila? Were they not barbarians also?'

The Duke's small face contorted into an expression of first surprise and then delight. 'What a curious creature you have here, Dom Vittorio. I've not noticed him before.'

'In truth, neither have I.' Vittorio lifted a sardonic eyebrow at Katāros.

'Impertinent *and* intelligent. With nerve like that, he's wasted as a notary. He'd do better serving on the city council. It might put one or two I can think of in their place.' The Duke turned to Katāros. 'In any case, young man, your master's point still stands. The city was sacked, true. But neither Goths nor Vandals could hold onto Rome. Even now, she is, and always will be, an independent power. This is ordained by God.'

'Does not the Duchy of Rome fall under the authority of the Exarchate of Ravenna, Your Grace? And that under the aegis of the empire?'

'By the sword of Saint Paul, he has a rare impertinence, this one! He seems determined to prove me wrong.'

'I suggest you hold your tongue, Amadeus,' hissed Antoninus, grasping nervously at his law books. 'No one asked your opinion.'

'Easy, Antoninus, easy,' soothed the Duke. 'We're not so fragile that we can't suffer a little correction.'

'Perhaps he has some personality after all,' observed Dom Vittorio.

'I wonder,' went on the Duke, 'do you also have an opinion on King Liutprand?'

'None of any value, my lord. Although in Portus I did hear he was partial to a cut of swordfish. They say, thanks to him, it is served every evening at the court of Pavia. Some fisherfolk are getting rich off that.'

'Hah! The things one hears! I dare say it's true. If the worst should ever befall us, Dom Vittorio, perhaps a dish of poisoned swordfish would be the answer to our troubles.'

'Ridiculous,' muttered Antoninus, glaring daggers at Katāros, then turning to offer wine for the Duke.

But just then, a small but lively group approaching along the colonnade distracted all of them. The newcomers had the look of travellers, judging from the long walking staffs. Probably pilgrims, who were common as gutter rats in this city of saints.

'Still more foreigners,' muttered the Duke.

'The price of our prestige, alas,' returned Dom Vittorio, as the leader of this pack of beggars drew up before them and bowed a small and nearly bald head.

'A fine day to you, my lords,' he declared, while his companions gaped with open mouths and vacant expressions from the noblemen to the frescoes and pillar surrounding the colonnade. 'Pray could we humble travellers beg a moment of your time?' His accent was foreign – of the north – and the Latin idioms he used were rather archaic, like the orators of antiquity. His cloak was threadbare, of coarse grey cloth, and worn right through in places. On his feet, several thongs of his sandals had come unstitched or snapped. His fellow pilgrims were similarly attired.

Antoninus stepped forward defensively. 'Move along, pilgrim.'

'Oh, let's hear the man out, Antoninus,' said the judge. 'I'll warrant he and his companions have come a good distance to stand here among the ghosts of our ancestors.'

'So have we, my lord,' returned the pilgrim. 'We've been upon the road for most of the summer.'

They smelled like it too, thought Katāros, his nostrils rankling at the collective cloud of sour sweat that rose off them.

'Where began your journey?' asked the Duke.

'Francia, my good lord. The city of Mettis.'

'A seat of Lord Chilperic, our noble king,' volunteered another.

'I heard he's not so noble,' muttered Dom Vittorio in the Duke's ear. 'They say his days on the Frankish throne are numbered.'

'None of us knows when our time is come, my friend...' the other replied behind his hand. 'Say, fellow, what brings you so far south?'

The leader's face glowed with piety. 'We come to Rome on pilgrimage...'

'Yes, this much I had surmised.'

'... to seek the blessing of the soldier saints on our lord king's behalf. Alas, ours is a land at war with itself.'

'Show me the land that can ever truly call itself at peace,' remarked Vittorio, with a wry tilt of his eyebrow.

'By God's grace, I trust we all journey towards heaven's high plains where peace will reign forever, my lord.' The pilgrim smiled. 'Our road has been long and weary. Yet nothing could have prepared us for the astonishing things we have already seen in this city.'

'You flatter us,' said the Duke.

'Not a jot.'

'Well then, you are most welcome here, ah...'

'Brother Narduin.' The pilgrim gave a fleeting bow. 'And these are my compatriots and fellow monks—'

'Yes, yes, no doubt,' cut in the Duke with an impatient glance at Dom Vittorio. 'But we must set you on your way. You say you seek the church of the soldier saints? You must mean Sergius and Bacchus. By good fortune, it is not far.' He pointed to the converted temple standing a little way up the slope towards the Capitoline Hill. 'There, you see—'

'In fact we seek another shrine, my lord,' interrupted this little Narduin. 'That of the Forty Martyrs. They too were soldiers, and my Lord Chilperic was most particular that we should seek their blessing, whose story so impressed him. But, alas, we have yet to find our way to it.'

'The Forty Martyrs? You must mean the oratory. Why,

91

that too is close by.' The Duke explained how they could find their way south along the Via Sacra to the church of Santa Maria, wherein, he said, they would find a new fresco, dedicated to the Forty Martyrs. 'It is a remarkable work. One which I commissioned personally.'

'How extraordinary,' declared Dom Vittorio, 'that such a tale should reach the ear of a Frankish king.'

'Even in our lands, it is well attested how forty soldiers made a good confession of Christ in the city of Sebaste,' replied Brother Narduin, with great eagerness. 'And how the prefect of that district, being hateful of all Christians, ordered them stripped and exposed naked on a frozen lake close to that city.' Katāros watched as, with cloying piety, the pilgrim pressed his hands together and gazed upwards to the heavens. 'The night, they say, was bitterly cold. Yet every one of the forty chose death rather than renounce his faith in Our Lord.' The monk lowered his pate, sun-raw and peeling, and beamed at the two noblemen. As if the thought of snuffing out forty souls of a winter's night was inestimably pleasing to him.

'But surely you have left out the most interesting part, man!' cried the Duke.

Antoninus cleared his throat. 'May I, my lord?'

'If you know it, Antoninus, go right ahead,' said the Duke, with an encouraging slap on his back.

Vittorio's secretary, clearly relishing his opportunity to shine before his master and no less a personage than the Duke of Rome, set about explaining how the prefect of Sebaste had warm baths prepared on the shore of the lake a short distance from those freezing wretches out on the ice.

'A temptation to succumb to their fleshly weakness and so prove inconstant to their faith.' As night drew on and the cold bit sharp as wolf fangs, one of the forty did indeed succumb. But no sooner had he slid in great relief into one of the cauldrons of warm water than his body stiffened and he dropped dead.

A collective gasp went up from the little gang of pilgrims. ''Twas the judgement of God,' murmured one of them, and there was a general nodding of tonsured heads.

'In any case,' continued Antoninus, 'one of the guards keeping watch over the forty, having witnessed this, looked out over the lake and suddenly saw overshadowing the wretched men a supernatural brilliance. Like rays streaming from the face of God.'

'How very poetic, Antoninus,' said Dom Vittorio, with a sarcastic glance at the Duke.

Antoninus gave him a simpering nod, taking the compliment straight.

'Well, go on with the story, man,' said the Duke impatiently.

'Of course, my lord. Where was I...? Ah, yes. This guard, then, beholding the vision, stood and declared himself a Christian on the spot. He threw off his clothes and went out onto the lake to join the remaining thirty-nine. Thus, their number once more complete, they all perished by the morning, and afterwards their bodies were burned.'

'An act of true courage,' pronounced the Duke.

'And faith,' added Brother Narduin.

Or else an act of incalculable idiocy, thought Katāros, but he kept his opinion to himself.

In fact, he had heard the story many times. The cult of the Forty Martyrs was widespread across the eastern empire. And never once had he been able to fathom the act of that Roman guard.

Why had he surrendered his life like that? What had he really seen up there in the cold winter sky?

'Well told indeed, Antoninus,' declared Dom Vittorio. 'I didn't know you had it in you, frankly.'

'I'm glad to be of some small service to our visitors, my lord,' said Antoninus, fairly basking in his master's tepid praise.

Seeing his gloating expression was more than Katāros could bear. 'The man's name was Aglaius,' he stated. All eyes turned to him.

'Whose?' demanded the Duke.

'The guard,' said Katāros. 'Aglaius of Nicomedia.'

'Was it, by God!' The Duke gave a hearty chuckle and turned to the judge's secretary. 'Well, come now, Antoninus, you must get these details right. Aglaius of Nicomedia. Next time you tell it you'll know, eh?' For this, Antoninus threw Katāros an acid smile.

The eunuch now felt strangely compelled to rub salt into the secretary's wound. 'It's true they say he saw a vision,' he continued. 'Although how anyone could know that, I cannot say, since the man went straight to his death.'

At this, there were a couple of doubtful looks among the pilgrim brethren.

'Ah, but such details must surely be in the knowledge of the Holy Spirit,' said Brother Narduin, frowning unctuously, as if the point was a genuine puzzle to be solved and these were not simply the unrealistic flourishes of a made-up story. 'Perhaps revealed to the authors of the martyrs' *passio* as they wrote it.'

'Mmm. That must be it.' Katāros offered him a thin smile. 'In any case, the details are what make the story. There is more, at least in the version I heard.' He found he was enjoying the attention, probably more than he should.

'Haven't we had enough of this tale?' muttered Dom Vittorio, taking another draught of his wine.

'Not at all,' cried the Duke. And to Katāros: 'Well, good God, man, don't keep us in suspense!'

'The martyrs were singing hymns of praise as the cold pressed harder. One by one, the voices fell silent. Until only one voice remained, singing over and over: "Our help is in the name of the Lord, who made heaven and earth." And then, at last, that voice failed as well. That was the moment Aglaius rose and threw down his cloak. He walked out on the lake, assumed the empty place and took up the song. He chanted until the first light of dawn. Then he, too, succumbed to the cold. The number of the forty was complete.'

He finished his story. For a while no one spoke, the silence lasting long enough for the moment to feel almost sacred. Like the silence before a great voice is about to speak. Katāros found the feeling decidedly uncomfortable. 'Of course there are many versions of the tale,' he said, breaking his own spell. 'But this is the one I have heard.'

'By heaven! Where *did* you find this fellow?' cried the Duke to Dom Vittorio. 'He knows more than the rest of us put together on almost every score. Don't you agree,

Antoninus?' He gave the secretary another hearty slap on the back.

'Indeed. He does seem to, my lord,' agreed the secretary, with a rictus grin. But Katāros saw in the secretary's unsmiling eyes that Antoninus did not share the joke.

That evening, they returned to the Palazzo Massimo. Katāros was tired and already looking forward to the seclusion of his own room. They crossed the great courtyard and reached the staircase that led up to the family wing of the palazzo. But before setting his foot to it, Dom Vittorio turned to Katāros.

'You intrigue me, Amadeus. I must say that.' He nodded thoughtfully and raised a bejewelled finger. 'Tomorrow we shall see whether there isn't something you can do for me which is more in accord with your particular... shall we say, talents? Good night to you.'

'Good night, my lord,' both servants echoed. And the judge disappeared up the stairs two at a time. Once he was out of sight, Katāros stifled a yawn and turned back towards the servants' wing. But Antoninus stopped him with a palm on his chest. 'I know what you're doing, boy.'

Out of pure reflex, Katāros jerked up his wrist in defence, knocking away the secretary's arm. 'Oh?' he snarled back. 'And what is that?'

'I know a cuckoo when I see one.'

'Is it my fault you can't remember a simple story?'

Antoninus's hand struck fast as a viper, the slap stinging Katāros's cheek like fire. 'I'm warning you. Humiliate me again in front of our superiors and—'

'And what?'

The Latin's bared teeth glared white in the gloom. 'You've had one piece cut off you, freak. There are always more, you know.'

A bold threat. But Katāros already knew Antoninus wasn't the man to follow through on it. He put a cooling hand to his own cheek, recovering his composure. 'I shouldn't worry, Antoninus. I'm sure the master has plenty of work matched to your talents, too. Sleep well.'

That night, Katāros lay on his bed, thinking of a thousand things. Of a thousand reasons, a thousand choices, but all of them led back to that same cell. That same cracked ceiling he was staring at.

The threads of the past bound him to this place and no other.

At last, his mind grew weary and began to drift, although he did not yet give in to sleep. Instead he stared up into the shadow of the rafters, his thoughts untethered, loose, on something vast and shifting, like his raft drifting out at sea.

After a while, he began to perceive things in the darkness, began to experience different sensations. Perhaps he was already dreaming, yet he still felt strangely alert.

He feels the cold first. Then the huddle of his body, his knees hard against his chest. On his shoulders, a heavy weight of wool – a cloak, maybe. And his breath billowing in frosty clouds before his face, his hand clutches around something solid and rough.

He looks up. Sees stars scattered across the firmament, the heavens gaping wider than he's ever known. As if the sky has been torn open, revealing hidden mysteries beyond, something too wonderful for a mere man to behold. Suddenly afraid, he averts his gaze, feeling something like shame as he drags it back to the earth. There, all about him, the snow lies sparkling. Then he hears it, barely a murmur at first, almost like the sigh of the wind, and yet... As his ears touch the sound and take hold of it, he perceives what it must be. Singing. The soft rise and fall of men's voices. Not sweet. Not even in tune. But assured. Defiant.

Now out in all that white, he sees darker shadows, each one a huddled heap of limbs crouched in the snow. At last, he understands. Together, they remind him of those old arrangements of rocks, laid out in remembrance, which he and the shaman would sometimes stumble across in the forests of the north. Places of ancient sacrifice, the shaman had told him.

He thinks how this place is not so different.

He watches, too afraid to look up, too fascinated to look away. The voices are fewer now; some shadows overcome by a deathly stillness; some still moving now and then. A roll of the shoulders, a twitch of the knee. Something inside him is stirring. Something in his heart. A kind of longing. But he knows he must resist.

Only two voices left now. He can hear them quite distinctly.

And then one.

And then silence.

He feels something flooding up into his throat. Words, a declaration... a *song*.

But he swallows it back.

He wants to rise. Wants to stand. Wants to be remembered.

To be seen by that awful presence looming high above. That awesome presence.

To be counted…

But will he stand?

He rolls his shoulders, testing the weight of the cloak. He squeezes his fingers, gripping the shaft of the spear more tightly, and all the while the silence calls out to him…

Will you stand?

CHAPTER ELEVEN

Damn that stubborn ox.

D	Erlan would have bet his eye that Einar would come, for an hour at least. But by now he had to concede that maybe he'd been deceiving himself that their friendship meant that much.

'Piss on it,' he muttered to himself, and tossed the empty melon rind among the other detritus bobbing in the harbour's dirty water. *It's past time anyway*, he thought, wiping the sweetly sticky residue of melon juice off the bristles of his chin.

Alone, then. So be it.

He stood up and shuffled down the steps to the stone jetty, the pain in his ankle growling softly. There, to join a flock of passengers shading their eyes against the westering sun as they waited patiently to load onto a *dekáliro* ferry. The Julian Harbour stank, as usual, and Erlan found himself hungering after the blast of fresh sea air out on the Straits. It had been too long since he'd been out of the city.

'One for Chalcedon,' he said when his turn came round, pressing a pair of copper pennies into the ferryman's hand.

'Return tonight?'

'Erm... no,' he said uncertainly. Who the Hel knew how this evening was going to turn out?

'Hold up there!' called a rasping voice behind him. 'You'd better make that two.'

Erlan turned to see the battle-scarred Sveär he knew so well trotting down the jetty towards them, looking for all the world like a common street vendor, in a tan tunic, a thick belt round his much-depleted belly, and a broad-brimmed sun-shader pulled tight on his bald head. 'My friend here is paying, of course.'

'Nice hat, fat man,' said Erlan, supressing his delight. And relief.

'Oh, this.' Einar rolled his eyes and flicked at the drooping brim. 'Orīana insists on it.' Then he hopped into the ferry with a thud while Erlan tossed the ferryman another two coins.

'And what Orīana insists, she gets, does she?'

'What do you think?' Einar said, with a scowl.

Erlan chuckled, and the pair settled down opposite each other as the ferryman got underway. 'So...' began Erlan. 'You came.'

'Figured I couldn't miss the chance of watching you make a total ass o' yourself.'

'Glad to give you some entertainment. I guess it's been a while since that wolf pit.'

'Gaaah! You know I've got your back, lad, when it counts.'

'So you're with us then? All the way?'

The fat man grinned, a grisly sight that was far from reassuring. 'All the way to Hel. And whatever lies beyond.'

'By the Hanged!' Erlan grinned back. 'I can't deny that's damned good to hear.' He reached out to join hands with his friend, but Einar held back.

'One condition though, Aurvandil.'

Erlan let his hand drop. 'Oh yes?'

'Orīana comes with us.'

Erlan snorted. He thought it had all come too easy. 'Orīana? Going north with us? Are you serious?'

'Well, there's no need to sound quite so incredulous. Listen, we've talked it through. Sure, she's worried as all Hel what it might entail, you being a reckless son of a whore 'n' all that. But she's game. That's if you talk these tricky bastards into it, which I seriously doubt.'

'But...'

'But what?'

'I mean... Orīana. I can see why you'd be smitten with her. *Here*. But think of what we're going back to. Think *why* we're going back. She doesn't want that, surely? Look, you've got a few days to say goodbye to her now. If you care that much for her then you must see that's best.'

Einar's eyes suddenly twinkled with mischief, and he shook his head. 'Too late for that, my friend.'

'Why? What are you not telling me?'

'The thing is, lad – Orīana and me...' A grin split his gargoyle face. 'We're married.'

'Married? You are joking?'

'And why the Hel not?' Einar replied, suddenly all indignant.

'I don't know,' fumbled Erlan. 'I mean, she doesn't seem the type. Hel, *you* aren't the type.'

'A man can change, can't he? Besides, it's done now. The priest said his words and it's done. So now, where I go, she goes. Simple as that. You want me, you get her. You don't want her, you don't get me. No fucking argument.'

'I still don't understand—'

'Because it were important to her, lad!' Einar blurted, leaning forward over his knees. 'When it wasn't looking so good for me, you get it... She said she wanted to see me again. On the other side, like.'

'Well...' Erlan blew out a long breath. There was no point fighting a battle already lost. 'Then I suppose congratulations are in order.' He held out his hand again.

This time Einar accepted it and pumped it for all it was worth. 'Thanks, lad – I know you mean it.'

'One thing, though,' said Erlan. The pumping stopped. 'What about Lilla?'

'What about her?' Einar growled defensively.

'Don't you think she'll want a say in who comes north with us?'

Einar dropped Erlan's hand like a hot coal. 'Not if she wants me with her, she won't,' he scowled. But then he looked up under his hairless brows, scratched at his beardless chin. 'Anyway, I was thinking, with Gerutha gone...'

'What?'

'Well, I figured Orīana could take her place, like.'

Erlan gave a short, sharp laugh. 'By all the gods! And you called us mad!'

'Why?'

103

'"Orīana, fetch my shawl. Orīana, pour my wine. Orīana, comb my hair." How the Hel is that going to go down with your new wife, eh, fat man?'

For a long moment, the two friends stared at one another across the little ferry, the plash and draw of the oars sounding in the background. Then Einar said, very softly: 'Ahh, bollocks.'

They found Demetrios, the *Fasolt*'s helmsman, in the tavern under the sign of the dolphin, as arranged. It was the only drinking house in the row of half a dozen brothels that occupied the rest of the Street of Sighs. The alleyway was cramped with coloured awnings of red and orange and yellow cloth, all sagging in the sultry heat. The cloying scent of cheap oudh perfumes wafted from the pleasure-house doorways, mingling with the smoky tang of agarwood flares and the fetor of the gutter running along the opposite wall.

'They hate her. Plain and simple.' Dimo – or 'the Greek' as the northerners called him – was propped against the tavern's counter, a cup of Thracian red hovering near his lips. A posture, Erlan guessed, that came only too naturally to him. 'Of course I've done my best to keep their spirits up. But it has been a most trying year, you understand – for all of us.'

'Aye,' muttered Erlan. 'For some more than others.'

Dimo gave an acknowledging glance in Einar's direction, the scalding kiss of the Greek fire all too evident on his hairless face. 'Even if none of them bear the wounds our fat friend here has endured, they still think themselves ill-used. Wish they'd never come, that sort of thing.'

'Hel, don't we all?' mused Einar.

'Well, you got a wife out of it, so that's something,' snapped Erlan irritably. Then he turned to Dimo. 'And you. Lilla paid you. And she's continued to pay you.'

'My lady has been most generous—'

'The crew was in your charge. So where the fuck are they, Greek?'

'Even gold cannot keep a pack of stray dogs.'

'Then what did it keep? Your cup full? Your belly warm?'

Dimo gave a shrug. 'My belly,' he conceded. 'And my bed.'

'By my reckoning, that makes you a thief.'

'Easy now. We're all friends here.' Einar laid a hand on Erlan's arm. Then to Dimo: 'So you're saying you don't know where they are?'

'I never said that. Only that I had no control over them.' His eyes narrowed with cunning. 'But even the wildest strays have their haunts.' He took another careful sip of his wine. 'One thing I've learned... If you want to catch a Northman, it's just a question of knowing where to look.'

'Welcome to the House of a Hundred Dreams,' said the door-keep, mouth wide in a hyena grin.

Erlan followed the others into the narrow atrium where reed-torches burned. Beyond Einar's bulky shoulders, he saw a lithe shadow pass in a billow of robes.

Dreams or not, the place was hot as Volund's forge. He felt sweat prickle all over his back as they entered. A few old divans were pushed up against the walls, arranged around low tables, about which were strewn several bodies, giggling and whispering and pawing at each other. There was a shimmer of thigh, a flash of half-covered breast. From somewhere concealed behind the acres of drapery covering the walls came the sound of a lyre, each note plucked languidly to match the mood of the place.

'Welcome, honoured guests, welcome!' exclaimed a voice that was neither man nor woman. Erlan was used to eunuch voices by now; the palace was full of them, and for the same reason as the brothels: eunuchs were reckoned trustworthy with the house valuables. The creature that materialised among them had long hair parted at the crown and dyed a shocking purple. Glazed lips curved in a simpering smile.

'A drink for such fine patrons!' He snapped his fingers at a servant boy lurking in a passageway. The youth vanished and reappeared moments later with a tray and three large white-bone beakers and a bronze pitcher.

'Please.' Their host ushered them towards an empty divan on the other side of the room. 'Once you're settled, I shall send over a selection of our most celebrated girls.' He cocked his carefully coiffured head. 'Unless you have more *specific* tastes. We cater to all.'

'We're here on business,' said Erlan bluntly.

'Business, pleasure,' soothed the eunuch, 'all is one here in the House of a Hundred Dreams.'

'Forgive my friend,' said Demetrios, deftly swiping a wine beaker off the boy's tray. 'Alas, Antipas, you see the company I must now keep. Northmen are barbarians and always will be. No sense of occasion, you understand.'

'Not even in a brothel,' muttered Einar.

'We seek our countrymen,' said Erlan, who had lost the last of his patience several cups of wine ago. 'Men of the north. They look like this one and me.' He gestured at Einar, although the two Northmen looked about as foreign to each other as they did to everyone else in that place.

'My lord, you understand that discretion is our most valued principle here in the House of a Hundred Dreams,' simpered Antipas.

'A whore-house with principles,' chuckled Einar. 'Now I've seen everything.'

'I don't give a rat's turd for your discretion,' said Erlan. 'Your patrons can rut away till their cocks fall off. Just tell me, are there any Northmen in here?'

'My lord, if you will insist on this approach,' Antipas trilled, turning to raise an eyebrow to two shadows hovering near the entrance, 'I shall be—'

'This way, is it?' Erlan shoved past the eunuch and, ignoring his flurries of protest, strode on into the passageway.

'Only paying customers are permitted behind the veil,' Antipas shrieked, then: 'Attilio, Attilio! After him, curse you!'

Erlan was already mounting the stairs two at a time, with Einar Fat-Belly thumping up behind him.

Moments later, he appeared on a landing swathed in shadow where the air was hot as Thor's breath and twice as foul. The walls reeked of stale sweat and the cloying stink of other bodily fluids, which clouds of cheap perfume had done nothing to conceal. Peering down the length of the corridor, he could make out a row of curtained cubicles.

'Now what?' said Einar.

'Stop here.' He could hear one of the doormen stomping up the staircase after them. 'Keep our friend occupied.' Einar turned while Erlan moved further down the corridor.

At the first cubicle, he snatched aside the drape. A woman with ebony-dark skin was bucking away atop a pair of pale legs and a mountainous belly. One glance around the mound of flesh at the man's face was enough to see he was no Northman. Erlan whipped the drape back in place, muttering apologies and feeling ridiculous.

Two more cubicles, another pair of couples in various states of sweat-slick congress; then a third, two women coiled around each other like serpents on the bed, while a bearded man watched them from a chair, wine in one hand, cock in the other.

'Oh, this is bloody hero's work, this is,' Erlan muttered, glancing back to where Einar was still blocking the stairway. He was about to give the whole thing up as a bad job when a voice came rolling down the corridor. Someone, drunk as a Dane and none too concerned to hit the right notes, was singing. And there was no mistaking it: the words were pure Norse.

Oh, I've sailed the circle sea,
  And never a wench did see
  A fella so fine
  For ale and wine
  To sink and drink as me.

Come friend, come foe
  Give the horn another go
  Salt and wind
  Reel 'em in,
  Bugger the bottle and start again.

And this northern ale-lark did just that, repeating the first verse in even more enthusiastic tones. Erlan knew the song. Most in the north did. Garik Long-Spear and his friends used to sing it late on a Yuletide evening after they were well on in their cups. It was called 'The Thirsty Viking'. And if that didn't mark the singer as one of their own, nothing would.

He followed the voice and soon came to the curtain, composed himself, then threw it aside.

A rump, pale as the moon, was hammering away at a woman on all fours, each thrust of his hips in time with the rhythm of his song, a gourd of drink swinging in his fist. The man's back was broad as a slab of granite. And, more importantly, he had white-blond hair.

'Good even to you, Estlander,' said Erlan in Norse, and the white head turned. Erlan was surprised to see the 'man' was barely old enough to grow a full beard. 'Forgive the interruption—'

But before Erlan finished his sentence, the massive youth leaped off the bed, flung the gourd at the wall in a spray of wine, snatched up breeches and tunic, and charged, bellowing like an angry bull, straight for him.

Completely off his guard, Erlan took the kid's boulder of a head in the belly and found himself launched through the cubicle doorway and slammed hard against the corridor wall. His head cracked against cheap plaster, sending blistering shards of pain through his skull. He crumpled to the floor, winded, while the bull took off down the corridor.

'Stop him!' Erlan yelled. 'EINAR!' He had little more to offer as he dragged himself to his feet. In the gloom ahead, there was more yelling, then an unearthly howl that would have put the fear into Fenrir Wolf himself.

He stumbled on down the corridor, dimly aware that the boy's flight had been checked and that two figures had crashed to the floor. He arrived moments later, breathless, with nothing injured so much as his pride. Einar and the Estlander boy were brawling on the ground, the brothel doorman looking on in stunned amazement. Einar had his forearm locked around the great bull's windpipe and was clinging on like a dwarf to his last scrap of gold.

'Stop your bloody flailing, boy,' snarled Einar through gritted teeth. The bull gave a gurning wail of protest, tongue thrashing wildly, face turning a deep shade of purple.

This needed to end, and quickly. Erlan dropped to one knee and drove the other hard into the boy's kidney. The bull bellowed with pain and he fell backwards.

Erlan flung himself down across the massive chest, pinning his arms to the floor. 'Catch his legs, fat man! Catch them!' Somehow Einar managed to manoeuvre past the boy's insanely large and half-swollen cock to flop his considerable weight on the boy's legs.

There was still a good deal more heaving and swearing and thrashing. But it was clear now that the bull wasn't going anywhere.

'Let me go, you filthy sack of whale-sperm!' he yelled.

'Just stop your wriggling, boy, and we will,' gnarred Einar. 'We only want to talk—'

'You cock-rot whoreson! Get the Hel off of me!' The bull was fairly foaming at the mouth.

'It's me, curse you,' croaked Einar from his stern end. 'Einar Fat-Belly.'

'Liar! Einar Fat-Belly is long dead!'

'By the Thunder,' Einar groaned, 'time's like this I wish I fucking were.'

'Ah, there you are,' said an unhurried voice in Greek from the stairs behind them. 'I see you've found young Vili.' Dimo had appeared at the shoulder of the ineffectual doorkeep, his brimming wine cup clutched doggedly in one hand.

'No thanks to you,' Erlan snapped in Greek.

'You did seem so determined on doing things your way.'

'Dimo?' The fight suddenly went out of the bull and his massive limbs stopped straining. 'What are *you* doing here? And who are these fuckers?'

'I am here,' the Greek replied, swaying gently on his feet, 'to be precise, because someone is paying me to be here... And these two friends of mine wish to speak with you.'

'Vili, you great troll, don't you recognise me?' said Einar.

Slowly the Estlander sat up, his flagstaff of a cock now wilting into his lap. 'Fat-Belly?' He took another hard look through the dust-clogged gloom. 'By Thor's beard, it is you!'

'The very same,' admitted Einar.

'But your face—'

'Still prettier than yours, boy.'

'We want to speak to you,' said Erlan. 'And the crew.'

'And who the Hel are you?'

'I'm your new skipper, kid. Erlan Aurvandil.'

The boy's broad jaw fell open.

Just then, soft footsteps came padding down the corridor. They all turned, and there, standing over the whole sorry heap of them, was the woman whose tender care of young Vili had been so abruptly interrupted. She looked proud as an empress, her willowy figure wrapped in a robe of yellow silk.

'Animals,' she pronounced, and went sauntering past them down the stairs.

They looked a surly bunch. Cocksure, indolent, stubborn as mules. In short, as mutinous a band of wastrels as ever took to the Whale-Road. And this was only the half-crew that had survived the journey from Dunsgard.

Once he'd got his clothes back on, Bull, as Vili was appropriately known, had led them through a warren of dimly lit streets, emerging at last into a little square somewhere in the eastern quarter of Chalcedon, where a miniature fountain chuckled away in the centre, and, on the far side, a tavern was huddled in one corner. It was little more than a hole in the wall, capped with a ragged awning, flanked by a couple of pitch flares, a scattering of tables and benches out front. And this pack of stray dogs lounging around them, while the taverner flitted between them like a hungry sparrow, recharging cups.

Their faces were ruddy from sun-burn, eyebrows bleached white on some of them, the embroidered collars and cuffs of their woollen shirts faded and worn, in dire need of repair.

They were men of the north, all right, but shabby as a barley field gone to seed.

'You should get that leg seen to,' croaked a bald man, older than the rest, who had the look of the leader. His jibe roused a few snickers.

'Keeping the lads busy, I see, Snodin,' said Einar.

'How goes it with you, Fat-Belly?' the other replied. 'Could say it was a pleasure, but I'd be lying.'

'There sure is less of him than there used to be,' said another man, further back.

'Ain't got no prettier, neither,' said another, this one with a thick Gotlander accent.

'These lads say the cripple's our new skipper,' said Bull, pointing at Erlan.

'We ain't got no skipper by my reckoning,' growled the bald one – Snodin, remembered Erlan, determined to learn their names.

'Oh no? Last I checked, you lads were serving a queen,' said Einar.

'No queen of ours,' Snodin returned.

'Yet you're happy to piss away her coin on cheap wine and cheaper whores,' said Erlan.

Snodin leaned forward over his table. 'Half of us are dead because of that bitch.'

'More 'n half,' threw in a long-shanked man with a gloomy face at the back of the company. 'Including my brother.'

'Valrik Viggorsson gave his ship to her,' said Einar, scanning the mirthless faces. 'You know that, Mikki Crow. Hel, we all do. We were all witness to it 'fore he passed. So no one here can deny it—'

'He was delirious,' called Mikki from the back.

'He was dying,' said Bull.

'All the more reason to honour his last command,' said Einar.

'Old Valrik promised us a fortune if we followed him,' said Snodin. 'But that woman got him killed. And since then, we've not seen so much as a silver buckle.'

'You were fools to believe Valrik then,' said Einar. 'No man could promise you a fortune. And you knew the risks well enough.'

'The risks didn't include being trapped here in another man's war,' growled Mikki.

'Truly said, Mikki Crow,' replied the Gotlander.

'All right then,' Erlan said, getting to his feet. 'So we all came here and got plenty of what we didn't want. But so far nothing tells me that you lot have any notion of what you do want or how to get it.'

'To get home,' said the small man with an elfin beard and clever eyes.

'To get rich,' said Snodin.

'To get laid,' laughed Bull. 'I got me plenty of that!'

'Shut your ale-hole, bollock,' said the swarthy man, the only one with jet-black hair.

'Go fuck yerself, Svali!' retorted Bull.

'Enough!' snapped Erlan. 'Lilla wants her ship back. And you with it.'

'Oh, your queen's welcome to her ship,' said Snodin. Wry looks passed between the men and there were a couple of knowing sniggers. 'Only it'll be without us.'

'Where *is* the ship?' cut in Einar, sensing, as Erlan did, that

114

they were hiding something. He turned to Dimo and repeated the question in Greek. The helmsman scrunched up his eyes in apology but said nothing.

'You, Snodin. Where is *Fasolt*?' demanded Erlan.

The old sailor shrugged. 'Well, it wasn't going to serve none of us if she fell into the hands of those Arab beggars, was it? She's a pretty thing, after all. He-heh! Bit like your queen.' More sniggers. 'So we took it on ourselves to make sure they weren't tempted.'

'She's hid in a cave a couple of bays to the east,' said Svali, cutting to the point. 'Though she took a bit of damage going in. That useless prick'll tell you why.' He nodded at the Greek.

Dimo frowned and took a sudden interest in the bottom of his wine cup.

'What happened?' said Erlan. 'Demetrios?'

'Erm, a small incident.' The Greek suddenly discovered the little Norse he knew. 'Nothing too serious.'

'You only went and stove the bloody bows in!' cried the Gotlander.

'Well, these shallow-bottomed hulls,' protested the Greek. 'It is not natural to sail a ship so big in waters so shallow.'

'Valrik coulda done it,' said the elfin man.

'But he took the Hel-road, didn't he, Kunrith?' snapped the dark-haired Svali. 'And there ain't no bringing him back.' He spat on the dusty pavings. 'There's a gash along her strakes under her steerboard bow. 'Bout an ell up from the keel.'

'Can she be repaired?' asked Erlan.

'Could be.' Svali folded his arms. 'Not saying we're of a mind to though.'

Erlan looked about him, seeing only obstinate, sullen faces. By all the gods, it was an uninspiring sight. 'You want to stay here. Then stay. Rut yourselves raw. Drink yourselves stupid. I don't give a rat's turd! Could be one day you'll find another ship to serve on. But looking at you flaccid bunch of fucks, I'd say you'd be lucky to find work shovelling sheep shit on a bath day.'

Mikki Crow kicked over a stool. 'Shit on that!' he swore. 'The bitch had her chance.'

Erlan stood up, surveyed the company of faces glancing darkly in all directions. 'All right. If that's your answer, then fair winds to you.'

He took Einar by the elbow and turned him round towards the square. He could tell Einar was confused, but the fat man didn't resist.

'Not sure you've quite mastered the art of persuasion there, lad,' he hissed as Erlan began to walk him away. 'You didn't even mention the bloody—'

'Shame though,' Erlan cut him off, calling back over his shoulder at the crew. 'All that *gold*… Someone's going to have it. Just none of you fellas, I guess.'

He hustled Einar to keep moving, but they hadn't gone five strides before Snodin's gruff voice called after them. 'Hey there, fellas. Perhaps we needn't be so hasty, uh?'

Erlan stopped, looked back. The craggy lines on Snodin's face creased into a smile. 'Reckon we got off on the wrong foot, is all.' He nodded at Erlan's crippled ankle. '*He-heh*. No offence meant, friend.'

Erlan scowled and made to turn away.

'Come now! Skipper!' Snodin lifted the pitcher in front of

116

him. 'This jug is brim-full. And paid for! Be a shame not to share it with old sea-brothers and their friends.'

Erlan shot Einar the ghost of a wink and turned back.

A few moments later, Snodin had pulled up more stools, poured out fresh cups, and invited them to take a seat. The other men drew in closer, ears a little sharper now.

'D'you know,' began Snodin in an amiable voice, 'I had heard of you back in Estland before all this began. A few of the other lads, too.' There were nods from several men. Though Mikki Crow was still sulking in the back. ''Course, we're river-men mostly. That's why Valrik picked us. None of us had much business in King Osvald's hall.' Erlan's expression soured at the mention of his former lord. Osvald was a dog's arse of a man whom he would sooner forget. 'But I did hear a tale or two.' Snodin wet his tongue with a slug of wine. 'The great Aurvandil! The Wanderer from the West! *He-heh.* And here he is. Sitting with us now.' He swung his gaze around his comrades. 'The honour, lads, eh? The honour! *He-heh.* We have us here a real hero. One of the *einherjar* through and through. Folks said you'd won some great battles near single-handed.'

'That true?' demanded Bull.

Erlan gave a dismissive snort. 'No one wins a battle single-handed, except maybe in the Old Tales. Sure, I've been in a few. Mostly I was scared witless, blind to everything but the blade in front of me, fighting to stay alive. That's all anyone does.'

Kunrith, the small man with the sharp beard, spoke up. 'They said Osvald had a taste for humiliating you. Is that why you left him?'

117

'I'll do the talking, Kunrith,' croaked Snodin.

Erlan thought back to the words of the strange mystic who had appeared one day in Osvald's hall. *Vassili*. That was a Greek name, he knew now, although what in the Nine Worlds had driven the little man so far north, Erlan had never really fathomed. But it was that encounter that had loosed him like an arrow hundreds of leagues across the wide world of Middle Earth, far more than Osvald's petty scores. 'It's all right.' He nodded at the elfin man. 'Kunrith, isn't it? Well, I had my reasons. But now I return north with Queen Lilla. We mean to raise an army. To take back her kingdom.'

'An army?' said Bull. 'How many do you have?'

He and Einar exchanged a look. Fat-Belly shrugged and nodded. Erlan held up two fingers. At this, the crew dissolved in a squall of laughter.

'Say one thing for you Sveär bastards,' said the Gotlander. 'You have a sense of humour.'

'Saying nothing of armies myself,' said Snodin. 'But I do believe there was mention of gold…'

'There was,' said Erlan. He cast his eye around his audience. 'By my reckoning, it takes two things to raise an army. A worthy cause—'

'Or else a whole shitheap of silver,' cut in the Gotlander.

Erlan grunted. 'I'm guessing gold works as well.'

'Don't tell me your queen's cause ain't worthy,' called Mikki Crow from the back, his voice thick with sarcasm.

'Whether it is or not, folk usually come round to seeing the right in a cause when there's something in it for them.'

'Such as?' asked Snodin.

'How about five hundred marks of gold for every man here?' said Erlan.

Even Einar's hairless jaw dropped open at that.

'*Five hundred* a man,' repeated Kunrith, his sharp eyes glistening. 'Why, that's... that's four and a half thousand marks just for us lads here.'

'So it is,' agreed Erlan. 'And we know where to find plenty more than that.'

'S'pose you just happened to dig it up or something, did yer?' drawled the Gotlander.

'Quit your ass-brain interruptions, Ran, and let the man speak,' said Svali.

So the Gotlander's name is Ran, noted Erlan. He licked his lips. He would get the measure of these motley bastards if it killed him. 'I don't promise you anything. Same as Valrik couldn't promise you anything. Not till it's in your hand. But I do know where – and when – to find it.'

'What's he on about "when"?' demanded Bull.

'I knew it,' spat Mikki Crow. 'I *bloody* knew it. Mark me, all of you. There's bound to be a catch.'

'Oh, there's always a catch, Mikki,' Erlan said, grinning up at him like a wolf. 'You want to hear what it is?'

CHAPTER TWELVE

Lilla's fingers rolled the arrow-shaft back and forth as she judged the distance. Though truly, she knew it perfectly by now. How many hours over the last months had she whiled away practising her shots in this quiet corner of the imperial gardens? It had been some small way of clearing her head. Focus on the tip – tip to target. And back again.

But today she felt restless. The days were passing quickly, and yet, perversely, the hours seemed to drag on forever. Preparations, Erlan assured her, were underway. She was to behave as normal. To go about her daily routines in the palace as if she meant to stay there forever. So she had come here, to the arboretum of dwarf trees collected from around the empire, to practise her skills, as she often did.

But all she could think of, one moment to the next, was that they were finally getting out. Finally leaving this place.

Erlan would never know the revulsion she felt for its cool marble halls and colonnades. Because she knew now what lay beneath its glittering grandeur. Those dark, dank dungeons cut deep into the bedrock below. Now, walking the pristine floors felt like walking on the shell of some monstrous egg, thin as a blade edge, which at any moment might crack beneath her feet and she would tumble down and down, back into the grasp of that hideous darkness.

She nocked the next arrow and drew back the bowstring.

Her chest tightened at the memory of the drip-drip-drip of the water over her face, the desperate panic in her throat for the next breath, the tinkling laughter of the eunuch standing by—

Breathe, she told herself, *breathe*… and she exhaled a long, thin stream of air through pursed lips. Then loosed.

The arrow flew with lethal precision, striking with a pleasing *thtock* dead in the centre of the circular target she'd had made for the purpose.

'Another fine shot, my lady.' Lilla turned to flick an acknowledging smile at her new handmaiden. Orīana had capped her eyes, peering at the target. 'I should hate to be on the receiving end any time you lost your temper.'

'Ha! If only disputes were settled so easily.'

Lilla had her doubts about Einar's woman – or wife, so Erlan had told her. But with Gerutha gone, she needed another to help her. To retrieve her arrows, if nothing else.

Orīana seemed willing enough. Although Lilla couldn't shake the opinion that she was playing a part. She had been what the citizens called an 'actor', after all – something, she gathered, akin to their own skalds of the north. Everything Orīana did was so over the top, performed with an exaggerated servility which seemed insincere. And it was beginning to get on Lilla's nerves.

'Would you care for a refreshment, my lady?' asked Orīana, gesturing at the fountain nearby. 'Or else I could send for wine?'

'Just fetch those five, would you? I wish to continue.'

Lilla watched the woman saunter down the path between the runt cedar trees towards her target, her hips swaying artfully from side to side. It was a practised walk, guaranteed to draw attention, certainly from the men around the palace. Indeed, Orīana's was a beauty that could not fail to attract admiring glances, even from female eyes. She was about as unlike Gerutha as Lilla could imagine.

My darling Grusha. How she missed her.

Of course, she had been thrilled to learn of Einar's survival. Horrified to hear of his injuries, wounded and perplexed at his reluctance to send word to her that he was still alive. She could have helped him, would have rushed to his side. But... he had preferred the care of this woman. Had been content to let Lilla believe him dead. It was hard to fathom, although, gods knew, she tried. And now this... *condition.* That she take on Orīana as her handmaid.

She had accepted. Could she have done anything less for a man who had proved so loyal? Yet there was something about the woman that made things awkward between them. Underlying this facade of servility, there was a kind of haughtiness. A kind of conceit. Orīana was a dozen years older than Lilla, at least. And to be sure, Lilla didn't require her to be abjectly humble. But she thought she detected a trace of hostility in Orīana's easy manner and honeyed words. A trace of hatred, even.

Orīana had returned. 'Your arrows, my lady,' she said with a deferential bow.

'Please, there's no need for that every time you hand me something,' said Lilla, taking the proffered shafts. 'You'll give yourself a sore neck.'

Orīana arched a finely plucked eyebrow and stood back. 'As you wish, my lady.'

'Einar tells me you are a celebrated name in the city,' said Lilla, laying aside all but one of the arrows and nocking that to her string. 'Some sort of singer.'

'Actor,' Orīana corrected her.

'That's right, "actor",' Lilla repeated, then loosed the string. 'Though I don't quite understand what that is. I'm told it's quite the spectacle.'

'So it is. But not for the eyes of one such as you, my lady,' Orīana added. There was that trace of superiority again. That downward slant. This time Lilla would not let it pass.

'Why is that?'

Orīana chuckled evasively. 'I think I would prefer not to say.'

'I insist.'

Orīana's full lips pressed into a thin weld. 'Very well, my lady. You are not one of us.'

'Us?'

Orīana shrugged a shapely shoulder. 'Those who must earn their bread by the sweat of their brow, the skill in their hands or the cunning in their heads.'

'Do go on.'

'Those who are only a couple of bad decisions from the gutter. Those who have to laugh at life because otherwise they would cry. Those who drink hard, eat little and must take their pleasures where they find them. It is people such as these come to see my "spectacle" as you call it.'

'I see.'

But Orīana was not finished. 'In short, you are a queen. You hold out your hand and someone is there to fill it.' To make her point, she held out another arrow for Lilla. 'No, my lady. You are not one of us.'

Lilla's gaze rested on Orīana for a while before she took the arrow. 'And yet I heard you're as popular with the patricians of the city as with the poor.'

'Hah! That's true, they did love me.' The actor sighed. 'But it's over now. The Hippodrome is closed, perhaps for good. The senate has decreed it. Even though it makes no sense now the siege is lifted.'

'Is that another privilege of rank?'

'What?'

'To make no sense.'

Orīana threw back her head and laughed. 'Quite possibly! But there's what they tell you and what they really intend.'

'What do you mean?'

'Money, it's always about money. Someone has paid someone. The Arabs are gone but the Hippodrome stays closed.'

'Who would benefit from that?'

'My bet is that old vulture Germanus.'

'The Patriarch?'

'Yes. If he had his way, you'd do better kissing the devil's puckered arse than raise a cheer for a Green or a Blue.'

It was Lilla's turn to laugh, slightly charmed by the coarseness of Orīana's language and her willingness to use it.

'These Greens and Blues... I'm not sure I understand what they are.'

'Horse-racing teams. Mother of God, that's what the Hippodrome is all about! Now *that* is something to be seen.'

Lilla shrugged. 'It has been closed the whole time I have been here.'

'Oh, but it's the greatest arena under heaven! Green and Blue represent the two factions in the city. Each supports a team of horses. And each faction hates each other with special loathing.' She chuckled. 'That is until a common enemy comes sailing over the horizon and then we're the best of friends again.'

'Then maybe it makes sense to have a period of unity in the city. It is so soon to open up any old wounds of division within the city.'

'Bah!' scoffed Orīana. 'No doubt that's what they'd say. But the fact is old Germanus can't stand to see anyone enjoying themselves. And his word stands.' Her face soured. 'The scabby hypocrite! I've seen his face in the crowd watching me, along with all the others.'

'Mmm,' mused Lilla. 'Well then... the city's loss is my gain.'

Orīana smiled. 'So it would seem.'

For a moment, the two women regarded one another. 'But only because you've nowhere better to be,' said Lilla.

Orīana's smile faltered.

But Lilla had already turned away from her, taken aim and loosed her next arrow. She saw, with satisfaction, that it had split the first shaft down to its tip. She was no one's second choice, no one's option of convenience – least of all this preening actor, who clearly needed a crowd's adulation like a drunkard needed a bottle.

'I don't take on servants just because it happens to suit them.' She turned and fixed Oriana's kohl-rimmed eyes with her own. 'You have no understanding of where we must go, or what I must demand of you. And not just you. Of Einar, of all who stand with me. I need an ally. An anchor. Someone of courage and resilience. Nothing makes me think that is you.'

'I have courage,' Oriana insisted, the lines of her face taut at the sting to her pride. 'And resilience. As much as you do. You don't know the life I've lived. And you don't know any more than me what is to come. The difference is, I don't need to know. I'll stand by Einar's side, all the same. And if he's with you then that's my place too.'

'Hm...' Lilla grunted. Not a bad answer. She turned and pointed through the arboretum to the target. 'That last arrow, I rather like it. Be good enough to fetch it back for me. And then you may go. I think I have no more use for you.'

With a disgruntled flick of her hair, Oriana spun on her heel and went to collect the lucky arrow. Lilla watched her go, wondering if the actor truly loved Einar Fat-Belly, and if not, what else she hoped to gain.

Oriana plucked the arrow from the target and started back towards Lilla, looking altogether fed up and preoccupied. Would she simply leave as ordered? Lilla wondered. If not, what argument might she bring next to win over a mistress she seemed to so despise?

But Lilla also wondered what courage she had. And what nerve.

Lilla still had three arrows in her hand. She nocked the first. 'Stay where you are,' she called, raising her bow.

Orīana was walking in line with the target, having reached about halfway back to Lilla's mark. Seeing the tip of Lilla's next arrow pointing straight at her chest, she halted.

'My father once taught me an unusual shot,' said Lilla, aiming down the line of the shaft. 'They say he was the best archer in Sveäland when he was a youth. He still had a few tricks even when age had worn the edges off him.'

Orīana didn't reply. She only drew herself taller, pressing her shoulders back, a statue of slender defiance. From Lilla's position, her head obscured the target entirely.

'I wonder if I can remember,' Lilla said, moving the nock higher up the string and tilting the bow to the left. She adjusted her aim a fraction to the right, then loosed, pulling her bow-hand inward at the last instant of contact. An eye-blink later the shaft thudded into the target. Orīana hadn't flinched.

'A hit!' declared Lilla. 'How funny that these old tricks stay in one's bones.' She nocked the next. It was swiftly done with two more arrows in her draw-hand. 'Shall we try the other side?'

Lilla repeated the action, mirroring the trick on the left side. Orīana's warm complexion had paled some, but she stood firm, a smile on her face, subtle and sardonic. As if she were used to dangerous games.

'You doubt my motives, my lady,' she said, once the second arrow had struck the target.

'Your motives. And your mettle.' Lilla thought back to the suffocating damp in that fetid cell, each desperate breath tearing at her chest. She knew that after that she could take anything. Perhaps already it was making her judge others weak.

'You can test my mettle all day long. As to my motive, it's simple. I love Einar.'

'Truly? You know I have great affection for him myself. That's why I wish to spare him any needless deceit or pain.'

Orīana scoffed. 'Was it you who found him on the brink of death? Was it you who nursed him back to life?'

'I didn't have the chance. Both of you denied me that.'

'You're blind, Lady. You owe me for his life. And more.' Orīana lifted her chin proudly. 'It was I who defied him and came looking for you.'

'Why defy him, if you love him so much?'

Orīana's lips pursed, considering her answer. 'He was tired. Tired in his soul. He had fought so hard to live... I guess a man does a lot of thinking once he's won a fight like that. He was resolved to stay dead to you because he knew what you required of him. He didn't think he could do it... But I could see the true desire in his heart.'

'What true desire?'

'The way he spoke of you. Of Erlan, and... Gerutha, wasn't it?'

'Yes. Gerutha.' At that name, Lilla felt grief squeeze her throat.

'You were his friends. And for a long time, it was as if all of you had died, and not he.' Orīana shrugged a shapely shoulder. 'I could not deny him what he so clearly loved. So I went to seek you out.'

'And to hell with the consequences?'

Orīana crossed herself. 'Providence rules us all.'

'Where I am from, we call it fate.' Lilla picked up two more arrows, holding three now in one hand. 'Shall we see whether ours are entwined?'

From that distance, it was hard to see Orīana's response. But she stood her ground. Lilla drew a deep breath. And then in rapid succession, she loosed the three shafts: right, left, and right again. Two of them whipped around Orīana as the others had. But at the third, the servant's arm shot out faster than thought and plucked the shaft from the air. For a second, she held it there aloft, long enough to fix Lilla's gaze. And then she spun it over her wrist and tucked it neatly under her arm with the other. 'Enough of this game, don't you think, Lady?'

Lilla lowered her bow, her eyes wide with astonishment. In all her days, she'd never seen a reaction so fast. And suddenly she could not contain her laughter. It came pouring out of her, long and free. Orīana, meanwhile, sauntered back to join her.

'Small wonder you drew a crowd,' Lilla said, once she had recovered herself sufficiently.

The actor laughed and handed back the arrows. 'Didn't I tell you, my lady?'

'You know, Orīana, I think you'll have to call me "Lilla" from now on.'

'Why is that?'

'Because although you might be a terrible servant, I've a feeling you'll make an excellent friend.'

'I'll call you whatever you want, if only you'll believe in me... Lilla.'

'One of us now?'

'You or me?'

Lilla smiled. 'How about both?'

It didn't take them long to gather up the remaining arrows and soon Lilla was sliding the last of them back into her quiver.

This was good. She felt satisfied that this new arrangement might work after all. And yet, she was still curious about this scarlet-headed enigma. 'Einar must have told you that we leave Byzantium in three days. You know we will not return?'

'I do.'

'And you have no regrets about leaving? Truly?'

'Well... Only one.'

'Your work?'

'No.' Her lips pressed tight with emotion. 'Something else... Someone I love very much.'

'Another man?'

'Heavens, no!' cried Orīana. 'I told you I love Einar.'

Lilla shook her head. 'Then who?'

'My daughter,' she said softly.

'Daughter?' Lilla was taken aback. Then again, Orīana was well over thirty. It should hardly be surprising that she had borne children. But Einar had made no mention of a child.

'She'll be fifteen this autumn. Her name is Marta.' Orīana sighed. 'I've not seen her in two years.'

'But where is she, if not with you?'

'She lives in a convent on the far side of the city. Under the walls of Blachernae.'

'But surely you can see her? It is not far.'

'It's not permitted. One day a year on the feast day of Saint Irene, we may speak through an aperture in the convent walls. That's all. Last year I was sick and could not go.' Her features clouded with sadness. 'The thought of leaving her forever is painful, I admit. Of never coming back...'

'But does Einar know all this?'

'No! And I would never tell him. If my heart must be split in two, it's my decision and mine alone.'

'But he should know. He's your husband.'

'One day soon I will tell him... But later, after we are gone.'

'But this changes everything. Surely you see that? I can't ask you to abandon your child. Not for me, not for any cause.'

'I've already made my peace with it.'

'For her sake, then. She needs you.' Lilla was remembering her own mother. She had been not a year older than Marta when her mother had passed on. Or chosen to leave, as Lilla saw it. She had been first to the body. Nothing but a hollow vessel by then, empty of her mother's soul, which had journeyed far and further, never to return. That wound felt fresh as the day it was inflicted. She shuddered at the thought that she would be responsible for wounding another girl in the same way.

'Marta doesn't need me,' said Oriana. 'She's a bride of Christ. The Church is her home, her everything now.'

'I don't understand. A daughter's place is with her parents.'

'Parents!' cried Oriana with a short, jagged laugh. 'Oh my, Lilla, we are from different worlds. I knew her father not even for a night. For an hour, at most. The Lord only knows where he is now. On this earth, in heaven? Or knowing him, most likely in hell.'

'An hour?' Lilla's expression must have betrayed her surprise.

'Hah! Does that shock you? That your new "friend" was once a whore?'

Lilla felt suddenly foolish, naive. 'No. Nothing shocks me anymore.' Nor should it. After all, could she reckon herself any less than Orīana after what she had done for Erlan? 'We all have our beginnings. It's how we end that matters.'

'Maybe. Sometimes it's hard to change the road you're on. I should know.'

'Well then, how much more important that you're there for your daughter, with her father gone.'

'You don't understand. Marta has the Church. She has forsaken me, forsaken everything of the outside world. I am nothing to her now.'

'That cannot be true.'

'If it isn't, it soon will be. In the spring, she takes her full vows. After that, I may as well be dead to her.'

Lilla could not say why but she found this deeply troubling. It just felt so unnatural – especially when Orīana clearly still held such affection for her child. A thought suddenly leaped into her head, a wild, joyful thought. And before she knew it, the words were out of her mouth: 'What if Marta came with us, too?'

'What?'

'Oh, but she must, don't you see?' she said excitedly, growing in her conviction.

Orīana peered at her, trying to discern in Lilla's face whether this was some insensitive joke at her expense. 'Is this another test? Surely you don't mean it?'

'I mean it with all my heart.'

Still Orīana could not believe it. 'Please, this parting from her is cruel enough—'

'Just tell me – could it be done?'

'I... I don't know. Perhaps. If she were willing. But Marta is devout.' Orīana put her hands to her cheeks and laughed. 'Mother of God, she is unlike me in so many ways! She believes the convent is her calling.'

'Her "calling", what's that?'

'What you might call her fate.'

A mischievous grin spread over Lilla's face. 'Why then, fates can be changed. Come, let's set ourselves to the task!'

CHAPTER THIRTEEN

Antoninus proved no great adversary, as Katāros had feared for a while. Nothing followed from his threats of that night. The only discernible difference in him was a sort of resentment, which simmered away whenever Katāros entered the judge's presence. There was a beautiful irony to it – that, despite his taunts, it was Antoninus who lacked the stones for ridding himself of his rival, and not the eunuch. Katāros was almost disappointed. A challenge would have been something: a whetstone on which to sharpen old instincts. Not that it changed his own schemes much. For he had quickly seen that, in order for him to rise, Antoninus must first fall. Or else be swept aside.

This was made easier since Dom Vittorio seemed minded to make more of Katāros's unused talents, just as he had avowed. This began, naturally enough, in the realm of Roman law, employing the eunuch as a sounding board for all manner of intricate legal questions. Katāros soon saw this was a genuine passion for his master who, while possessing far deeper and broader knowledge of the law than Katāros did, seemed to enjoy watching the way his new notary would think through any particular problem. It reminded Katāros of those former days – not unpleasant to him – of his training in the imperial schools of Byzantium. He had always been an enthusiastic student to any wise teacher, and there was no doubt Dom Vittorio had a kind of wisdom.

Oftentimes Vittorio would hold him back at the end of a working day. With Antoninus dismissed, the judge would furnish Katāros with a drink, invite him to sit, and steer their conversation into lighter realms. He wanted to know of the eunuch's past and how he had come to be – in Vittorio's words – 'as he was'.

Katāros had spun a little web of lies sufficient to satisfy his master's curiosity, imputing the Byzantines' crime against him onto their Arab enemies.

'It's not something we see much here in the old empire of the west,' said the judge, rising from his seat to go to the window and gaze out into the dusk. Beyond his shoulder, Katāros could see the nighttime flares being lit all across the Caelian Hill. 'I find it hard to fathom… what it must be like to be you.' He chuckled softly and raked fingers heavy with gold through his copper hair.

Katāros said nothing. After all, how could he begin to explain something like that.

The judge turned to him. 'I mean, you've seen what I do, Amadeus. In order to judge someone justly I must first put myself in their place. I must reason why a man would take one action and not another. But someone in your place, of your kind… I find I cannot do it. As if there is an invisible barrier between us.'

'My kind, my lord? I was a boy, as you were. I simply never became a man. At least not the man I might have been.'

'It seems a pity. Someone with your talents could have risen to great heights. With time and the right connections.'

I did rise to great heights, my condescending lord… Like the morning star, Katāros thought bitterly. *Yet like him, I too fell.* 'I need no pity, my lord. For there's one advantage I possess which you do not see.'

'What's that?'

'It is of a somewhat delicate nature.'

'Don't be ridiculous,' he scoffed. 'You may speak freely.'

'Well… You're a man. You are all which that entails. But I… I have been both man and woman. That is something you will never know.'

'Man and woman?' Vittorio gave an indifferent snort. 'Is such a thing so enviable?' But his look showed his curiosity was genuine.

'It can be.' Katāros held his master's gaze. 'It has been. Many times.'

Vittorio's brow creased a little, then he pushed a hand through his hair again, as if to sweep away whatever thought had lingered there, and turned the subject to something else. But Katāros had marked the moment, and knew it could be turned to his advantage. If he so chose.

He also knew that he had told only half the truth: that the man he might have been was not quite dead. The ghost of him still haunted this body, like a mournful echo in an empty cavern.

But even the longest echo must fall silent in the end.

One morning soon after this he was summoned to Dom Vittorio's quarters. There was no sign of Antoninus, and he found his master standing behind his desk, tapping pensively at its gleaming surface, a piece of vellum in one hand. Katāros saw at once the broken seal of purple wax. For a second, horror filled his veins; he was only too familiar with that colour of imperial authority. Was it possible that his past had hunted him down to this backwater of the empire? To Rome? His mind was suddenly crowded with sickening images of violent pain and torment, which were always there, lurking not far away in the shadows of his consciousness.

Yet there was nothing in his master's face that justified his alarm. If anything, the judge looked tired, the weary lines of care that came with middle age beginning to set into something more permanent.

'I've been summoned to Ravenna,' he said, flipping the parchment at Katāros.

'Ravenna, my lord? To what purpose?'

The older man sighed and flung himself down in his chair. 'The Exarch has called for a general council.' He reached for his wine – by this time of day, he was usually into his second flagon. 'You wouldn't believe the number of officials he needs about him to hold his hand while he muddles his way through his... difficulties.'

'Difficulties, my lord?'

'The usual. Relations with this new Lombard king, the trouble in the duchies of the south, Spoleto and Benevento, and such. Money, taxes. Always more taxes... That is unless word has come down from on high,' he said, fluttering his hand airily over his head.

'On high?' repeated Katāros. 'You mean the emperor?'

'Of course the emperor! The Great Lion, they are calling him in the east now – which only goes to show you how little originality those damn Greeks have. I think I preferred it when he was busy fending off the Arabs. Now the siege is over, he has time again to meddle in our affairs.'

Katāros stood frozen to the spot, like a man who has felt a serpent slither over his foot. Because although the judge had not said it outright, Katāros had already guessed he was not telling him all this for no reason. The idea that he might come face to face with Leo, or with any of his court, was almost too dreadful to contemplate. He would be unmasked in a moment. Shorn, shackled and shipped off to Byzantium the very next. 'But surely the emperor will not attend in person?' he asked, trying to sound indifferent, which was far from how he felt.

'Leo? Heavens, no! The Great Lion is not interested in the west, not really. He has too much of the east in him. No, he'll send some of his flunkies in his place to lord it over us.'

That was hardly less disturbing. 'How long will you be gone, my lord?'

The judge looked at him as if he were half-witted. 'Not me, Amadeus. Us! You and I, damn it.'

'You wish me to accompany you?'

138

'Of course I do! Why else would I be telling you this? By God, you're being obtuse today.' He glanced again at the parchment. 'And if we're to reach there in time for the opening of the council, we must leave within the week.'

'But... what about Antoninus, my lord?' God knows, if Katāros had thought this was coming, he would have remained in blissful anonymity and been damned content with his lot. He cursed his own ambition, and not for the first time.

'What *about* Antoninus?' Dom Vittorio snapped irritably.

'It's just... nothing, my lord. No matter.' There was no way out of this.

'Good. Then here's to the journey!' He raised his cup at Katāros, then drained it to its bottom. When he looked up again, his gaze settled on Katāros for a long while. The eunuch could see the swirl of the morning's wine in his dilated pupils, felt the invisible cords of inhibition between them loosen. 'It's funny, Amadeus. You ask of Antoninus... but d'you know, it's your company of which I've become very fond these last weeks.'

Katāros's mind was racing. Looking for angles, divining outcomes. 'And I yours, my lord,' he said carefully.

Vittorio smiled at him. 'Well, you don't have much choice in the matter, do you?'

Perhaps that was it. An idea was coiling around his mind like a serpent around its prey. 'No, my lord, but... I *would* choose it... if I did.' He spoke falteringly, as if confessing some secret. He lifted his eyelids a little and softened his mouth, a trick he had put to use many times in the City.

The judge sighed. 'Ah, you have a fine mind, young Amadeus.' His voice was thicker, his tone something more than admiring. 'And a fine face. A gentle face. I confess, the more I look at you... Well, your face becomes more indispensable to me every day.'

That night, when Katāros returned to his room, he did not light the oil lamp. Instead he took a small copper mirror he had acquired and stood in the puddle of moonlight spilling down from his little window. In the silvered gloom, he gazed at the face staring back at him in the mirror's polished surface. His face. A 'fine' face. The thin, dark eyebrows; the brown eyes, flecked with gold. He ran a finger down his lean, straight nose, over his lips, along the lines of youth in his cheeks, so true they might have been sculpted by the hand of Hephaestus himself. On his smooth brow, there was no sign of cruelty. No sign of courage, either. He saw a handsome nothing of a face. He turned away from it in disgust, threw the mirror on his bed, and wondered what this journey would bring.

Two weeks later, he was watching that same finger moving in a different mirror. The faint glow of dawn had begun to fill the window behind him. By its light, he watched his fingertip sweep down the bridge of his nose, under his right eye, down his cheek, and along the line of his hairless jaw.

He remembered the action from those days when he would prepare himself for some grand address of the emperor, or the audience of some puffed-up dignitary at the imperial court. The hours he would gaze at that face, applying a line of saffron-scented kohl under his eyelash, a dab of carmine to the arc of his lips. The muscles of his face remembered these movements, like a soldier strapping on his armour for war.

Indeed, it was very like armour. The mask he'd created had been a shield behind which he could hide, obscuring not only his true face but his true thoughts. It had served him well. Too well, perhaps. Since anonymity had bred complacency, and it was that which, ultimately, had been his undoing.

But today he had no such protection. Men did not wear make-up here in the west. It was considered shameful for a man to beautify himself too much. They did not make of themselves moving statues, as was the fashion in the imperial capital. No. Here, he would go into battle without armour or shield.

Outside a church bell began to toll the morning hour. A shape in the gloom behind him began to stir.

'You're up early.' Vittorio's voice still crackled with sleep.

'I wake with the dawn-light,' Katāros replied over his shoulder. 'An old habit.'

'For God's sake, come back to bed.'

His master unfurled his arms and stretched out the last vestiges of sleep. His copper curls were a ruffled mess, one lock draped rakishly over his left eye. He smiled at Katāros and lifted the covers. Beneath, Katāros could see the gleam of his hairless chest, the sweep of muscled arms.

'Hadn't we better get ready, Vito? The senate convenes in two hours.' Vito was the name his master insisted he call him now... a mark of their new arrangement. Their new intimacy.

'Damn the senate! Damn all of them!' He laughed, with that low, languid laugh, which declared that the world and everything in it was his. 'Come here. There's still time.'

It had taken a hundred miles on the road for the judge to make up his mind, the distance doubtless spent wrestling with his conscience or else some petty scruple. When Vito had finally come to his bed, Katāros had anticipated it. Had already seen in the man's looks the seed of curiosity take root and grow until it gave forth its natural fruit. They were in the mountains just north of Perugia, an unseasonably cold night, and had sought out rooms in a roadside inn. Katāros had woken to see a robed figure standing above him. 'Can't sleep,' his master's voice had murmured in the darkness. 'This cold and... And *you.*' It was an accusation – laced with hatred as much as desire. Slowly Katāros had peeled away his blanket and got onto his knees, eyes locked on his master's above him. Vittorio had let his robe fall open, reached down to stroke his hair...

The rest was as the rest always is.

Once the seal was broken, there was nothing much to stop them. No prying eyes from which to hide. The judge travelled light, with only his notary for company, and a drudge of a servant to attend to the basics – a squat man in his late thirties and a naturally heavy sleeper. But for his relentless snoring, they were never disturbed.

Katāros could not deny the thrill he felt at this new development. It was a kind of victory after all. A seal of assurance that he still had power over powerful men. And that feeling, so long absent, of being wholly desired, of satisfying his master's growing appetite for him, somehow restored him. With each passing day – and wakeful night – he felt his old self returning.

Now, in Ravenna, he felt almost free, even despite the risk he was running. Sometimes he would watch Vito sleeping next to him, imagining the judge's pale wife back in Rome,

142

sleeping alone. He was certain that was more thought than Vito ever gave to her. He wondered what would happen on their return. Surely, this could not go on in such brazen fashion. But for now, he would take what pleasure he could and worry about the morrow when it came.

Ravenna, at that time, was a grand city, second only to the Queen of Cities herself in the empire. The place seemed at first a sort of confluence of the sanctity of Rome and the imperial grandeur of Byzantium, with many more functioning imperial buildings than the former, and an even greater rash of churches than the latter. After all, Ravenna was chief city of the Italian Exarchate. The business of empire flowed from its halls. And it was for such business that they were there.

Already, they had attended several meetings of the Exarchate senate. None of the matters of the day seemed that pressing. Indeed, now that the great crisis of the Arab siege had passed, there was a general spirit of relief. Jubilation, even. One in which Katāros could not share – though he might at least have pretended to, had there not been one small fly, as it were, in the perfume.

A face he had seen among the multitude of officials when the senate first met. A face he knew well. A face that could be his undoing.

And that was why, before he returned to Vito's bed, he threw a final glance over the rooftops of Ravenna – and there he saw not the golden shards of morning sunlight darting between the bell-towers, but only the long shadows that each of them cast.

*

'Order, order!' cried the officer of the Curia, whose bleating yelps seemed incapable of bringing the numerous conversations to heel. Eventually, through some sort of cosmic improbability, there came a moment when everyone happened to draw breath, and that was enough for silence to get its foot in the door. A hush fell over the marble hall.

'Thank you,' declared the Magister of the Senate, with exaggerated exasperation. 'If we are to get through our order of business this side of Christ's Mass, I suggest we all pay greater heed to the exhortations of my esteemed colleague there for *silence*.'

There were a few scathing looks around the chamber. Grown men rarely enjoyed being talked down to like schoolboys – which the Magister did all too frequently – and these scores of high-ranking imperial officials did so even less. They had already endured two days of this, and although the hall of the Provincial Senate House was cool and airy, the sheer number of officials crammed along its benches was stifling. Every senator came with at least one junior, and many with more than that.

The fault lines between the Roman faction, aligned behind the Duke of Rome and Pope Gregory's delegation on one side, and the imperial faction in Ravenna under the Exarch, a man called Scholasticus, on the other, ran deep and divided them on nearly every issue.

On taxation: 'Despite the Great Victory which God has bestowed on us, the Arab wars continued,' the Exarch declared. 'His Majesty now intends to take the fight to the enemy. To strike a blow while the new Caliph is on the back foot. For that we must raise taxes.'

At this, instant jeering from the Roman faction.

'The papal patrimonies must shoulder their share of the imperial burden.' Scholasticus manfully pressed on in the teeth of the Roman barracking. 'In these uncertain times, we all must make sacrifices—'

'We all know the sacrifices *you* are willing to make, Excellency,' cried out a papal representative. 'Your own estates in the Pentapolis have increased five-fold since you arrived here.'

'Order, order,' bleated the Senate Speaker. 'Delegates must allow the Exarch to speak.'

Such was the nature of the debates on almost every point.

On the Lombard threat: 'Pope Gregory is undermining imperial policy by sending his own embassies north to King Liutprand, appeasing him when he ought to be resisted,' complained the Exarch.

'How can you possibly object to such diplomatic channels, Excellency, when you have so clearly benefitted from them?' shouted the highest-ranking of the papal delegates, a bishop named John, whose jutting chin and bunched fists minded Katāros more of a pugilist than a cleric. 'Classis would still be in Lombard hands had Pope Gregory not brokered its return.'

And so the arguments tipped one way and then the other – on doctrine; on military spend; on building projects; then looping back to taxation again – agreeing on almost nothing, clouds of anger and recrimination and mockery and frustration filling the hall.

The long hours on the hard marble benches should have been a purgatory of tedium. But Katāros was only half-listening to the endless debates, the far greater part of his attention fixed on watching every face that came and went from the hall. It was a wearying concoction of boredom and fear; the fear that he was not the only one studying faces in the crowd as the hours drew on. That one of these imperial delegates would see him, would know him, and he would be denounced.

It was the vagueness of this fear that made it so intolerable. So much so that when the threat became suddenly specific, it felt almost a relief.

It had been late on the first afternoon when everything had changed. When that new face had appeared among a group of scribes recording the debates on the far side of the chamber. Katāros had recognised him at once. They had known each other in Byzantium. Intimately so. And the recognition sent rivers of ice down his spine.

His name was Eucephius.

He had been – now, what had he been? – *kanikleios*, that was it. A senior official in the imperial chancery, a role that had given him some freedom around the palace. Hence, he had come into Katāros's orbit. Not for long, but long enough to better their acquaintance. Some whiff of scandal had brought all that to an end. A junior in his department had defrauded the imperial purse and Eucephius had carried the blame. He had been moved sideways into some more administrative role. One of the multitude of logothétai, if Katāros's memory was not playing him false. Most likely in the diplomatic service, given his presence here.

He was an ordinary man with ordinary tastes, a man of no exceptional talent. And yet this ordinary man now represented to Katāros a deadly threat – since if Katāros recognised him, there was every chance that Eucephius would recognise him back.

Katāros sat, his nerves stretched tight as bowstrings, his back streaming with sweat that had nothing to do with the oppressive humidity of the city or the number of bodies crammed into the senate hall. Dozens, then hundreds of times, since that first moment of recognition, he had glanced askance across the floor; and yet he dare not look directly. Sometimes Eucephius was present, sometimes he was elsewhere. After three days of this, Katāros was fractious with worry, although somehow he had managed to conceal his anxiety from Vito.

Each night he gazed at his face in the mirror, wishing he could somehow conceal it. He cut his hair till it was so short he began to resemble the statues of the old emperors that stood about the city with their close-trimmed curls. 'Makes you look younger,' commented Vito, 'if that were possible.' Katāros could tell he didn't approve. Men like Vito never did. They had always preferred him with long, sweeping hair that shone like polished jet-stone. In Byzantium, his hair had been his glory, lending him that allure of feminine beauty. The touch of the angels. Probably, it helped men like his master forget what it was they were doing. Cutting his hair only served to remind them that, when all artifice was stripped away, he was simply a young man of twenty-one summers, with an ugly scar where his penis should have been.

At the end of the third day, with only one day of the convention remaining, he began to dare hope he would escape detection. When the day's debate was concluded,

147

Vito lingered only for a few trifling conversations before he signalled to Katāros that he wanted to leave, perhaps eager to get him alone. He took his elbow and began to steer him through the crowd when a high nasal voice stopped them both.

'Dom Massimo, as I live and breathe!' They turned to see the vulture skull of Peter, Duke of Rome, weaving a path towards them through the other delegates.

'Good day to you, Your Grace,' returned Vito with a formal bow.

'Where the devil have you been hiding? I missed you at the Exarch's palace.'

'We've found ourselves other lodgings,' Vito replied, sounding admirably nonchalant. 'The centre of the city is too damn choked with dust at this time of year. Our rooms are out at Classis.'

'Aha, the harbour. I see,' Duke Peter chuckled knowingly. 'A plate of mussels, a jug of wine, then a quick fuck before a gentle stroll home to bed. That it?'

'I beg your pardon.' The judge's ears instantly turned red. By the Virgin, thought Katāros, the man would make no spy.

'The brothels, man! Classis is famous for them.' The Duke sniggered. 'Heaven may forgive you your little foibles, old man. Although I doubt Cornelia would if she ever found out.'

'Yes, well, happily she never will,' Vito growled. 'So then, what do you think? Much has been said.'

'And little decided. As usual.'

'There is still one more day.'

148

'One? Great God! Scholasticus could have another fifty and still be no closer to making any real decisions.'

'Well, one thing is clear. We'll get no help with recovering Cumae.'

'That is undoubtedly true,' lamented the Duke, then all of a sudden ducked his head behind Vito's shoulder. 'Agh, by the balls of Saint Paul! Don't look now but there's a delegate from the capital heading straight for us. Damnation! He is the most insufferable bore. Eucephius, by name. You should make good your escape while you can.' He shot Vito a wink. 'Back to those mussels, eh?'

'Your Grace,' exclaimed a strong, low voice, smooth as liquid honey, which Katāros remembered all too well. His senses became alert at once. He turned his body a fraction, offering only an oblique angle of his face to the newcomer behind him. Even so, a man whose very body odour he now recognised was standing only two feet away from him. He suppressed his panic, streaming long, thin breaths through his nose. 'Your Grace,' Eucephius began again in heavily accented Latin, 'I'm so glad to have caught up with you finally.'

Duke Peter spread his hands. 'A man in my position finds himself well supplied in many things. Time, alas, is not one of them.'

Eucephius responded with a simpering laugh. 'Indeed, Your Grace. I find myself in the same position.'

'We were just leaving,' said Dom Vittorio smoothly.

'A wise decision,' smiled Duke Peter. 'Oh, I suppose I should introduce you before you escape. This is Eucephius Palamas, *logothetēs tou genikou*—'

'*Tou dromou* now, Your Grace,' Eucephius corrected him.

'Well then,' chuckled the Duke. 'Going up in the world, eh?' Eucephius gave him a gracious nod at the compliment. '*Logothetēs tou dromou* of the Western Diplomatic. This is Dom Vittorio Massimo, *iudex maximus Romae*. A man of impossibly noble heritage. Cut him and I swear he bleeds purple.'

'Truly?' said Eucephius, turning now to Vito. 'I fancy I met another Massimo the last time I was in the west. Valerius, I think it was. A cousin perhaps?'

Dom Vittorio offered him a cold smile. 'There are many of us.' He gestured at Katāros. 'This is my secretary, Amadeus.'

Few noblemen would have bothered with an introduction. Secretaries were there to observe and assist, barely worthy of acknowledgement to those of the patrician class.

But there it was, already done.

Eucephius turned to face him. Katāros felt the cold coil of fear deep inside him. For a chilling moment, their eyes locked. The eunuch had never felt so exposed in his life. But he couldn't look away. He saw the same striations of gold in the dark blue irises, the same double-crease between those thin eyebrows. Mother of God, he knew every detail of that face. But what did Eucephius see? A young man in a plain tunic, wearing not a single ornament of gold or even silver. Shorn hair, face plain, unpainted. For once, he thanked the Virgin that almost every encounter he'd had with Eucephius, his eyes had been masked with kohl shadow, and he was pretty sure his hair had been dyed red at the time, too.

He watched for any flicker of recognition. But there was nothing. '*Yassas, kyrios.*' Eucephius spoke the greeting in Greek with curt formality, then turned back to the Duke.

150

Meanwhile Katāros's breath remained still as a tomb; it was premature to feel relief.

He waited while Vito excused them with a quick bow, then turned to leave with his master. Whether it was the change in angle or some other movement that goaded Eucephius's memory, he'd never know. But in the tail of his eye, Katāros caught a sudden change in the Byzantine's expression. A tiny contraction around the mouth, a wince of shock. There one moment, gone an eye-blink later. He concealed it well. But Katāros didn't miss it.

He didn't miss anything.

And as he followed Vito through the crowd, he felt the weight of those Byzantine eyes on him with every step.

CHAPTER FOURTEEN

Erlan gazed on the sword hilt in amazement and shame. Leo had once again summoned him to his personal solar, high in the Daphne wing of the palace. But never in a hundred moons would he have guessed it was to present him with a new sword.

'That is Damascus steel,' said Leo. 'Strong as a titan's bones.'

'It's... astonishing.'

The emperor chuckled. 'Thought you'd like it. It was forged by a smith from Frankia. A kingdom not a thousand miles from your own land, I believe. The best workmanship there is, I'm told.' He ran his fingertip from the cross-bar up the base of the blade where a line of runes were stamped into the metal. 'This man's name is Alf-iya. See, it is graven there.'

'*Ulf-rað*,' Erlan corrected him slowly, noting each rune with care. He was better at reading them since Lilla had insisted he master the skill. 'It means something like "Mighty Wolf".'

'What strange names you northerners take.'

'It's not so different from the Great Lion.'

'No, I suppose not. Anyway, the man lives here now.'

'Here in Byzantium?' The notion seemed bizarre, so out of place. A Frankish smith in the imperial capital.

'He does busy trade here in the Strategion quarter. There's no finer bladesmith in all the empire.'

Erlan's eyes flit jealously over the remarkable artistry of the blade. Wrathling had been the best he'd ever held. Sometimes the ghost of it still haunted his hand, even now. But he'd never seen the ring-sword newly forged. Wrathling had already served five generations of Vendling lords when he'd taken it from his father's hall. But this...

He gazed on rainbow rivers of steel, the metal folded over itself, again and again. Pattern welding was a rare skill among the smiths of his own lands. Even the richest lords there would struggle to find the silver to pay for a blade forged like that. Yet here was one being gifted to him, its hilt plated with gold, inlaid with silver, marked with tiny Frankish runes and also letters of the Greek tongue. A meeting of two worlds. The north, and the empire. Two worlds. Divided loyalties.

Aye. This was a blade destined for him, all right.

'Majesty, I have not words—'

'Oh please, I need no words,' cut in Leo. 'You've earned it. Besides, any envoy of mine must look the part.'

Erlan clasped the weapon to his chest, where his conscience was burning with shame.

Leo clapped his shoulder. 'This mission cannot fail. You understand its importance.'

'I do. But it is simple enough, is it not?'

'Nothing is simple in this world.'

'You're not worried, though? The empire is secure, the enemy beaten.'

'Thwarted, maybe. But, by heaven, this is not over.'

'The Arabs will not come again, surely?'

'The Arabs are merely one of my enemies.' Leo gave a rueful snort. 'Seven times the crown has changed heads in the last twenty years. I'd be a fool to think that just because the Caliph's forces have withdrawn, my place on the throne is assured. The devil works through the dreams of ambitious men. If I were an ambitious man, if I wanted to make a play to win the throne... it would be now. Now, while the sweet lull of victory still clouds our heads and dulls our wits.'

'But the people have hailed you their saviour. Without you, the city would have fallen.'

'Such acclamation only goads the envy in other men's hearts.'

'Do you suspect treachery?' Erlan wondered whether his own dark eyes betrayed the secret purposes of his heart.

Leo inhaled, grimaced, then expelled a long sigh. 'I have a son now, an heir to the throne. But an infant heir is a seedling. It can easily be crushed. And meanwhile, I am only one cut of an assassin's blade from death at any moment.' He drew his thumb across his throat. By the Hanged, he was in a grim mood, to be sure. Soon to be a lot worse if their plan succeeded. 'Vigilance, always. That is my watchword.'

'Your people love you. You're their protector. They would support you against any usurper.'

'I wish I could be so sure. After all, I took the crown from a weaker man. Why would another not seek to take it from me? Or from my son?' His face looked dark as thunder. But then, he seemed to shrug it all off, and as quickly as it had come, his melancholy evaporated. 'Bah! Enough of these dark misgivings! These are not your concerns. You serve your mistress now. Or you will soon, once this last service to me is done.' He clapped Erlan's shoulder decisively. 'You leave in two days, yes?'

'We do, Majesty.'

'Then I wish you God's speed.'

Erlan took his leave and made for the door, relieved to be escaping. The deception in his own heart was becoming suffocating.

'And keep hold of that sword better than you did the last! I won't tell you how much the damn thing cost me.'

'I will, Majesty.' Erlan closed the door.

He limped away, his relief soon giving way to a sickening guilt. The emperor was a decent man, undeserving of this betrayal. This had never been Erlan's way. It was honour above all that counted; that much his father had always tried to hammer into him.

And yet...

Hadn't he already murdered his kinsman? Hadn't he been the ruin of his sister, oath-breaker to his father, traitor to a king? Why not a common thief as well?

He stopped and looked down at the gilded hilt of his new sword. Abruptly he unsheathed the blade a few inches till he could see his own eyes staring back at him in the gleaming metal. After a few moments, he shoved the blade back in.

Gold is gold, he thought. *And our need is greater.*

CHAPTER FIFTEEN

They had failed.

And following Orīana up the stairs to her apartment, Lilla could not help but feel sympathy for her. Their trip out to Blachernae had not gone as either had expected. The convent of Saint-Andreos-Without-the-Walls was an austere place from the outside, an impregnable box of stone. But once inside, they found a serene haven of running fountains and blooming flower-beds, the cool air fragrant with the scent of miniature fig trees and jasmine climbing the cloister pillars.

They had been ushered into the office of the abbess of the convent. Mother Anna-Sofia listened patiently while Orīana made her appeal – a mother's plea from the heart. Marta must make up her own mind, was the abbess's response. The girl was summoned and Lilla saw her for the first time. She was short in stature, her head entirely covered with a scarf of turquoise blue, and dressed in a robe of the same. She glanced at neither her mother nor Lilla when she entered. Her gaze was fixed rigidly on the floor. Even so, Lilla could observe her face: eyes of a dazzling dark blue, like sapphires. She was young, not yet seen fifteen summers, with eyebrows black as a raven's wing and a bonny face. But when she spoke, her voice was flat and toneless. The interview that followed was one of the strangest Lilla had ever witnessed. It was almost as if the girl's wits were not wholly there. She reminded Lilla of the mystics of her own people, the *valar* and *spakonur* and such. And she seemed impervious to her mother's pleas. When Orīana told her she was leaving Byzantium and wanted Marta to come with her, the girl simply asked: 'Why?'

'Because I... I love you, of course. I want you with me... if you want that too?'

Marta had answered that what she wanted for herself was of no account. All that mattered was what Christ wanted for her. 'His is the path I must walk. His, the life I must live.'

Orīana had continued to plead with her, but her words met only a cold and impenetrable wall of refusal. To Lilla, it seemed such a waste. This bright, attractive girl with her life before her, choosing to entomb herself in a prison of stone. But there was no dissuading her from the choice she had made. And so they had left Marta to her cloister.

Perhaps, thought Lilla, it was simpler this way.

'We're late,' said Orīana, leading Lilla down the landing to her door. 'The others should be here already.'

Lilla touched her elbow. 'Before we go in... You're not too distressed to do this?'

'Distressed?' Orīana snorted. 'I'm not distressed, I'm livid. That little vixen! It was all an act, you know that. Playing the little saint in front of her precious abbess. An act, I tell you!

Although she's probably convinced herself she believes it. But sooner or later, she won't be able to deny the blood that runs in her veins. Under that pious facade, she's wild, that one. She always has been.'

Lilla could not imagine a girl less wild than the jewel-eyed doll she had encountered earlier that day. 'Then you're ready for this? For all of it?'

'I am.' Orīana nodded. 'Heaven may take Marta, if that's her path. The rest of us can walk the road to hell.'

The hour was late.

Already their little band of conspirators had talked through half a dozen different plans, and every one of them seemed bound to end in failure.

'It's like one of those riddles in the Old Tales,' said Erlan, taking an angry pull at the cup of wine with which Orīana had furnished them all. 'How do you separate twenty thousand marks of gold from three fully armed chelandions?'

'At least we know it's in the *Stilico*,' said Lilla.

'Yes, but I don't see how that gets us any closer to separating it from the others. Short of starting a naval battle which we're guaranteed to lose.'

'Even if we did separate off the *Stilico*,' said Einar, 'it's still armed with at least three of those infernal fire-syphons. The *Fasolt* wouldn't stand a chance.'

'But we still have the element of surprise,' countered Lilla. 'If we found the right place from which to launch an ambush. At night. Dimo, can you think of anywhere that would serve?'

'I can think of several coves up the straits, and others along the coast where we might hide. But as soon as we showed ourselves…' The helmsman shook his head. 'We might get close but it wouldn't take much for them to react. And we'd be in the same position.'

'Huh,' grunted Fat-Belly. 'You mean down on all fours and ready to be fucked—'

'Einar!' exclaimed Lilla. 'Please.'

'Anyway, what would you know about that, you great wine-skin?' observed Orīana.

Einar raised his cup to her. 'Not as much as you, my dear, I have to admit.'

'*Malakia*,' she said, thumbing her chin at him.

'I love you too, *Agápi Mou*.'

'Are we not straying somewhat from the point?' asked Demetrios from over the rim of his cup.

'Indeed.' Erlan scrubbed pensively at his beard. 'It's about narrowing the odds. Yes, we have to separate the *Stilico*. But then find a way to deal with the men onboard.'

'Do you know which ship you will be on, *bárbaros*?' Demetrios asked Erlan.

'Not yet.'

'We need you on the *Stilico*,' said Lilla.

'Obviously. But I can't guarantee it.' Lilla glared at him and he added, 'I'll do what I can.'

'Could you take Einar with you?' said Demetrios. 'As your *spatharios* or something.'

'That will provoke too many questions. Everyone will wonder where he's been.'

'What if you drugged the crew?' ventured Orīana. 'Like

159

the witch, Circe… You know I played her to a packed crowd in the Hippodrome not two years ago.' She sighed at the memory. 'Hey, those were the glory days.'

'A fine performance,' said Demetrios, raising his cup to her. 'I remember it well.'

'Again, off the point,' said Erlan.

'Maybe,' said Lilla. 'Maybe not. I could make up a sleeping potion from the herbs in the palace gardens without much trouble. Root of valerian, for example. A concoction of lavender, galphimia, passionflower. They're all there. Even poppy seeds. I could gather the ingredients tonight. Have it ready by morning.'

'We are not drugging an entire shipload of marines,' said Erlan. 'It's far too risky. You'd probably poison them all to death anyway.'

'Well, maybe that's the price of our success…'

'No. *No!*' Exasperated, he leaned back on his stool against the wall and rubbed wearily at his eyes. '*Streð mik!*' he swore in Norse. 'Maybe it just can't be done.'

'I don't accept that,' said Lilla firmly. 'I can't.'

'The priests do say,' chuckled Demetrios, 'that with God, all things are possible.'

'Then we'd better get down on our knees and pray,' said Orīana. She looked at the two Northmen. 'After you, *bárbaroi.*'

But before any of them had a chance to do that, Einar rose to his feet and planted his knuckles on the table-top. He leaned forward, his fire-ravaged face twisting into something like a smile. 'I reckon we've got this all back to front.'

'How so?' said Lilla.

'Well, we're all sat here thinking how do we lower the odds? How do we shave down the risk? But what if going all in is our best chance? What if it's our only chance?'

'What does that mean – going all in?' asked Demetrios.

'I mean, stealing the gold before it's even left the city. Right out from under the emperor's nose.'

'By the Hanged,' said Erlan, 'you really have lost your wits.'

'If I have, it's only 'cause I've been following you around all this time.'

Just then Lilla heard a faint tapping sound on wood. Her whole body stiffened. 'Quiet! What's that?' she hissed.

'I heard nothing,' said Demetrios.

'Nor I,' said Einar.

But there was the sound again, louder this time, floating down the corridor and into the room. 'The door,' said Orīana.

Guilty glances shot between them. Orīana began getting to her feet.

'Sit,' said Einar. 'I'll go.'

Lilla watched the other faces as Einar went to the door and the rest of them listened. Orīana, a hand clasped protectively to her breast; Erlan leaning forward, fingers resting lightly on the haft of his knife. Even Demetrios had put down his wine cup.

She heard the door open, the creak of hinges, a low murmur of voices, too soft even to know whether the newcomer was man or woman. The pad of footsteps back towards them. And finally, ahead of Einar's bulky frame, a small figure emerged into the dim lamplight of the parlour. Lilla recognised at once the neat oval shape of her head, bound tight in her novice's headscarf, and those fiery blue eyes.

Orīana's hand flew to her mouth. 'Marta!' She rose and went straight to her, folding her into her arms. 'Oh, my child!' Marta stood passive as a statue as her mother showered kisses on her face. Einar stood by, looking somewhat bewildered.

'She says she's your daughter,' he said. There was no mistaking the edge to his voice.

'Yes. Yes,' confessed Orīana. 'I know, I know, I should have told you.'

'Oh, do you really think so?' returned Einar. 'I mean, I'm only your husband.' Sarcasm didn't suit him.

But Orīana was too focused on Marta to take notice of Einar's indignation. She ushered the girl in, found her a stool, sat her down. 'Are you hungry? Or thirsty maybe? Here, have a drink.' She pushed her own cup of wine in front of the girl. Marta peered gingerly into the cup, then picked it up between two fingers and took a swig.

'What happened? Why are you here? After all you said.'

'I had to come,' the girl said softly. 'The Lord showed me something after you had gone.'

'The Lord? What do you mean?'

'Does Mother Anna know you've gone?' asked Lilla. She was already imagining the abbess alerting the city guard, and wondered how long it would take them to find the dwelling place of the missing girl's mother. How long before another bang on the door?

'It's possible by now. But anyway, it doesn't matter,' said the girl defiantly. 'She, too, will submit to the Lord's will. As I must.'

'But how did you get out?' demanded Orīana.

For just a second, mischief glimmered on the girl's face. 'Please, Mother. You think I don't know by now how to quit the convent if I really wanted to? In any case, the Lord told me to come.'

'Come where exactly?' said Erlan in a low growl. It was the first he had spoken since the girl had entered. And Lilla saw now he was looking anything but happy.

Marta looked at him. 'With you, of course.' As if it were the most natural thing in the world.

Erlan's dark gaze swung to Lilla. 'Did you know about this?' From his expression, she realised that she too probably should have forewarned him of their plan.

But Marta spoke before she could: 'A great light has dawned on those living in the shadow of death.' The girl's words were sticky with enchantment.

'I don't understand, my love,' murmured Orīana.

'After you left, I went to my cell and met with the Lord in prayer.' She reached out and took her mother's hand in her fervour. 'He gave me a vision, Mother. A *vision*. So clear... He showed me a cross as tall as the sky... burning, burning. I was standing alone in a dark forest. There were trees all around.' Lilla tried to remember how much they had told Marta about where they were going, of Sveäland and the north. She thought very little, if anything at all. Marta had certainly never thought to ask. 'And I saw a great moon shining down upon the flames. But as I looked, it changed. The light turned from bright silver, darkening and darkening until it ran red, the colour of blood... I was there,' she whispered. 'The air was biting cold. My breath clouding before my face. And then I heard a voice speaking out of the flames. It said, "A great light has dawned on those living in the shadow of death..."'

She stopped. As if these words, so strange and obscure, were sufficient explanation for her sudden appearance.

Orīana cupped her daughter's cheek, as one might touch the face of a child sick with fever. 'Here, let me take this off you.' And with the practicality of a mother, Orīana began loosening the headscarf and unwinding it from Marta's head. The girl sat there, passive as before, allowing her mother to fuss over her until eventually the blue-green covering was removed and only a cap of old white cloth remained, holding up her hair. When Orīana slipped this off too, the girl's long hair tumbled in a sudden rush down her back, waves of long, looping curls the colour of oak that fell to her waist. Her sapphire-bright eyes looked up at her mother. 'I will come with you. Wherever you are going. The Lord has willed it.'

'What the hell is this?' said Erlan, the sharpness in his voice breaking the spell that had held them all entranced. 'Where we're going is no place for a child. Lilla, you know that.'

'I am no child,' Marta said defiantly.

'She's my daughter. I can't leave her now she has come.'

'Lilla?' Erlan said again, ignoring them. 'For Frigg's sake, talk some sense into them.'

'I... I said she could come with us,' Lilla admitted. 'And if the girl wishes it – which she plainly does – there's no argument.'

'No argument?' Erlan swore. '*Sorðinn!* You know there's no guarantees for any of us. Who knows which of us will see even the day after tomorrow?'

'If she does not come, then nor do I,' insisted Orīana.

'Nor I,' growled Einar automatically, staring deep into his cup, as if he wished he could crawl right into it.

Erlan shook his head. 'By the Hanged.' He looked at Lilla. 'You had this all worked out. You didn't think you might have told me?'

'I would have but I didn't see the point. Until now, she had refused to come.'

'You don't think this changes things?'

'What does it change? We all know the risks.'

They stared at one another a long moment. Until at last he shook his head with another scowl. 'Just so we're clear,' he jabbed a callused finger at the girl, 'I'm not responsible for that.'

'I can look after myself,' returned Marta sharply.

'Really? By all the gods, that's more than the rest of us, girl,' he muttered, and took a long swig on his wine. This seemed to signal the end of his opposition. Once he'd drained the cup, he thumped it down on the table and wiped his lips. 'All right then. Where were we?'

'Under the emperor's nose,' muttered Einar.

'Ah, yes.'

'You said the more we're prepared to risk, the greater our chance of success,' said Lilla, wanting to move on from Erlan's reluctant acquiescence to the girl's presence. 'D'you mean stealing the gold here, while it's still in the city?'

'Exactly,' nodded Einar.

Seeing the focus of their talk had moved away from her, Marta slipped quietly onto her mother's lap and settled in to listen, allowing Oriana to tease at the tangled tresses of her hair.

'Arbasdos told Anna that he intends to load the gold tomorrow night, ready for their departure the following dawn,' said Lilla.

'Then that's when we'll have to take it,' said Einar. 'Once it's on board.'

'But how?' asked Orīana.

Einar shrugged and blew out his lips. 'Buggered if I know. That's where my thinking runs out.'

'Christ's blood, this is insanity,' scowled Demetrios from his corner, and poured himself another cup of wine.

'Insane... but not impossible.' Erlan leaned forward, a lupine glimmer in his dark eyes. 'I think I begin to see it now.'

'I'm glad someone does,' sighed Demetrios.

'It's going to take all of us to play our part.' Erlan jerked his head at Marta. 'Even her.'

'We're ready,' said Lilla, putting down her cup, her eyes scanning the room. 'All of us are ready.'

'Fine,' he nodded. 'Then here's what I think we should do.'

CHAPTER SIXTEEN

They lay beside each other, panting in the gloom.

The sweat on Katāros seemed to grow cold quickly this night. Everything seemed cold. The long walk back from the senate hall. The staircase up to their rooms, draughty with the winds off the Adriatic. The spiced wine, the touch of his master's hands. Even the fire of desire within him, which at times had burned white hot, tonight remained obstinately cool.

This night.

He was distracted, that was all. He was not himself. Mother of God, nor was he supposed to be! Was that not the very point?

Did Eucephius recognise me?

It was the unanswerable question that had filled his mind, far more than what Vito had been doing to him the last hour. He had watched the shadows deepen, each passing moment drawing him closer to the anonymity of night. Surely if they were coming for him, they would have done so by now?

Vito heaved a sigh and reached for the wine by the bed. 'You're tiring of me, Amadeus, I can tell.' The tone of his voice was so matter-of-fact that Katāros wondered whether he was almost glad.

'No, I—'

'You don't need to lie.' His master took a long gulp of his wine then wiped his lips on the back of his hand. 'I was curious. I'd say you've more than satisfied my curiosity.' He turned his head, his steady eyes anchoring Katāros's gaze. 'Wouldn't you?'

Katāros allowed himself a flicker of a smile. 'It's been a long day, that's all. A long day to do nothing but listen.'

'That's the whole point, sweet boy. They grind you down with boredom,' he traced a teasing finger down Katāros's hairless chest, 'then *strike* when you're at your weakest.' At the word 'strike', he gave a smart flick to Katāros's nipple. The shock of pain shot up and down his body in a jolt of exquisite pleasure. He sucked in his breath and Vito laughed. Maybe this arrangement between them had not quite run its course.

'Vito,' Katāros murmured. 'My Vito. I don't think I can face it all again tomorrow.' He drew a finger down the line of Vito's jaw. 'Is there any way that I can—'

'Skip it? You are joking. If I must attend another day, I'll be damned if I'm doing it without you.' Even so, he was smiling.

'Bastard,' Katāros whispered, easing back on his elbows and running a tongue across his lips.

Vito chuckled. 'I see you need reminding who's master again, boy.' Katāros watched the lust flooding into Vito's eyes, felt its rush into the ghost of his own loins as well. He reached out, slid his hand down Vito's stomach.

'Turn over,' Vito muttered, gripping hold of the eunuch's hip and pulling him closer.

Katāros inhaled, drawing the effusions of sandalwood perfume that mingled with Vito's sweat deep into his lungs, readying himself as he rolled onto his side. But before he even felt his master, there came a loud pounding from below and the sound of a man's voice beyond the courtyard gate.

Vito's head turned. 'What in God's name is that racket at this time of night?' The knocking continued. They waited, neither moving, although dread was already crawling unseen under the eunuch's skin. 'Where is that blasted inn-keeper?' Still the knocking, fit to shake the gates off their hinges. With a sigh, Vito gave Katāros's rump a slap. 'Well, boy, it seems our lesson must suffer a slight delay.'

Vito jumped up, snatched a robe from the chair and, wrapping it around himself, went to the window. He peered down into the courtyard. Somewhere below a decrepit voice was croaking: 'I'm coming, I'm coming, rot you to Hades!' followed by a stream of incoherent mutterings.

Again, the knocking.

Like a hare before the hounds, Katāros found his senses darting in all directions. His clothing, the window ledge, the landing, the stairwell to the roof, the balustrade outside, his master's dagger – all flashed through his mind in an instant. Yet there he remained, limbs locked, still as a pagan idol.

At last came the sound of the gate being opened, the weary groan of unloved hinges, the tramp of feet. Half a dozen at least. The noise finally broke Katāros's enchantment.

He sat up. 'What's going on?' he called across the room, trying to sound unconcerned.

'Looks like a troop of imperials,' replied Vito from his lookout. 'There's someone else with them. I can't tell... The old fellow's stalling them. I wonder...' Suddenly he cursed. 'Damnation, I feared as much. It's me they want. The inn-keeper just pointed up here. God rot the man! Now the fool's leading them up here.' He turned and hurried to the door. 'I'll head them off.'

'I could go for you—'

'No, no. By heaven, no! I can't let them see us like this. I'll go. Whatever it is they want, I'll send them away till morning.'

And before Katāros could kick off the covers, Vito had slipped out of the door and down the hallway. The eunuch didn't waste a moment. He pulled on his woollen leggings, knotted the drawstring and had his cotton tunic over his head almost before the door was closed. Thus half-dressed, he opened the door a crack, and seeing the landing was clear, he went to the rail. Already he could hear voices. He peered down the stairwell. At the bottom, three flights below, there were shadows moving. He strained his ears. He could hear the bass tones of his master's voice, but at that distance only certain words reached him, floating up like murmurs of the dead rising from the underworld.

From his master, he caught words like 'absurd' and 'mistake'. From the other, some officer of the guard, he heard the Latin words *'imperator'*, *'camerarius'*, and then, distinct as the chime of a bell, his own name. *Katāros.*

In an eye-blink, he'd turned back to the room. Would have fled that very instant, but for a change in the timbre

170

of the voices. They were rising now, in anger and dispute. Until, with sudden ringing authority, his master's voice came clear: 'Wait! *I* will go. If what you say is true, I'll bring him to you.'

In reply, a grunt of acquiescence, then footsteps climbing the stairs. Solitary steps. Katāros stayed only long enough to hear whether the tramp of hobnailed sandals followed them. Once he was sure they didn't, he sprang to life.

He was back in the room, snatching up his own sandals and cloak. *Did he even need a cloak?* His mind worked fast. There was money in a leather pouch on Vito's belt, golden bracelets, a silver brooch. He snatched up his master's tunic and threw it aside, then stopped. There was Vito's dagger. Long, broad, the pointed sheath concealing the steel within, suddenly full of malice.

He snatched it up and surveyed the rest of the chamber, their strewn possessions, the scrolls, the chests, the chairs, the table. Nothing that could help him. He went to the window. Below, he could see two soldiers posted at the gate, spears tall and sharp. Hidden in the shadows, his mind leaping like a hind in terror of the huntsmen, he assessed his escape. There was a narrow balcony a floor below to the left. Beyond it, and another floor below, the courtyard side-wall met the front corner of the inn. Beyond that, a river of shadows. Doubtless some shit-slop alleyway that led the devil knew where. From his window, he could see that it was narrow. That at least would provide some cover. A head start, maybe. A thread to clutch at, nothing more.

He gulped. He was a man of no great physical courage. Yet he was also a man who had run out of road. A man with no options. The alternative was too terrible to contemplate. He had been the tormentor too often in those dank dungeons beneath the Great Palace to believe that he would be spared the worse of what the emperor's enemies must suffer. Wasn't his crime the greater? Traitor to the city. Traitor to his lord. Betrayer of the Faith. By God, they would slice him up piece by bloody piece.

Still, he wasn't in their hands yet. And he was determined to steal for himself some small advantage if he could. If he could just slip away unnoticed... Down below, he saw one of the guards looking up at their window. *Once he looks away,* Katāros told himself, he would climb onto the sill and jump. *Once he looks away...*

'Come on, come on!' he snarled, eyes welded to the man's face.

Then he heard footsteps on the landing. The door behind him opened. And there was Vito, silhouetted in the doorway.

'Amadeus?' Their eyes met across the room. There was a slow, stupefied note in his voice. Like a child who had walked in on his parents' coupling, innocence falling like scales from his eyes. 'What are you doing?'

'I am...' *By Christ, what was he doing?* Looking out the window? Leaving? Running for his life? 'I am *not* Amadeus.'

'They said your real name is Katāros. Is it?' He advanced across the room, his wild wave of copper hair dancing like a cockscomb on his head.

'Don't come any closer,' Katāros hissed. He knew time was short. He glanced down. The guard was still there.

'They say you're a traitor to the empire. That you were High Chamberlain to the emperor himself. These are lies, surely. Tell me they're lies.' That note of shattered innocence again.

'It's better to let me go. You don't know me... *No one knows me*.'

'But... but... what we have?' Vito shook his head in confusion. 'Why would you lie to me like that?'

'Why do you think, fool?' Katāros snarled. 'Survival. It's always survival.'

'But I trusted you.' Vito moved closer, only three paces off now. 'How can you say—'

'Stay where you are!' Katāros threw down the cloak, revealing the sheathed dagger beneath.

'You wouldn't use my own dagger against me. Not after everything we've done.'

'Don't test me... *master*.'

'I cared for you.' Another step forward. 'There's nothing I wouldn't have given you.'

Katāros threw off the sheath. For an instant, the dagger flashed silver in the smoky gloom. 'I mean it.'

'Liar! You're a god-damned liar!'

That was the instant Katāros realised he'd been tricked. Vito leaped at him, closing the final distance.

Katāros lunged in turn, the wicked-sharp point thrusting for his master's heart, but Vito clubbed away his arm so hard he thought the bone must break. Somehow, he held onto the haft, but now Vito's fingers were clamped around his wrist, his right hand clutching at the eunuch's throat. Katāros gagged as Vito slammed his skull against the window frame, his vision blurring like a drunkard's, seeing only glaring eyes and the snarl of teeth.

'That angel's face—' Vito growled, his wine-sour breath filling the eunuch's mouth, fingers choking tighter, 'hides the heart of a devil!' Katāros's sight was tunnelling. He was losing this fight. He heard his master's voice, muted by the ringing in his ears, cracked with betrayal and despair. 'Why, in God's name, why? I gave you all of me... I would've loved you like a father.'

Father.

Didn't the fool understand? Katāros had already murdered the only father he ever knew. He would murder this one, too.

Head boiling with rage, he pushed back, fighting to stay conscious, his left hand grappling for some purchase. He'd fought dirty before, when living no better than a rat in the gutter. But even rats fought to stay alive. He reached down, seized a fistful of genitals and twisted as hard as he could. Vito screamed like a boar on a lance. There was a shout from below as their shadows slipped across the window. Vito drove forward, his greater weight bending Katāros backwards over the sill. But the eunuch wouldn't yield his grip. Not on Vito; not on the knife. Instead he twisted harder, with a savagery he didn't know was in him. Vito buckled in pain, face jammed against the eunuch's chest, and for an eye-blink his grip on Katāros's wrist weakened. The dagger sprang inward. And before either knew it, the blade had sunk inches deep into Vito's neck.

The shock of it stopped them both.

Those languid eyes stretched madly. Then Vito sagged backwards and flopped down onto his backside. Katāros gulped air hungrily, blinking down at his master. The mass of copper hair was slumped forward, blood already streaming

174

down his chest and pooling in his crotch, while his legs jerked the life out of him.

Katāros drew himself up and pulled his tunic straight. A moment of stillness. Somewhere in the back of his senses he heard shouting, military boots clattering up stone steps.

He sighed, then snatched hold of that thick copper mane and yanked the dagger free. When he let go, the judge fell backwards, blood gouting from his neck into a puddle of silver that shone in the gloom.

'I'm sorry,' Katāros whispered. 'It wasn't meant to be like this.'

There was time for nothing more.

Impelled by fear, he stepped up onto the window sill. At once, shouts in the courtyard. He didn't care now. His fate lay in the hands of something greater than him. A higher power, maybe. But a power for evil or for good? How was a man to tell when all about him was nothing but a fog of lies, greed and death?

He looked down. There was the balcony and the courtyard wall beyond it. Behind him, footsteps rolled like thunder on the landing.

He jumped.

Hours later, he was crouched, breathless, in the dark.

He had run and run, losing himself in a maze of filth and slime and shadow. All about him the city watchmen hunted, their numbers growing, the alarm spreading, first around the port, then throughout the wider city.

He was tired. The fierce energy of fight and flight was ebbing away, leaving his limbs hollow and weak. He needed to stop and rest. To collect his thoughts.

He judged that he was now far from the harbour. Somewhere near the main sewer that ran under the city wall and into the swamp. That ruse had worked once before. Why not again?

He sat on his haunches, panting, his back against a windowless wall, listening to the tramp of a patrol hastening by the entrance of the alley where he was concealed. A mist-wreathed moon lit the wall on the other side, its thin light glinting off the stinking puddles of slop that pocked the alley. The jangle of boots and buckles faded into the night. Feeling more secure, he shifted his weight forward onto all fours, like an animal, listening, his breathing quick and shallow. Just then he caught a glimpse of his face in the surface of the rancid water. His expression was strange, almost inhuman. He was the hunted. The prey. A beast, wearing the face of an angel.

A face that had betrayed him in spite of all.

A face…

How can a man change his face? This face that had done him untold harm. 'Pretty One' the shaman had called him a lifetime ago. In the capital, they had called him 'Beautiful', even as they used him for their filthy pleasure. He scowled. Images, memories, came rising in a tide of foulness, till he felt suffocated by them. Drowning in a sea of other men's illicit desire.

He looked down at his hand in the gloom. The dagger rested there, whispering to him.

His face had made him a murderer. It would not do so again, he promised himself, as he slid off the sheath and dropped it into his lap.

You cannot escape the threads of the past, the shaman had always told him. *There is always a debt to pay.*

Maybe. But not yet. Not while there was still breath in his body.

He put the dagger's tip to his cheek. And with sudden resolve, he pressed and pulled it down. He was surprised to find the first cut came as a relief. The pain of it flew out of him like a bird that had longed for its freedom, released from its cage at last.

Clamping his teeth shut, he put the blade to his face a second time.

By the time he was done, no one would recognise him ever again.

CHAPTER SEVENTEEN

Erlan gazed up at the stars, thanking the gods that there was no moon in the heavens. Tonight they needed all the cover they could get. Satisfied, he pulled the hood of his stinking cloak down over his brow and resumed his watch on the quayside.

The Prosphorion harbour was the reserve of the imperial naval division, known as the *Karabisianoi,* and even then only for those vessels about to be deployed on service. It was a small arc of stone in the immediate lee of the promontory that formed the southern bank of the *Chrysókeras*: the Golden Horn. To enter the harbour from the city meant passing through the ancient Gate of Eugenius, the Prosphorion's sole access point.

Erlan sat hunched in front of a begging bowl on the corner of a military storehouse, a heel of mouldy bread and a broken water pitcher on the ground between his sandalled feet. His seax and a hand-axe lay beside him under the tails of his cloak, along with a length of rope. In the shadows, he was all but invisible. The citizens of Byzantium noticed a beggar on a street corner no more than they marked a stray dog scavenging for scraps in the gutter. The city was littered with them. But just across from him, by the entrance to a narrow alley, another beggar sat. A sharp eye might remark on the length of the man's legs tucked under his cloak. But no one could have guessed that the other vagrant was none other than Mikkel Crow.

It was past midnight. Already well on in the third watch of the night. The looming shadows of the three chelandions rocked gently on their moorings, knocking with rhythmic monotony against the quayside pavings.

To the casual observer, both beggars looked fast asleep, heads dropped, shoulders slumped. But Erlan could see Mikki's damp eyes darting under the brim of his cowl as they followed the harbour guards back and forth on their patrol beside each ship. Now and then, his gaze would rise to the deck of the *Stilico* each time the shape of the guard appeared at the midships bulwark. The marine would stop, cast his eye over the harbour, then turn again on his beat.

Erlan, meanwhile, had his eye on two other figures approaching along the quayside from the Gate of Eugenius, one of them holding a small lantern. Orīana's silhouette was unmistakable, the curves of her body artfully on display in the light's shifting glow as she hip-swayed her way up to the guard stationed in front of the *Stilico*. Marta was smaller in every way, but even at that distance, there was something of her mother about her. A kind of lightly worn confidence that drew the eye. He never could have imagined it was the same demure girl who had walked into Orīana's apartment the night before. She was hard to read, that kid – no doubt of that.

It was late, to be sure. But for some in the city, it was never too late to make a coin or two. He tried to imagine the lie Orīana was spinning now. The sway of her shoulders, the swing of the wine pitcher in her hand, the easy way she threw back her head and laughed at whatever inanities the guard was offering. All of it suggested she was a little drunk. Perhaps a little free with her favours, if the guard played it right. Even from there, it looked damned convincing. And all Marta had to do was smile and play along. And not drop that bloody bottle.

Erlan looked along the quayside for any signs that some officer might appear from the *Karabisianoi* headquarters that overlooked the harbour and move the women along. But no one came. Everyone was sleeping. And soon, the night grew merry with the jingle of Orīana's tambourine and the skipping notes of Marta's flute. Erlan watched Orīana's lissom figure spinning and turning to the rhythm of the music, flaunting and teasing in equal measure. Soon the soft tinkle of laughter added to the music, drawing in the other guards from further along the quay. At this hour, it would be an unlucky man to be caught not minding his duty. Besides, they must have thought there was strength in numbers; and a woman like Orīana didn't cross a man's path every day. And all the while, Marta went from guard to guard, encouraging them to drink, re-charging their cups. The gods only knew whether this part of the plan would work. Though they'd find out soon enough whether Lilla knew her business. It could be that the brew she'd concocted would poison them all to death – or else have no effect whatsoever. Erlan wasn't sure which outcome would be less welcome. In any case, all he and Mikki could do was wait. They had time. It was still many hours till first light.

Orīana's dancing soon attracted the attention of the guards on board the *Stilico*, and after a small measure of flirting, they too were inviting her up to entertain them. Of course, she agreed only too willingly, and moments later she and Marta were being hoisted on board, the other guards climbing up after them.

Who could blame them? It was the dead of night. The chain across the mouth of the Horn was secure and in place. Nothing could come into the harbour. Nothing could get out. What harm was there to enjoy the entertainment that had fallen into their laps? A couple of drinks to see them through the watch. It would only cost them a copper coin or two.

Erlan imagined the scene. How expertly Orīana would keep their attention on her, even as one by one they fell asleep. His own arse was getting numb from sitting cross-legged for so long, and his ankle felt stiff. He glanced across at Mikki, who was so still he might have been made of stone. But when Erlan exhaled a low whistle, Mikki's cowl turned and he gave a quick nod, the movement exactly like a crow's.

Erlan smiled to himself. Still awake then.

He'd chosen Mikki Crow because he was the most reluctant. That, and he wanted to keep him away from Lilla. But if he could win *him* over... Well, the others would fall like autumn leaves.

Suddenly a small figure appeared at the rail. Marta. The weak light of a lantern rose and fell, rose and fell. There was the signal.

As one, the two beggars got to their feet.

Einar Fat-Belly had never much enjoyed creeping around in the dark. Stealth was not his thing. And he was pretty damned sure it had never been Bull's thing either. He'd herded pregnant heifers who were lighter on their feet – and been a damned sight less stubborn to manoeuvre as well.

Which was why he favoured straightforward boldness over sly cunning any day.

It was all about timing, of course. Carrying yourself with confidence, looking the part.

Erlan had given up his old palace guard uniform for Einar to use. Einar's had been burned right off him in the sea battle under the walls. The bright white cloak and tunic meant he was lit up like marble under the starlight. No thief would dress like that – not unless he had sheep dung for brains. Which, Einar had to admit, was at least conceivable in his case, given everything he had agreed to so far.

Bull was dressed alike, although his white cloak was fashioned from Queen Lilla's drapes. Einar wondered what the palace servants would make of that, come morning time.

But that wasn't his concern. Lowering the great chain that sealed the mouth of the Horn, on the other hand, was.

'Ready?' growled Einar.

'Aye,' grunted Bull. 'Shitting myself. But ready.'

'That's how you know. Come on.'

The two of them stepped out from under the cover of the archway where they had been waiting. He'd seen Orīana's light, watched the two cloaked shadows of Erlan and Mikki Crow steal across the open quay and clamber up over the *Stilico*'s gunwale, disappearing onto the deck.

It all seemed to be going swimmingly, far as Einar could tell. Although this next bit might be tricky.

'Remember what I said. These Byzantine monkeys like to march in time.'

'Righto, Fat-Belly.'

They set off, striding along more or less in line, if not exactly in step, towards the small stone turret at the eastern end of the harbour that housed the mechanism for releasing and raising the harbour chain. It didn't take long to cover the distance, but Einar was glad when they had crossed the open space and tucked in under the shadow of the chain-house turret. The two Northmen stopped, looked at each other, and Einar nodded at his companion. 'I'll do the talking, lad. You stick to... well, what you're here to do.'

Then he thumped hard on the little studded door.

A few seconds later, he heard noises on the other side. A voice demanding to know their business.

'Message for the kentarch from the Comēs of the Opsikian Theme,' answered Einar in his best Greek, which had improved a Hel of a lot since he'd fallen in love with Orīana.

'From the Comēs? You mean Nikolaitos?'

'Erm... yes.' He shot Bull an uncertain look and rolled his eyes. 'Comēs Nikolaitos, exactly... Of the Opsikian Theme,' he added for good measure. And then wished he hadn't.

There was a long silence, some half-concealed whispers, then: 'What the hell does he want at this time of night?'

'Fetch the kentarch, open this god-damn door and I'll tell you, shall I?' Einar hissed. 'Or would you like to go on report?' He knew how the lower ranks of imperial soldiers and marines dreaded nothing so much as going on report. He reflected, and not for the first time, how he'd never figure these people out.

'All right. One moment.'

And soon enough, there was a snapping of bolts and the little door opened. 'Well?'

'Are you coming out or are we coming in?' said Einar.

'Just deliver your message.' This was a different voice. Perhaps that of the duty kentarch.

'I was ordered to present it face to face,' countered Einar.

'By the Virgin! Oh very well,' snarled the voice. 'Come in.'

Einar nodded at Bull, then ducked down and went through the little door. Inside, the air was close. It stank of tallow candles. Einar straightened up and found himself near nose to nose with the duty kentarch. He was quickly followed into the room by Bull, who, once he had squeezed in through the little doorway, straightened himself up and peered down his nose at the chain-house guards. He looked absurdly oversized for the confined space inside the little turret, and the white drape serving as his cloak looked... well, exactly like that.

Already he could see the kentarch's irritation turning to confusion. 'Wait, what unit did you say you were from?'

'First Sveäland,' said Einar. 'By the way, have you met Private Bull?'

184

And before the kentarch could blink an eye, Bull's massive fist shot out and up from his waist like an ascending comet. The kentarch was halfway across the little room before he'd even felt it. And an instant later, he was slumped against the wall, out cold. Bull now turned with awful deliberation to the other man, who was fumbling for his *spatha*.

'I'd leave it where it is. There's a good lad,' said Einar, the point of the long-knife he'd had concealed at his side now jabbed up under the man's jaw. 'So, where's this lever then?'

Erlan was just tying off the final knot around the last unconscious guard's wrists when he heard the shriek of metal and the prolonged splash of the chain dropping into the water.

By the Hanged, it was loud as Heimdall's horn. It was sure to bring troops running. He waited, waited some more. But nothing happened. He looked across at Mikki, who, like him, had stopped what he was doing to listen.

'Well, let's not stand here waiting for Ragnarok to break. Let's get on with it.'

Orīana and Marta were busy securing the ankles and wrists of the other unconscious guards behind their backs.

'Beautifully done, ladies,' said Erlan, with genuine admiration.

'We've done our part,' Orīana said. 'How about you get on with yours?'

'Not quite done. The signal.'

'I know, I know.' Orīana was already on her knees, pulling out the little pack of folded material from the pouch at her belt. She began spreading it carefully on the deck.

Erlan turned to Mikkel Crow. 'All right, Mikki, start bringing up the gold.'

As he said it, one of the guards lying nearby moaned. Mikki was on him at once. He pulled back the man's helmet, exposing his throat, and had his knife to the flesh in an eye-blink.

'Stop!' hissed Erlan. 'No killing. Not unless we have to.'

'Why the Hel not?'

The truth was, Erlan's conscience had enough to deal with just stealing the gold. The last thing he wanted was a glut of Byzantine blood on his hands if it could be avoided. 'Just knock him out. And stuff this in his mouth in case he wakes up again.' He cut off a piece of another guard's tunic and tossed it to Mikki. There was a short, violent thud while Mikki dealt with the man and dropped him to the deck.

'All right, let's go.'

By the gods, he wished he had more men. But Lilla needed the rest of them just to get the *Fasolt* moving. There was a modest lick of wind about which might serve them if they ever got out of this. But she needed the men on the end of oars to come into the harbour. The loss of two was already a significant setback.

'Is that thing nearly ready?'

Marta was holding the top of the linen sack while Orīana was crouched holding the lantern beneath it. The material fell out into a kind of bell shape. It looked pathetically flimsy. The idea was, Orīana assured him, that it would gradually fill with hot air and then rise up and up into the sky, high above the city: easy to spot from any ship floating out on the straits. Lilla and the *Fasolt* and the rest of the crew were out there somewhere, watching and waiting for the signal, anticipating their moment to enter the lion's mouth. Erlan had favoured a horn, but they had decided that was too risky. Any noise that could be heard out on the straits was likely to wake the whole city. Orīana had suggested this idea instead. It was some fire-trick she'd seen, brought to the city down the trade routes from the distant east. But the flimsy lantern was taking agonisingly long to fill with hot air.

'It will work, I promise,' she said. 'Just hurry up with shifting the gold.'

Erlan shook his head, swore, then grabbed Mikki and pulled him down the squat, broad step-ladder that led into the hold. Below the main deck, it was pitch black. It took several thumping heartbeats before his eyes started to adjust. Then he saw something amorphous, a kind of monstrous shape, materialising out of the black, like the first god Búri when he was licked out of the rime stones of Ginnungagap.

'There,' he said. And they were both on it at once. They felt their way as much as saw it, over a great orderly heap of boxes. Each box was small, no more than a couple of hand-breadths in length, half that across and about three inches deep. Erlan took out his long-knife and prised open the top of the nearest one. Even in the darkness, the contents glistened tantalisingly, as if by some dwarf-magic the gold could draw to it whatever tiny particles of light there were to be found in that dark place. Erlan reached in, picked up a handful of coins and let them trickle through his fingers back into the box.

He started laughing. 'By the Hanged!'

'Fucking beautiful,' murmured Mikki in wonder, pushing Erlan's hand out of the way and burying his fist into the golden solidi up to his knuckles.

Suddenly Orīana's head appeared in the hatch above them. 'It's away! The signal's away. Hurry up, will you?'

The two men looked at one another. Then Erlan replaced the lid on the little box and picked it up.

'Mother of God,' he said in Greek. It felt like he'd picked up a boulder. He put it back down. 'Try it.'

Mikki did so. 'By the Thunder. How the Hel are we two going to shift all this?'

A fair question.

'Well, you're not going to do it by talking about it, are you?' hissed Orīana from above.

That was true.

'One at a time then,' said Erlan. 'Two if you can manage it.' He hefted the improbably heavy container and turned for the steps, knowing whatever time they had left was surely running out.

Lilla stood fore of the mainsail under the shadow of *Fasolt*'s prow-beast, gripping her bow, her weight shifting with the swell of the currents. Gone were the patrician robes of a noble lady of the empire. Instead, she wore the practical breeks of a man, linen hose, goatskin boots, a fitted leather jerkin over a fine wool tunic. She felt free already – like a she-wolf escaped from a snare.

By the gods, it was good. Even if, mingled with the feeling, was the unbearable tension of waiting. For a signal that might never come.

Everything around her was dark. The crew had spent the last day painting the oars black, along with their shields and the outside of the top strakes and gunwale that sat above the water-line. Demetrios had even got his hands on a huge vat of black dye which had served to darken the sail. Not a perfect job, but then time was not a luxury they possessed.

But on this moonless night, any guard standing atop the sea-wall would have to have the eyes of an owl to notice the darker shape in a sea of shadow out on the straits.

'There!' said Demetrios, clapping his hands in triumph. 'D'you see it?'

An instant later, Lilla saw it herself. How could she not? The little bubble of orange light rose higher and higher above the long, low shadow of the promontory, soaring like a second moon.

'Go, go!' she called.

At once, the men on the oars started pulling. They were away.

She felt the tension draining out of her, leaving behind it only a wicked-sharp focus, like a great jagged rock emerging out of an ebb tide. She jumped down and made her way aft towards Demetrios, who was hanging off the steer-board in the stern. Even he looked alert and attentive for once.

Upon reaching him, she murmured: 'You're sure about what you told me?'

'It's standard protocol in the Naval Theme. At least it was in my day. I doubt it's any different now. Especially for a mission like this.'

'In the hold, you said?'

'Yes. A full cask of the liquid. And another chest containing a full set of replacement parts.'

'Good. Can two men carry it?'

'They should be able to, my lady... Just make sure they don't drop it,' he added. 'Nasty stuff that.'

Mmm. That was the idea. She hadn't told Erlan this part of what she intended. She knew he was already at the limit of what he could bear. It didn't matter. He didn't need to know. She would take care of this.

She watched the point of the promontory draw closer, then cast her gaze over her crew, looking for the right men. *Dreng*, she thought. *The boy never questions anything, but he's strong.* Who else? *Ran. Yes, Ran.* He was calm and deliberate about everything he did. And seemed less hostile to her than some of the others.

Gold and fire, she thought. *If she could win these both, who could stop her?*

'How many's that now?' Erlan dumped the box he was carrying with the others already on deck and palmed the sweat from his brow.

'I count fifty-three,' panted Mikki, behind him.

'We need to go faster. A lot faster.'

Judging from the amount they had eaten into the pile in the hold, he guessed there had been maybe three or four hundred boxes down there. It would take all bloody night to move them.

'Where are they?' he snarled, glaring at the harbour entrance, willing the night to coagulate into the menacing fire-worm prow that would announce Lilla's coming.

'Anyone fancy giving us a hand up?' said a voice down on the quay. Erlan recognised the gruff Sveär accent of his friend. He limped to the gunwale and took hold of Einar's meaty fist. 'Up you come! We need you on the gold at once.'

'There they are,' cried Marta excitedly. She was on the harbour-side bulwark watching for the first sign of the *Fasolt*.

'About bloody time,' muttered Mikki Crow.

This was when it would get interesting. If there were any guards left on the other ships – the *Theodora* and the *Aspar* – they must surely raise the alarm, seeing a strange ship like the *Fasolt* calmly gliding into the Prosphorion.

Bull and Einar were on deck now. Orīana ran to her man and threw her arms round his neck. 'You're safe!'

'Bit early to say that, elskling,' he growled back, gently extracting himself from her embrace.

'Bull, help Mikki,' ordered Erlan. 'Bring up as many boxes as you can shift. And get them into the *Fasolt*. Throw them in if you have to.'

Suddenly a horn blast from up on the walls cut through the night like an axe through dry kindling. Erlan cursed. 'That's us out of luck then. Now it's down to speed and steel. Fat man.' He touched Einar's elbow. 'With me.'

This was the contingency if things started to unravel. The Gate of Eugenius to and from the rest of the city was a single stone gatehouse, from which spread fortified walls that curved round to the water. In other words, if the gate was closed, the Prosphorion was sealed like a small fortress. Besides the guards already in the harbour, any troops arriving there would have to enter through that gate. Now that the element of surprise was gone, Erlan's goal was to seal them inside. But there was only one way of doing that.

And it would doubtless mean blood.

He trotted with Einar across the quay towards the gate-house, his long seax slipping easily into one hand as he unhooked his hand-axe from his belt with the other. 'Speed, speed,' he hissed.

'Aye. Speaks the cripple,' returned the fat man, easily moving ahead of Erlan in spite of his bulk. He reached the door to the gatehouse first, didn't break stride, just smashed the latch open with his boot. The guards inside were still arming themselves, doubtless confused about what was going on. Unhappily for them, they would never find out.

Einar knocked aside one guard's *spatha* and drove his seax up through the man's ribs, then flung him aside. Erlan slipped past him to the other guard who was desperately trying to raise a mace and shield. Erlan spread his arms and blocked both, then stepped up to the man's chest and head-butted him. The guard went down like a felled tree.

'Where the Hel's the ratchet wheel?'

'Well clearly not in here,' said Einar, blood dripping from the tip of his knife.

Erlan took the steps two at a time, emerging into a dimly lit upper room. There was a low cot pushed against a wall, another guard trying to get up out of it. The man cried out as Erlan crossed to him, raising his empty hands in defence, but he could do nothing. Erlan slashed his seax across the man's throat before he could even get to his feet, feeling sick to his stomach as he did it.

But behind him was the mechanism that would lower the gate. The gate itself was only small but it was solid oak, held up by a thick length of rope tied around a massive iron bracket in the stone. It took two blows of his axe to cut through. Einar's head appeared in the stairwell as the rope flailed upwards into the pulley system and the sound of the gate crashing down into place shook the whole gatehouse.

'How long will it hold?' asked Einar.

'Let's not wait around to find out. Move!'

'Oars in!' called Snodin in a hushed voice as Demetrios pushed on the steer-board and swung the bows round at the last moment. *Fasolt* went slewing in sideways to hit the broadside of the *Stilico* with a loud scrape of wood.

Snodin, Krok and Kunrith lined the gunwale to palm off the worst of it, and then Mikki was there at the rail a few feet above them. 'Toss me a rope,' he called down, to which Dreng obliged.

A few moments later they were in position, with Mikki already passing down the containers. Lilla felt her blood surge with the thrill that the first of the gold was on board. But it seemed a painfully laborious process, even to pass down a single box. All the same, the men had soon figured out a system.

Lilla, meanwhile, clambered up onto the *Stilico*. She found Orīana and Marta there, doing their best to heft more portions of gold. 'Orīana – you and Marta, in the ship now.'

'But we need every pair of hands—'

'I know we do, but you've done enough. I'm not risking you any more than we have to.'

Already she could see men filing along the tops of the walls. She had heard the great crash of the gate falling. If the Norns were smiling on them, it would buy them enough time—

There was a whizz and a thud as an arrow struck the deck beside her. Then another. 'Quickly,' she said to Orīana. 'Get on the *Fasolt* and under cover.' Seeing the new threat, Orīana was now only too happy to obey, coaxing her daughter over the gunwale into the arms of the men below. More arrows fell, one of them scoring a direct hit on the prostrate body of an unconscious guard. He kicked at the boards, flapped like a landed codfish for a few moments, then lay still.

'Dreng! Ran! Up here now,' Lilla ordered. A few moments later, the two of them were there. 'You know what to do.'

'How about the gold?' said Ran in his unhurried drawl.

'Just get this done and you can go back to helping the others.'

Ran gave an insouciant shrug and led the way down into the hold. Almost immediately, he called back up, 'You can't tell shit from clay down here.'

'You will. Your eyes will adjust.' *Quickly*, she hoped.

She waited, trying not to duck every time an arrow landed on the deck. There was another terrific crash, drawing her gaze towards the gate. She realised they must be trying to batter in the wood, although it must be pretty unbreakable, supported in its stone frame. Evidently someone on the other side had come to the same conclusion, and instead of a ram, the sound of axes slamming into the wood soon struck up like drums before a day of battle. Lilla guessed those might have more effect. But it would still take time to hack through. Up on the walls, more archers were appearing. The distance between the wall and the ships was to the northerners' advantage, but sooner or later the numbers would tell. So far, there was no sign of the guards coming over the walls, but that too was surely only a matter of time. Certainly if Lilla was in command, that's how she would get her men into the fight.

As if reading her mind, ladders appeared above the crenellations, waving awkwardly from side to side like giant fingers of reproach, while the guards manning the walls hefted them up and over and slid them down on the harbour side. Where the first one touched the ground, she suddenly caught sight of Erlan and Einar below. Braving a hail of arrows under the scant cover of a Byzantine shield, Erlan darted forward and yanked out the foot of the ladder with the beard of his axe. It came clattering down to the stones with a man entangled in it, who hit the ground hard and struggled for a moment. Erlan's axe fell once, twice, and the man stopped moving.

Another ladder appeared. The same thing again: Erlan moved in and toppled the ladder, his shield now peppered with arrow-shafts. Lilla wondered how long he could keep that up.

On the other side of the gate, a third ladder came over. This time it slid down and stayed in place, and guards began lining up to come down it, some of them carrying torches. Lilla unslung her bow and pulled out two arrows. She ran to the *Stilico*'s quayside bulwark, nocked an arrow, took aim just below one of the torches, and loosed. She marked the count of two, three… and then the beacon fell. She grunted with satisfaction.

'Lady, this what you're looking for?' said Ran's voice behind her. She turned and was thrilled to see the Gotlander and Dreng emerging from the hold, carrying a sizeable wooden barrel between them. *Liquid fire!* she thought in triumphant vindication. *Dear Gods, how I suffered for that!*

'Is the rest of it there? The pipework.'

'Aye. It's all there, just as you said.'

'Well, hurry up then. We need it all if it's to be any use to us.'

Ran tipped his head and hustled Dreng off to deposit the first of their loads. They were soon back for the rest. Meanwhile, Mikki was still shuttling back and forth with the boxes of gold like a squirrel provisioning for winter. The heap of boxes on deck was getting smaller. She wondered how many they had loaded now.

Ran and Dreng emerged a second time, lugging a large chest with metal handles. 'You could give us a hand, eh?' said Ran.

Lilla lay down her bow and went to one end. Compared to them, she was weak, but her arms filled with the urgency of the moment and together they soon had the thing at the gunwale. After much swearing and cursing and bitter complaint, the chest went over and down into the waiting ship. That done, Dreng and Ran returned to help Mikki.

Lilla fetched her bow. It was strange. She felt an astonishing power filling her body, a feeling of invincibility. Now, perhaps for the first time, she dared to believe they could actually pull this off.

But when she returned to the other side of the *Stilico*, she saw more and more guards pouring over the walls. Too many for Erlan and Einar to handle. They had pulled halfway back towards the ship, making a stand in the gap between two heaps of disused cargo boxes. Several guards were fallen around them. But more were coming. Archers, too.

Lilla nocked an arrow instinctively, seeing one draw and take aim nearly point-blank at Erlan.

Greed will be our undoing, was the thought that flashed through her mind. *It was time to flee.*

Erlan ripped his bloody axe from the wreckage of the man's skull and turned to face the next. Too late, he saw the tip of the arrow pointing straight at his face not ten paces away. He didn't even have time to duck. But next moment, an arrow appeared in the archer's chest, seemingly out of nowhere, spinning the man at the instant he loosed his bow. His arrow whipped past, inches from Erlan's head.

Next to him, Einar was roaring defiance at each man that came. So far the guards' attack had been disordered, reaching them in ones and twos. But that was changing. Erlan heard an officer bellowing orders, sensed a battle-line forming. There was no way to hold against a concerted attack. They didn't even have shields.

'Back! Back!' he yelled at Einar, and the fat man didn't need a second telling.

But two more guards were already running at them, so close they would have to face them. Again, two arrows whipped out of the darkness behind them. Both guards fell, skidding along the pavings on their face.

Snatching greedily at their instant of reprieve, the Northmen turned and sprinted for the *Stilico*. Not fast in Erlan's case, but he was damned if any Byzantine was going to best him in a footrace now. Einar was first to the ship, launching himself up the side without breaking stride, and he was over the gunwale with an agility that belied his hefty byname. Erlan saw Lilla slapping arrow after arrow against her bow, loosing them off at an astonishing rate.

But if they didn't leave now, they never would.

'Go, go, go!' he yelled as he scrambled up and over, landing in a sprawl on the deck. Lilla released her bowstring for the last time then turned and ran. Now it was a simple race.

Some of the men were still working at the dwindling heap of boxes by the outward bulwark, almost throwing the gold into the *Fasolt* below.

'Get in the boat,' shouted Erlan. 'All of you! Make ready to row.'

One by one they snatched up a last load, looking absurdly awkward as they tried to hustle but weighed down with each little box. Over they went. Lilla threw down her bow and what arrows she had left into the *Fasolt*, hefted up a box and scrambled over the side.

Black Svali was screaming, 'Ready to shove off! Dreng, you dopey bastard, on that oar!'

Mikki was in. Ran was in. Einar picked up a box in each hand and threw them straight over. Down below there were curses as the boxes hit the thwarts and smashed, scattering solidi in every direction. But no one cared so long as the coin was in the hull. Erlan did the same, then both men lifted a final pair and jumped as a fresh volley of arrows rattled into the woodwork behind them and went skittering over their heads into the water.

Erlan landed painfully. Gods only knew what hit him – in the shins, in his arm, in his head. But if he could move, he needed to row. The bows were already swinging away. Demetrios was screaming orders at the top of his voice. Black Svali was cursing everyone blind. The oars in the bows were the first to be clear. Ran and Mikki started pulling, and one by one the others were able to join, Erlan with them. By the Hanged, it was like pulling on the carcass of a dead bull. The inertia of all that gold in the hull was something none of them had fully anticipated.

But they had no choice now. Guards appeared on the deck. Spears lanced through the air. But they were moving. Not fast, but drawing away from the *Stilico* and the quayside and all that Byzantine rage. As the *Fasolt*'s own momentum started working for them, Erlan started to believe they could at least escape the harbour. Every man of them was already covered in sweat from toting the gold. Now they had an even harder task.

'Once we're round the promontory, we'll put up the sail,' said Demetrios.

That seemed like a hideously long way at this rate. Erlan's back was on fire, his lungs were bursting, his heart was screaming at the rest of him to stop. But they could not stop, not now.

They moved clear of the prongs of the harbour. They were out on the Horn now, soon they'd be on the straits—

'There's another boat!' Snodin yelled in alarm.

199

'What?' cried Demetrios on the steer-board. He looked behind, but the rest of them didn't need to. A small vessel was emerging from the Neorion, the harbour adjacent to the Prosphorion, where other naval vessels were moored. Seeing it, Dimo swore. 'That's a fire-runner! They're small but damned fast.'

'They armed with that devil's fire-piss, Dimo?' demanded Einar through panting breaths.

'Every ship is, you know that!'

'Once *Fasolt*'s sail is up, she'll fly,' said Lilla. 'They'll not catch us.'

'I wouldn't count on it just yet,' answered Demetrios.

Erlan could have done with a little more optimism from their helmsman. But it didn't change their situation: they just had to row their guts out.

'They've more oars than us,' growled Snodin, who was nearest the stern and setting the rhythm.

'They're catching us,' wailed Dreng.

'Then row fucking harder,' called Mikki from the bows. 'Come on, you whoreson cunts! Pull!'

Erlan had been through a lot. But that next stretch of back-breaking, lung-raking pain was as tortuous as anything he had ever endured. And the sense of building dread as the bows of the fire-runner drew closer and closer, whatever their effort, didn't make it any more comfortable.

'The wind's good,' said Demetrios, trying to give them some sort of encouragement.

'How much do you want that fucking gold, lads?' Mikki Crow's bellowing voice again. Seemed like he wanted it anyway, and plenty.

'Get ready to hoist sail,' called Erlan. 'Sval, are you on it?'

But before Black Svali could answer, there was a rasping rush of sound from astern, and the night lit up like a vision of Muspelheim. The jet of fire arced high and far, driving a wave of heat before it. But the burning oil splattered into the water behind them, well short.

'Harder,' yelled Einar, 'pull harder!' The note of terror in his voice was all too obvious. Demetrios, knowing he was first in the line of fire, kept glancing nervously over his shoulder. 'How's that sail coming, Sval?'

'Bastard thing's stuck!' Black Svali croaked in reply. 'Too much blasted clutter on this boat now!'

Orīana and her daughter were crouching in the midships just fore of the mastblock. 'Orīana,' cried Lilla. 'You and Marta help him!'

Evidently fear lent them strength because after only a few seconds of frantic tugging at the mass of black wool, the sail came free of its snag and Svali set about hoisting the rig. They were past the promontory now, moving out into the deeper waters of the straits where the currents ran faster. But the fire-runner was closing at a disturbing rate.

'They're moving on us,' called Erlan. 'If we get to the straits first, lads, we've still a chance!'

The Byzantine crew were no novices. Now they had the distance, they weren't going to waste another shot if they didn't have to. But the awful pause before the next blast of liquid fire came raining from above was a torture of the mind only a devil could devise. No wonder the Byzantine fleet instilled such fear in its enemies.

Lilla was moving back to the stern, bow in hand. Instinctively, Erlan reached out to stop her, knowing that way lay the most danger. 'Where the Hel are you going? Stay in the bows, for Frigg's sake!'

She rounded on him, iron determination stamped on her beautiful features. 'Just keep rowing! I know what I'm doing!'

That instant came the second hiss and roar of the syphon as orange flames launched high in the sky behind them. This time the blast of heat that came barrelling over them all felt like opening a door to Volund's Forge. Erlan closed his eyes in expectation of the searing splatter of oil and pain.

But still it fell short. Only Demetrios let out a screeching cry: 'My arm, my arm!' he cried, beating at himself. Erlan saw a flicker of flame. Then Dimo's hand was on fire. 'Put it out, put it out!'

Suddenly Marta appeared from midships, crawling over the thwarts, tearing off her shawl. With no thought for her own safety, she balled the cloth around his forearm and hugged it to her chest. What she was doing was crazy; the liquid fire was notoriously hard to extinguish. But maybe her God was with her after all. The fire was smothered. Erlan couldn't see the expression on Demetrios's face but he imagined it was grim. Still, the helmsman held his course.

Lilla, meanwhile, had taken up position next to the Greek with her bow.

'They'll have us on the next shot,' wailed Dreng. 'We're done for!'

'Save your breath and row, pretty boy,' snarled Kunrith, who for a small man was showing himself mighty game for the task.

Lilla nocked an arrow, drew back the string till the tension made her hands shake, checked her angle and line again, then released. The arrow launched at precisely the moment a third jet of liquid flame erupted from the fire-runner's bows. And it was still ejaculating like some phallic nightmare when the stream suddenly slewed off line, landing harmlessly to the larboard side.

'You hit him!' Ran crowed for joy. 'By all the gods, you must have hit him, you goddamn beauty! You actually took down the bastard!'

The men couldn't resist a roar of victory and defiance, despite their huffing and blowing and sweating and straining.

'Sail's going up,' croaked Black Svali, as if it were the most mundane thing in the world, and not the difference between life and death for every one of them. And he hauled and hauled on the halyard as the sail rose and began to fill with the wind.

At once Erlan felt the pressure diminish on the end of his oar.

'You're sure about this course, Dimo?' he called.

'South to go north,' the Greek croaked, stifling the pain in his voice. 'I told you. If you trust me on nothing else, you must trust this. It may be longer, but by God it's easier.'

Now was not the time to revisit their debate on whether they returned north via the Euxine or the Inner Sea. With this fire-breathing devil on their stern, the question was moot: they had to go with the wind and the currents or else they would not go at all.

Fasolt was sleek as a she-wolf once the wind started to lift her. And though the Byzantines attempted one more shot, it now fell far short. Within moments, Snodin was yelling: 'They've stopped rowing! They're giving up!'

Another cheer went up from the men as they watched the shape of their pursuers fall back and the distance of water between them grow.

'Ease it out now, lads,' called Demetrios, his voice clenched but less urgent. And after a few more strokes, content they were properly underway by sail, he called them to stop and ship the oars.

Too exhausted to celebrate yet, the men slumped forward or fell off the thwarts, gasping down air, groaning as the pain in their muscles ebbed away and their galloping pulses eventually slowed. Meanwhile, *Fasolt* glided past the shadow of the city.

Erlan dragged himself upright, the blood still beating in his head, and looked over at the passing city. They were level with the section of sea-wall that defended the Great Palace. For a moment, all was relatively quiet after the hiss and roar of the flames. He heard the wind, the creak of the wood, the panting of his crew. Then a voice rose up into the night. The wind must have carried it since it was several arrow flights behind them, rising from the city walls.

'*AURVANDIL!*' the voice cried. '*AURVANDIL!*' How, he didn't know, but in that moment Erlan was certain who it belonged to. '*Doúlos! Kléftis! Prodótis!*... *DOÚLOS! KLÉFTIS! PRODÓTIS!*' Over and over, the voice cried the words, like a great lament over the city.

'What the Hel is that idiot saying?' asked Ran through heavy gasps.

'Slave. Thief. Traitor,' said Demetrios from the stern. Erlan

204

looked up at the Greek. In the gloom, their eyes met, and he could see a smile forcing its way through the little helmsman's grimace of pain.

'He's right, skipper,' croaked Mikki from the bows. 'You are a fucking thief!'

'Aye,' laughed Bull merrily. 'And a bloody good one.'

All the crew laughed with him.

Erlan knew they meant well. But somehow it still rubbed sore. 'We didn't steal it all,' he said to no one in particular. Maybe to his own conscience. 'Reckon what we took is no more than fair payment for what we've done.'

Einar was up from his row-bench now. He reached forward and patted Erlan on the back. 'Whatever you have to tell yourself... *skipper*,' he said.

'How much *did* we get exactly?' asked Bull.

'Still counting,' answered Kunrith quickly. *Fasolt* meanwhile had found her wings and was picking up speed with every moment as she moved further out into the open sea of the Marmara.

'Erlan.' Lilla came and sat down beside him. She was grinning like a little girl. 'We did it,' she whispered, as if she couldn't quite believe it. She pulled him towards her and he was so tired he half-collapsed against her shoulder.

'I don't know how,' he muttered, laughing into the warm nape of her neck. 'I really don't.'

She kissed his cheek. 'You've set me free, my love. You've set me free.'

She had all she had come for now. From half a world away. He had to admire her for that. And as her 'gilded prison' slipped further behind them, he heard more of her whispered words close to his ear, words only meant for his hearing. And he smiled and drew her tighter to him.

'A hundred and fifty-seven by my count,' declared Kunrith.

'How much is that exactly?' asked Snodin.

'Exactly a shit-ton!' crowed Bull, clapping his hands in delight like some infant *jötunn*.

'I'd say, very roughly,' continued Kunrith, plucking thoughtfully at his little beard, 'just over eighteen thousand marks.'

'Odin's eye!' exclaimed Snodin. And there were other such cries of astonishment from the rest.

'We left a lot behind,' Erlan said.

'Well,' drawled Einar. 'Would have been rude to take it all. Don't you reckon, skipper?'

'More than double what we took.'

'Bah! You always were a horn-half-empty kind of fella,' said Einar, with a shake of his head.

'Hang on,' cut in Mikki from the bows. 'Is he trying to say we get less than what we was promised? We did everything you asked. No one could have done more and come out of there alive.'

'No,' said Lilla firmly. She hopped up on a thwart. With her wild train of hair and leather *brynja* clinging tight, she looked every inch the warrior queen. 'No, he's not saying that. You all get what we promised you in full. Five hundred marks a man. Not a coin less. But the rest is to raise an army in the north. When we get there, I want you all with me. If *you* are willing…'

There was a moment of quiet, filled only with the bubbles rushing under the hull and the soft sighing of the wind. Long enough for a few darting looks between the river-men. And then, as one, their faces cracked into smiles and they raised another cheer.

Hel, thought Erlan, looking up at her. *If she can win this stubborn bunch of bastards to her cause, maybe we stand a chance after all.*

'Even you, Mikkel Crow?' demanded Lilla. 'Will you have a part in this?'

Mikki stood.

Seeing his sullen look, for a second Erlan anticipated a fight. But instead, a grin crept across Mikki's craggy face, too. 'Reckon any lass who could make that last shot gets my oath,' he said, and graced Lilla with a flourishing bow. 'I'm yours, my queen. For as long as you need me.' Then he began to laugh like none of them had ever heard him laugh before.

'By the Thunder, Mikki,' bellowed Einar merrily. 'If that's what it takes to make you happy, no wonder you're such a miserable fucker.'

And for a time they all laughed with him. Until, their mirth subsiding, they broke into smaller huddles, slapping backs and reliving tales of their daring exploits, which were already growing taller in the telling.

Meanwhile, those words were turning over and over in Erlan's head:

Slave. Thief. Traitor.

Aye, he may have been all those things at one time.

But now he was also a man heading for home.

PART TWO

Verðandi

The Weaving of What is

CHAPTER EIGHTEEN

A pitiless wind was curling in from the north, driving the rain straight through the black wool of his Benedictine robe, turning his pale Anglian skin to gooseflesh.

It was the second time Wyn had crossed the Frisian Sea, and neither had been to his liking. Almighty God, Creator of all good things – including this hellish wind – had made him no sea-farer. That much he could admit. But after all that he had heard… Well, he'd had no choice but to make the journey.

Wyn's stomach felt hollow. No surprise that, since he had voided its contents many leagues back, most of it off the Kentish coast, barely an arrow's flight from the wind-whipped point of Sheerness where his voyage had begun. His throat was still raw with the taste of vomit.

Yet his spirit, at last, was soaring. It seemed to him that the very gulls, turning high on the wind overhead, shrieked with joy in union with his soul. Because ahead, through the rain, he could just make out the steel-grey seam of land appearing on the horizon.

Frisia.

He made the sign of the cross, muttering a prayer of thanks to the Everlasting Father under his sour breath. In an hour, maybe two, they would be out of these gale-blasted waves and in among the relative shelter of the Frisian isles. Come noon – by His grace – they would be landing at Dort. And from Dort, the great lands beyond opened up. The Rhein and the Mosella cut south, deep into the Germanic marches, where dwelled the cousin tribes of his own Anglo-Saxon people.

Dort itself was a dirty smear of a settlement, barely rising above the levels of the mud-banks among which it was nestled. But it was dry land, firm land, a place to seek out a fire and even a roof over his head, if only for a night. Right now, that was all Wyn cared about.

Blood and fire. The crackle and the screams were still fresh in his memory, even a year on.

Aye. That had been an evil day.

It would have been easy to stay in Wessex. After what happened the last time he crossed the Frisian Sea, who could have blamed him? Another man might have taken that failure as a sign of God's will; that mission – and adventure – were not to be his path.

Could be that was the truth of it.

After all, Canterbury had promised everything which, if he were honest with himself, a large part of him would have dearly loved to pursue. Learning, teaching, the scriptures – the deep and holy thoughts of men and women long dead. The sweet silence of the cloister and the scriptorium.

Wynfred the Scholar. Wynfred the Wise.

Aye. It had a pleasing ring to it, a definite plausibility. And all the markings of the sensible choice, too. Wyn had seen forty winters come and go by now. And as old Winberth, his late mentor and the Abbot of Nursling, had said shortly before he passed: 'Forty years is an age by which a man ought to know his path.'

That was the trouble, though, wasn't it? Wyn had known his path a long time. Had seen it in his dreams. Heard it whispered in his prayers. He just hadn't walked it, is all. Had been living in the denial of it for too long.

It had taken the horror of that vision to move him off of his comfortable sin of omission.

He thought of it again as he watched the grey seam of land roll closer, remembering the words he had written of it to his beloved sister in Christ, Eadburga, only that year. Of the Wenlock brother who had died, and then, by some miracle of Christ, lived again. Of the visions the man had seen. Horrors beyond nightmare; marvels beyond dream. The black pits of hells, flame-filled and ringing with the cries of the damned. Foul demons accusing him of every one of his sins, those known to him and those unknown. He had seen beyond the veil of this world, seen angels in their glory and perfection, seen the souls of wretched men in the likeness of black birds sat upon the margin of the pits, clinging there for a while, wailing and howling and shrieking with human cries, mourning past deeds and present suffering. Seen gardens of wondrous beauty where the souls of the blessed walked, their breath a fragrance of wonderful sweetness. Trembled at a pitch-black river of fire, boiling and glowing, dreadful and hideous to look upon.

Such were the monk's own words.

And they had forced Wyn to look upon his own sin. His own denial. It was the sin of Jonah: that he knew his call, felt it like an ache in his bones, and yet for how long did he not obey?

The shame of his obstinacy scalded his conscience.

Still, as old Bugga used to tell him: better a son who says Nay, but does, than one who says Aye, but doesn't.

And the time for refusal was over now.

He looked down at his hands, at his palms mottled white and purple with the cold. They were a scholar's hands. A monk's hands. Hands hidden away from the world. Well, maybe hands could change. And maybe a life could change, too.

The Lord had called him out of Albion, he was sure of that. Called him across the grey waters, called him to love the Frisian folk. To preach the Blood. To carry the light. To be a bearer of the Holy Flame.

Blood and fire... Aye, of a different sort.

The first mission had ended in failure. Bishop Willibrord's community at Traiectum had been attacked, overrun, the church burned to the ground. It had been the work of King Rathbod of the Frisians, a man whose hatred of the Cross was only surpassed by his hatred of those who carried it. But it had also been the fruit of their own naivety. *The devil prowls like a roaring lion, looking for someone to devour.* They had not taken the necessary precautions. Had not taken any precautions, if the truth be known. So many good folk had been devoured that day. Wyn remembered the cries of terror, the chaos, that hellish stench of bodies burning. A foul mockery of all their good intentions. In the aftermath, Willibrord had fled south to the safety of Frankish territory while Wyn had returned across the sea to Kent. To lick his wounds and seek some guidance in the fog of darkness that had come to cloud his heart and mind.

And God had been gracious, as always. He had come to find His servant, to speak with him. Wyn was wiser now. He knew that first mission had been a test of his resolve. Was he ready? Was he willing?

Here now was his answer, in the cold and the wind and the rain.

He smiled. *Aye.* By the Great God above, he was willing…

Whether he was ready or not… well, that he would soon find out.

'Hey, oaah!' cried the helmsman as he swung the bows of the cargo skiff into the jetty. Wyn had to steady himself on the starboard gunwale, his stomach giving a final lurch to send him on his way. He was happy to see the back of the open sea for a good long while. The other passengers – few enough – clambered out onto the jetty and Wyn was close behind them, eager to get his feet back on solid ground.

Solid, but far from dry. The dense veil of drizzle fell in depressing sheets all about them, turning the path and the gangplanks into rivers of slime and oozing mud. Everywhere he looked was mud, like the primordial world without form or memory that their pagan forefathers used to sing of in the old tales of creation – before the light of Christ came to speak a better word. The great life-giving Logos that began it all.

215

'If it's vittles you're needing, the meet-hall always has a good fire going,' called the helmsman as he coiled the forestay around his arm. 'You'll be dry quicker 'n you could empty your bladder.'

Wyn called back his thanks and followed the others trudging ahead up the gangplank onto the marsh banks. Aye, heat and an empty bladder felt like the consolation of paradise to him just then. That and a little ale, mayhaps, just to settle his belly.

Dort was a place of traders, and a monk was not such a strange sight among them to draw any particular notice. Indeed, he knew a good few folk in the settlement had already accepted the new faith and were guarding its little flame with care, against the cold damp of the place and the blasting winds that might extinguish it before it had a chance to grow.

As he followed the path towards the stacks of wood-smoke and the stench of the first smithies, he fell into some friendly talk with another traveller, a merchant of wool, feeling his way round the Frisian tongue for the first time in a while. He'd always liked it. Frisian was not so different from his own tongue, in truth, but something about wanting to understand the other, listening just a little more carefully, reading the man's face a little closer. Aye, he liked that well. He was a better man in another tongue, a humbler man. And his pride was long in need of a popping. He had to smile to himself at the irony of it: books were no way to teach a man how to be the best of himself; the Lord had made living for that.

The merchant seemed to know Dort better than he and played the part of host, pointing out the 'best baker in this miserable place' down one lane of low rain-soaked shacks, then confiding there was a cloth merchant he had come to outwit whom he was due to catch up with in the meet-hall at noon. 'If the tight-fisted devil shows up,' he added, with a wink. 'He likes his ale, God forgive him.'

'God forgive us all,' returned Wyn with a grin. 'On a day like this, who could blame him?'

'Well said! Would you join me for one, Father?'

'Ha! I'm no priest, friend. Merely a humble monk. I go by Wyn.'

'Well, Wyn, pleased to know you. Me, I go by Lorik,' nodded the merchant. They had reached the open space before the meet-hall where folk were coming and going about their business in spite of the weather. Lorik gestured at the door. 'Come – I can tell you my life story while we wait for my spinner!' He pulled aside the sodden drape.

But before Wyn let himself be swallowed up in the warmth of smoky air and sour breath that leaked out into the rain, he heard a quiet but urgent voice cry out, the note of distress in which would have stopped a far harder heart than his.

He turned to see the source of it, and among the figures hunched against the drizzle, he noticed one moving at pace towards him. A woman, by the looks. Unlike the others, her head was uncovered, her hair plastered across her face, giving her a wild appearance.

'Father! Father, please wait!'

She rushed straight up to him and flung herself down upon her knees, oblivious to the cloying mud, clutching at his robe like she wished to save herself from Noah's flood.

'Father,' she wailed. 'You must help me! Please, hear me, hear me.'

'Do I know you, woman?' said Wyn, perplexed at this sudden accost.

'He's a monk, woman, not a priest,' the merchant corrected her, evidently lively to the distinction.

'But you are a man of God?' she said, looking only into Wyn's green eyes.

'I am that, by His grace,' answered Wyn, sinking to her level. 'Come, you've no need to kneel before me.' With gentle insistence, he prised her hands from his robe and drew her to her feet.

'I must speak with you, sir. I... I am troubled. My soul... my heart is torn.'

'Of course, child.' The woman was young, no more than twenty if she was even that, though the lines of hard living were already marked upon her thin face. Strings of snot and rain drooped from the tip of her sharp Frisian nose, only adding to the picture of anguish. 'Be calm. I will hear you.'

'How can I be calm, sir? I've lost everything. *Everything*. My soul before all else.'

'It need not be, my child.' Wyn clasped her hands together. 'God forgives a repentant heart. The scriptures say where sin abounds, grace abounds all the more.'

'I fear no grace can blot my sin, sir.'

The merchant scoffed and said in a voice none too soft, 'A whore, no doubt, who by the looks has come to the end of her business.'

Wyn rounded on him with a sudden snarl. 'Bridle your

tongue, man! If Our Lord did not judge a fallen woman, nor should we.'

The merchant was taken aback by the unexpected ferocity in Wyn's face. He scowled and gave an indignant shrug. 'Know what, *monk*? You can get your own damn ale.' With that, he vanished into the hall, the drape falling behind him.

Wyn turned back to the woman. 'No matter your sin, you may tell me your trouble. God hears you as much as I.'

'I am no harlot,' she said, her voice weak and broken. 'Would that my sin were so simple. No... I've done far worse.'

'What is it? Unburden your conscience,' urged Wyn, and as he awaited her answer, a sudden chill snaked through his bones that had nothing to do with the wind and the rain.

'It's my child,' she whispered. 'My own child.'

'Go on.'

'I... sold her.' She covered her eyes in shame. 'I must have been possessed by some evil spirit to do it but...' She shook her head again. 'It seemed the only way. And they... they were so persuasive.'

'They?'

'The men who took her.' She seized his robe again, pulled him close. 'They offered me gold for her. More than I had ever seen. They said they would care for her, give her a good life.' Her fists bunched in the rough wool of his tunic. 'Understand, we had nothing. It was all I could do to feed her. Myself, I ate but little.' Aye, she looked like it, too.

'Have you not a husband?'

'I did. Cold in his grave two summers past.'

'No other who could help you?'

219

'Maybe. But my own folk are far from here.' Tears welled in her eyes. 'I lied to myself – telling myself they would be kind to her. But then last night...'

'What happened?'

'I had a dream. I saw it all. It seemed as if an angel showed me the truth of what I had done. The horror of it. And I cannot bear it!' Her voice broke down into heaving sobs. Wyn put his arm around her shoulder.

'There is no chance of finding her? Of taking her back?'

'The money is all gone,' she sobbed. 'They are gone. Upriver, I know not where.' She suddenly pulled his tunic tighter, glaring up at him with desperate eyes. 'Can God forgive me my terrible sin? My greed. When I saw that money, I... I *wanted* it.' Her eyes now stared right through him, as if remembering with horror that same desire. 'I know now I allowed myself to be persuaded. Yet I knew in my deepest heart it was wickedness. I lied to myself. And now she's gone.'

Wyn did not know what to say. He had heard such things before. Pitied the desperation to which a mother or father must be driven to take such a step. But never had he been confronted with the raw wound of it.

'You must take your confession to God,' he said quietly. 'The blood of Christ covers your sin.'

'Oh, I confess it, I confess it to him, I do. But can nothing be done to undo the wrong I have done?' she wailed. 'Can you not help me find her?'

'Me?'

'I have no one else, sir.'

'I...' Wyn's voice faltered. This was not why he was here.

He already had a clear plan and purpose. And yet... had not God put this woman in his path also to some purpose, if only to salve her troubled soul? 'They went upriver, you say?'

'Yes!' she cried, catching hold of his halting words like a drowning man to driftwood. 'Do you go that way?'

He turned to gaze off towards the grey expanse of water, wending its way into the flat white mists that cloaked the land. The source of the great Rhein river lay that way, Wyn thought. That was his direction and his goal. That, and much further. He meant to voyage to Rome, there to seek an audience with Pope Gregory, to win his blessing. 'What is her name?' he murmured.

'My little Fenna,' the woman answered. 'She's seen but five winters. She's so small.'

'Fenna.' He nodded. 'Come, child, off your knees.' He lifted her a second time and, like a father himself, gently tipped her chin so he could look directly in her eyes. 'If God is willing, He may lead me to her. Meanwhile, you must pray – for your own soul and for your daughter. And the Lord will hear your prayers.'

She buried her face in his shoulder, murmuring her thanks into the sodden black wool of his tunic.

'Can you tell me anything more of the men who took her?'

She shook her head. 'Nothing,' her muffled voice muttered. And then, slowly, she looked up at him. 'No. One thing, maybe. They all of them were blond. So blond, their hair was almost silver... Bright like the moon,' she whispered.

Wyn frowned down at her. That anything could seem bright in this drab and dreary place was startling enough. But silver hair? Like the moon? It was a curious choice of words. Yet he didn't want to discourage her. 'I will pray that God guides my steps, child. And meantime that He keeps your Fenna safe.'

Fresh tears broke from her eyes. Tears of gratitude no doubt, although in his secret heart, Wyn feared they were premature. Or worse, unwarranted.

Fenna was the first of the missing children of whom Wyn heard in his journey upriver.

But she would not be the last.

CHAPTER NINETEEN

Whichever gods ruled over the winds and the seas, Erlan reckoned they must have been smiling on the *Fasolt* and her crew.

With their pulses still racing, they had run before a brisk north-easterly wind that had carried them far beyond the Marmara Sea and the immediate clutches of any imperial pursuit. The *Fasolt* flew westward like an eagle on the wing, passing through the thin bottleneck of the Hellespont and onward into the Aegean Sea, long before any word could have reached those places from Byzantium ordering their interception. Since then, the days that had followed had been easy voyaging. The worst they had faced were a few brooding stacks of clouds and a boisterous northerly breeze, which brought with it a modest swell, pitching and rolling the *Fasolt*'s sleek hull, but nothing to worry even a man as ill-favoured towards the sea as Erlan.

All the while, the mood among the crew remained buoyant.

After all, not one of them had truly believed they could actually pull it off. At least, so they said a hundred times afterwards, reliving their success nearly every night as they ate and drank together, until the telling of it became so entangled with Erlan's memory of how it had been, that he could not have sworn to the truth of anything that happened. But if they ever doubted their memory, their eyes were proof of the result. There was the gold, all eighteen thousand marks of it, securely stowed in the midships hold. And each day that passed, Erlan's guilt at his betrayal of Leo abated a little more, like a tide ebbing away. Soon he would be left only with the cold, hard fact that they had needed it. Because the gold would buy them the spears that would start a war. Whether it was enough to finish one was a harder question to answer.

There, too, was the syphon and its barrel of liquid fire.

Erlan suffered more disquiet from that.

He and Lilla had argued vehemently when at last he had noticed this addition to their cargo. It looked innocuous enough in its barrel and box of piping, but he had grave misgivings about bringing any of that Devil's Piss, as Einar called it, back to the north. And even graver misgivings about Lilla's hunger to acquire it. A hunger that had already brought her to the brink of death. Even if she was sure of herself and made light of his fears, he could not shake the feeling that carrying such a weapon to the north – if it didn't blow up in their faces before they got there – risked doing them more harm than good. Sure, it was powerful; he knew that as well as any man still living, and many who were not so lucky. But if it fell into the wrong hands, what horrors could it inflict?

Or worse, what could it do in the right hands?

Perhaps it was this doubt that had come between him and Lilla. Something had, anyway. He told himself it was all her, that she had withdrawn from him. And although they slept under the same fur at night, their bodies pressed close as arrows in a quiver, the stars a bright blaze overhead, he felt far from her. Could sense her apprehension growing with every league they journeyed closer to home. But what could he say to allay it? *The Norns have graven all?* The words had never seemed much more than cold comfort. In any case, words would change nothing. Whatever fate the three sisters had spun for them would be clear soon enough, one way or another.

At least the gold seemed to have won an uneasy truce between Lilla and the crew. Even Mikki Crow's long scowl was gone. Although the gods knew he was a bloody hard man to please. And Einar... Einar was quiet. If he spoke at all, it was with Orīana, away from prying ears, their voices soft with understanding. Gods, but that woman was a find, thought Erlan. No doubts about it. Without her, they would still have been stuck in Byzantium, still scratching their heads, the chance long slipped them by.

No, he was glad for Orīana's company. It was her daughter who troubled him most of all.

Marta... Marta...

She was in his thoughts more than she ought to be. Even though the reason for it made no real sense. He had awoken before dawn one morning with a start. Bad dreams, again. He pushed tousled strands of hair out of his face, rubbing at his eyes to try to erase the image of the face burned inside their lids.

225

It was *her* face. The face of Inga, his sister.

She had come to him again. The third night in a row she had done so. But why? Why should she haunt him out there on the blue emptiness of those waves? Had she not yet gone to the gloomy halls of Hel? Or was she not at least at rest in the quiet of her barrow grave on the hill above Vendlagard? What had brought her back to him?

The answer eluding him, he stretched, snatched up his tunic and pulled it over his head. Only then did he notice the bright, clear eyes on him, peering out from a body under a cloak huddled beside the mast block. Beside him, Lilla was still sleeping. Most of the crew was asleep. But Marta was awake. And for a lingering moment, they had looked at one another, his mind still groggy from the wine the night before, or else the dregs of the dream before it drifted away. And for a second, she looked at him exactly as Inga once had, hiding nothing. A look that even now undid him, that transfixed him, locking his limbs as if by some black craft.

That was it. Different eyes, different mouth, different nose, but somehow altogether... *Inga.*

Marta's smile broke the spell. She lay down her head and turned away. And Erlan was left with the strangest certainty that he had just given something away.

He shook the incident off quick enough, and soon thought no more about it. Or at least persuaded himself that it signified nothing.

But then came Syracusa.

*

Demetrios said it was a calculated risk. No imperial dromon or karabion could have made the port ahead of them. The little Greek had boasted they were likely days ahead, and that was if any imperials were in pursuit at all, which he doubted. Even so, Erlan wanted to take no unnecessary chances. They would stop only for a day, long enough to take on vittles and fresh water and wine and then move on.

'And ale, if we can find it!' Bull had insisted.

Demetrios assured him there was no finer beer to be found in all the wide world than in Syracusa. 'They have the best of everything.'

Of course, the town had nothing to match the overbearing grandeur of Byzantium. But when Demetrios explained that fifty or so years before, an emperor named Constans had thought to make it his capital, Erlan could well see why. The marks of that imperial favour still endured. Temples of the old gods refurbished into richly adorned churches, municipal buildings with myriad pillars, busy porticos full of trade. The port reeked like an open shitpit, but then what port did not?

Perhaps it was that which encouraged them all to throw themselves into the town, if only for a day, each in their own way. That, and a desire to stand on solid ground after two weeks at sea. Bull nearly broke his ankle in his haste to find the best brothel in town. And for once, most of his crewmates were content to go with him, except for Black Svali and Ran, who offered to safeguard the gold.

'Don't do nothing I wouldn't do!' Ran called out merrily to the rest of them.

'Ran, you lazy whoreson, that don't leave 'em much!' sniggered Snodin.

'Well, whatever else you do,' returned the Gotlander, 'I'd put our little bullock on a leash. He's liable to do himself an injury.'

Erlan was inclined to agree. But he knew it would do them good to let off some steam. And besides, they had the coin for it. Who was he to deny them the fruits of their spoils?

Meanwhile, he went with Einar to scour the market for various items Black Svali wanted. Nails mostly, and replacements for tools that had broken or worn out, some lengths of new rope, strong thread for the sails. Lilla felt unwell, had done for some days, and said she would stay with the ship. Although Erlan suspected that she, too, didn't want to let the gold or the liquid fire out of her sight. Finally, Orīana took Marta with her to wander around the town.

Oh, it was a proper little invasion.

It was a hot afternoon, getting on towards dusk when Einar and Erlan concluded their business among the stalls and porticos of the main market-street. Einar was haggling with a boy with a handcart about how many copper coins the lad would get for toting their gear back to the harbour when Orīana and her daughter appeared.

'Stay with us!' exclaimed Orīana gaily. 'It's too soon to go back to that stinking fish bucket.'

'What d'you say, skipper?' Einar grinned. 'A jug of the local, huh? My tongue's dry as Hel's crotch.'

'Your tongue's always dry as Hel's crotch and no amount of wine'll change that.'

'Well, always worth a try.'

'You go.' He glanced at Marta who was paying more attention to the trade-folk passing by. With her placid

228

expression and novice headscarf, she looked a long way from her cloister. 'And you, girl,' he added. 'Family time, eh?'

'I have a name,' she replied indignantly.

'Marta, then,' he said, irritated she felt so free to correct him.

'Thank you, *Erlan*.' She looked down, the corners of her mouth curling a fraction.

'Ha! Better get that right, skipper.' Einar nodded at Orīana. 'Get wrong off these ladies and how they make you pay!'

'*Várvaros ilíthios*,' said Orīana, giving her man a loving shove.

Erlan excused himself and made his way through the crowd, irritated again. But whether more at himself or at her, he couldn't say. She was fourteen. Or was it fifteen? A young woman perhaps in body, but in all else a child. Yet his mind kept returning to her. *Her, or who she reminded him of?* Did it make a difference? By all the gods, he didn't need this... distraction. Didn't he have enough to worry about?

As the crowd thinned, he quickened his pace, suddenly craving the company of Lilla. She was a blast of familiar wind to clear the miasma of confused emotion that girl stirred in him.

He turned off the portico down a side street, reckoning from the slant of the sun that it must be a short-cut back to the harbour. But he was hardly out of the thoroughfare when a voice called out to him: 'Erlan! Wait!'

He turned.

'Erlan!' It was Marta's voice, but full of laughter and gaiety. So unlike her usual rather solemn monotone that for a moment he wondered whether it was truly her. But then there she was, standing before him, those penetrating eyes uncomfortably close.

'I thought I should leave my mother with Einar. They're so rarely alone.' She smiled at him. He said nothing, struggling to fathom this sudden change in her mood. Wasn't she snapping at him a moment ago? 'I told them I'd catch up and go back to the boat with you.'

Erlan raised an eyebrow. 'If you like. I think this is a short-cut.' He turned to continue down the alley but she caught his hand.

'There's no hurry, is there?'

He looked down at her hand on his, her smooth olive-skin fingers against his worn, dry knuckles. 'What do you mean?'

'They are not the only ones who wish to be alone. Are they?'

Erlan frowned down at her, seeing expectation glowing in her eyes. Gods, was it him who'd put that there? 'Look, Marta—'

'But you agree we need to talk?'

He realised she still had his hand. He took it back. 'What have *we* to talk about?'

'I've seen the way you look at me.' The corners of her mouth turned up again.

He shook his head, thoughts in there stumbling, slow-witted. 'I don't... look at you. I don't know what you mean.'

'It's all right. God knows how I have tried to quell my feelings. But... I can't deny that I feel the same. It's obvious there's something between—'

'Don't,' he cut in. 'Don't say it.'

Suddenly she laughed gaily, the sound of it free as running water. 'Sometime it's all I can do to stop myself from reaching out... and touching your face,' she added in a murmur. To prove her point, she did just that. But Erlan caught her hand.

'Aren't you a nun?' he said, his brain quickly trying to marshal his defences. Weren't there so many reasons to douse this flame before it got out of control? 'Sworn to chastity?'

'I...' She looked down, then demurely stroked his fist clutching hers. 'I've not yet taken my vows. Maybe now I never will. I ask God why He has brought us together...'

He brushed away her hand, pulled back his own. 'You're delusional, Marta. Imagining things that are not there.'

'It's no delusion,' she insisted, her voice growing in boldness. 'You can't deny what you feel, Erlan. I certainly will not. It's too pure. Too good. To deny it would be a sin.'

'Now listen to me,' Erlan said in a gruff whisper, and in his urgency to persuade her, he found he'd pushed her back against the wall. 'Get these thoughts out of your head. Lilla is my woman.'

'Lilla! Bah!' she scowled. 'You don't want her. I see you with her. There is nothing.'

'That's not true.'

'Now who is delusional?'

He had his forearm across her chest. Her face was close now, just below his. She was looking up at him, eyes intense... her mouth so close he could smell her breath, with its lingering sweetness. Youth in full bloom. 'You'll not speak of this again.'

'You want me. As I do you.'

'I do not.' Yet at that very moment, he didn't rightly know whether he was lying or speaking the truth. 'Understand?' He summoned all the coolness he had in him. 'Now run along back to your mother, little girl.'

All at once, her expression changed. 'The devil take you then!' Her sapphire eyes flared like blue flames in a forge.

'Aye. Probably one day he will. Now off you go,' he growled, shoving her back up the alley the way she'd come. But the action was harder than he'd intended and she stumbled, falling to one knee on the dusty cobbles. She gave a little gasp of pain, then slowly picked herself up.

'God sees your heart, Erlan,' she hissed. 'You're a liar. *A liar!*' And with that, she hurried away back to the portico and the passing crowds.

Erlan expelled a long sigh, relieved she had gone, but somehow disturbed. At what Marta had revealed, perhaps in his heart as much as her own. No. It wasn't her. It was Inga. It was the memory. *By the Hanged!* Wasn't that wound a scar by now, long sealed? He must not let it re-open. He must bury the ghost of his sister as their father would have buried her body. And he must watch himself. The present days had sufficient troubles of their own not to go digging up the past.

He turned and limped back towards the ship, quickening his uneven steps. The sooner he saw Lilla, the better.

All was calm when he reached the *Fasolt*. The cart-boy had already been with his delivery of provisions and spares. Ran was sorting through it all. Lilla and Svali were talking in the bows, apparently oblivious to the noxious air of the harbour. The stink of it made Erlan feel nauseous. But maybe that had more to do with the encounter he'd just had.

He went to join them, smiling at Lilla and taking her hand without a word, not wishing to interrupt them. Svali seemed to be in some story of his past. The carpenter had lightened up considerably since they had got away from Byzantium. Erlan guessed gold had that effect on some men, although he wasn't one of them; it only made him more nervous. Anyway, Lilla seemed absorbed in the story.

She squeezed his hand to let him know she was glad he was there. It made him think of that wood on the ride home from Freya's Fair at Sigtuna. The sound of the rain falling through the blood-beech canopy. It must be standing there still, waiting for their return.

Waiting for the return of its rightful queen.

Dusk was coming on. The taverners were lighting their torches. Gods only knew what debauchery the crew were deep into by now, with no doubt Demetrios at the head of the pack. *So long as they're back by morning*, he thought. A few hours at sea would soon clear their heads.

Something caught the tail of his eye, drawing his gaze back to the quayside. Three figures advancing at pace. It was a moment before he recognised Einar, then Orīana and the slighter figure of Marta.

Something was wrong. The girl was clutching herself, her head down. Orīana's arm was round her shoulder. As they walked down the jetty, Einar saw him and shook his head. He wore a look dark as thunder. Erlan bristled.

What the Hel has she told them?

As they reached the gangplank, Lilla saw them too. 'Is something the matter?' She got to her feet. 'Look at you all! What's wrong?'

Orīana ushered Marta across the gangplank and into the hold. 'Marta was attacked.'

The girl was visibly shaking, her shoulders hunched.

'Attacked? Is she all right? Are you hurt, child?'

Marta looked up, forced a brave smile. 'I will live.'

'By all the gods!' exclaimed Lilla. Even in the dusk-light, Erlan could see the whole left side of Marta's face was swollen, the skin on her cheekbone grazed bloody. 'What happened? Who did this?'

'She doesn't know,' said Einar. 'A man, is all.'

Perhaps only Erlan was aware that Marta's glance kept shooting in his direction.

'Here, let me see. Give her space.' Lilla drew Marta to her and sat her down on a thwart.

'I fought him.' Her voice was back to that soft monotone. Marta the novice had returned. 'He dragged me into a passageway. I tried to scream but he had me round my throat. I couldn't...' She broke off, her voice now cracking into short, staccato sobs. 'I couldn't breathe...'

'Your arms.' Lilla pushed back Marta's sleeves. There were livid scratches all over her forearms.

'There was a struggle,' Marta continued. 'Then all at once he was gone. He must have been scared off... So I went to find my mother.'

'I thought you were all together.'

'She wanted to come back here,' said Einar. 'We sent her to catch up with Erlan. He'd only just left.'

234

They all looked at Erlan. He sucked in a breath, his mind trying to process all this. What could he say, that they had argued and he sent her back. But that would only elicit more questions.

'I couldn't find him.' Marta's eyes fixed on his. She paused, perhaps waiting for him to contradict her.

'I... I just came back to the ship,' he said. 'Just as I said I would.' Did something in her eyes shift then? Maybe it was a trick of the fading light. But now she knew he would lie. Or at least he was prepared to conceal the truth.

'I got lost. I didn't know the way back to the port so I came back to find the two of you.' Marta reached out to her mother. Orīana took her hand and kissed it. 'That's when the man grabbed hold of me.' Marta suddenly winced and put her hand to her neck. 'It hurts here.'

'Take this off.' Orīana's fingers were already working at unwinding Marta's headscarf.

Moments later, her hair tumbled out and she tipped back her head. 'Is it bad?'

There was a thick band of bruising already, an ugly purple necklace of swelling around her throat. Einar swore and ground his fist into his palm. 'Son of a whore! If I ever catch up with him—'

'Poor baby,' interrupted Orīana, pulling Marta to her chest. 'You're safe now,' she murmured. 'Safe with us.'

Erlan watched them, this newly forged family, with Einar as protector. He didn't know what to make of it all. But before he looked away, he could have sworn he saw the flicker of a smile cross the girl's lips.

CHAPTER TWENTY

They sailed the next morning.

Despite having managed to re-provision and re-fit without incident, and that most of the crew had been in good spirits after their night of carousing, the attack on Marta soured the mood considerably.

Lilla felt for the girl, remembering that sickening vulnerability of being at the mercy of a man much stronger than herself. In truth, though, she considered Marta had got away lightly. How many less fortunate women had suffered rape or worse among the warren of Syracusa's streets? she wondered.

Still, the girl was not looking for her sympathy. She had her mother for that, and Einar of course, who was proving himself quite the doting father. But the girl's bruised face served as a sobering reminder to everyone on board that their luck could run both ways.

With little more she could do about it, Lilla busied herself with more practical matters about the ship. Black Svali seemed satisfied that the new caulking in the bow strakes was holding. 'Though she ain't been tested too much yet,' he said, always ready with a gloomy qualification. He wasn't wrong, though. Demetrios marvelled at their continuing good fortune when the wind swung round into a warm south-easterly. 'A wind straight from the desert's throat,' he called it, which rendered the air unseasonably hot and coated *Fasolt*'s woollen sail with a sheen of red dust that glistened copper at sunset.

They passed abeam of Kalaris on Sardinia after only two days. Demetrios was in an ebullient mood. 'If we keep on like this, we'll be clear of the Pillars of Herakles in under a week. That's where it gets interesting.'

'The Pillars of Herakles?' Lilla asked. 'What is that?'

'Gateway to the end of the world,' the little Greek grinned knowingly. 'The ancients tell that the demi-god Herakles smashed his way right through the mountain of Atlas. All he left standing were two pillars and a great gulf of sea-water between them.'

'Truly? The place must be a great wonder.' Since leaving the choking constriction of Byzantium far behind her, she'd found that a new expansiveness had opened up within her spirit. The hunger to return had been the necessary spur to summon the will to escape the City. To do what they had done. But now, for a time at least, she could allow herself some respite. To wake each day and see what it would bring. The time would come – and perhaps sooner than she would like – when she would have to hone that will to a wicked point again. When she would have to face her enemy and the challenges that lay before her. But for now... there was time to wonder.

Demetrios shrugged. 'All I'll say is, I've been a lot of places and there's nowhere quite like it. You'll see for yourself.' He chuckled. 'Anyway, it makes a good story.'

'I'd like to hear more of them.' She gazed off to the western horizon. 'And after the Pillars, what lies beyond?'

'The ocean,' was all he said. And in that one word, he seemed to convey a great mystery – of something so large and unfathomable as to be impossible to capture in mere words. 'You'll see that, too.'

She nodded, realising that what she really wanted was assurance. That all would be well. If only they knew what was to come. But the truth was, no one knew. So here they were, suspended between what had been and what would be.

The present. What is… *Verðandi*.

A path as sharp as a blade-edge.

Since Syracusa, Erlan had seemed subdued. Even more absorbed in his own thoughts than was his habit. She often wondered what was in them. He had confessed so much to her before the Night of Fire. His name. His wound. His people. Maybe that was as much as he could ever tell her. It was something, though. A bond that only she shared with him. Sometimes she would look at him from a distance and just murmur his true name, feeling its shape over her lips. *Hakan. Hakan.* Uttering it like a spell, as if somehow it would call him back to himself. But she suspected that man whom he once was no longer existed. When they returned to his native Jutland, as they intended to, she guessed that both of them would find that 'Hakan' – whoever he once had been – was already long dead. Sometimes she feared who they would find in his place.

One morning she went to him and laid her hand on his shoulder as he was looking out west to the seam of land growing thicker on the horizon. 'You seem troubled, my love.'

He smiled up at her and shook away his pensive look. 'Tired, maybe.'

'Then rest some more. Dear gods, there's little else to do.'

'I will, I will.'

'Do you think of your home?'

'Mmm. I wonder what we'll find there. My father...' His words trailed away. She knew better than to press him to pick them up again. Instead she sought something practical to say.

'Do you think he'll add his spears to ours?'

'To ours? You mean all dozen of them.'

'A dozen is a start.'

'I suppose it is.'

'And gold is a convincing argument. Isn't that what you say?'

'For most it is. But you don't know how it was left with my father. I can't say how he'll receive me... Bah! I can't say I deserve much of a reception. I dishonoured him. Probably started a feud for him.'

She brushed a windblown lock out of her eyes. 'Still, you said he hates the Wartooth... Or hated him,' she corrected herself. King Harald Wartooth had long since ridden to the Halls of the Slain, from the bloody fields of Bravellír, taking thousands with him. 'Surely he would stand with me against the Wartooth's son?'

'Like I said, I can't tell you what he'll do.' A trace of impatience had crept into his voice. 'Let's reach Jutland first.

We still only have the word of that drunkard,' he gestured at Demetrios, 'that the north can be reached this way. I have my doubts.'

'We had little choice but to trust him. Besides, Dimo seems to know his business.'

'So far he does.'

They fell silent for a time. He, looking out to sea; she, looking at him. She liked looking at his face. Liked tracing the lines down his cheek, watching the darting movements of his wolf eyes, always alive, always alert. Liked that there was still mystery there.

He gave a little snort of amusement. 'Am I so fascinating?'

'To me, you are.'

'Gods,' he breathed a long sigh and turned to her. 'I don't deserve this.'

'What?'

'All of this.' He shook his head. 'My life. Where we are. How we got away. How I'm still alive when so many have died... How I have you.'

'You'll always have me.' She touched his cheek. 'You're the man I choose. The man I will always choose.'

'You know, my love...' He stopped. Then, with sudden vigour, he swung round to face her square, clasping her hands between his. 'I need to be more than that. I want to be your husband.'

A small laugh escaped her lips. '*Now* you tell me this? Here?'

'Here.' He was grinning. A rare sight these days. 'Anywhere.'

'Yes, but... we're hardly alone, are we?'

Erlan looked around at the crew sprawled about the ship. 'Come up here with me.' He led her over the thwarts into the lee of the great curved prow. 'See out there,' he murmured into her ear. 'I don't know what lies that way. Or what fate awaits us over that horizon. Maybe it's victory – a crown, vengeance, your land. Maybe it's a short and bloody death. But whatever it is, I want to face it bound to you.'

'We are already bound together.'

'Heart and soul. Our wills united.'

She found her soul rising with each of his words, like a swallow upon the air – but then an ugly thought brought her back to earth. She was barren. Nothing to be done. 'You know I can't give you sons. Or daughters.'

'You are enough.'

'You think that now—'

'It will always be so. That is *my* choice. I choose you just as you choose me. Over all that is past. Over all that may be.'

The words sounded very fine. As a younger woman, Lilla would have heard only them. But her older self had learned to listen for the whispered meaning behind mere words. Half-wise as she was, she couldn't yet fathom it. Anyway, why should they not marry? Must she forfeit her happiness forever on account of Saldas's curse? Her womb was barren, yes. That did not mean her life had to be.

And yet…

What power had she really if she gave away her hand so… cheaply? She already had Erlan's loyalty. She had his love. Beyond that, what did he bring? No army. No lands. No wealth. Were these not things she must consider? Queen Lilla Sviggarsdottír certainly must think of such things, though

241

the girlish Lilla of her youth would have skated right over them.

'And so?' he said expectantly.

She opened her mouth, but even in that moment she could not have said what her answer would be. The chafe of a divided heart burned inside her.

'*So-hoooa!*' cried a voice from the stern. Lilla turned, and there was Demetrios, leaping up and down on the stern-most thwart, pointing to the west. 'Look yonder, my lady! Didn't I tell you? Behold, the great Pillars of Herakles!'

She looked ahead and, true enough, in the distance, either side of the prow-beast, two shivers of land rose up out of the sea like rivets on a shield. Dimo's yelling had roused the rest of the crew, who all poured forward in their curiosity.

She'd almost allowed herself to feel relief, but Erlan took her wrist. Gentle but insistent. 'What's your answer?'

The first of the crew – the boy Dreng, in fact – reached the bows and jumped up beside them, whooping and hollering excitedly. But Erlan held her gaze. 'Lilla?'

'It's yes, my love,' she said, with something that felt a lot like fear coiling in her guts. 'Of course it is. *Yes.*'

And as the rest of the crew crowded round them, Erlan pulled her to him and kissed her fiercely, deaf to the goading jeers of the Estlanders filling their ears.

Absent a priest or a goði, Demetrios and Svali married them that very evening, under a crimson sky as the *Fasolt* slipped smoothly by the twin mountains, one to the north, one to the south. Erlan insisted they had no cause to wait. As though, having made the decision, he wished to be the other side of his vow before anything could get in its way.

'I swear this oath to you,' he said, her hand clasped in his. 'It is the last I'll ever swear.'

Demetrios raised his arms high above them, calling out in a loud and ringing voice for the blessing of the Almighty God of the Heavens. Then Black Svali got up in turn and called on the blessing of the sea-god Njord, and his wife Skadi if she were around and in a blessing kind of a mood.

And everyone reckoned it a pretty thorough job. And a brief one at that, which was equally welcome.

All the while, Lilla swallowed down her doubts and smiled, as she knew she ought to. And Erlan kissed her and Einar grinned and Orīana laughed. Even Mikki's long mouth was tilted in something approaching good humour.

Lilla saw only one face in the onlooking crowd that was the same as ever. Impervious, unfeeling, the bruise purpling one cheek adding a shadow of darkness.

Marta's face.

Cold as marble.

CHAPTER TWENTY-ONE

Katāros stopped, leaned on his staff, and took a moment to look back down to see how far he had come.

The valley spread out below him, the path up to where he stood switching back and forth like the coils of a serpent. Granite-grey peaks rose all around him, piercing the azure sky like the jagged spear tips of ancient titans. Many were streaked white with snow, as if daubed with the pure blood of the gods whom those titans hated.

But such dark comparisons were out of place.

Truly, the eunuch had never seen anything so beautiful. Far below, the greens of the valley bottom stretched away into the distance, far as his vision could fly, curling south and east. And closer, higher up the mountain, the leaves had already begun to turn, orange and red and yellow, shining gold and copper in the noon-high sunlight. The air was crisp and fresh but the cold was not yet penetrating. It was too soon in the year for that. Though it would surely not be long before the first snows fell.

He sucked in a deep breath, filling his lungs. Air so pure. So innocent. As if the blight of mankind had not yet reached this place... yet here *he* was.

His journey had taken him far. By his reckoning, over five hundred miles and the best part of a month. At first he could only walk a small distance each day. But now, his steps could swallow up vast tracts of land between the rising and the setting of the sun. His body was lean, his muscles strong, the soles of his feet hard as plate iron.

Once clear of Ravenna, his fear of exposure had begun to subside. Although on the road, there were always dangers, even for a beggar as wretched and penniless as him.

As soon as he was able, he'd had his wounds cleaned and dressed. One of them had given him real trouble, the seam where the knife had cut blowing up bright scarlet for a time. He had feared the infection would eat right through his face, but, doing his best to keep it clean, somehow his body had met the challenge and the swelling had subsided. The last time he had gazed at his own reflection, in the public fountain of Osta thirty miles back down the valley, a web of scars had stared back at him. An unrecognisable face. Someone else's face.

His own was now gone forever.

As a fugitive, his choices had been limited. Once clear of Ravenna, he had decided to come north. For a while, he thought to take himself to the court of the Lombard king, Liutprand, in the city of Pavia, having heard so much of him. But when he reached that city, something in him kept his feet moving. Maybe it was the unappealing prospect of being caught in yet another web of intrigue, a hapless fly at the mercy of yet another bloated spider. Or maybe it was that he had at last found some peace upon the road. Whichever, he kept moving. And each step further north seemed to awaken in him more memories. Few enough of them were happy, to be sure, and yet they were a part of him. He could not deny it. Many things came back to him: towering trees of oak and beech, and sprawling forests of fir, the biting cold, frosts and snows abounding, great rivers and rolling hills of green, the call of cuckoos in the dewy evening mists, the flutter of pigeon wings roosting in the branches of hawthorn bushes. These all called to him – an echo of his life *before*…

And so he kept walking.

In Vercelum, he had exchanged his ragged tunic and hose for a monk's habit: a gift from the abbot of a hospice which lay on the Via Francorum, the ancient pilgrimage trail that ran – so the abbot said – all the way north to Anglia across the sea, and south to the Holy See of Rome. 'Alas, this poor cloth is all we have to spare,' the abbot apologised. 'But it should keep you warm on the road, and the worst of the rain off you.'

Katāros soon realised the habit not only kept him warm, but it was as good as a cloak of invisibility. In it, he became just another pilgrim returning from Rome. To complete the illusion, he cut his hair into a tonsure. His bronzed skin was already fading to his native pallid colour. He spoke only Latin. To any whom he met, the idea that here was a once High Chamberlain of the far away empire… why, it was a plain absurdity.

He turned from the valley back to the path and began trudging on uphill. The last food in his belly was a heel of bread begged from a baker in Osta. The last water from a cattle trough filled by a mountain stream in the little village of Saint Remigius, just a couple of miles back down the valley. At this pace, he hoped to reach the Poeninus Pass long before nightfall. There, so he had been told, a small hospice stood on the saddle across the Pennine Alps where he could at least expect to spend the night in safety, if not in great comfort.

A bank of clouds was moving in, drawing with it a dark pall across the mountain range, moving slowly from east to west. He marvelled at how the landscape could change from a place of such glory to one of menace and threat in less time than it took to sharpen a knife. It made him think of the shapeshifters of whom the old shaman used to speak – friend one moment, foe the next.

And with the shadow came a lick of colder air. Perhaps it would rain later. The thought made him quicken his pace, even though with each step upward, the air grew thinner. He was panting even now, just to keep moving.

Ahead of him, fifty paces on, he saw among the trees in the gathering gloom the next turn in the path. Somewhere close but out of sight, a mountain stream chuckled by. There was no birdsong, only the rustle of the wind in the treetops. And then came the first spattering of rain.

He shuddered and muttered a curse, calculating how much longer it could be to the pass. Perhaps another hour. Surely not much more.

It was then he saw a figure step into his road.

He stopped, watching them. The figure stopped as well. Whoever it was had something propped over their shoulder.

There was something haughty, nonchalant about the way they stood. Then, with an unhurried movement, the figure swung the object to the ground and Katāros realised it was a club.

'Good evening, pilgrim,' said a laughing voice at his back.

Katāros spun around as a second figure detached itself from the trees and hopped onto the path behind him.

'Who are you?' demanded Katāros, with as much command in his voice as he could muster.

The man downhill answered, 'Does it matter?' He also carried a heavy stick, held across his waist. 'You're a bold man, travelling up here all alone. Some folk would say it ain't safe.'

'I have no reason to fear. I have nothing of any value.'

'Oh, don't say that!' The other gave a guttural chuckle. 'I've yet to meet the man who ha'n't got something worth the taking.'

His companion laughed, so close behind him now that Katāros whipped around his head. Both men were moving in, only a few paces away. 'Truly, I only have a couple of tremissis.'

'Well, there you are! That wasn't too hard, was it?'

Katāros poked his fingers into the makeshift cloth pouch on his belt, fishing around anxiously for the two little gold coins in there. They had been an act of charity from a passing merchant on the road south of Osta. Useful, no doubt, but they weren't worth dying for.

'Here.' He tossed them at the feet of the robber below him. Casually, the man stooped down and plucked them from among the stones on the path. 'That's all I have.'

'Come now, you're very modest. Young lad like you.' The man ran a black tongue along his lips. In the greying light, his teeth flashed like wolf fangs. Katāros tightened his grip on his staff, wishing he had something heavier.

'I mean no harm to you. Let me pass on.'

The robber sniggered. 'Wish we could say the same, pilgrim. Eh, Bepp?'

And before Katāros could even raise his stick, his skull exploded in a starburst of pain. He sank to his knees and toppled sideways, his vision a blur of reeling shadows. Before he knew it, his staff had been plucked from his hands and he felt himself being dragged by the heels away from the path and into the trees.

'Please,' he heard himself mutter. 'Please...' But there was no pleading to be done.

Instead he found his face screwed down into the forest litter. The smell of dead pine needles and loamy soil filled his nostrils. 'Come on, come on,' said one of them behind him, voice coarse and thirsty as a devil's on the day of judgement. Katāros tried to struggle, but the back of his neck was pincered, his arms and shoulders pinned helplessly to the ground. 'Quit your wriggling, you bitch monk!' snarled the second robber, whose voice was deeper than his accomplice's. But who could comply with a demand like that? Only a man already dead. So Katāros thrashed and kicked and tried to get his knees up under his chest. His reward was another blow to the head, blunter, heavier than the first. He felt his eyes roll back in his skull, the sting of cold

249

air as the hem of his habit was thrown over his rump, a trill of nasal laughter. He screamed into the dirt. Another blow.

And then, by the mercy of God, the world went black.

When he came to, he was alone.

At once, his whole head was filled with an intolerable throbbing pain, like some monstrous beating heart. He reached back and felt his skull where he had taken the blows and was astonished to find the back of it blown up big as a cow's udder. He couldn't feel his legs. His most intimate nether parts were burning like a forge-fire. He slid his hands over the rest of his body, tentatively exploring the damage. His fingers smeared in something sticky. He brought them back up to his face. When at last he managed to train his eyes on them, even in the half-light, it was obviously his own blood.

He wiped his hand on his chest and rolled onto his back with a deep groan. And there he lay, staring up through the pine branches.

Breathing. Breathing. Bitter tears burning his eyes...

How long he stayed like that, he could not have said. Only that it was night when at last he could summon the will to get to his feet. His sandals were gone. His belt was gone. His staff was snapped. They had left him only the habit.

He stumbled back to the path, his mind overwhelmed with pain and a growing delirium. Yet somehow, even in the darkness, the pale stone of the pathway was just visible. He set his feet to the task, falling forward more than walking. The spitting rain thickened and grew colder. The wind was picking up, whistling through the soaring peaks which towered above him like the devil's own citadel.

On and on he staggered, gulping down cold air, the rain now become sleet, driving into his eyes and open mouth. The rocks beneath his feet became slick as ice. He slipped and fell more times than he could count, skinning and slashing his knees till the blood stained the habit to its tattered hem.

At last, he thought he saw ahead of him, in the dark, a single pinprick of light. Quavering, but constant. He moaned with relief and pushed on. The light shone.

A rock beneath his foot gave way. His ankle twisted and he fell down, lying helpless on his back. He looked up at the starless night, summoning one last bellow of rage and despair, and then he lay still and closed his eyes...

He felt peaceful then, his whole body bathed, as it were, in pain – like a newborn babe swaddled in soft, warm cloths.

Surrender. Surrender...

If he heard voices, he knew it was only another lie.

Or else another dream...

He found himself walking in a passageway that had no doors and no windows. A gentle gradient, downwards. Slow and steady. He walked and walked, seeing nothing above him, nothing ahead. Only the darkness. And this thought, this same refrain, repeating over and over in his head... Let me die. Please let me die. Only let me die... *But instead of the peace of death, or else its horror – whichever was the truth of it – a soft whisper came echoing down the passageway towards him, filling the confined space with its sound.* Go back. Go back. Go back...

Katāros opened his eyes. He felt warm.

He could smell the heavy lanolin scent of cheap tallow candles, hear the murmur of low voices outside.

He seemed to be in some kind of small room. Almost a cell, with bare grey walls and a simple square window through which daylight shone with unnatural brightness, too painful for his eyes to behold for long.

His body still ached, his head worst of all. But he was comfortable. He felt the weight of a blanket on top of him, a surprisingly sympathetic mattress underneath him.

Where was he?

He tried to speak but only a croak came out. Yet the sound was enough to start an avalanche of movement. Someone out of sight near the doorway leaped up, and he heard footsteps scamper away and then an excited exchange of voices down the corridor. Moments later, two faces appeared around a jamb of the door. At first he thought them both strangers, one with ragged clumps of oak-brown hair and round, ruddy cheeks. The other was brown as a nut, with hardly a hair on his head, but such smiling eyes under deep rivers of wrinkles across his brow, and a wide-open grin. Something in it was familiar.

'You are awake then!' declared the ruddy-faced man.

'God be praised! Let Him be praised!' said the man with the twinkling eyes, looking to heaven.

'I'll fetch vittles and water.'

'No, wine, wine!' said the twinkling man. 'We must build up his strength.' There was something about him that was

252

familiar. But in the haze of his befuddled mind, Katāros could not yet place him. Had he seen him on the road, perhaps further south?

'Water... is... fine,' he managed to utter. 'For now.'

'Very well, water it is,' said the old brown nut, and he hustled the other man out of the room and urged him to hurry back. Only then did Katāros notice both men wore the light-grey monkish habits of the same order as his.

The older man turned back to him and came to his bed-side. 'Brother Cadwin is a diligent man and surely has healing hands. He has nursed you through a most tempes-tuous fever.'

'How long?' muttered Katāros.

'Six days in all.'

'I've been unconscious for six days?'

'Ha!' laughed the monk. 'I thought it would be much longer – if you ever woke again! You were in a terrible state when we found you. Your poor head was swelled up like a melon. Those wicked men who set upon you on the road had done you most grievous harm.' The webbed wrinkles of the old monk's face contorted in sudden anguish. 'Terrible indeed.' But the look lasted but a moment, and the irrepressible brightness soon returned to his face. 'Still, by God's good grace, our party found you and brought you here.'

'You stayed with me?'

'Of course.' The monk grew serious for a moment. 'I felt the charge upon my shoulders. I promised my companions we would stay here no more than a week. And here you are awake. In six days! A miracle! And I may keep my promise.'

'You are pilgrims?' Katāros enquired weakly.

'Indeed we are. Like you, brother! Returning from the Holy City, our pilgrimage complete.' The monk's face beamed with piety.

Katāros recognised that expression.

'But now that you are well...' The monk squeezed Katāros's hand, which was resting on the covers. 'Brother! We shall go onwards together!'

He knew this man.

The monk was Brother Narduin.

CHAPTER TWENTY-TWO

'The Ocean of Atlas is not like any sea.'

So Demetrios had said. And so it had proved.

And if Erlan had not already a well-founded fear of drowning, a day and a night at the mercy of Atlas and the great stirring of his waves would have been sufficient to give him nightmares for a lifetime.

As if he needed fresh nightmares.

He remembered the storms on the Western Ocean after his first battle in the north. How he had cowered in terror against the lowest strakes of the ship, among the slop and the piss and the vomit. Three days it had lasted. But they had lived through it – those not already dead – and he had come home with his father. Come home to *her*...

Demetrios assured him that this was the same ocean but, by the Hanged, it did not feel like it. The huge surges of water that came rolling in from the vast wilderness of blue to the west rose and fell like the great coils of the Midgard Serpent, lurking in the deep. Waiting, waiting for the Final

Fires, for the Ragnarok when Loki's kin would rise and make itself known to the world of men. Then to do bloody slaughter with Thor and all the gods, until all was burnt to ashes... and memory.

Aye. Out on the ocean, those stories did not seem so hard to believe. It would take an ocean to hide something so terrible.

And yet, for all his fear, he could not show it. He was leader of these men, skipper of this ship, captain of their company. Fear was not a luxury he could afford.

'We've had a good run thus far,' declared Demetrios one morning, looking up at the scudding clouds. 'We must pray our luck holds.'

'Any luck we have needs to hold a good deal longer than we're on this ship.'

'No doubt. But that'd be a start.'

The days since the Pillars numbered many now. A dozen at least. Their water supply was low, and Demetrios had recommended they ration the wine barrel too, for the time being, which pleased Einar none. The Greek said he knew a place where it was safe for them to come into shore again and re-supply. 'North, north, further north,' he always said. And then swept his arm over the distant shore to their east. 'All this is Arab territory now. My guess is they'd take an unhealthy interest in our cargo there,' he said, gesturing at the stack of boxes containing their myriad coins. 'And they'd probably have the means to have it off us, too.'

To Erlan, it beggared belief that the armies that marched from Damascus, a city already far to the east of Byzantium, should also hold dominion out here. But again the Greek assured him that this was so.

They were over two weeks at sea before Demetrios finally allowed them to come to shore on a long ness of land he called Bertayne. Or Brettany, as another name had it. The folk there were simple, the little harbour where they sought shelter more like the market harbours of Erlan's homeland than the great stone ports of the Marmara or the eastern Inner Sea. They found no trouble there. On the contrary, the local merchants were glad of their business as the men bought up great quantities of furs and thick woollen homespun and deer-hide strips for their boots in preparation for the cold that was to come.

Autumn was on them. As they continued north and then north-east, the woods carpeting the hills that rose out of the bleak coastline were on the turn. And with each league northward, the air grew a little colder, the teeth of the wind-whipped sea-spray a little sharper. The cover of cloud sank lower, darkening the days, and with it the spirits of the crew.

At last Demetrios said they were reaching the limits of his sea-knowledge. He waved his hands vaguely due north. 'I know the tin mines of Albion lie that way beyond the horizon. But further on up into the Northern Sea...' He shook his head. 'These are your lands now, *bárbaros*,' he said with a dry chuckle. 'I am but a poor *civilised* man.'

Erlan felt the moment growing. The on-rush of fate. It would not be many more days before they would be rounding the Skaw, running their shallow keel into the bleached strands of his boyhood home where the marram grass swayed in the low dunes. He tried to imagine the meeting with his father. How would it be?

He gazed around at the faces of the crew. At Lilla, at Einar, and the women...

Truly, how will it be?

One morning he noticed Marta standing alone in the bows, lost in thought it seemed, gazing northward. The hems of her blue-green robes now had white tide marks from the salt-spray and sea air. Her shoulders were wrapped in a Breton blanket against the cold. The wind was worrying at the headscarf that bound her long dark hair. It was a gusty day, and the waves were boisterous, heaving the bows up and down.

He clambered forward. 'You should come back from there,' he called. 'It's not so safe.'

She turned and saw him, but stayed where she was. 'I was just thinking how far we are from home.'

'You think your god journeys this far with you?'

'My God does not journey. The whole world is His and everything in it.'

'Then he must be used to the cold already... You should come down.'

But she remained where she was, her gaze fixed on the horizon. 'What happened that night?' she asked. 'When the daemon came out of you.'

The shock of the memory was like pressing a finger to an unhealed wound. Especially on the lips of this curious maid. 'Who told you of that?'

'Who do you think?'

'Einar.' Erlan found himself irritated to be the subject of

family chatter. 'He's no business talking of it to you. Now come down—'

'I have a warning for you.'

The certainty in her voice took him by surprise. 'A warning?'

She was still looking ahead, gripping the prow with her small hands, her slender shoulders buffeted by the gusting wind. She was back in the guise of saintly mystic, the laughing girl of Syracusa a strange memory, at least for the moment. 'Our Lord once said that when an impure spirit comes out of a person, it goes through arid and empty places seeking rest. But rest it does not find. And so it says to itself, "I will return to the house I left." And returning, it finds the house empty, swept clean and everything put in order. So it goes and brings with it seven other spirits more wicked than itself, and they go and make the house their home.' She looked back at Erlan, her dark blue eyes bright in the dull grey light. 'And the final condition of that person is far worse than the first.' She nodded at him. 'You are that empty house. Until you receive the Lord.'

'You're saying I must be a Christian then?' said Erlan, unable to hide his disgust. 'Of course you would want that.'

'What I want clearly means nothing to you. I only give you this warning.' Her mouth creased into an enigmatic smile. 'You and your men – and your *woman* – ' she said the word with an acerbic bite, 'mean to carry war into the realm of your enemies. An invasion, so you hope. Make no mistake, I bring an invasion of my own. I carry the light into the darkness. And so long as I stand with you, then all the powers of hell will come against you.' She turned away again. 'But they will not prevail.'

'Like all holy folk, you speak in riddles.' He hesitated, then added, 'But I've seen you also tell lies.'

'Do I…? The Lord will reveal all mystery in its time.'

Erlan's patience with this peculiar girl had run dry. 'Thank you for the warning.' He held out his hand. 'Now for the last time, will you come down?'

Suddenly she rounded on him. 'No!' she snapped. 'I like it here!' And in that moment she seemed every inch a mere child. Erlan shook his head. The girl didn't speak in riddles; she was a riddle.

'Skipper!' came a yell from the midships. 'See there! The white cliffs of Albion!'

For once, Erlan was glad for the distraction. *An empty house? An invasion of light? By the Hanged! Hel could take it all.* He climbed aft and slipped under the mainsail. Several of the crew were gathered by the mast on the larboard side.

'Gods, would you look at that?' marvelled Bull. 'They're white as fresh milk.' To the north the channel of sea narrowed, and there, lining the horizon, was a wall of chalk cliff that shone brightly amid the drab of the sea and sky.

'That's Anglia, right enough,' said Mikki Crow. 'My old man once harboured there, he did. That's just how he described it.'

'Not far now, eh, fellas?' chuckled Ran. 'Couple more sleeps 'n' we'll be dipping our beards in the East Sea.'

'You look worried,' said a soft voice at his shoulder. Lilla had come up beside him and slid her hand into his. 'Husband.'

He looked down and saw she was smiling. 'Be of good cheer. The worst is behind us now.'

'I wish I believed that were true.'

'What is it then?'

'Hm… Nothing.' He could hardly share Marta's obscure riddles with Lilla. She had cares enough of her own. 'Nothing important, anyway.'

'Erlan.' Einar touched his arm. He pointed astern, back to the south-west. 'That don't look too pretty.'

Erlan swung round and saw black clouds boiling up out of the western horizon like a cauldron left too long over the fire.

'Demetrios,' he called. 'Should we bring in the sail?'

The little Greek hooked an arm over the tiller and looked back over his shoulder. 'Looks to be heading north on this wind. I think we'll outrun it.'

'We'll tie everything down, just in case. Bull, Dreng,' Erlan grabbed the two youngest crew members. 'And you, Ran,' remembering the Gotlander's skill with knots. 'Make sure it's all lashed tight. The gold, especially.'

'You don't say,' muttered Ran.

'And the syphon,' added Lilla.

They were all looking astern now. And though the Greek knew his business, for once Erlan wouldn't have bet a soft sheep's turd on Dimo's weather prediction.

'Maybe we should make for land?' suggested Lilla.

'Let's see how it develops. If Dimo's right, it'll pass astern.' But as he spoke, the black clouds were fanning north and south, swallowing up the sky. Even at this distance, he could see sheets of rain pounding the waves. He went aft. 'D'you get the feeling our luck might be running out, Dimo?'

261

'A good helmsman makes his own luck, *bárbaros*,' growled the Greek. 'Now pass me that wine.'

It took less than an hour for the weather to overtake them. Even if they'd wanted to make for either shore, they never would have reached it before the whistling winds closed around them. There was only one thing to do, said Demetrios, and that was to run before the storm.

It was not yet noon, yet the sky was turning dark as dusk, a pall of gloom flying over them and plunging to the horizon far ahead. The *Fasolt* raced on, swift as a sea-eagle over the top of the rising swell, her sail full, her prow shooting down the face of a wave one moment, mounting up to the peak of another the next. Sometimes the gradient was so steep that Demetrios, clinging to his steer-board, tipped twenty feet above Marta at the prow. The girl had wrapped the bow-rope around her arms and was hugging the carved neck of the fire-worm, riding the storm like she was part of the ship.

Erlan had to admit, it was damned exhilarating as well as terrifying. The sheer speed at which they flew with the wind was like nothing he had ever experienced. 'Hold her straight and we may yet see this out,' he yelled at Demetrios over the wind.

'I know my job,' bellowed the Greek in turn. 'You just be sure that gold isn't going anywhere!'

Erlan dragged himself forward, skinning his knees on the sea-slick thwarts. Dreng was throwing up. Kunrith was huddled under a thwart and muttering prayers. Krok was hugging a sea-chest like a drunk would his favourite whore.

He reached amidships where Einar and Orīana had wedged themselves in between the mastblock and the strakes. 'Can't you control your damned daughter up there?'

'I told you she's wild,' screamed back Orīana over the wind.

'She'll soon be drowned if she's not careful.'

'Then go talk sense into her!'

'Me?'

'Yes, you! Aren't you the captain of this ship?' Orīana snarled at him. Beside her, a pale-looking Einar merely shrugged.

The rain was beating down hard now, lashing his face, whipping his hair in his eyes. Erlan crawled further forward, bowels alive with the first twitches of terror. Then, somewhere in the galing winds, he thought he heard laughter. But surely that was his imagination? There was certainly nothing to laugh about.

'Are you afraid, Erlan?' cried a shrill voice above him. 'You know you can't outrun the will of God!'

He looked up. Marta was peering down at him a few feet ahead. Her headscarf was shaken loose, strands of black hair plastered like war-paint across her eyes. Erlan watched in amazement, clinging to the foremost thwart, as she turned back to the storm.

'Hear me, O God!' she screamed at the wind and the waves and the slanting rain. 'See me, O My Creator! Here I am, Lord! Here I am!'

She's lost her mind, he thought.

The waves were mountains now, lifting the prow-beast to the height of a giant's hall in the space of three heartbeats, then flinging it back down in half that time. Marta, meanwhile, shrieked wild laughter at the storm. Suddenly she turned and stretched her hand to him. 'Is this not living, Erlan? *Come!*'

'Get down!' he yelled, in vain. She only laughed again at him and turned back to the storm. Incensed now, he struggled forward the last few feet into the scant shelter of the prow. 'Have you lost your blasted wits, girl?' he shouted over the howling air.

'Maybe I have!' she cried gaily. 'But what else can we do but ride the wind?'

By the Hanged! he thought. *What else indeed?*

He grabbed a rope flapping loose around the prow and wound his fist into it, then braced his legs.

'Don't you see, Erlan!' she shouted. 'Don't you see?'

And the marvel of it was that he did begin to see. As if her insane confidence was rising off her in clouds of contagion. He glared up into the black fury of the storm, the prow-beast rising and falling above him, fear rinsing off him with each passing second. Instead, he found himself howling like a wolf at the moon.

Dear gods, he had never felt more alive.

'There, you see, sweet Erlan!' she cried joyfully. 'Were you not made for this moment!'

A voice bellowed a curse behind him. He looked round and saw a figure on the starboard side, bent double with his head in the bilge.

'Svali? What is it?'

'She won't hold, skipper! The caulking – I bloody knew it!'

'How bad?'

'See for yourself.'

Erlan climbed back towards Svali. He didn't need to go far before he saw black water frothing up through the strakes at an alarming speed.

'What can we do, Sval?'

'Ain't fuck all we can do but bale like fury and pray Njord is in a forgiving mood.'

Snodin and Kunrith were wedged between the gunwale and the gold on the steer-board side. 'You two – on these!' Erlan tossed them a couple of balers which Svali had fished out of the bilge.

'Skipper!' Another bellow from the stern, this one from Demetrios. 'The wind's swinging west. The waves are driving us onshore!'

Erlan looked to the eastern shoreline and saw it was an awful lot closer now than it had been. 'Hold your course parallel to the coast!'

'If I do that, the waves will break over us…'

'Hold your damn course! If we're driven onshore, the whole lot of us will go to the bottom, gold and all.'

'Skipper, you don't understand—'

'Just do it!'

Demetrios scowled and shook his head, probably cursing him too. But he did as ordered, swinging the prow to larboard across the roll of the waves.

'Mikki, bale with the others! Use whatever you can find.'

'I've only got my hands!'

'Then hands will have to do!'

With no warning, a huge wave came barrelling in from the north-west, lifting the hull like some giant's hand, so that both bows and stern came right out the water. A deluge of

265

saltwater came crashing in over the gunwale. For some moments, everything was buried under a tumult of wash and white foam. Erlan was thrown flat against the thwarts, then swept against the mastblock, the force so great he thought his spine would snap. But just before it became too much, the pressure eased.

'Snodin!' wailed a voice from the bows. 'Snodin's gone over!'

Mikki was leaning over, a hand on the gunwale, peering off into the roiling sea.

'He's gone – he's bloody gone!' stammered Kunrith, blinking like a mole.

'Keep baling, you whoreson bastards!' shouted Black Svali, for once looking like he gave a shit.

It was a moment before Erlan realised that Marta had vanished as well. 'Where's the girl?' he bawled, already throwing himself forward. 'Marta's over too!' Then he saw a small fist and forearm with a rope wrapped around it. 'There! She's still there! Go, go!'

But he was first forward. He threw himself full tilt and grabbed for her arm, half-expecting to find nothing but a dismembered limb and the rest of her swallowed in the maw of the sea. But the girl was still there all right, hanging on, doggedly refusing to die. Her robes were dragging her under with at least as much strength as Erlan could pull her up. 'Help me, damn it! Mikki, over here!'

But then Bull was there, one meaty fist locked onto a thwart while the other reached over Erlan's head, grabbed Marta by her long hair and hauled her back over the gunwale. All three collapsed in a heap behind the prow.

Erlan cursed as another wave broke over the larboard side.

'Turn for shore,' he yelled. But Demetrios couldn't hear him. 'Fat-Belly!' he shouted to Einar who was closer to the stern. 'Tell him to go for the shore.'

'We'll be smashed in the surf!'

'We have to take our chances. We can't go on like this. Do it!'

So Einar relayed the message, and moments later the prow swung to starboard. Almost at once the running was smoother.

Erlan looked ahead through the sheets of steel-grey rain at the shadow of land looming larger with every moment. 'Got any more prayers in you, girl?' he muttered grimly.

Marta grinned, her eyes bright as stars. 'Always.'

CHAPTER TWENTY-THREE

L illa was soaked through and shivering.

Not from the cold. From excitement. Or maybe anticipation, since she knew their fates could be decided in the next frantic moments.

She glanced around. Every last man of them – those that were left – was crouched down against the gunwale, eyes trained on what lay ahead, like eagles on their prey. The speed was terrific now. Valrik had surely known how to build a ship. Even with the bows slowly filling with water, with the blast of the storm filling her sail, the *Fasolt* planed along the surface like a gull swooping on the wing.

But that couldn't last. They needed to keep baling.

There were four of them on that now. Lilla reached out and laid her hand protectively on the boxes of gold. A cruel irony – to win such a prize only for the Thunder God and his underlings to snatch it from them when they were so close.

She glanced back at Einar Fat-Belly, whose face of webbed scars was a mask of grim resolve.

He caught her look. 'Which do you want to save, Lady? Our lives or the gold?'

She didn't answer at once, though she knew what the next decision would have to be. 'We can still make it.'

'Aye. As I thought.' Einar scowled in disgust and looked away.

Anger burned in Lilla's throat. Who was he to judge her? They were nothing without the gold. Nor was she.

Erlan was forward, tearing at the water in a relentless rhythm, stopping every now and then to peer ahead. As the ship tilted back and forth with each rolling wave, the bilge water sloshed and splashed, showering everything.

Beyond the prow, she could see the shore. Pale grey, low and formless, pounded by the storm. She imagined sand bars lay before it. The *Fasolt* had a shallow draught, but if they caught on one of them, it was over. Yet they would have to take the risk. And so they went streaking in at the shore like a lancing spear.

Suddenly there was another cry from the larboard bow. Ran was pointing wildly to his left. 'There! See where the shore breaks up! Dimo, you see it?'

Not only the Greek but all of them looked. And sure enough, just visible through the gloom of the storm, the fast-approaching strand curved inland away from them.

'What is it?' Erlan yelled, crouched to the deck.

'Not sure,' returned Ran. 'Could be an estuary, maybe. If we can get in there…'

Erlan didn't waste any time. He came scrambling aft and soon had Demetrios altering course for the widening gap. The change meant the waves began coming across them again, but if there was a chance, they must take it.

'On the oars now!' Erlan yelled.

Svali swore and told them to keep baling.

'You keep on it, Sval! The rest, get on an oar. It's going to get rough.'

As if it wasn't already.

But Ran was right.

There seemed to be some great river discharging into the sea. The storm surging up into the estuary was throwing up a torrent of white-water, waves bucking and roiling like bubbles in a cauldron. Einar and Dreng began pulling out the oars, slipping and scrambling with each wave that broke over them. It was a mess. It was a panic. But somehow two, then three, then four of them were pulling away.

The storm suddenly intensified, throwing fresh fury at the languishing boat, and with one huge blast of air, the sail, having withstood so much, at last succumbed. There was a cracking sound as the top yard folded in two, showering splinters of oak down onto them.

There was a loud squall of cursing from every man aboard. But the bows were aimed upriver now. 'All of us on the oars,' bellowed Erlan. 'We row for the southern bank. Leave the baling.'

'I ain't leaving it,' snarled back Svali. 'I ain't going down.'

'Fine, you stay. But the rest of us, row for your lives!'

'And for your gold, right lassie?' Einar growled at Lilla's side.

There was no time for argument. Just a frenzy of effort as each man tried to find the rhythm as the waves crashed about them. Einar was nearest the stern. Stroke by stroke they fell in with him, as much energy spent on fighting to bring their oars forward as heaving them through the swell.

But they were making headway, even as the depth of the water around Lilla's ankles grew.

Gods, Lilla thought, but it must be some river to contest the surge of the storm. The *Fasolt* seemed locked between the weight of the two bodies of water. But then Demetrios let out a loud cry and hauled on the steer-board, swinging the fire-worm's head to the south for the last time.

'Ready to jump!' he yelled.

There was a loud hiss as the keel touched bottom, the stern was instantly lifting high, throwing all of them on their face, then the bow-keel gave a little more, slipped forward over the sand-bed, and then they were stuck fast, the waves pounding them from all sides.

'Out, out!' screamed Erlan.

Lilla stood up to comply, but the broken yard and ruined sail were whipping all around her. She ducked, took a step forward towards the side of the boat and the surging waters beyond, ready to jump. Too late, the tail of her eye caught a flash of movement as the heavy oak yard cracked against her skull.

And just like that, the storm – and everything – was gone.

What woke her was the whistle of the wind, high and shrill.

She opened her eyes. The first thing she saw was Orīana's mouth, and the ropes of her long scarlet hair hanging around her face. 'Lilla… *Lilla,*' the mouth said. Then she felt herself scooped into her servant's arms and hugged tight, Orīana's

271

cheek against hers, cold and sleek as salmon-flesh. 'Thank God, you're alive.'

'Gently,' Lilla groaned softly. 'My head.'

'Of course.' Oriana laid her back down and Lilla propped herself on her elbows, wanting to see where she was. The throbbing pain in her head made her blink, but she'd had worse. She tried to count the times she'd been knocked senseless. One day, she wouldn't wake up.

And looking at the mess around her, part of her wished this was that day.

Equipment and gear and oars and sea-chests were strewn on the muddy strand below her. The *Fasolt* looked stricken. Flopped over on its side, its keel exposed, the steer-board snapped and twisted skyward in its mounting, the waves of the storm alternately butting and sucking at it as they moved in and out, the ship helpless to resist. What was left of the sail was hanging from the remnant of the yard, flapping like a broken wing in the still shrieking wind.

Several of the crew were moving about the shoreline, dragging things further up the beach. There were oars discarded, thrown up on a low bank of dunes, and now Lilla saw, to her profound relief, a jumbled heap of the little wooden boxes up on the rise among the whipping marram grass.

'The gold. Is it all out?'

'Don't know about all,' replied Oriana. 'Soon as you were safe, Erlan organised the men to get it out while they could.'

'And the syphon,' she said anxiously. 'The fire.'

'Yes, that too.' Oriana nodded over to another pile of salvaged equipment. 'Over there.'

Lilla collapsed onto her back, feeling the shock of the cold suddenly deep in her bones, alongside a good measure of relief. Although their situation hardly merited much of that. Gods only knew where they were. It was damned bleak, wherever it was.

But she was alive. They still had the gold.

'I want to see Erlan.'

'You should rest—'

'I want to see him.' She forced herself to her feet and, as she did, realised how groggy she felt. 'Help me.' Orīana obliged, supporting her as she stumbled down the shallow dune onto the flat where she could carry herself more easily.

Erlan was by the growing heap of gold. Some of the boxes had split open – fortunately only a few – and Ran and Dreng were busy trying to gather the spilled coins onto a sodden cloak spread on the ground. Even in the grey, the gold glistered prettily.

When Erlan saw her, he hurried over and swept her into his arms. 'My love... my love,' he murmured, squeezing her tight enough to stop her breath.

'Our luck ran out then.'

'We're not finished yet.'

'Is the *Fasolt*?'

'Hard to say. She doesn't look good, though.'

'Snodin went over.'

Erlan nodded grimly. 'Aye. Reckon we were lucky to lose only one.'

'One is too many.'

Abruptly, he held her away from him. 'Lilla. You know we're going to lose a lot more than that before we're done.'

He released her gaze with a sigh. 'Come. You can see what we've salvaged.'

In truth, it was remarkable. What they'd lost was mostly replaceable. Furs, shields, sea-smocks, food and drink, some tools and weapons, buckets and such. But the things of essential value were still there.

What was in poorer shape was the *Fasolt* herself. The strakes in her steer-board bows had taken such a beating that Lilla could slip her fingers between at least four of the clinker layers. And they had lost most of the tools and materials for Svali to repair her.

The rain was still falling in thick sheets, but the wind was abating some. They called everyone together for a conference to figure their next move. They'd need food and fresh water before long. After that, they'd have to give some thought to repairing the *Fasolt*. If that was even possible.

Svali was at his blackest, determined to sour any hope of restoring the ship to a sea-worthy condition. But as the alternative was too depressing to entertain, everyone else refused to accept that nothing could be done.

'We need a fire going soon as there's a break in the rain,' said Erlan. 'And a scavenging party will have to go inland to find provisions.'

Einar touched Erlan's shoulder. 'Skipper.'

'What is it?'

Fat-Belly nodded up the estuary. 'Company.'

They all turned to look. There, about half a mile down the shoreline, rising from among the low-lying dunes, was the silhouette of a lone rider. For some moments, no one moved. No one spoke. They watched the figure watching them, the spell only broken when the horseman turned and put his heels to his mount. A few moments more and he disappeared from sight.

'Hel,' said Erlan. 'I thought we'd have more time.' He scratched fretfully at his beard, eyes flicking between the empty horizon and the unruly heap of crates beside them. 'Do we still have any picks?'

'What for?' asked Lilla, a dread cold creeping into her guts.

'The gold, of course.'

'Why? What do you mean to do?'

He looked around the circle of haggard faces. 'Bury it. And fast.'

They did work fast.

But not fast enough.

They were twelve now; three of them women. Even with nine men digging and toting the boxes from the beach to a place further back from the sea, while the three women watched for any sign of the horseman's return, they had only managed to bury half the gold when Marta's sharp eyes spied spear-tips hovering over the swaying grass and coming towards them.

At the signal, Erlan told the crewmen to cover everything already in the hole. 'It's all we can do. At least this much may be safe.'

Lilla was boiling with fury at the prospect of forfeiting any of it, but Erlan tried to contain her despair. 'Some of it is safe. Even if we may not be.' He kissed her fiercely on the mouth, neither of them knowing whether it might be for the last time. 'Don't lose hope. Stay alert. Stay close. I love you.'

'Do you?' she said, with the thunder of hooves rumbling through the sand, not knowing why that doubt should suddenly prick her now.

His eyes hardened. 'Just be ready.'

They'd already decided they didn't have the means to fight their way out of this. And once they saw the number of horsemen in the approaching troop, it would have been folly anyway. There were twenty of them, if there was a man. Warriors with short, round iron helms and close-cropped hair; beardless men strapped in oiled leather byrnies armed with ten-foot-long spears mounted on corn-fed war-horses.

How a war-band as strong as this had been alerted so fast to their presence was a mystery. Unless this was already a land at war.

The riders circled around the shipwrecked survivors, eyes glaring with hostility, the jangle of their bridles a metallic challenge to the gusting wind. Their leader seemed to be a man draped in a yellow cloak which spread back over his horse's rump. His hair was almost as yellow. He looked ill-tempered and restless. All of them were soaked through with the rain.

The leader pulled his mount back and forth a few times before he addressed them, barking words which were unintelligible at first. But the more Lilla listened, the more she started to grasp the shape of his speech. It was not her own tongue, but also not so very distant from it. Since no one answered, the man tried in another. This time, Demetrios answered him, and for a time they conversed freely. Lilla recognised that the tongue they were speaking was Latin, but no more than that.

She heard the word 'Austrasia' pass between them more than once. It was not a word or name she knew. And 'Frisia' too, which she did know. Frisia – or Friesland – was a land to the south of Jutland and the Danish Mark.

'What's he saying?' she asked Demetrios in Greek.

'He says this land is the northern boundary of Austrasia. He seems to think we are Frisians. But I assured him none of us are of that people.'

'Frisia. Is that not the realm of King Rathbod?' she said to Erlan in Norse.

To her surprise, the yellow man answered before Erlan could, and she found she could now follow his words. 'Rathbod is our sworn enemy. Any man pledged to him found in these lands forfeits his life. Do you come from his realm?'

'Are you Frankish?' she asked.

'Answer my question.'

'No. Of course we are not from there. We are traders, returning much further north after a long voyage in the south.'

Erlan took up her thread. 'We were caught in the storm. You can see for yourselves the sum of it. We were wrecked and forced to strike land here. We have nothing to do with King Rathbod. And no argument with your lord, whoever he may be.'

While they had been speaking, several of the other horsemen had wheeled their mounts to amble among the detritus of the *Fasolt*'s cargo. Einar and the others were watching them like sparhawks. It wasn't long before one of the riders prodding at the remaining boxes looked startled and immediately rode up alongside the yellow man to speak low and quickly into his ear.

Leaving Erlan's words unanswered, the leader went to see for himself what his men had discovered. Uneasy glances darted between the crew while he flicked his long cloak off the rump of his mount and jumped down. Drawing his dagger, he knelt beside one of the boxes and levered off the lid. For a moment he stopped, as if astonished. Then buried his hand in the small fortune of coins. He lifted them to his face, examining them in wonder, slowly letting the coins fall back into the box between his fingers.

He got to his feet and returned to where they stood.

'Traders, you say?'

'Aye.' Erlan hawked and spat into the sand. 'We've done good business down south.'

'I can see that,' he said with no little sarcasm. He turned to one of his men. 'Ride to Breezant. Send for a cart and four strong oxen.'

'At once, my lord.'

'A strong cart, mind you,' the yellow man called after him.

Lilla felt hope crumbling inside of her. And in its rubble, sharp thorns of anger began to spread. She thought of all they had suffered to possess the gold, all that they had achieved. Only for fate to pluck it from their hands as easy as taking bread from a babe.

'My men and womenfolk are exhausted,' said Erlan. 'Will you at least feed us and give us fire?'

'We are confiscating this… cargo.'

'You've no right,' protested Erlan. She could see the same thoughts as hers swimming in his eyes. But what could they do? 'We are traders, nothing more. We bear you no ill. We need your help, not this.'

'By the ancient Salic law, all flotsam belongs to the crown,' returned the yellow man. 'Or in this case, to my liege lord.'

'You can't simply steal what is ours,' snapped Erlan.

'We're no thieves,' the other countered, a warning look in his eye. 'But a quantity of gold like this must be taken before my lord.'

'Who is your lord then, if not the king?'

'Duke Karil, son of Pepin.' The man said it as though the name should mean something to them.

Erlan glanced at Lilla. She nodded at him, understanding. They couldn't be separated from the gold. Not if they could help it. 'If you mean to deliver our gold to this Duke Karil, then we demand you present us before him too.'

The yellow man gave a mirthless chuckle. 'Don't worry, trader,' he said. 'I will.' And with that, he signalled his men to lower their spears.

CHAPTER TWENTY-FOUR

Autumn was already well established by the time Katāros and his small party of pilgrims reached Basilia and the great Rhein river.

Mile after mile they had toiled over hills and down valleys, around lakeshores, along woodland streams. The old way, the pilgrim way. The Via Francorum. All the while, Katāros played his part. The part of piety, of monkish reticence, of holy contemplation. But all the while concealing the scorn he felt in his heart, the black bitterness at the god his companions worshipped. And far more besides.

But in truth, there was little danger of discovery.

If the impish holy man, Narduin, had lived for a thousand years, he never would have made the connection between the poor ill-used 'brother' whom he had rescued on the mountain and brought under his wing on the pilgrim trail, with the boastful notary of the Roman Forum. The scars on Katāros's face concealed all.

He was glad.

If nothing else, it proved that his old self was truly gone. Erased forever.

So he played the part of the reticent, which didn't stop Narduin talking all the livelong day. Some holy men found reverence and worship in silence. Not Narduin. If words were a sign of riches, then Narduin had the deepest coffers in all the wide world. Whether you spoke any back to him didn't seem to matter a whit.

But you could say one thing for the man. There was nothing – no discomfort, no abuse, no hunger, no thirst, no foul tempest, no blazing heat – could shake his damnable good cheer. He took a kind of fathomless pride in the ability to be joyful whatever the circumstances. The more miserable the journey, the more exuberant he became.

Katāros found it all quite intolerable.

Yet he did tolerate it because the cover this afforded him was unparalleled.

He *was* a monk, to all appearances. He prayed with the little band of brother pilgrims, sang with them, walked with them, ate with them, slept with them. They treated him as one of their own.

Together, they had descended from the great heights of the Poeninus Pass, through the market town of Octodurus, skirting Lake Lausonius and heading north, through the ruins of Aventicum where the ghosts of the amphitheatres and aqueducts of empire told of a far grander past. Now the ruins were silent and still as graveyards, good for nothing better than stone robbers, or giving shelter as the haunt of thieves.

At last they had reached the new city of Basilia and the Rhein itself, where Narduin had sought the aid of the newly appointed bishop to secure passage on a merchant barge which planned to navigate nearly the entire length of the mighty flood. All the way north to the ancient Roman town of Colonia, or Koln as his Frankish companions knew it in their native tongue.

If Katāros had found peace walking on the road, it was on the river that he found serenity. After hundreds of miles on foot, to sit and feel the river carry you in its powerful embrace... well, it was sweet respite indeed. For that, he could even endure old Narduin's chatter. And, to his surprise, sometimes he would even enjoy it, since the old monk was a fount of stories, and the pleasant progress downriver seemed to enliven the old wordbag's memory.

True, most of his stories concerned the lives of other long-dead monks. But their scope was so wide that Katāros learned many things of many different places. He was reminded of that feeling – when once he had accepted his lot as a young eunuch, newly cut – of settling into a time of pure learning. There was a pleasure to it which, now re-awakened, he enjoyed again.

Besides this, the landscape itself was invigorating. A long spell of autumn sunshine turned the valleys of the high Rhein into a shimmering tapestry of green and gold and copper hues. Along the riverbanks grew a ceaseless procession of vineyards and orchards, meadows and woods, the orchards especially perfuming the air with their harvest crops. The water seemed to be a perfect blue, still glowing with the freshness of the mountain streams which filled the valley from high, high above.

There was something of the dream to that journey. And he should have known – had not life taught him the lesson enough times by now? – that soon enough, every dream must turn into a nightmare.

He had called himself Skírpa.

It was, in fact, his own name. Before he became Katāros, he had been Skírpa. The name meant 'ill-fated' in the Norse tongue. A jest of the old shaman who had named him, who had been the closest thing to a father he had ever known. The vile old bastard had said young Skírpa was bound for an evil fate. It was only out of his own folly and soft heart that he had taken the boy into his care. Certainly it had been an ill-fate that had put him in the shaman's path at such a tender age. In truth, at a time before memory. 'My little Skírpa', the man would call him, fondling the lobe of his ear. Well, fate had overtaken the shaman instead. And now he was rotting in the blackest halls of Hel, while his little Skírpa still walked the earth.

Narduin and his friends didn't need to know all this, of course. But the eunuch had needed to give them a northern name, so that was what they got.

Skírpa.

There was a beautiful irony to it after all that had happened. He was the shadow now to the 'Amadeus' he had been – beloved of God.

He was loved by no one. And he would wear his lonely name with pride.

One night after supper, as the stars came out and the rush of the river made soft music to lull the pilgrims to sleep, Narduin came and sat by him and asked if they could talk a while. A full moon was rising, shedding its silver light over the smooth waters of the Rhein.

Skírpa sighed and sat up, hugging his knees to his chest against the evening chill.

'There is something I wish to ask you, Brother Skírpa, since you have not volunteered it yourself.'

'What's that, Brother Narduin?'

'I trust you will not be offended.'

'How can I say until I know what you wish to ask?'

'True, very true. Though to take offence is of the world. Did we not give up the right to be offended when we took up our cross to follow our Lord?'

Skírpa shifted impatiently; Narduin was full of such pious rhetoric. 'Ask your question, brother. Please.'

'I can see the wounds you carry. Oh, I don't mean the attack you suffered, though the Lord knows that was bad enough. No, I mean...' He hesitated. 'You carry a great sadness in you.'

'Do I?'

'Is there not something I can do to lighten your burden?'

'I... don't know what you mean.'

Narduin's eyes twinkled in the shadows. 'I do not need to know your secrets. You travelled alone. I never asked why. We have carried you as our own.'

'And I am grateful for it—'

'That is not what I meant at all! I am not seeking your gratitude. Rather...' He paused again. 'Hah! See how abashed I am, even to ask. So I shall just jump on it, like a child catching a frog, heh? Best done without delay.' He reached out and clasped Skírpa's hand. 'Would you not come with us back to

Mettis? Our life there is simple but it is good. I see the light of intelligence in your eyes. You would find rest there, my boy. Rest for your weary spirit.'

'Mettis?'

'It is a royal city, seat of the Merovingian house in Austrasia. Worthy of a fine mind such as yours.'

'Who says I have a fine mind?'

Those twinkling eyes again. 'You cannot hide it, my boy. You are a patient listener, a profound thinker.' *Indeed,* thought Skírpa, *but you would not like to know the thoughts that fill my head.* 'You have a good heart, indulging an old man's silly need to talk. We could surely find a place for you at the Abbey of Saint Pierre. Oh, you should see the basilica! It is a venerable old building. Quite the wonder.' *Me?*, thought Skírpa indignantly. *One who has stood in the most august place, second only to the emperor himself, before the altar of the Holy Wisdom of Byzantium?*

He smiled. 'Dear brother. You paint quite the picture. And truly, I am tempted. Your kindness to me has been beyond anything I deserve.'

'God's grace sustains us all.'

'Truly,' said Skírpa. 'Yet my own home is fair Albion across the sea. My journey must take me to road's end at Cantwareburg. The full measure of my penance demands it. You must understand. It would be to rob Our Lord of what I have promised him. Does the scripture not tell us, when we make a vow to God, do not delay to fulfil it? He takes no pleasure in fools.'

Certainly the Almighty took no pleasure in him, Skírpa thought bitterly. *Did that make him a fool?*

'Forgive me,' said Brother Narduin, his voice warm with self-reproach. 'I see there is much I do not know. Perhaps it is my pride only that believes we could offer you a good and holy life among us. I am sorry. I will not ask again.'

'Please. Do not reproach yourself on my account. The offer was kindly meant.'

'Perhaps… if you do mean to go on, though, there is a great favour you might do me. Do all our people.'

'A favour? What could I do to help you? It is you who have done so much for me.'

'And yet there is something,' said Narduin, lowering his voice to a whisper. 'A message which you could bear. One, I believe, spoken by God.'

'Go on.'

'Ours, as you know, is a land riven with strife,' Narduin said sadly. 'The divisions between each faction run deep. It feels like ambition and greed are master over all.'

'It takes a strong hand to unite a people. I have seen it in my own lands.' Seen it all over the known world, in fact. Wherever there was power or money, ambition grew beneath the surface like fungus beneath the soil.

'Indeed. I fear the rightful king, Chilperic, is not strong enough to tame those who stand against him.'

'Who are they?'

'A powerful duke named Karil Martel has raised rebellion against the crown. Were it only he, I believe the king would triumph and thus secure peace in our land. But there is another – the Lady Plectrude – whose power is centred in the city of Koln. She also has designs upon the throne for her grandson, who is not yet of age, but who she avows has a stronger

286

claim than any to the throne of Merovech – King of All Franks. She also has considerable military power. It is to Plectrude that I would ask you to bear my message.'

'What message could I bring?'

'You will think me…' Narduin paused and heaved a weary sigh. 'Oh, agèd man! You will think it a witless notion, that a humble monk such as myself should play at power among these princes. But…' He shook his head. 'Listen to me. When I was in Rome, we came specifically to seek a means for peace. To hear Our Lord and hope that He might reveal a word to us.' Narduin's eyes twinkled again with mischief. 'He honoured me with just that. A word in prayer. Almost a vision, I say. But the meaning of it was this: the key to peace is Plectrude. She must send overtures to King Chilperic. A settlement between those two powers will free Chilperic to subdue Karil and his rebellious followers.'

'Surely Plectrude must see this for herself if it is obvious to a simple monk such as yourself?'

'Hoho! Simple I am, you are right. But I think she is blind to it. It is her pride that blinds her.' He scraped his hand over his face. 'Hm! As pride blinds so many of us. No. She will listen because she is a superstitious woman. If you, a stranger and a monk, come bearing a message that purports to be from God Himself…' Narduin chuckled again. 'Can you not see the potency in it? Would it not make *you* think, if someone arrived in your hall and declared himself a prophet, bearing the very word of God?'

'I suppose. Is this Plectrude a God-fearing woman?'

'They say so. But I myself could not swear to it.' He suddenly seized Skírpa's hands. 'Bear this message, dear brother. And I will have discharged my duty to God. It saddens me that you will not join us, but with this…' Here, he needed a moment to control his emotion. 'With this, you will have made an old man very happy. I long for peace among us. Too much Frankish blood has already been spilled to satisfy the thirsts of ambitious men.'

'And ambitious women, by the sounds,' said Skírpa without thinking, his tone more biting than he'd meant.

Narduin sat back on his haunches with a chiding look. 'Now is not the time for cynicism, dear brother, but for hope.' But quickly the old monk relented, leaning forward again and gripping Skírpa's wrist. 'Blessed are the peace-makers,' he murmured. 'For they shall be called children of God.'

'Then I will gladly do it,' agreed Skírpa. 'For you, for peace – and for Our Lord.'

Naturally Narduin fell into paroxysms of gratitude at that. And soon, satisfied that his young companion was an answer to his prayers, the old monk fell asleep, leaving Skírpa to his own thoughts. He lay back on his bed of sacking and gazed up into the clear night sky.

This woman Plectrude sounded interesting. At least she sounded like a player in a wider game. A grandson not yet of age, a city in her power. She must have riches and land, *and* she would be obliged to him, should he decide to carry out Narduin's little mission from God. What she would make of it, he could not say. But Narduin was right on one score. The improbability of it alone would surely give her pause. And into that pause, Skírpa could pour his own quick wits and sharp mind.

Little figures on a large board.

Suddenly he remembered how one of the few joys from his boyhood had been the game of *tafl*. Little figures on a large board of a different kind. No one could ever beat him. And once joined in this game among princes, he would wager any amount of coin that none would be his equal. The north called to his soul, yes. But so too did his own ambition. Perhaps this Godly mission could be, for him, a new dawn. And soon the dark night of recent times would fade to memory.

With such sanguine thoughts pleasantly circling in his head, he let sleep slowly overtake him, not marking that the river had carried them beyond the fragrant orchards and vineyards of its southern course, and instead plunged deeper into forests dark with shadow, in which creatures of the night went prowling, looking for their prey.

The first that he knew something was very wrong was a sound like splitting timber. Immediately he opened his eyes, alert. So many times had he faced danger that he could summon his senses to a razor-edge in the blink of an eye. He felt his balance shift, and a sudden irresistible force roll him off his bed of empty sacks to slam against the barge's starboard bulwark with a jolt of pain. *What the devil is happening?*

There were shouts of confusion as other passengers woke – merchants and monks equally ignorant in the face of their alarm. Only the steersman was on his feet, but he was clutching tight to his rudder and struggling to stay upright.

'Ambush! Ambush!' he cried.

There was a strum and fizz in the darkness, and before the

fellow could shout the warning a third time, an arrow skewered his neck. Skírpa stared in horror at the man spluttering his own blood, pawing pathetically at the arrow-shaft as he sank to his knees. Beyond the steersman, the shadow of the forests slewed across Skírpa's field of vision. Then he heard the rush and roar of the water as the full weight of the Rhein piled against the bows.

But how could that be?

The barge was swinging across the flow of water towards the western bank and the pitch dark of the forest. And then, in the moonlight, he saw a rope, taut as a bowstring, running out from the bows and disappearing into the forest.

He swore. This was some kind of bandits' trap which had caught the barge like a fish on a hook. He followed the line of the rope and in the moon's glint saw there was a grappling iron fixed onto the bows of the barge. The tension had flipped the barge midstream, pulling the bows right round and swinging the whole vessel in towards the bank. It must have taken some skill to attach the grappling iron to a moving boat, even one as slow as the big barge. But understanding what had happened and how it had been done was not nearly as important as figuring what was coming next.

Nothing good, of that Skírpa was damned certain.

On the deck of the barge, chaos reigned. The monks were calling to one another, checking all of them were all right. Everyone was asking questions to which no one had an answer. Two of them had crawled to the stern where they were trying to help the luckless steersman. But he was beyond any man's aid.

Meanwhile, Skírpa had recovered himself a little and got as far as his knees when the huge heavy vessel swung the last few degrees and slammed into the riverbank with an almighty crash, sending a violent shudder through the whole structure of the boat. Any man on his feet was knocked over a second time. There were more curses and wails and yelps.

And then... silence.

For the second time, Skírpa picked himself up, unsure now what to expect.

The spill of the moon was glimmering on the water. But where they were, tucked into the bank, was swathed in moon-shadow, under the lee of the forest where all was black as tar.

'The rope,' Skírpa hissed when no one else moved. 'Some-one cut the blasted rope!' Still no one moved. And then he realised that in his haste he had spoken Greek.

'Skírpa,' a voice near him said in Latin. 'What's happening, brother?'

'It's a trap, isn't that obvious?' he snapped back. 'We're ambushed.' He stood up and meant to look about for a knife or an axe, anything with an edge that could cut them free, but he was still amidships, some distance from the bows. The foliage spilling over the bank was pushed up against the starboard gunwale, the first line of trees no further from the water's edge than the toss of a stone. 'God's blood, we need to cut that—'

Another weird whistling sound.

Instinct spun him towards the danger, but only in time to glimpse a shiver of movement in the blackness, then feel a burst of savage pain as an arrow struck his arm. He cried out and fell to the decking with the force of the blow. His solitary shriek was answered by a new sound: a weird wailing, a discordant chorus of inhuman barks and yips and shrieks from voices hidden in the darkness.

A sudden cold and racing terror in his blood overtook the sensation of pain in his arm. Men whimpered around him. Then, without warning, out of the darkness came the flash of metal. More grappling irons landing with heavy thuds on the decking – three, four, five of them now, raining down like iron hail. One hit a monk on his head, sending blood bursting from the blow, a splatter of black in the monochrome light of the moon. Then a fearful scraping noise as the grapples were pulled taut, only finding their teeth on the lip of the gunwale. As if with one unseen force, the ropes snapped tight and the barge was locked against the riverbank, fast as if it had been welded there.

Someone else was bleating to cut the ropes but it was all too slow. Far too slow. Skírpa felt the burn in his arm. The shaft was barbed but, by some good fortune – if it were possible to speak of such – it had pierced his bicep right through. He locked his arm, sucked a breath, then snapped the longer end of the shaft clean off. Only the stump of it remained, the ugly barb scraping against his rib cage. Carefully he held out his arm, took hold of the metal barb and pulled the remnant of the willow shaft clear of the muscle.

He cried out with the pain of it, bile rising in his gorge, but he managed not to vomit.

'Brother Skírpa, are you hurt?' That voice was Narduin's.

'Yes, I'm hurt, by the devil!' he snarled back, angered by the idiocy of the question. 'But by God, not nearly as badly as we're about to be.'

He could smell it. Smell the bloodlust on the air. And he knew that he was one of the prey. He looked desperately behind him. For all the gold in Damascus, he would not have fled the boat on the bank-side. And for a fleeting second, he considered whether he should take his chances in the mighty river.

But if there had been any such chance, he had missed it.

There was a rush of movement behind him, the swish-swish sound of men sprinting, the crack of undergrowth, the jangle of combat metal. Then that unholy shrieking began again. He turned to face the danger, and out of the shadows came a line of creatures who made no sense. They came at the speed of jackals, barking and yipping to the bright and fulsome moon. But these were beasts on two feet, beasts with the heads of wolves, brandishing steel and savagery.

The passengers on the barge backed away. A few stood frozen in place, limbs locked with terror. One man flung himself overboard, hitting the water with a pathetic splash, disappearing into the depths. Skírpa never saw him surface. Others might have followed him but the wolf-savages were on them too fast.

Skírpa dropped to his knees, his legs failing with fear. Then everything around him dissolved into bloody mayhem.

Arrows came whipping out of the night. Axes thudded. Men screamed and scrambled to hide. Voices begged for mercy. But there was none to be found amid the silver-gilt slaughter and lupine howls.

It was only pure chance that kept Skírpa alive in those first few seconds when other men around him fell like barley in the harvest. His mind was stuck fast until a thick spatter of blood hit his face, bringing him to his senses. There before him a huge shadow rose, its silhouette in the shape of a wolf standing on two legs, an axe glinting high above it, dripping blood that looked like black ink.

Skírpa, seeing a pitch-black square in the middle of the deck and realising it was the opening to the hold, flung himself into it. A pile of dusty grain sacks broke his fall and he went tumbling head over backside into the corner. The wound in his arm rammed against the hull, sending another shot of pain to his brain. He groaned, then sat there for a moment, stunned, staring up at the square cut-out of night sky visible through the decking. Above him, he could hear the scuffle of naked feet and heavy-hide boots shifting and darting. Little clouds of dislodged dust came raining down on him in silver swirls. He heard moans and wails and death cries, but even these were fading away.

After all, there were only so many people to kill.

The inhuman howling had stopped at last. He edged forward, curiosity challenging his fear, wanting to see more.

All of a sudden a body flopped over the lip of the hold. He recognised the shape of the head at once, not a hair on it, ears crooked as blackbird wings.

Narduin.

At first, the monk didn't move. Then he uttered a quiet sob and lifted his head. Skírpa froze, hardly two feet away. But to his surprise, Narduin was more than merely conscious. His old face lit up for a second and he held out his hand, his bright twinkling eyes imploring Skírpa to take it. 'Help me, brother. *Help… me.*'

Goaded by some unfamiliar impulse, Skírpa reached up to support Narduin's head.

Narduin seized his hand. 'Pull me down there, for the love of heaven!'

Skírpa hesitated for a moment, then pulled. Narduin shifted forward, but not quite far enough to tumble down into the hold. Skírpa made to pull again when he felt a terrific force seize the other end of Narduin's body. The old monk gripped his hand even tighter. 'Help me!'

'Let go, you old leech!' said a brutally hard voice above him. But that Narduin would not do. Instead, Skírpa found himself in a tugging contest with the wolf-killer on deck.

'Hold on, brother,' whimpered Narduin, his gnarled fist locked like a vice. 'Please, hold on.'

'What's the little cocksucker got hold of?' another voice demanded up above.

'Let go of me,' Skírpa hissed softly, daring nothing louder.

'Brother,' moaned Narduin. 'Help me, brother.'

'I'm not your goddamn brother,' Skírpa snarled in panic, and with a vicious jerk, he bent back Narduin's thumb. The old monk yelped, a look of horror and betrayal on his weathered features. But his grip loosened at last. Immediately his body was jerked back out of the hold and onto the deck. Skírpa heard the crackle of cruel laughter. 'Finish the cunt,' said someone.

There was a sudden startling bang on the deck above him. A couple of seconds, and then another. Droplets came filtering through the wooden planks, falling like rain onto his upturned face. Except it wasn't rain. He smeared them away. He didn't need to know what it was, didn't want to know.

After that, everything went quiet.

Skírpa could hardly breathe with terror – that at any moment one of these monsters would jump down to claim their ill-gotten booty and see him and then…

But the moment never came.

He willed it to, the strain of anticipation almost breaking him apart. But instead he crouched alone in the darkness, like a rat in its hole, while everything else fell to silence.

He lay there a long time.

At least it felt like a long time. Maybe it was only seconds.

At length, a trickling sense of security began to fill his consciousness. Cautiously, he wriggled his body until he could clutch his arm to stem the worst of the bleeding. He thought it best to deal with that as soon as he could, so while he lay there, he undid the bit of hemp rope that had served as his belt and wound it around his arm, pulling it tight with his teeth. In a few moments, it was done.

When he looked up again, the shards of moonlight lancing into the hole had shifted. He listened but could hear nothing.

Slowly he pulled himself up and moved closer to the hole. He hovered there, like a fox sniffing the wind before it left the safety of its den. It didn't make any sense though. Why go to all the effort of snaring the barge and killing its passengers without taking its cargo? There was enough grain in the hold to feed a village all winter.

But then maybe these wolf-men lived by different customs to ordinary folk.

He pulled himself up, half-expecting an axe-blow to take him between the shoulders. But when he got on deck, he saw only the formless lumps of dead bodies, many of them so fresh they were still leaking blood. The nearest seemed impossibly small. As if shrunken in death. But the bald head was unmistakable. Narduin lay in a spreading black lake of his own blood.

A sudden wave of nausea overwhelmed him. He hurried to the side, bent double, and vomited into the water. He had to get off this boat.

Wiping his mouth, he hitched the hem of his habit, mounted the gunwale and leaped as far onto the bank as he could. He landed in a heap, his arm snarling with pain. The shock of the wounding was wearing off now. The whole limb and shoulder were starting to throb.

Slowly, he picked himself up and peered into the darkness of the forest.

Empty. Silent. Vanished.

He felt the weirdness of it. Or the *wurt* of it, as the old shaman used to say. It was uncanny, in that twilight place between the seen and the unseen.

He glanced back at the barge. Would he be safer there? Or...

No. It had a kind of sepulchral glow to it now, its outline rimed with the silver of the moon. He shuddered.

He would take his chances and go onward by foot.

North. By any means, north.

He turned, the decision taken. But he was hardly five strides downriver when he heard a guttural laugh.

He halted, his blood curdling with fear.

A figure stepped out in front of him, crouched like some wild beast, ready to spring.

Now another sound at his back. He spun in terror. A second of the wolf-men had risen behind him, the ears on his wolfskin hood standing sharp as demon's horns. Skírpa opened his mouth to speak, or to scream, or plead for mercy. But nothing happened, only a kind of strangled, staccato panting, quickening with the beat of his heart.

'Eh, look at his face,' said the shadow behind him.

Suddenly, he felt strong fingers in his hair and his head yanked back and twisted to the moonlight. The other had crept up on him without a sound. His fetid breath fumed into Skírpa's mouth. A sharp kiss of cold steel pressed against his throat. 'Thought we'd gone, eh, handsome?' the foul breath sniggered. 'There's always another rat comes crawling out if you wait long enough.'

Skírpa closed his eyes, ready for the end. The blade pressed deeper.

'No!' barked the other.

'Why not?'

'Look at his clothes.'

'What about 'em?'

'He's a monk, in'ee?'

'So?'

'You know how *he* likes a monk.'

'Baah,' scowled the second wolf-man, then laughed his ragged laugh. 'Ugliest fucking monk I ever saw.'

'Even so, the One Eyed will want to see him.'

Something about the words 'One Eyed' sent a shiver of terror right through Skírpa. And before he could do anything about it, he felt hot urine streaming down his legs.

CHAPTER TWENTY-FIVE

Erlan and his company made a sorry sight, slung on the back of two hay carts, trussed up like hogs on the way to market, swaying and jarring with every rut on the road. Erlan stayed alert at first. But even he succumbed to the tedium and fatigue as mile piled upon mile, league upon endless league, his head bobbing and rolling as he drifted in and out of sleep.

On and on they travelled, through the featureless flatlands of the northern marches of Austrasia and still onwards, heading south and east towards the great cities of the Rheinland. At least that much the yellow man – the leader of their escort – had told them.

The bleak, sandy marshes and causewayed swamps at last gave way to more fertile farmland, criss-crossed by long-harvested strip-fields, and orchards, rutted roads and hedge-rows, the land bubbling up with small undulations, then swelling into low-lying hills. All of it depressingly smothered in rain and more rain. Each day, the clouds were overcast, hanging with grey oppression a few hundred feet above their heads. And many days, the cloud descended into fog, enveloping the world in its dewy white. In his wanderings, Erlan had known some gloomy places, but, by the Hanged, none so miserable as this.

Besides the grey and the damp, they had to wear the utter despondency and humiliation of being bound and disarmed, stripped of their hard-won gold and any notion of where they were being taken or why. So far, there had been little chance of escape. They were flanked at all times by mounted spearmen who looked like they knew their business. The griping from the crew did nothing to lift anyone's spirits, a drip-drip-drip of complaint like a leaky roof, fraying nerves as much as the endless rain. Didn't seem to matter how many times Erlan or Einar told them to hold their damn tongues. *Drip, drip, drip.* The only two who never said a word of complaint were Orīana and Marta.

The story Erlan had spun, that they were simple traders, was evidently not believed. Instead, it was clear these Franks still suspected them of being Frisians, or at least sell-swords in the pay of this King Rathbod, of whom Erlan had only ever heard distant rumour. Although, he thought, the presence of the womenfolk must have given their captors cause for doubt. But solving the mystery of who they were was apparently the preserve of greater men.

It would have been easy to despair. The uncertainty of it, the unfairness even. And as the miles slowly passed, Erlan found himself oscillating between disappointment and determination. Between grit and devastation. But he couldn't show it. He mustn't show it. If he succumbed then what

300

chance stood all the others. But it was hard to see what pieces they had to play.

When he had tried to discuss it with Lilla, they had argued over whether they should tell these Franks exactly who they were and what they were doing.

Lilla favoured honesty. 'I am a queen,' she had whispered to him over the rattle of the cart, her voice shaking with emotion, 'and I am worthy to be treated as one. I'm not going to hide behind some feckless lie.'

Feckless or not, Erlan could not see how conceding the truth would improve their chances of survival or regaining their freedom. 'As soon as you admit that, they're hardly going to pat us on the back and send us on our way.' The rightful queen of the Twin Kingdoms could not stand aloof from whatever conflicts were troubling Francia. It was clear they would have to pick a side. By Erlan's reckoning, the longer they could avoid being forced to that choice the better. At least until they understood more of how the powers in this warring land lay. Lilla didn't like it, but she could see the reason in his thinking, sinking into a kind of sullen acquiescence which, Erlan suspected, had more to do with the hateful weather than any real complicity between them.

The yellow man's name was Childebrand. A nobleman by birth, and brother, he said, to this Duke Karil. In spite of their predicament, he seemed to Erlan a thoughtful man, reasonable in his treatment of his prisoners, and honourable towards the womenfolk. At least so far. But as to his intentions once they reached their destination, the Frank refused to say more.

301

At night time, Childebrand allowed his captives to sleep under their carts to shelter from the worst of the rain. And he insisted at least four men stand guard around them through the night. He said any man or woman trying to escape would instantly forfeit their life. But judging from the Frank's shifting looks around his own men, Erlan wondered whether the guards were as much for the women's protection from his other men as to keep the captives under guard. If so, Erlan was grateful for that; it meant he could sleep easier. Although, without arms, they were powerless to resist much at all.

Eventually they reached a town of some considerable size, which the Franks called Traiectum, fording the Maas river. As this appeared to be a town of some import, Erlan expected it must at last be where they would come face to face with this elusive Frankish Duke.

But to his disappointment, and his companions' dismay, it was soon obvious they were there only to cross the river, and then continue on their journey.

That night, on the road again, Childebrand came and squatted by their fire. He told them that in Traiectum he had sought word of his brother and discovered that Karil's last known whereabouts was in the forests south and west of another town called Durum. The Hurtgen forest, he called it.

'Rightful rulers of a land don't hide in forests,' Erlan observed.

Childebrand snorted. 'Our fight is not about the right of it. In these troublous days, the strong must take control.'

'That at least is honest. So, this brother of yours means to make himself king?'

'No,' the Frank replied sharply. 'He would never presume

302

to take the crown for himself. Rather, he sees fatal weakness in the king. Chilperic is corrupt and surrounded by the counsel of devils. Ragenfrid, the Mayor of his Palace, whispers poison in his ear. It is he who has sought alliance with Rathbod of the Frisians against us.'

'Threats from both north and south then.'

'Austrasia is beset on all sides by its enemies. But my brother is a good and worthy man. The man our people need to lead them.'

'Evidently not all of your people agree.'

The Frank glared at him. 'Those Austrasians who stand against us have been led astray... But united, they – and then the Franks – could be strong again, as we once were. We could even be great.'

'Under your brother.'

'You will see. He is not like other men.'

'Huh. He sounds very like several men I have met. Hungry for power and the wealth it brings.' He threw a rueful glance at the cart containing the gold. 'Perhaps you feel your own coffers could be fuller, too.'

Catching his look, the Frank shook his head. 'None of us fights for greed. But fighting a war costs money.'

'Preferably someone else's.'

'If Providence has seen fit to place this... *blessing*... in our hands—'

'You'd be fools to refuse it.'

'We're no fools.' Childebrand got to his feet. 'Now sleep as you can, Erlan Aurvandil. We have a long ride tomorrow.' And sweeping up his long cloak behind him, the yellow man returned to his own fire.

After he had moved off, there was some talk among the captive crew, but none of it conclusive, stirring up only more questions, and never any answers.

At length, Erlan told them all that the time was better served with rest. And one by one, they lay down their heads and took his advice, so that a kind of uncertain peace settled over the camp, among captive and captor alike.

Yet Erlan himself could not sleep. For all his reassurance to the others, he had little confidence that the road ahead held anything good for them. To make sleep even harder, his bladder was as full as his mind. Wearily, he slipped off his cloak and got to his feet. One of the guards immediately challenged him. He held out his palms and gestured to his crotch. After all, where the Hel was he going to go in the dead of night, unarmed and in a strange land? The guard relented and waved him off into the shadows.

He limped to a nearby tree, loosened the drawstring of his breeches and flopped himself out. A few moments later, he expelled a long breath, listening to the pitter-patter stream of piss falling among the dead autumn leaves. Yet as he listened, he thought he heard another sound, far away, drifting on the wind. Singing... Or rather, song.

As the sound of his own making died away, he stayed still, his ears searching the night. There it was again... Music, ever so faint; so faint that for a second he wondered if it was inside his own head, its melody *so* beautiful... Dancing harmonies, voices interwoven, moving through and inside and around one another like oil-skinned serpents, coiling and twisting and turning in perfect unison, weaving a spell in his head.

Suddenly an arm slipped around him. He was startled, instinctively catching the wrist, realising at once that it was a woman's hand. Then he felt a body close behind him, pressed up against him, the other arm slipping round.

'Lilla,' he murmured, with a half-smile in the dark, wondering how she had slipped past the guards unnoticed to join him in the shadows. Although it was just like her to get what she wanted.

'Shhhh.' A sound hardly more than a breath, as the firmness of her body, the swell of her breasts, gripped against him. Then her hand travelled downwards, slowly... teasingly... through the hair at the root of his manhood, venturing out along its length. He felt the blood rush to his loins, limp flesh filling in the warm cup of her hand. He closed his eyes with the unexpected pleasure of it – *Gods, of all places!* – when suddenly there was a giggle behind him. A laugh nothing like Lilla's. He spun around and there was Marta, her small face tilted up to his.

'I knew that you liked me,' she murmured.

He shoved her away so hard she fell on her backside in the leaves. 'What the fuck are you doing?' he hissed.

'Only what you want. You seem to enjoy it...' She looked down at his semi-erect penis and laughed, her face creasing into something almost mad, oblivious to the fact that she might wake someone else or bring one of the guards running. No sign of the chaste nun, with hair bound and face expressionless as a holy icon. Instead, her blue eyes flashed with a wildness that he could scarcely have imagined.

Hastily, he tucked himself away and pulled his drawstring tight. 'Get away from me.'

'I know your heart, Erlan. I know you only married Lilla to hurt me. But I *forgive* you. Stop lying to yourself. We must tell her how we feel, she will understand.'

'You really have lost your mind.' He turned to return to the fire but a gruff voice challenged him.

'Here, what are you doing there?' It was the guard, not two paces from them. 'Both of you.' He made no effort to lower his voice and already Erlan could hear others stirring by the fire.

The guard's spear-tip was lowered in threat. Marta began slowly picking herself up. Erlan cursed, wondering how in the Nine Worlds he could explain this. Explain any of this. 'Well? You've had your piss. Now get back—'

But before the guard could finish his sentence, an arrow-shaft appeared in his temple, as if at the conjuring of witchcraft. His eyes went wide with shock. Erlan started backwards, his spine butting against the tree-trunk. Marta screamed at the top of her lungs, the sound of it more chilling than the blood bubbling out of the man's skull. The Frank stood for the count of two, three… then he fell forward onto Erlan.

Erlan collapsed against the tree under the weight. A second arrow came streaking out of the night, skittering past Erlan's ear, then a third, thudding into the dead man's back. Erlan slung him away and reached down to snatch Marta's hand. 'Move!' he snarled, seeing shadows, five, eight, a dozen, running through the trees. 'Attack!' he screamed. 'We're under attack!' He hefted the girl's light frame off the ground and swung her towards the camp where already the Frankish guards were rousing each other. He needed a weapon.

The guard's spear lay on the ground. Erlan had but an eye-blink to drop to his knees, grab the spear and drag it upright as a dark figure ran at him. He saw the glimmer of an axe raised overhead, thrust the spear low, and the man impaled himself on the point. Erlan twisted the shaft and ripped it clear, glimpsing a skin cloak and wolf head, hardly any detail that seemed human. He glanced left and right, seeing other shadows whipping around them, similarly attired, armed to the very fangs of their hoods.

'*Sorðinn,*' he swore softly.

These were *ulfheðnar*, he thought with grim certainty. Wolf-warriors. And by the sound of the growing howls in the woods, there were plenty of them.

Another figure sprinted into the camp, shortly followed by another, and another from the other side. Erlan snatched up the fallen *ulfheðinn*'s axe and retreated towards the fire and his friends, feeling the horrible nakedness of being un-armed in the face of the terror spilling out of the darkness.

He started yelling, 'Shield-wall, shield-wall!' But that was pure instinct. He'd been in this situation before – a surprise attack at night. But that had been as one of a band of trained warriors. Here, none of them had any shields or any sense of order, and Childebrand's men were hardly going to take orders from him. His own, those still alive, were all river-men, and the women...

By the Hanged, the women!

The night was filling with sound. Shouts of command behind him, the dread howls of their attackers, the dull ring of iron against iron, the thrum and whip of streaking arrows.

He had a creeping sense that the numbers were with the

attackers as more and more of them poured out of the night. He scrambled back to the fire. Einar was bellowing at the Franks, 'Arm us! Arm us, damn you whoresons!'

'Here, Fat-Belly!' Erlan lobbed the axe he'd taken off the *ulfheðinn* at Einar, who snatched it out of the air and spun around to meet the threat, which wasn't long in coming. Two men came racing in, leaped over the corpse of a Frankish guard, and dashed through the fire, sending sparks showering up into the sky. Einar side-stepped to the right, ducked under the swipe of an axe, then drove in his shoulder with a body-blow that knocked the *ulfheðinn* off his feet. Mikki Crow didn't waste a second, throwing himself on the wolf-hood, his fists bludgeoning away like cudgels until the wolf-hood was smashed to ragged pieces and stained red with blood. Mikki bellowed in triumph and came up clutching an axe of his own. Bull was just beyond him, roaring in fear or defiance – it hardly mattered which – his massive bulk silhouetted by the flames, bracing himself for another attack. Next moment a warrior was on him, trying to sink a long blade into his neck, but the kid caught his wrist and the pair of them fell to the ground, rolling and wrestling for the upper hand until suddenly Bull threw the other bodily into the fire. The *ulfheðinn* shrieked with pain and Erlan stepped forward to skewer him with the spear still gripped in his hand.

In his periphery, he was dimly aware of other fights all around him, of Childebrand scything broad and bloody swaths with his nobleman's sword, of a handful of Franks forming some semblance of a battle-line, of horses screaming like dying men. But the surprise had been complete. Any defence was too little too late. The attack had broken up into a scattering of desperate skirmishes as every person fought to stay alive.

'Erlan!' He recognised Lilla's voice and turned towards it, trying to pick her out of the maelstrom of bodies and faces and pelts and masks. 'Help them! For Frigg's sake, Erlan! Help Orīana!'

Then he saw her, on the other side of the fire, yelling at him but pointing wildly to her left. He followed the line of her arm and saw three *ulfheðnar* dragging Orīana out of the camp by her hair. And beside her, two more had Marta.

He swore, ashamed that his first thought was to protect Lilla, but if they were to stop them, they had to move fast. 'Einar!' he yelled. 'With me!'

But the fat man was busy, locked in a struggle with a huge *ulfheðinn* at least half a foot taller than him. Each had the other by the wrist of his axe-arm. Erlan drew back his long-spear, took aim, and would have launched it but for Mikki rising in front of him, blocking his line. Erlan cursed and screamed at the long-shank river-man to get out of his way, but Mikki was no coward. He moved in, driving his boot hard into the tall warrior's kneecap. The *ulfheðinn* roared in pain, falling to the ground, pulling Einar down on top of him. There was a momentary flail of limbs, then the fat man rose up on his knees and brought his axe slamming down. The blade bit deep into the angle of the *ulfheðinn*'s neck and, a second later, the struggle was over.

Erlan looked again for Orīana and the girl but in the darkness and confusion he could no longer see them. Behind him, the noise of a stampede of hooves, while he scoured the shadows. Then a long horn-blast sounded from a distance off. And everywhere, all at once about the camp, the *ulfheðnar* were pulling back, leaving behind their own dead and the corpses of those they had killed. A receding tide of violence and destruction, leaving behind it the pathetic wreckage of Childebrand's camp.

'The gold,' Erlan heard one Frankish voice call. 'They've taken the cart and the gold.'

Erlan was blowing hard, his muscles heavy with exhaustion, the iron taste of blood in his throat. His mind said they should go after them – *now* – while they were still not far off. But his body wouldn't respond. He was suddenly a shattered sword, a broken bow, his energy completely spent.

He sank to his knees.

'Where is she?' Einar was looking about him, his fire-ravaged face a mask of desperation, scouring the wreckage around the still-burning fires for any sign of his woman. 'Orīana? Did you see her?'

Erlan could hear in his voice the edge of madness. 'I saw her,' he nodded wearily.

Einar came up to him, grabbed him by the collar of his tunic. 'Where? Where is she?'

'I'm sorry, my friend. She's gone… They're both of them gone.'

CHAPTER TWENTY-SIX

It was a terrible thing to see Einar Fat-Belly like that.

Till now, Lilla had thought of him as a boat with plenty of ballast: essentially imperturbable. But love changed a man. And evidently Einar loved Orīana.

In the aftermath of the attack, he'd almost lost his mind. It had taken all of Lilla's calming words to bring him back to himself. Even once he grew more tranquil, he seemed not wholly there. He was silent and morose, and sharp with anyone who tried to speak with him. As if he blamed all of them for Orīana's disappearance, and not the misfortune of the attack.

Maybe he was right to.

As for Marta's disappearance, Lilla felt an ugly splinter in her secret heart that was almost glad of it. Why, though? When she examined her feelings, she found that there was something about the girl, about her presence, her preternatural calm, that felt somehow ominous. As if it presaged some great evil... But the better part of her knew that whatever doubts she had about that girl, whatever strangeness Marta seemed to carry with her, she did not deserve the fate that must be playing out, even now. No one did. It was a horror to even think of it. And, alas, Orīana and her daughter were not their only loss.

As a sullen autumn sun rose through the grey gruel of the Hurtgen dawn, they took stock of what the night had left them. Not far from the fires, near the cart and oxen, they found the bodies of Dreng and, sprawled over his legs, Kunrith. Kunrith, whose sharp mind had been no match for the *ulfheðnar*'s sharp steel or towering fury. Dreng, a sweet, handsome boy, so timid Lilla hardly knew the sound of his voice. Krok must have run for it. But he hadn't got far. His corpse lay twenty paces into the trees, his face smashed in, all but unrecognisable.

Demetrios was alive, just. His left buttock had suffered a deep cut as he had wriggled on his belly under the wheels of the cart to escape the wolf-men's blades. He considered the wound very bad sport, even though Erlan persuaded him he was damned lucky not to suffer far worse. He would live, provided he kept the wound clean.

Childebrand had them burn their dead together with his own in a clearing. But of the *ulfheðnar* corpses, he said: 'The wolves can take their own.'

They left them to rot where they fell. But not before they had examined them closely. Beneath their wolf-pelts and fearsome masks, they were ordinary men. True, they had the bodies of strong, well-trained fighters, but there was nothing mysterious about them, with the exception of one feature. Every one of them had bright blond hair. Not just the honey-

312

gold colour of Lilla's own hair, but so blond it was almost white. It reminded her of Gellir the White, who had come within a whisker of taking her life. But these men were not freaks of nature, as he had been, with pinkish eyes and skin like a revenant wight. These were just men with silver-blond hair.

She found it very curious.

Childebrand, meanwhile, smouldered with rage. It was interesting to her how men expressed their anger so differently. She'd known men boil and thunder and flame like the fire-mountains in the tales of the Old-Time. Others turn white with cold fury, their anger silent and cruel. This Childebrand, she decided, was like a forge-fire, its embers turning over, grey and red and white, while the invisible heat of his vexation grew hotter and hotter.

He was most angry, of course, at the loss of the gold. Far more about that than his dead and wounded men, and that most of the horses had been driven off. And while Lilla, too, was by turns distressed and angry at the turn of events that had upturned her world, she soon understood the real cause of Childebrand's upset. He was embarrassed to report to his brother what had happened. That he had, from one day to the next, lost such a quantity of gold, which could have been a boon to his brother's cause, was not something he wished to report. And, what was worse, he had no idea who the wolf-warriors were. They were as much a mystery to him as they were to her and the sorry remnant of her crew.

Thus, it was in every way an unhappy column that continued on its way through the Hurtgen forest the next day. And although she, Erlan and the rest of them rode in the

313

one remaining ox-cart, they now felt as much fellow survivors as captives of the Franks, most of whom continued on foot.

Upon one point Childebrand was adamant: there was no question of them hunting down their attackers, as Einar demanded they do at once. 'Not before we've made contact with my brother. We're not trackers,' he said in answer to Einar's plea. 'Besides, I have never seen warriors like this before.'

'Could they be some sort of vanguard of your enemy?' suggested Erlan.

Childebrand only glowered at this. 'King Chilperic follows the Christian god. These men were followers of the old ways.'

'How do you know?' asked Lilla.

But the Frank ignored her question. 'My guess is they are Saxon raiders from the east. Though how they could be this deep into Austrasian territory is beyond me.'

'You don't have to be a Christian to fight for a Christian king,' Erlan said. 'I should know.'

'You know nothing of this war,' returned Childebrand impatiently. 'And nothing of those who are waging it.'

'You're wrong, my lord,' said Lilla. 'We are part of your war now.' She gave Einar a significant look and squeezed his meaty hand. 'Whether we like it or not.' The fat man acknowledged her look and nodded his appreciation, the furrow in his brow deepening. But he said nothing. Nor did Erlan, though she could tell he too was troubled.

Later that day, their party came across a small homestead where an old woodcutter said he had seen an armed force matching the description of Karil and his men heading north

314

and east not two days before. 'There weren't many of 'em was over-talkative, like. But one of 'em said he was looking forward to a proper roof over his head and a decent hearth to lay by. Day after tomorrow. In Durum, so he said.'

'That means they plan to reach Durum tonight.' Childebrand considered this and suddenly his mind was made up. 'We make for Durum then. It is only half a day's march from here with the cart in tow.'

They all agreed it was their best course of action. The comparative safety of the small town would be welcome after the shock and terror of the night attack. And once they had found the path that would lead them north and east out of the forest, Lilla sensed an improvement in the mood of the Frankish men.

Her own company were less enthusiastic. She tried to reassure them that the sooner they came before this Karil Martel figure, the sooner they would know their fate – for good or for ill. But that felt as cold comfort as it sounded.

The nearer they approached the town, the better the roads became, lined and reinforced with large blocks of stone that reminded Lilla more of the great thoroughfares of Byzantium than the mud-packed tracks of even the greatest roads in her father's kingdom. And when, next morning, the town at last came into view, she had an even stronger impression of a power greater than almost anything she had yet seen. But one fading away to dust and memory.

Durum was surrounded by a large wooden stockade with a strong stone gateway and guardhouse on both the west and the east side of the town. It was through the western gate that their much-diminished column entered. Lilla noticed at once the signs of a land at war. The bustle of the smiths, the great piles of arrows and spear-tips and shields, conspicuous in their heaps by the wayside and outside the garrison barracks. Sacks of grain from the recent harvest, quantities of wood for fuel.

Childebrand led them through the stinking market square to a hall which still bore faint vestiges of its past grandeur. There were a few stone pillars still standing, supporting a kind of partial colonnade, and a broad limestone staircase, broken in many places, which led up to a raised stone platform, giving the building a semblance of authority: the elevation of a ruling elite. Despite these remnants, the roof of the hall was timber and turf, as it might have been in her own homeland in the north.

Their guards were told to watch the prisoners and await further orders while Childebrand went inside, flanked by two of his men. It was some time before he returned. Long enough for Mikki and Ran to have a good long croak about their predicament, and how they could have been spared all of this if only they'd told Valrik he could stick his promises of fame and fortune very far up his bony arse.

'Aye,' agreed Bull, 'but think how you never would've seen all that gold.' His face fairly glowed at the memory of it.

'Listen, you beef-headed oaf. Seeing it ain't much fuckin' use,' countered Mikki. 'It's spending it I'm interested in. And there ain't the hope of a maid's virtue in Valhalla that any of us'll be doing much of that.'

'Hold on to what hope you have,' Lilla said, to herself as much as to them. 'The Norns are fickle. Their weaving may yet turn in our favour.'

But that only earned a gloomy scowl from Mikkel Crow.

At last they were summoned. Some of them, anyway.

Lilla, together with Erlan and Einar, was led inside. They found themselves passing through a strange fusion of the airy stone palaces of the empire they had left behind, and the smoke-filled oaken halls of the north. Tapestries hung on the walls, along with long-dormant weaponry of many kinds and of another age, while every table surface or stand was cluttered with all manner of intricately fashioned ornaments, vases and bowls that had never been seen in the lands around the East Sea.

But the moment they were led into *his* presence, there was nothing to look at but him.

Lilla needed no telling which of the men gathered around a table on a small dais was Karil Martel, although his back was turned to them as they were brought in.

He was wearing a sky-blue cloak, trimmed with fur, with long strands of blond hair swept off his face just touching the collar. But it wasn't that which held her eye. It was something about the way he stood, and the way all these other, evidently important, men were positioned towards him. Almost like worshippers before an idol. A kind of subservience, a willingness, a readiness to obey in the angle of their faces, in the tilt of their shoulders.

It was this, maybe, that fixed her attention. But also the sound of his voice.

She had never heard a voice so striking. She would soon forget what he was talking about. After all, it was not quite clear. But she would never forget the sound – mellifluous as honey; rich like the dark wines of the emperor's table; smoky like the great hearths of the Uppland halls in the snowbound north. She had never been enchanted by a voice so instantly. And that was before she had seen his face.

They were led up onto the little dais and stood between the group of counsellors and the edge of the platform. Erlan reached out and squeezed her hand. She squeezed back, but only mechanically, an automatic response, since her attention was still firmly on the man in the sky-blue cloak.

Childebrand was one of the circle of nobles – for such, Lilla guessed, they must be. They all had the same haircut, short at the back and sides of their heads, cut straight across their brow. Unflattering, to her taste. And they all had the same style of wearing their cloak, pinned at one shoulder, leaving their right arm free.

Childebrand leaned forward, touched Karil's arm in a manner so familiar it could only pass between brothers. Karil stopped what he was saying. When he turned, his head moved first, the rest of his body following, and she saw that Karil was not the same as the others. Under his sweep of blond hair, his brows were solid but not heavy. His cloak was pinned at each shoulder, in the manner of the military commanders of the empire. His eyes were piercing as rays of sunlight, but there was something in the lines of his face, a slight scarring or a pocked mark on one side, that gave his resting expression a kind of sneering quality. Something between a smile of amusement, a joke that only he understood, and the assured glance of authority. The knowledge that he was the centre of attention in any room he walked into.

And his gaze was fixed upon her.

For several moments, no one spoke. Then he gestured at their hands, which had been bound in front of them. 'I think we can dispense with those, can't we?'

It was barely a fully formed thought, let alone a command, yet immediately a guard stepped forward and went down the line of the three of them, cutting their bonds.

'I understand you are traders,' he began, still looking at Lilla.

'We are,' said Erlan.

'We are, *my lord*,' Karil corrected him, his gaze still not shifting from her. Then, abruptly, his eyes snapped to Erlan. 'From what my brother tells me, you must be very good ones.'

'We do fine. At least we were doing fine. Until ill fortune cast us into a storm and... well, here we are.'

'Ill fortune.' He nodded drily. 'It will have the better of us all.' He moved closer. Lilla found she had turned a fraction away from him, was standing a touch taller, her shoulders held back. *Dear gods*, she thought, *I'm showing myself off to him.* Yet it felt like she could do nothing else.

'Funny, isn't it?' he continued. 'How the moment a little gold is involved, the truth flees for the hills.' He smiled at all three of them. It wasn't sinister exactly. But there was an underlying steel in his eyes. 'Although I hear you possessed more than a little.'

Erlan said nothing.

'Shall we try this again? In case there is any confusion... I ask a question, you give me the answer.'

'Was there a question, my lord?' said Erlan. 'I must have missed it.'

The scar tightened into a sneer. 'Who are you? Why are you here?'

She knew the pieces Erlan wanted to play. Knew they had agreed upon it. But she still couldn't stop herself stepping forward. 'My name is Queen Lilla Sviggarsdottír,' she said. 'I am the rightful ruler of the Twin Kingdoms in the north. We were shipwrecked off your coastline. We claim your protection and the proper honour which is our due.'

That penetrating gaze swung back to her. 'Well, that was unexpected, I must say.' The sarcasm in his voice was undisguised. 'Not traders, then. Royalty.'

Lilla could feel Erlan bristling like a hedgehog beside her. But the truth was always more powerful than a lie. In any case, it was clear that this Karil was nobody's fool.

'Sviggar... Sviggar...? I feel I know that name.' Karil turned to survey the faces of his retinue behind him, most of whom wore blank looks. And finding no help from that quarter, he pinched at his brow, rinsing his memory. 'Ah, yes. Of course.' He turned back to Lilla. 'The Bastard King of Sveärika. That the fellow?'

It was Lilla's turn to bristle. 'My father may have been bastard born, but he was a nobler man than any in his kingdom.'

'I've no reason to think he was not. But please, don't be too quick to take offence, Lady. Your father is in good company.' He pointed at Childebrand. 'It's widely said that my brother there suffers from a regrettable lack of legitimacy.' He turned and gave a small bow. 'As indeed, do I.'

Not knowing what to make of that, Lilla said nothing.

'At least, that's what they say of us. It might distress my

late mother to hear it, but who am I to correct them? A certain notoriety has its uses.'

'Families are complicated,' she said.

'Now that *is* the truth,' he laughed. 'If my own stepmother Plectrude had her way, I would still be locked in her cellar. She feels herself to be infinitely better suited to rule than her boorish stepson.'

Far as Lilla could tell, there seemed nothing boorish about him.

'But what are we to do with you, Lady?'

'At least treat us with the dignity we deserve. So far, there's been precious little of that.'

'In fairness to my brother, you withheld the truth until now.' He arched a fair eyebrow. 'If you are indeed a queen.'

'It would be an absurdity to claim so if I were not.'

'Wouldn't it though?' Karil chuckled, then took a few paces along the platform, thinking. He suddenly turned. 'Is there a king of these Twin Kingdoms?'

Lilla and Erlan exchanged glances. 'There is a usurper who claims to be king—' began Lilla, but Karil cut her off.

'Yes, yes. No doubt there are complications. We shall come onto those. But what I mean is – have you a husband?'

'No,' she declared, feeling shame burn her ears, not daring to glance in Erlan's direction. 'My husband died from his battle wounds.'

'Mmm.' Karil nodded thoughtfully, but took the point no further.

Erlan suddenly spoke up. 'My lord, what do you mean to do about these attackers? They have taken two of our people. Will you help us find them?' Lilla could hear the trace of anger in his words, knew that it was meant for her.

'Your people? You mean the two women?' Clearly Childebrand had told him more than they thought. 'I suppose they are more important to you than the gold?'

Erlan glanced at Einar, who stood quietly glowering like a vengeful bull. 'They are.'

Karil looked all three of them over. 'Hm. Well, the truthful answer is that even if I wanted to help you, I have no men and no time to do it. News came this morning that King Rathbod is approaching from the north with a force of at least a thousand. I cannot spare a single spearman just now.'

'We would promise you a portion of the gold.'

'Ha! A portion? Why, that's very noble of you! Believe me, if I had the luxury of time and men and *peace*, damn it, I would think nothing finer than to ride to the aid of a pair of luckless women, with the promise of winning a king's ransom in gold to my profit. And from nothing worse than a pack of heathen robbers.'

'They seemed more than mere robbers, my lord,' said Erlan. 'They were organised. And well equipped. Perhaps a shield-band of your enemy?'

'A "shield-band"?' He chuckled but with little mirth. 'Some quaint idiom of the north, I take it.'

'Whatever you call them. To have a force of warriors like them moving unchecked makes you vulnerable to further attacks. They could strike you at any time.'

'If I wanted your advice on how to conduct my military affairs, believe me, I would have asked for it.' Lilla noticed how the lines on Karil's face tightened the shorter his patience grew, drawing his handsome face into that cold sneer once more. 'The gold, and your friends, must wait.'

'My lord, I must speak.' The voice belonged to someone whom Lilla had not noticed before but who now stepped forward from the circle of counsellors. At once she saw he was dressed differently to the others, in a long black tunic with a muddy hem, cinched with a simple bit of hemp rope. His head was tonsured from his crown to about a third of the way down his head. Lilla had seen enough holy men now to know this signified he was some sort of monk. He was an older man with the web of age in the corners of his eyes, a man so lean he seemed made of stone, with a short, dense bloom of grey stubble on an angular chin. Yet she saw gentleness as well as intensity in those eyes. 'If you will,' he added.

Karil acknowledged the monk with a weary sigh. 'Wynfred of Nursling. You are rapidly becoming a thorn in my side. Must I hear you again?'

'If your conscience is not yet dead, my lord.' Lilla was surprised at the firmness with which he spoke; he had not the deference of the others.

Karil rolled his eyes. 'How can it be when you are constantly on hand to revive it?'

'Can you not see these two things are connected, my lord? My own pleadings and those of these outlanders.'

'You yourself are an outlander, monk. Let's not forget that.'

'Yet my heart aches at what I have seen in your land as if I were native-born.' His accent was different to Karil's – somehow flatter, his voice a little rough. ''E'er since I set foot in the Rheinlands, and the further upriver I've travelled, I've heard tale after tale of sorrow and mystery.'

'Yes, so you said.'

'But you must admit the details correspond,' the monk urged. 'At almost every settlement up the Rhein I've heard of children going missing. Either purchased for a pittance or else simply vanished. And the connection seems always to these men with the silver hair.'

'Yes, yes, yes.' Karil sighed impatiently. 'I agree, Wynfred – it's all very mysterious and distressing.'

'But if they are now operating inland of the river. Even as far as the Hurtgenwald—'

'As I have said to you before – I cannot spare the men to go chasing about the woods hunting ghouls. If these are men living outside the law, or Saxon slavers of some kind, they will doubtless have some bolthole to which they return. Like any wolves, they will have their den. It will take time to sniff them out. Time which I do not have. And while I am sorry for these children you speak of—'

'You cannot simply abandon them to their fate! Many, I'm sure, must already have been horribly ill-used.'

'Yes, my thanks to you, Wynfred. You need not paint us a picture. I know how keenly you feel for them.'

'This is not about my own sensibility, my lord. This is about the weight of obligation. Of what is right. If we can do something, we must.'

'Brother Wynfred, I grow tired of repeating myself! Plectrude holds Koln fast with a garrison of thousands immediately to my east. King Rathbod is marching south from Frisia, and my scouts along the Neustrian marches send reports that King Chilperic and that upstart dog of his, Ragenfrid, have been raising an army against us. Did Our Lord not say that each day is sufficient for its own trouble? I'd say enemies on three sides is already a sufficiently troublesome day not to go looking for more. Wouldn't you?'

'If you would rule this land, Karil, son of Pepin, as your father did before you, you must protect the weak.' This Wynfred spoke as if it were he who held authority here, not the man in the sky-blue cloak.

'Do you dare to tell me my own business, monk? Here, in this hall.' Lilla saw Karil's sneer turn cruel. The monk was a brave man to rile him.

But before Wynfred could give an answer, a man entered at the far end of the hall and strode with ringing steps up to the platform. 'I bear news, my lord, from the fortress commander at Bitburg.'

'Go ahead. Make your report,' said Karil, turning his back on Wynfred with a snap of his cloak.

'A Neustrian column has been seen north of the Eifel mountains, Lord. They take the Koln road through the forest.'

'Their numbers?'

'At least five thousand.'

'And was the king's banner with them?'

The messenger nodded grimly. 'The triple lily was seen, Lord, yes.'

This caused a stir among the noblemen of Karil's retinue. The Duke glanced at the monk. 'Enough of this, Wynfred, I beg of you. My own sympathy for those missing children is worth nothing if we are crushed now. We've been caught unprepared. My forces are scattered. If we are to stand any chance, I must concentrate them all here, at Durum. And at once.'

This new development had stolen the wind from Wynfred's sails. If he had anything more to argue, he did not offer it, perhaps seeing the futility of his cause, at least for now. Karil turned back to his nobles to take counsel.

'My lord! A word first, if you would.' To Lilla's surprise, it was Erlan who spoke. 'We are strangers here. But we've seen enough to know you have hard choices to make. Hard battles to win. If we could help you, we would stand with you against your enemies. Alas, we are but eight souls. Seven men and one woman cannot make a difference to your fate. But we still might change the fate of our friends. Please… I appeal to your honour. To your mercy. Return us our arms. Give us food and clothing and fresh horses. We will take up this monk's cause and our own.' He looked across at Einar, put his hand on his friend's broad shoulder. 'Let us be your arm of justice. If there is still any chance for them, we will find our friends. And the children.'

It was a fine speech. Erlan had taken a chance and, for a moment, Lilla saw hope rise in Einar's face, yet with it the fear that this Frankish lord would crush it with his next breath.

'Eight,' said Karil, half-turning only. 'What can you do with eight? My brother tells me there were dozens of these villains.'

Erlan spread his hands. 'What can we not do with eight, my lord? The world was often changed with fewer than that.'

At this, Karil gave a laugh like a thunder-clap. 'By God, I like a man with some stones! Very well then. You shall have your weapons and whatever supplies and horses I can spare. I can't promise my best, but...' He nodded to himself, as though satisfied the business was now concluded. 'So then, I send you out – as sheep among wolves, eh?' He turned to the monk. 'How d'you like that, Anglian?'

Wynfred's lined face betrayed nothing. 'I like it well enough, sire. So long as the Lord goes with us.'

'May He go with us all,' returned Karil drily. His eye fell once more on Lilla. 'I have one condition, however. Your queen, Lilla Sviggarsdottír, will remain here. Under my protection.'

Lilla felt foolish not to have seen this coming. She and Erlan exchanged uncertain glances, his with more than a measure of anger in it. 'With respect, my lord, I need no protecting,' she said. 'My place is with my countrymen.'

'I have said you will remain and that is how it shall be.' Despite his shallow smile, Karil Martel's tone brooked no dissent. 'After all, we have to keep your friends honest somehow, don't we?'

CHAPTER TWENTY-SEVEN

Skírpa's feet were a bloody ruin.

He looked down at them miserably. In Byzantium, a servant used to come to his rooms in the Daphne wing of the palace once a week, with oils and creams from the best apothecary on the Mese. Skírpa would read the latest business of the day while she massaged his feet for an hour, then trimmed and filed his toenails. Sometimes he would have her adorn his toes with rings if he was feeling decorative.

Now his toes were so swollen he could hardly tell one from another, and the sole of each foot was so shredded he dare not touch them, let alone massage any relief back into them, for the pain that he knew would come shooting up his leg.

His captors had driven him through forest and field, marsh and moor, like a hind before the hunt. Five days of hell, a hundred miles or maybe more. The wolf-men moved fast and had no sympathy. They didn't care whether he, or the other captives, lived or died. Though he'd thought himself the only survivor, in fact three others had been taken from the bloody wreckage of the barge. Another monk, even younger than he, who was so buried in his own misery he never said a word. A young wench, who had worked as serving girl to the captain of the barge. And a grain merchant, who had been shipping his harvest yield north to the river town of Confluentes.

Each night was filled with the horror of the girl's screaming. The wolf-men would use her, each of them in turn, deaf to her pleadings and screams both. Until, at dawn on the third day, they found her face down in a puddle of her own blood. Somehow she had driven the jagged stub of a broken branch into her throat and bled out during the night.

She was free of them now anyway, and there were moments when Skírpa envied her. But he resolved to himself that *he* would stay alive. Whatever it took, whatever was demanded of him, he would do it. Even if it were only to live on in this hell.

And though he was not a man who believed in such things, he could not imagine a hell much worse than the place they brought him to. By then, he was delirious, his senses staggering in and out of reason. He remembered a river crossing, being pulled and shoved into a boat and dragged out by his hair the other side. Then clawing his way up a steep hill as the sun was setting under an overcast sky. And just before darkness fell, the whole sky lit up in crimson colours. A sea of blood crushing him from above. And the stench of death below, growing stronger with each faltering step. Then the sun fell beneath the horizon, and with it came a black and moonless night.

He remembered nothing else of his arrival.

Plainly, things could always be worse. Only the fool thought otherwise.

And yet the place he now found himself in was beyond anything in the imagination of the 'civilised' citizens of empire. This was a world that those peoples had long forgotten.

'Get up, monk!' A sharp kick accompanied the vicious snarl, bringing Skírpa back to full wakefulness. He had long given up pleading that he was no monk. His robe and his hair marked him so. What else was there to say?

He had been left until last. The girl was dead. The merchant had been dragged out of the place the previous morning; the younger monk, the evening before. They had left Skírpa alone in the pit, shivering with cold and the numb ache of terror that would not leave him now. They had put him in a kind of circular hole, dug out of the earth but lined with rotten bracken, and covered with a roof of wooden spars in which was cut an ill-fitting door on rope hinges. That was where he had awoken after his arrival. But he soon realised this was only a kind of holding pen, a temporary place. Because now and then other cries reached his ears, wretched and weak. Unanswered except by the dull thud of blows and angry curses. If his ears did not lie, many were the plaintive voices of children.

What dread place is this? he wondered.

Seemed he was about to find out.

Until now, he had thought of all his captors as 'wolf-men', although the man in the pit with him now wore no wolf-skin. But his face was as cruel as the rest, fixed in its familiar sneer of malice, as he seized Skírpa's hair and dragged him to the hatch opening. 'Out!' he barked, administering another kick to the hamstrings that dropped Skírpa to his knees. That barking 'out' and then denying his captive the means to do it revealed a man of no very great intellect was something Skírpa thought best kept to himself. Instead, he scrambled up and out of the hole as best he could, flinging himself face first onto the ground. He lay there a few seconds, blowing his own stinking breath into the dirt.

Then, as he knew it must, came the raking snarl of pain as his hair was seized again and he was hauled to his feet. Even then, he could hardly stand.

'Move,' said the guard. So he moved, not knowing where, his only imperative to avoid the butt of the man's spear, which jabbed in his back if he didn't keep his bloodied feet stumbling one in front of the other. Slowly, shyly, he lifted his eyes to look around him. He soon wished he hadn't.

The stench of death and rotting viscera was everywhere. He had seen only one battle in his time: the Arabs' attempted storming of the Walls of Theodosius. And the stink reminded him very much of that. Back then, the air had been filled with the acrid heat of burning oil and the fumes of quicklime, mingling with the raw fetor of mutilated bodies. Here, though, there was decay as well as death and destruction. The smells were old, rancid, putrescent.

He soon saw the source.

For dominating the whole settlement was a huge tree. It rose like a mountain into the sky. Dark and bleak, in spite of the fullness of its autumnal foliage. From its leaf and bark, he saw it was of the family of ash. But it was an ash tree like none he'd ever seen before. A giant of a tree, towering over all the others, as Goliath must have towered over the young David before the boy struck him low. Its trunk was, he guessed, at least twelve feet across, its lowest branches another twelve clear feet from the ground. And hanging from the branches he saw the dark shapes of human bodies. They were naked, bound hand and foot, each with a noose around their neck. And a strange black apron hanging around their bellies. For an instant, his eye judged them further away, which made the tree even more monstrous. But he soon realised his mistake. They appeared that size not because they were further away, but because they were children. And then, to his disgust, he saw the black aprons were not cloth of any kind. But rather an absence, an abyss. A great void where each child's intestines should have been.

He fell to his knees and retched into the mud.

'On yer feet, monk!' came the inevitable bark. 'The One Eyed don't suffer no waiting.'

Skírpa struggled back to his feet. In any case, his retching gave him no relief since his stomach was long empty. He turned away from the horror, only to be confronted by other sights almost as grim. There were five or six low long-houses laid out in a row. They had no windows and a small square door at one end, so low a dog would have struggled to pass through. They had the look more of animal byres, except it would have been impractical to husband any livestock in and out of there. In any case, the pathetic cries and moans muffled behind the dark wooden walls, climbing with moss, betrayed their true occupants.

Further back, across an open space, where the white-haired men came and went, for now behaving as close to ordinary men as anything he'd yet seen of them, was another wooden construction, this one in the form of a pyramid. A temple of sorts, perhaps. Or maybe it was just a triangular facade, he could not tell. Only that near its top, just below the peak, was an empty aperture. From there, it had the appearance of a large eye, dark and menacing, peering down at him. At all of them. But it gave the whole structure a weird imbalance. As if the triangular face had been cut into two pieces near its summit, separating the top portion from the rest.

He hobbled on, seeing some womenfolk now going about their business, carrying pails and firewood and such, as if this place were any other village in any other land. He could not see any kind of wall or stockade, but he suspected there would be one. Whoever this One Eyed was, no man would put himself at the centre of a place like this without protection from the outside world. And suddenly, the prospect of meeting a man like that face to face felt like a weight crushing him down into the earth.

There were still other structures – he could not think of them as dwellings, even though in the wanderings of his childhood he remembered witnessing many homes yet more meagre than these – but to call anything in this place a 'home'... even he, Skírpa the homeless, could not bring himself to that word. These were places where people existed, nothing more. And one of them seemed larger than the others. They were heading towards it, and as they drew closer, another warrior – Skírpa recognised him as one of the two men who had taken him captive by the river – appeared

333

from inside and approached them. He had a piece of sacking in his hand.

'Cover him up. Same as the others.' He tossed the rag to Skírpa's guard. 'He'll be the last today.'

'Heard there's more coming in,' said the guard.

'Maybe. Maybe not,' growled the other. 'Not our business. Yet.' And then Skírpa's world went black as the cloth went over his head. Being blind now, as well as disorientated and afraid, didn't make walking any easier. He fell perhaps five times before he reached the threshold, and even then he was reluctant to go over it.

'Get in there, you skinny prick,' his guard gnarred.

When Skírpa didn't move, he got the butt of a spear in his kidneys. He groaned, staggered forward, then tripped over a step he couldn't see and went sprawling face first into a room. He knew better than to curse his captors out loud, but he did so inwardly with violent prolixity. He lay there, panting. Waiting. But nothing happened. The guard seemed as still as he.

Then, as if by some sixth sense, he intuited the guard's own fear. And another presence in the room with them.

'Leave us,' a voice said. Low. A rumbling whisper.

He heard footsteps scuffle out of the room and the door snap shut. Then other footsteps. Heavy padded steps, slow and ponderous. A moment later, he was seized under his armpits with a strength that was quite incredible, plucked from the floor like a little child and thrown down in a chair.

He waited, pain ebbing from his spine, terror seizing him like physical hands at his throat.

'Monk,' said the voice. 'You believe a lie. A foul, tyrannous lie.'

334

'I don't know what you mean.' His own voice barely audible, a scrape of sound.

'You know, monk. You are a deceiver. A purveyor of darkness, blindness, falsehood.' He spoke as he walked, with that slow, heavy tread.

'No, not I... I...' He was stammering with fear. He swallowed hard, trying to get a hold over himself. 'These clothes, this hair. They are nothing but a... a ruse.'

'Your lies will not save you.'

'I am not lying—'

'The Eye sees all.'

'But I am no monk.'

'Blood is the only truth. Blood...'

This last word was spoken mere inches from Skírpa's face. In a sudden rush of air, the bag was snatched from his head. For a second, his eyes couldn't focus. He sensed only gloom around him. Despite the daylight outside, in here there was precious little light. He saw only one feature, hovering before him. It was a huge unblinking eye, the pupil dilated to an astonishing size. He could see a kind of yellow rim to it, the vessels swirling from there to its black centre like a hundred tiny vipers. It was several moments before he was able to place it in a face. And such a face...

Pale as chalk dust, with cracked lines running in all directions, a nose large and hooked like an eagle, and a great gash of a mouth that gave the lower half of the face the look of a monstrous toad. And the eye had no twin. In its place was a gaping hole of darkness. Mesmerising as a whirlpool – horrifying, and yet with a weird magnetism all of its own.

335

Without warning, an enormous hand seized his chin and turned his face first one way, then the other. The hand was a marvel in itself – big as an ogre's, the grip of its fingers strong as death. 'Who gave you these scars?' asked the One Eyed.

'I did,' Skírpa hissed, a spark of defiance flaring somewhere inside him.

'You?' the creature said – for Skírpa could not think of him as anything but a creature, certainly not a man.

'It was no other. I swear it.'

Suddenly the toad mouth fell open, and some guttural sound beat at the air, pulsing foul breath into Skírpa's nostrils. It was moments before he realised the creature was laughing. 'You must have quite a story, Monk-That-Is-No-Monk.'

'I... I...' Skírpa closed his eyes, trying to give his mind a moment's respite to order his thoughts. 'My story has but one thread. The will to survive. It's all I've ever done.'

'Truly? Then perhaps you have come to your final test, Monk-That-Is-No-Monk.'

'My name is Skírpa.'

'Skír—*PA!*' Another wave of foul air engulfed his senses as the One Eyed exhaled his name. 'What kind of a man are you? Why are you here?'

Skírpa opened his mouth to respond, though he had no clear idea what he meant to say.

'No! Do not speak.' The great yellow-rimmed eye peered closer at him. 'The Eye sees you. *He* will tell me all I must know.'

Before Skírpa could make any sense of this, the two enormous hands seized his head. Between them they enclosed it as though it were no bigger than an egg. They squeezed, and the whole of his world became a red fog of pain. The hands crushed harder and harder, the pressure in his skull building, so that even through the agony, his mind was seized with the horrible image of his entire head imploding like a duck egg in the hands of a clumsy child.

He experienced heat, saw bright scarlet lights, heard a weird chittering sound coming from his tormentor's mouth, like the clacking of teeth, and then a sudden high-pitched ululation from the One Eyed's throat. He couldn't see. His eyes were screwed tight shut, but now he could hear the stream of strange words spilling over those hideous lips. As if the One Eyed were summoning some spirit. The unseen summoned to the seen. It was a long, long time since Skírpa had witnessed anything like it.

'WOTAN!' the One Eyed suddenly bellowed, the word exploding with a percussive blast in Skírpa's senses. 'WOTAN! See this one! See him – and *SPEAK!*'

Skírpa's whole body was shaken like prey in the jaws of a wolf. His skull could surely not endure much more, but strangely, racing through his mind, came all kinds of other memories long buried. Of things the shaman had taught him which he had forgotten years, no, decades before. The spells and utterances and *galdr*-song of the Other Folk that he had once known. He remembered curses he had placed on the vile ones who had mistreated him after he had escaped the shaman's clutches. The tricks he had played on other children for spite. And many, many details of his childhood came flooding back to him in a deluge of sound and image.

Then, just as suddenly, it all stopped. His mind was still. And he was back in that small, spotless chamber, the stone

337

pavings swept clean, the walls painted white as fresh snow, the small cauldron of water spitting and babbling over the fire-hearth. Those implements laid out on cloths of pristine linen, each one sharp as a razor. Gleaming with menace despite the sympathetic smile on the physician's face. Dread bubbling like bile in his stomach. And then the feeling of that burning, burning heat between his legs, the scream emptying his lungs, his body writhing, rinsed with pain; his soul dying, drowning in shame.

Suddenly the One Eyed let out a bellow of triumph. The pressure in Skírpa's skull vanished and he was lifted onto his feet. Those enormous hands seized the collar of his monk's habit and, in one swift movement, the robe was torn from collar to hem. He stood broken, naked, before this strange creature. This man. This one-eyed man who was laughing at him. Seeing him, seeing his shame, and laughing and laughing.

At length, Skírpa became aware that the room had returned to silence. Then a gruff voice ordered him to open his eyes. But the voice no longer carried that weird chitter of before.

Skírpa opened his eyes, hardly daring to behold what they revealed. His head felt big as a watermelon. Before him was a man, broad of shoulder, a great barrel chest and thick powerful arms. But he was not tall, perhaps a couple of inches shorter than Skírpa himself, yet somehow with five times the presence of any normal man.

The solitary pale eye blinked. 'Wotan has shown me who you are,' the One Eyed said. 'Wotan has shown me what you can do.' Here, he struck himself hard upon the chest. 'I am

Alvarik. Seer of Wotan. Master of the Moon.' Skírpa was suddenly conscious that he was naked. He clutched the wreckage of his robe around him but the seer snatched his wrist with a powerful hand. 'There's no shame among us, friend. Wotan has shown me. Come.' And before Skírpa could respond, this strange square man had stepped forward and put his long arms around him, holding Skírpa in an awkward embrace. In his confusion, it took some moments for Skírpa to realise he was being comforted, that gigantic hand now stroking his filthy hair like he was a lovelorn maid. 'I have seen how you have suffered. Don't be afraid. You will suffer no more.' Skírpa felt tears rise, stinging his eyes as he sank deeper into the embrace. 'We have a place for you here, Skírpa... A very special place.'

A full moon was shining through the trees, streaks of moonlight cutting through the branches like silver lances launched from the heavens. Darkness and light. Tumbling over each other till he could almost not tell one from the other.

He stood high above a sea of upturned faces, the crowns of white-blond hair like the crests of breaking waves. They were looking at him only because he stood behind the four figures positioned further forward. Three women, who represented the Norns, that much he had gathered – Urthr, an old crone: *What Was*; Verthandi, an expectant mother, her robe stretched around her distended belly, there for all to see: *What Is*; and Skuld, a young girl, hardly reached the age of womanhood: *What Will Be*.

And before them, Alvarik – the One Eyed, the Master of the Moon – an enormous head-dress capped with two long goat-horns on his square head.

Skírpa did not pretend to understand what was happening. He had made his resolution. He would do whatever was demanded of him. He would bide his time. He would stay alive.

Alvarik had given him a new robe, a cloak made entirely of raven feathers. He twisted his neck slowly, still adjusting to the weight of the head-dress. It had antlers attached, making it hard to balance. He held antlers in his hands, too. Alvarik had put them there, but to what purpose, Skírpa could not say. More raven feathers hung off the head-dress, down over his brow, nearly covering his eyes, a strange filter for everything he was seeing.

He felt the presence of the great tree behind him, conscious of it as he might be of a prowling lion. But he dared not look around at it, nor at the small bodies still hanging there or the bloodied runes carved into its bark. Yet he could feel its spreading branches reaching out over his head like the claws of a tiger. Or something far worse.

Wait for my word. That had been Alvarik's sole instruction.

Wait. Hadn't he been doing that his whole life? Waiting for that supreme moment when it would all make sense. Maybe this was it, here and now. Or maybe it had passed him by and still he knew no better. Or maybe – and this he feared to be the truth – there was no coming moment. There was no meaning. There was only this.

It started with a faraway sound. If there had been a breath of wind, it would have smothered it. A low humming, very deep, but too soft to call a growl. It was several moments before Skírpa realised its source. The humming came from the throats of the wolf-warriors spread below them. There had been no signal that he had discerned. Only a collective sense that now was the time. And so it had begun.

A hundred voices humming like the first word of creation. And then, above them, Alvarik raised a goat's horn to his lips and blew. The notes he made were mournful, moving over one another slowly, tentative, patient. Pitched low at first, but rising higher, drawing the hum of the onlooking crowd with them, until the voices of the three women swooped in above it all, each moving around the others, like the strands of fate which the Norns wove to forge the lives of men.

Their music was enthralling, as it had been then. He felt himself falling under its spell in a way he never had in the great basilicas of Byzantium. A peace seemed to settle over him, a kind of harmony with all that was around him. The trees, the earth, the beasts of the forest. Even these strange folk under whose sway he had fallen. The wind, the sky, the moon. All of it seemed beautiful to him for one sublime and piercing moment.

Then Alvarik let the horn fall to its sling at his side. He lifted up his massive hands, and with them his great booming voice:

'See here, O Wotan!' he cried. '*Aldagautr! Báleygr! Ancient One! Lord of the Earth!* Gaze on us with the flaming light of your eye!'

It seemed as though this were some kind of signal. Because opposite from where they stood – beyond the gathered crowd – the monstrous black triangle suddenly lit up. At least the pinnacle of it did. A beacon flame. The effect was remarkable. And now he saw the purpose of the thing: the summit of the facade now seemed like an enormous staring eye. The light of it dancing and quavering with the flame's flicker, glaring down at the gathered company with a baleful and unforgiving gaze.

'Bring forth the offerings!' bellowed Alvarik, looking no less the daemon in his twin-horned crown.

And now, somewhere in the crowd, a drum began to beat, insistent, hypnotic. The three women were still singing but their song turned, as if their voices had come to a fork in the road and here they chose the darker path. The harmonies diverged, became discordant. Men in the crowd began to growl and hiss. And suddenly a procession of flaming torches appeared from the back of the triangle. At this, the warriors nearest them started barking and yipping. One by one they pulled masks over their faces. Most were wolf-masks, although there were some other creatures among them. Skírpa saw stag, bear and fox skulls. A menagerie of savage beasts, frozen in death. The yips became a cacophony of howls and other deranged bestial noises. And through them all came the torchlight procession. The crowd parted before it, leaping and lunging as they passed. But it continued to make its way through. The party was close to the rise on which they stood before Skírpa could see what – or who – was being led.

They looked wretched, even from there. A collection of nine or ten heads; at first he could not tell exactly their number. But immediately he could see the youthfulness of them all. Boys and girls, young women. The oldest must have been, well… perhaps a woman of thirty summers. She was

342

the exception, in fact. Her hair already marked her as something different. If the flame light did not lie, her tresses were red as vermillion. A bright scarlet colour which Skírpa had only ever seen among the highest patrician courtiers in the emperor's palace, or else the lowest whores in the city. How strange, he thought, to see it here, in this place.

She was beautiful, too, and, unlike the others, her face was calm. Serene. Christ's blood, she looked almost saintly. The others needed shoving forward and up onto the rise. Not she. She walked with graceful dignity, looking neither to the left nor the right. He noticed her lips were moving but silently. Speaking to herself – or else her Maker.

Aye. Whoever that was would need to hear her now.

The drum was beating faster. Alvarik stepped forward to the great slab of rock – or altar, for it was clear now that that was its purpose. The music was filling Skírpa's head – or was it the dread of what was to come? No, he realised, it was something worse than that. It was anticipation. He actually *wanted* to see what would happen now. He could feel the ancient power swirling like a dark mist through the crowd, spilling down from the all-seeing eye, exhaled with the women's song, rising up with the terrible hands of Alvarik.

'Blood is the only truth!' the One Eyed cried as the scarlet-haired woman was laid down upon the altar. Several of the corralled children screamed. 'Blood is the only power! Shine forth your light on us, great Wotan!' he declared to the burning eye. 'Your light that is darkness made visible!'

With no more warning, he turned and beckoned Skírpa. 'Come,' he said, his voice a soft growl for only his ears. 'Now is your time.'

343

Without thinking, or perhaps not daring to resist, Skírpa felt himself step forward. And suddenly all was like a dream, like he floated outside of himself. He looked down at his hand and found in it a long knife, wicked-sharp, glinting in the moonlight. He could not remember taking hold of it. His mind was a flood, overwhelmed with the smell of the raven feathers, the shrieking song of the women, the whimpers of the children, the pulsing rhythm of the drums, the muttering of the red-haired woman, while his heart filled with rage and bitter resentment. All the manifold ills that had been visited on him, all the wrongs ever done to him, would now be settled. All would be paid for.

The pale light of the moon fell across the woman's restless lips, while they whispered over and over: 'Receive me, O my Lord, receive me, a sinner.' Her eyes were closed.

A small corner of his mind thought: *how strange she speaks in Greek.* But mostly he heard nothing but Alvarik's raw bellow, ringing through his skull: 'Blood is our only truth, Wotan! We offer it to thee!' He turned to Skírpa. 'Now, boy,' he rasped. 'Do it now!'

Skírpa raised the knife high, feeling the Eye's power surging through him like a wild wolf in his veins. Then he brought it flashing down.

The first blow took all his will and all his strength.

The second, though, was easy.

CHAPTER TWENTY-EIGHT

Erlan's pride was still smarting. Not only his pride. Lilla's denial of him was a wound that had cut him deep; her explanation afterwards had only riled him all the more. Her aim had been to protect him, she said. But he could not see how it would have made any difference; they had been in the hands of this warlord, Karil Martel, anyhow. Life or death was already his to deal as he saw fit. But, she argued, it gave them options, means of persuasion.

Means of persuasion. Hah!

She didn't spell it out; she didn't have to. Erlan knew she must be thinking of the man's obvious interest in her. The weaker part of him feared the feeling was mutual, and her convoluted explanations only seemed to confirm that notion. He couldn't help but think back to the deal she had made with herself in Byzantium: his freedom for her virtue. A selfless act. Yet it still burned him to his core, the idea of Arbasdos enjoying her. Or worse, her enjoying him.

Then again, who was he to judge? A damned hypocrite if he did.

Well, the Norns would have to keep Lilla for now, and the dark slitherings of jealousy in his heart. She was a 'guest' of Karil Martel – which meant his prisoner. And gods only knew what would happen when they returned. *If they returned.* In any case, it sounded like this Frankish lord had plenty of troubles of his own. And as to how safe Lilla would be in the meantime, no man could be certain.

Erlan and his companions had been on the road for a couple of days now. Einar Fat-Belly was not proving much company, it had to be said. His usually jovial nature was gone, driven out by a morose and dark mood which had settled on him and saw no sign of shifting, no matter how much Erlan tried to raise his spirits. Mikkel Crow, Bull, Ran, Black Svali... All of them had assembled their gear without much complaint, glad to be free of Childebrand and his Frankish spear-men. But once clear of Durum, and confident that their destiny was once more in their own hands, the Estlanders' griping soon took up again, steady as the rain which kept up for hours on end as they headed east.

By the Hanged, it was sour company, and no mistake – enough to sink a man's will into his boots. The only source of any kind of cheer was from the monk, Wynfred, who must have been older even than Einar. Yet he seemed hardy and uncomplaining for all that, impervious to fatigue, the cold or the wet. And though he was no warrior, he sat well astride his horse. It was he who led them, since he had the clearest notion of where their hunt should begin.

346

Bonnborg, he said. That was where he had left the Rhein river to seek audience with Karil Martel. Unfortunately for him, six men of the north was all the succour he had won. But he seemed content enough. 'Do not despise the day of small beginnings,' he'd said with a knowing smile at Erlan, soon after they had set out. 'For the Lord delights to see the work begin.'

'Maybe he does. As for me, I'll delight to see it ended,' was Erlan's terse reply.

They had left Demetrios with Lilla. With his arse sliced up the way it was, he'd be more use to her than to their own enterprise. And though they were short on numbers, Erlan wasn't disheartened by the men he had left to him. Though he would have to keep an eye on Einar. Erlan sensed he was like to do something unexpected. Not to say, drastic. Aye, he would watch Einar closely.

Bonnborg proved to be a day and a half's ride from Durum, and that along a half-decent road. It was a stronghold of some antiquity, Wyn explained, enclosed with walls of black stone that were well maintained, punctuated by great round towers and strong gateways that seemed older even than the great fortifications of Byzantium. The fort was smothered in sheets of rain when they arrived, which didn't let up a whit the whole night they rested.

While the men found shelter in a stable yard and settled themselves in for a damp night, Wynfred took Erlan down to the riverbank where they began their enquiries. Erlan was impressed with the monk. Wyn seemed adept at striking up a rapport with total strangers and was scared of no man. Tanners, smiths, bailiffs, merchants. He had turned them all inside out for information within a few short minutes of talk. His fire for the cause still burned hot, that was clear. And either the Norns or else Wyn's god must have been smiling on them that night, for they left the riverside with something to their profit.

A trader of wool had heard tell of an incident further upriver. Some sort of attack that had left a number of folk who were known up and down the trading places of the Rhein missing. Then a cargo barge had been found with all kinds of stinking bodies rotting on it. None knew who was responsible as they'd been dead some time. But the wool-trader had also heard of some unknown 'hooded' men seeking out children, in particular, at the slave market in a town called Two-Rivers. 'Couldn't swear whether them fellows had silver hair, like you're looking for, but...' The trader shrugged. 'Hooded men?' He shrugged again. 'I don't know – if they didn't want to be marked as all having the same hair... Guess folks would remember a thing like that, eh? Either way, that's the closest I know to what you're asking.'

'You've been very helpful,' said Wyn, thanking the man and offering him a coin for his trouble.

'Keep your coin, monk,' said the trader, pushing his hand away. 'I'll take your prayers instead, if you like. Can't see much help in what I've told you myself, but still.'

As they walked back to the stables where they had left the others, Erlan could already anticipate Einar's frustration at the vagueness of what they'd found out. He was acutely aware that they seemed to be heading away from where Orīana and Marta had been taken. And still with no clear trail or scent.

'What d'you make of it?' he asked Wyn as they trudged through the sludge back to their comrades, their own hoods pulled deep over their faces against the rain.

'It makes some sense.'

'Does it?' Erlan grimaced. 'By the gods, it surely doesn't to me.'

'You forget I've been following this trail some time. I've learned to notice the signs. Imagine your wolf-warriors – or the silver-haired slavers, as I think of them – as wasps going out from a nest. They go in all directions. Some stray far. Some stay close. But all return to the nest eventually, and carrying whatever prize they have won.'

'Hmm. Doesn't feel like we're any closer to finding a nest.'

'I disagree. It must be upstream. Upriver. That much is clear to me. Whether your friends have been taken that way...' Wyn stopped, turned to Erlan. Under his hood, his face was all shadow, except for a broadening smile. 'The Lord is guiding our path. I believe it.'

'Well, wherever we're going, I wish your lord would get us there quicker. And more directly.'

'That is always the way it feels, my friend. But take heart. We must only have faith.'

'So all you holy men are fond of telling me.' Erlan hawked and spat into the mud. Truth was, he wanted to have something more substantial than mere faith to give Einar. 'Just tell me where we go next.'

'South to Two-Rivers, of course. The Romans called it Confluentes. I'm told it stands where the Mosella joins the Rhein. There, we will find more answers.'

'How can you be sure of it?'

'How can you doubt it?' Wyn smiled. 'I prayed for help and – lo! – here you are. Now I pray for guidance, I know the Lord will not fail us.'

Mad men, these monks, thought Erlan. *Every one of them.* And yet he found himself strangely encouraged that Wyn was with them.

He had more trouble convincing the others.

They found them huddled around a wretched little brazier in one corner of the yard where they had paid for lodging, of a sort. The thing was belching out far more smoke than heat from the charcoal inside it. Between them, they had scrounged a few soggy heels of bread, hunks of hard cheese, and half a dozen eggs which the stable maid had given them for nothing. If she felt sorry for them, it was no surprise. They looked a miserable crew to a man.

'Well?' growled Mikki Crow. 'Got anything to tell us?'

When Wyn explained what they had found out, there was little in the way of celebration. Just dark scowls, mutterings and curses. And silence from Einar.

'Fucking rain,' snarled Mikki. 'We'd ha' done better to stay in Chalcedon.'

'Aye, but you were no happier there, were you, Croaker?' said Bull.

'Hm.' Mikki Crow pulled his cloak further over his bony shoulders. 'Least it were fucking warm.'

'It's a sorry show, that's for damn sure,' said Ran, settling back in a small clump of damp hay he had commandeered for the night. 'But there ain't nought to do but get some rest.'

'That's your answer to everything,' gnarred Black Svali.

'Well,' Ran chuckled. 'It ain't failed me yet.' And he shut his eyes.

'He's right, though,' said Erlan, crouched down beside the brazier, trying in vain to warm his calloused hands. 'We've a long ride tomorrow.' He nodded at Wyn, who had taken himself off to pray, which he did each night. For once, Erlan hoped someone was listening. 'Up river, so the man said.'

'How long?' asked Svali.

'It's another day and a half to Two-Rivers, according to the trader fella. But he said the going was good. We follow some old military road beside the river. All being well, we'll reach there noon on Thor's Day—'

'We'll get there tomorrow night. We rise before dawn. We don't stop. No fucking complaining.' The voice was Einar's, rough as rust, but his eyes glinted in the gloom, sharp as steel. It was the first he had spoken all day. No one contradicted him. No one dared.

Erlan reached out and patted him on the shoulder. 'You heard the fat man. No delays. If we are going to find them, it has to be soon.'

After that, they all settled in for whatever sleep they could eek out of the night, despite the cold and the damp. Erlan made a place for himself next to Einar. He was worried about him. But as he sat down, the fat man rolled over to face the wall.

'You all right, old friend?' Erlan murmured.

The only reply was a gruff 'hoom' in his throat under the sound of the rain.

Erlan wanted to say something encouraging. Something hopeful. 'Reckon that once we're—'

Einar suddenly spun over to face him. 'Ah, what do you fucking reckon, Aurvandil? Gods, I should have run you off into the street, the moment I saw your face by my bed.'

'I know you're upset—'

'No, you don't know shit, Aurvandil,' he hissed under his breath so only Erlan could hear. 'And you don't know me. Not anymore. We do this together. We get it done. And then we're through. Understand? You and your woman – you're poison. Now... let me sleep.'

Erlan sank away from him. For a long while, he lay there staring up at the leaky thatch, sleep eluding him. By the Hanged, the stitching of all this was coming apart and no mistake. The weight of the burden he was carrying rode sore on his back. *This is the price of persuasion*, he told himself. *After that, anything that goes wrong is your fault.*

It had all unfolded so fast, he'd not really asked himself what he thought about what they were doing. Was it all just chasing after shadows? What chance did they stand with their little crew of bickering misfits anyway? And without Einar in step with him?

He couldn't blame the man for how he felt. He could only rely on the fact that their friendship stood on solid ground. Or rather hope that it did. Folk said many things in anger, felt many things in despair. But Erlan was determined to do all he could to get Oriana back. And Marta...

He thought back to the strangeness of their last encounter. The gall of her, right there. But whatever notion she'd got into her head, whatever trouble it was likely to cause him, in the end she was just a young girl who didn't deserve whatever fate those *ulfheðnar* had in mind for her. He must find her too.

His eyes closed, his weary mind drifting off into the oblivion of sleep. But not before some devil in him had recalled the feel of Marta's hand around his cock. He turned over, forcing his mind back to rest, focusing on the drip of the rain and the soft snores of his companions. And soon he was asleep.

Of the gold, he had not given a single thought.

They reached Two-Rivers just before nightfall the next day without incident. They had ridden hard, with little rest, and their mounts were grateful when they slowed within sight of the settlement. The rain had moved away to the south-west, and a north-easterly wind had at least dried them off, even if it brought the cold with it. The old town of Two-Rivers lay on the far bank of the Mosella river, on a flood plain between two high ranges of hills, and fitting snugly into a point of land, sharp as a spear-tip, where the two rivers met. They crossed with their horses on a broad barge that ferried travellers coming and going from the town across the river.

'Are we on the edge of the Frankish territory?' Erlan asked Wyn.

'No, no. I think we're deep in its old heartland,' replied Wyn. He chuckled. 'Although, of course, I've never been here myself.'

'He's right,' said the ferryman, pointing up the Mosella. 'Follow this far enough and you reach Mettis. That's the seat of King Chilperic.' He spat over the gunwale. 'One of 'em, anyway. Sometimes he comes here. Though how long he'll be king, these days few can tell.'

'How far to Mettis?' asked Erlan.

The ferryman shrugged. 'Dunno. Can't say as I've been there myself.'

'We may find sharper counsel in the city,' muttered Wyn, for Erlan's hearing only. 'Do you know of any taverns in Two-Rivers that would welcome travellers such as we?' he asked the ferryman.

The man looked them up and down, his bovine gaze lingering a while on the weaponry they carried. 'Try the inn under the sign of the dove. Ask anyone, they'll know it.'

'A dove for peace,' said Wyn. 'A good sign indeed.' Though Erlan had his doubts.

The walls of Two-Rivers were not as imposing as those of Bonnborg. They were made of wood and earth instead of black stone, although rising from the heart of the town was a building that might have passed for a palace. Or at least a hall worthy of a royal visit. But having no wish to encounter whichever authority held sway over the town, they entered discreetly, splitting into smaller groups, and leading their mounts through the gate and past the guards without more than a cursory inspection.

They re-assembled in the central market square and, with the help of a local fletcher, soon located the inn the ferryman had recommended. By now, evening had become cloudless night. The moon was on the wane but still gave off enough light to make out the white shape of a dove blazoned on the sign hanging over the door.

Wyn went in ahead of the others, telling them to wait outside. Erlan was coming to realise how useful it was to have a monk in their company. Folk seemed to trust him, and by extension them. That suited Erlan. Though they had not quite the look of a band of warriors, they were at least strangers and carried arms. The less attention they drew to themselves, the better.

Wyn re-appeared a short while later, having agreed with the inn-keeper that they could keep their horses at the back of his property for the night. And once their mounts were settled there, they all crowded into the warmth of the inn's main parlour, where a hearth fire burned brightly and a dozen or so patrons sat drinking in a hubbub of talk. The smell of boiled pork and stale beer was pleasantly familiar to Erlan after the spiced wineshops and skewers of braised meat of Byzantium. A smell of the north, and one he'd missed.

'Split up,' he told the others. 'And Bull, Mikki, we want no trouble,' he added.

'Don't you trust us yet, skipper,' grinned Bull. While Mikki just scowled and went to find an empty place on the long table that dominated the room. Perhaps pointedly, Einar went with him while Svali, Ran and Bull made their way to a smaller side table and immediately called over the serving wench.

'Well?' said Wyn. 'Shall we begin our enquiries?'

It took some time, some ale, and a fair amount of the coin which Karil Martel had given Wyn in lieu of his aid, to make any kind of headway. There were several dead-end conversations. A few had heard of the attack on the barge upriver but none had any more details than the wool-trader had already told them in Bonnborg. Erlan listened while Wyn talked, his ears on what was said but his eyes on the others in his crew. Bull seemed to have taken a fancy to their serving wench, who was at least willing to entertain his less than subtle advances while Ran laughed at him, Black Svali scowling in the background. Meanwhile, Mikki and Einar had struck up conversation with some others at the long table and joined in some game they were playing. Looked similar to *tafl* from where Erlan sat, but with a different kind of board.

'What about missing children?' asked Wyn of their current interlocutor, a grain merchant from Swabia in the south. 'Or child slaves?'

'Oh, I wouldn't know anything about that. I'm only here twice in the year. I hear stories from the river, but not of this place so much. Have you asked old Besso there?'

'Besso?'

'The inn-keeper.'

'Well, no,' admitted Wyn. 'Not yet.'

'Try him. Ain't no story comes to Two-Rivers that he hasn't told a dozen times himself.'

Turned out Besso was more than willing to talk, now that most of his patrons had taken themselves home. When Wyn put his usual questions to the man, it was the detail of the wolf-warriors that he picked up on first.

'Men dressed as wolves, you say.' Besso took a pull on his own ale cup and wiped his mouth. 'Aye, I could tell you stories enough of them to keep us here till Christ's Mass. But they all of them end badly.'

'Be specific,' said Erlan.

'Well... it's almost like folklore round here,' he said, propping his elbows on the counter. 'Wolves in human form. "Man-wolves", some folk call them. They only appear under a waxing moon. Terrible killings, mostly. Bad business.'

'That attack upriver, for example?'

'Mmm, I did hear about that. But no, I couldn't say. No one survived to tell what happened or who done it, as I understand.'

'Other stories then,' asked Wyn.

'We're looking for their stronghold... Where they come from,' said Erlan. 'Tell us anything that might help us find it.'

Besso gave him a look like he'd lost his wits for a moment, then blew out his cheeks. 'Well, there was one...'

'Go on.'

'This was a year past. No, nearly two. A girl walked out of the Immerwald.'

'The Immerwald?'

'It's the ancient forest that spreads to the west of here.' Besso waved his hand vaguely as if the detail was not so important. 'It's vast. Anyway, this kid was in a terrible way. Half-starved, bloodied and bruised. Had a kind of haunted look, they say.'

'What had she seen?' asked Wyn.

'Well, that was the thing, no one could get a word out of her. Lost her voice. No, not her voice, lost her will to speak,' he corrected himself. 'Except during the night when she would sleep... but she'd have such nightmares. Shrieks and mutterings was all she'd utter. I had one in here who had heard her hisself.'

'What did she say,' asked Wyn, 'during these nightmares?'

'It was nonsense, mostly. About a gigantic eye in the forest. Dwarves and wood sprites and howling wolves – that's what made me think of it. Oh, and a tree. Big bloody thing, by the sounds. Seemed like she was scared of that most of all.' Besso took another swig of his beer. 'Poor kid. Probably lost her wits from the fright she took.'

'Where is she now?' said Erlan. 'Can we see her?'

'Not possible. She died of a fever last winter. Her mother buried her at the shrine of Saint Castor outside the town walls.'

'Who told you all this?'

'It was the trapper who found her out in the woods. Not knowing what to do with her, he brought her into town. The bailiffs put the word out and eventually found the girl's mother.'

'Where can we find him, this trapper?'

'He lives up the Mosella valley. About five miles south-west of here on the northern bank. He keeps to himself. Lives alone. But you can usually spy the smoke from his cabin up in the hills. Can't tell you more 'n that.'

'What's his name?' asked Wyn.

'Berengar.'

Erlan and Wyn exchanged glances. 'And you've seen no slave-traders pass through here with chattels in tow? Or up either river?' said Wyn.

'Or a woman with red hair?' cut in Erlan.

'Well, red hair,' said Besso with a shrug. 'You do see women with it now and then—'

'No, I mean, bright red, crimson-coloured hair. Like blood.'

Besso frowned. 'No... no one like that.'

Erlan rubbed his eyes in frustration. This felt like those boar hunts back home that dragged you leagues and leagues through forest and fen, and never a glimpse of a boar hide or anything else.

Suddenly there was a yell behind him. He turned to see Mikki Crow on his feet, reaching across the table, the scruff of his opponent's tunic bunched in his fist. 'That's right, I'm calling you a fucking cheat, my friend!'

And before Erlan could open his mouth to stop him, Mikki had rammed a fist in the other man's face. An instant later, several bodies were sprawled across the long table in various states of struggle, sending cups and pitchers and gaming pieces in all directions. The soupy air of the inn reverberated with the thud of fists, the clatter of tableware and the strangled grinding and gurning of angry men.

'Oh, Hel,' muttered Erlan, knowing it would only be another few moments before someone drew a blade. This was exactly what he didn't need. 'Here,' he said to Wyn, 'hold my ale, would you?'

Erlan waded in. In a glance, he saw Mikki and his opponent were more or less evenly matched. Mikki's lip was split and bleeding messily all over the other as he did his best to strangle the life out of him on the tabletop. In a couple of swift movements, Erlan crossed to them, seized Mikki by the back of the collar and swung him off the other man towards Bull and the others.

'Get a hold of that fool and don't let him go!' he snarled at Bull, who dutifully obliged, putting Mikki in a headlock before he could get to his feet.

Erlan turned back. The other man was squaring up to Erlan now, like he was ready to continue the fight. But Erlan just shoved him backwards, sending him flat on his arse on the bench. 'Back off!'

Meanwhile, Einar was beating merry Hel out of the other player. He had him on the floor, his great bulk standing over him, stamping on his head again and again.

'That's enough.'

But Einar continued heedless. The man's face was a bloody mess already. A couple more blows from Einar's boot and he wouldn't be getting back up again. 'I said, enough!' Erlan grabbed Einar's arm and yanked him away from the juddering wretch on the floor. At his touch, Einar spun round and seized Erlan by the throat, his fist drawn back ready to strike. Erlan could already see blood dripping off his knuckles, the mad glaring rage in his eyes.

'Easy, big man. Easy…' He held up his palms. 'It's me.'

But instead of releasing him, Einar's fist squeezed his throat a little tighter. 'I know it's you, lad. Don't I fucking know it's you.'

For a long moment, neither moved. Erlan gazed at the scarred features of his friend, the brow creased in anger, that weird twist of flesh pulling at the corner of his mouth. Of the old Einar Fat-Belly, Erlan could see almost nothing.

'We have a lead,' he hissed through his constricted throat.

'Huh,' grunted Einar at last. Slowly his grip loosened, the great slab of his fist uncurled, and he patted Erlan's cheek. 'We best get on with it then, eh?'

They left Two-Rivers before dawn, having handed over most of the rest of their coin as a kind of wergeld for the beaten man and his friends, at Wyn's insistence.

'Intemperance is an unhelpful sin,' was his verdict as they rode south-west along the left bank of the Mosella that morning, the mist lingering on the surface of the water long beyond the break of day. 'In drink, in gambling, in women... All the pathways of sin lead to death. Sooner or later.'

'Tried them all, have you, monk?' asked Erlan, feeling more cynical than usual.

But Wyn seemed unperturbed. 'Hah! I must be twice your age but maybe with half your experience in some of those. None in others. Although Jesus said, whoever looks upon a woman with lust has already committed adultery with her in his heart.'

'What chance does any man stand then?'

'Oh, none at all,' said Wyn, with a light-hearted chuckle. 'But for the grace of God. For me, those were the sins of youth. These days the sins I'm tempted to are worse. Too often I seem wise in my own sight. Then there's spiritual pride, sloth, envy.'

'Envy! What could you be envious of?'

Wyn sighed, rocking back and forth with the gait of his mount, considering the question. 'A great name, I suppose. And adventure, believe it or not.' He laughed. 'Perhaps that comes from a lifetime of only reading about the deeds of great men. Of brave men.' He turned to fix Erlan with his age-worn eyes. 'You can talk about beer forever. But it's simpler just to taste it.'

'Is that why you left your home? Adventure?'

'You could say that...' He looked south, and for a moment seemed to be thinking of somewhere else, somewhere far, far beyond the river and the distant hills. 'Perhaps in part I left to be here. With you.'

'You speak of fate?'

'I call it providence. The will of God – which is wild as any wind.' He gave a rueful chuckle. 'In any case, I am here.' He nodded on to Einar, who was riding alone up ahead. 'Your friend there suffers greatly from the anger he carries.'

'He has good cause to feel it.'

'No doubt. But I think it will not help him to get what he wants. You two are close?'

'I owe Einar my life. Several times over.'

'Then you must care for him. Help him carry his burden. There is a line between wrath and righteous anger that is fine as a blade's edge. It cuts through every man's heart.' He sighed. 'The Lord knows I struggle with it every time I think of those children.'

'Einar has a right to feel angry,' Erlan said, feeling defensive on behalf of his friend. 'At fate. At me… That's why I let him blow off at me.'

Wyn nodded to himself, looked up at the ponderous grey clouds rolling low and slow overhead. 'We will all be tested, I think. But in different ways. Perhaps his anger will be his test.'

'See there, skipper!' yelled Bull suddenly, interrupting their exchange. 'There's smoke up ahead.'

Ahead of them, and a distance off to the north away from the river, a solitary skein of smoke was curling up out of the dense copper canopy of trees.

'Is there a path up that way?' Erlan called forward.

Einar didn't answer or even look back. He only pointed ahead and to the right, and soon enough turned his horse up the fork in the road.

'The inn-keeper was right then,' said Wyn. 'Who knows? Maybe he was right about everything else as well.'

362

'Aye,' growled Erlan. 'That's what worries me.'

They rode on, deeper into the woods that spread up the valley hillside towards a low and rounded ridge, following the path through beech trees mostly, their foliage already turned to an autumn rainbow of copper and gold, yellow and orange. In another week or so, all the leaves would have fallen. The place felt swollen with the recent rain, the earth soft-going for the horses, their hooves crunching the split shells of beech nuts underfoot. At last, high up the slope, the path led them to a small glade, covered in moss and the first fall of leaves. The clearing formed a crown of treetops, which surrounded a little dwelling. The place was hardly bigger than a shieling, but it was made from strong, well-cut logs, with a good turf roof. And from the odds and ends left strewn around it, it was clear the place was inhabited.

There was no longer smoke rising from its smoke-hole, but this had to be the place they had seen from the river. There were no other signs of human life up this way.

Ran hopped down off his shaggy mare and went to the door. He tapped the wood, waited, then gave it a prod. The door swung easily on its hinges. Gingerly, he stepped inside.

A few moments later, he re-appeared. 'Embers are still warm. But there ain't no one in there.'

Erlan hissed a curse. 'In that case, we wait.'

'It's not even noon,' snapped Einar with an angry snort. 'Could be all bloody day before he comes back.'

'Then we wait all day. There's nowhere else we can go, is there?'

'This whole thing stinks like fresh horse-shit.' Einar slid off his beast and stomped towards the nearest tree. 'I need a leak.'

'Einar,' Erlan called after him.

'Let him go,' said Wyn. 'His frustration is natural. I feel it too.'

'Don't we bloody all.'

He watched Einar fight his way through his buckles and drawstrings till he got himself out. The sound of his streaming urine was audible and went on and on.

'By the Thunder, Fat-Belly,' chortled Bull. 'How much did you have to drink last night?'

But the words were hardly out of the Estlander's mouth when a thrap of air cut the clearing, ending with a loud *thtock* as an arrow slammed into the trunk of Einar's beech. The tip had missed his ear by a whisker.

Instinctively, Erlan ducked. His whole body tensed, his hand moving to his hilt, as his eyes scanned back and forth to find the source of the danger.

'What in the Halls of Hel!' cursed Bull.

Heads darted in every direction, while Einar froze, his bladder draining the last of its contents into the dead leaves in a dwindling trickle.

'The next one goes through his skull,' a voice sang out. ''Less you tell me who you are and what you're doing here.' It came from behind them. Erlan pulled round the head of his mount, still scanning the woodland but seeing nothing. He swore under his breath.

'Up here,' said the voice.

Erlan lifted his gaze to the branches of a large blood-beech, whose thick trunk soon broke into dozens of smaller limbs, on up into the common foliage of the wood. For a few seconds, he still couldn't see anything until, all too abruptly, he realised he was looking straight down the shaft of an arrow and into a pair of small, hawk-like eyes.

'We seek Berengar the trapper,' said Wyn. 'Besso of Two-Rivers sent us.'

'Besso?' The voice was laced with suspicion. 'The taverner? What does that ale-sot want? And what are you to him?'

'Besso wants nothing. It is we who need your help,' replied Wyn.

'That arrow is still pointed at my eye,' muttered Erlan out of the corner of his mouth. 'D'you mind?'

'Perhaps if you came down, Berengar,' called Wyn, peering up. 'It would be easier for us to talk. We mean you no harm.'

Erlan wished he could have guaranteed it.

'I'm fine where's I am, thank you very much,' returned Berengar. 'You do your talking from there. I'm listening.'

'I'll have him out of that fucking tree quick enough,' growled Mikki Crow, slipping his hand-axe through long fingers. 'Only say the word.'

'No one move,' hissed Erlan. He suspected Berengar was a man whose aim seldom missed, and it was damned un-nerving feeling that arrow-tip trained upon his eye.

Wyn, however, paid Erlan no heed whatsoever, and instead swung off his mount and advanced towards the tree, hands spread out before him in peace. 'Besso told us of the young girl you found in the Immerwald. How you brought her into Two-Rivers.'

'If you're looking for her, she's dead, I heard.'

'Yes. So Besso told us.' Wyn crossed himself. 'But it is not her that we seek. It's whatever it was she saw.'

For a few heartbeats the branches made no reply. Then: 'Whatever that kid saw is best left well alone.'

'It was deep in the Immerwald, so we understand,' Wyn said. 'We hoped you might lead us there.'

'If you hoped that then you know nothing of Berengar son of Berulf.'

'We have coin to pay you.' Although, in truth, not very much.

'Ain't no amount of coin worth looking for that sort of trouble.'

'Why? What more do you know?'

'Aye. You of all folks should stay well clear of that kind of trouble, monk.'

Wyn shot an uncertain glance at Erlan. 'At least tell us what you know. If you have warnings, we would hear them. But nothing you say will deter us from our quest.'

'Then you're even stupider than you look,' said Berengar.

Wyn gave a wry smile. 'Sometimes the right thing to do seems also the most foolish.'

'Reckon you'd know the right of it better 'n me, monk. But right or wrong, I keep to my own business. Find I fares better that way.'

'Berengar, you know better than anyone what that girl saw,' said Erlan, finding his voice at last. 'How many more are there like her, d'you think? The ones that don't make it out?'

The branches stayed silent.

'This monk here is set on finding those children. And we

are looking for our friends. All we know is they've been taken by a band of warriors in wolf-pelts. The trail has led us here.'

Einar, losing patience, strode forward suddenly. 'Listen to me, Berengar son of Berulf. They took from me a woman with red hair,' he said. 'Long red hair, the colour of blood. And there was another girl with her. You seen anything like that in these parts?'

Again silence. This time it seemed to stretch for an age. Erlan watched the hawk-eyes glint among the branches. 'Like blood, you say,' the trapper replied at last.

Einar nodded, gazing up at the tree like he was stood before the judgement seat of God, hope and fear dancing in his eyes.

'Aye.' Berengar lowered his bow. 'That I did see.'

It still took a lot of persuasion to get Berengar out of his beech tree. And a good deal more to convince him to lead them to where he had seen a company of slavers making their way through the forest.

It sounded promising. He reckoned it was four or five days ago he'd seen them pass. 'O' course, it could have been less. These days, I find it hard to remember one day from the next.' He described hearing a kind of procession along a little-used woodland path a dozen or so miles to the west of there. He shadowed them a while, staying well clear. That was when he saw the crimson hair. But they kept moving on into the dusk and fading light, heading into a part of the forest where, Berengar said mysteriously, no man who still had command of his wits would go.

'Why not?' asked Erlan.

'You'll see,' was all he would say.

Berengar was a small man of darting, agile movements, restless in mind and body both. Physically, he looked like he'd been cut from wood. His hands were stained brown and supple, like oak carvings that had come to life; and his eyes were constantly shifting, so that when you spoke to him, it felt like his attention was more intent on the trees and the forest animals all around you, than on whatever it was you had to say. Everything he wore was made of the skin of some animal, not a stitch of wool on him.

Berengar preferred running alongside their horses to riding behind one of the men. He said he could never keep his seat on a horse anyway, and he didn't see the point since he was fit as a wolf-hound and had no trouble keeping up.

He led them west, then south-west, then south, in what felt like a sweeping arc through the forest, though it was hard to keep track of their precise bearing and the position of the sun, of which there was precious little anyway. And if Berengar had decided to drop them and simply melt away into the woods, Erlan and the others would have found themselves irretrievably lost.

'How far back to the river from here?' he asked Berengar, well on into the second day.

'A day, maybe two due south and you'd come to it. Depends how fast you move.'

'Is this what you call the Immerwald then? The Forever Forest.'

'Aye, but only the edges of it. You've seen how the beech give way to oak. The true heart of the Immerwald is all pine.

Black as the devil's soul in there.' He pointed up into the treetops. 'Sunlight can't hardly get through the canopy. Still as death, too.' He chuckled to himself, although Erlan had no idea why.

Late on the second day, they struck upon the track where Berengar said he had seen the 'red-haired woman', as he called her. 'It was only 'cause it seemed so off-kilter with the rest of the forest that I marked her,' he said. They hunted around in the undergrowth and soon found the imprints of a slow-moving wagon pressed into the earth.

'There's no road here, though,' said Wyn. 'Or even a path-way. How could they get a wagon this deep into the forest?'

'They could if they knew the woods like the back of their hand. Must have been back and forth a good few times to find a way through with something like that.'

Even Erlan, who was no tracker, could see the direction of travel. 'So we just follow then. Deeper into the forest.'

'No,' said Berengar firmly. 'I say we camp here tonight. And tomorrow I go back. I said I'd take you this far, that's what we agreed. You want to go deeper in, that's your business. But this is as far as I go.'

'Why? What are you afraid of?'

'Just exactly what I need to be. And you'd be wise to be afraid yourselves.'

'But we're on the right trail. We must be.'

'We're on a trail all right. But I'd wager all I owned you're not going to like what's waiting for you at the end of it.'

They set up camp there, dividing up between them the tasks of cooking, gathering wood, and rigging up some perfunctory shelter for the night.

It was not quite dark when Einar came up to Erlan while he was trimming branches off brushwood to ready it for the fire. 'I found something,' he said.

'What?'

'I'll show you.'

Erlan followed Einar through the trees, feeling strangely relieved that the fat man was still at least willing to approach him, whatever it was about. Einar led him about fifty paces from the camp, then stopped. Erlan saw why, catching the glimmer of white among the shadows even before Einar had pointed it out. 'There.'

'What is it?'

'Looks like a goat to me.' Clearly it was a skull, with two large, thick horns – dark, almost black in the gloom – rising sharply out of the long-blanched face, curling twice before reaching their tip.

'Or else a ram,' suggested Erlan. 'What's it doing all the way out here?' He went closer and examined it. The thing was nailed to the trunk of an oak tree. From below, the empty slits of its eye sockets felt like they were peering down at him. There was something chilling about it, almost sinister. But he shook it off. It wasn't as though he'd not seen every kind of animal skull adorning all manner of ritual places and halls in the north.

'There's more.' Einar led onward, and within a dozen paces they came to another. This time, a different creature. 'That's a fox.'

On and further on, one after another, until Erlan had counted eight in all. Some were creatures of the forest: fox and wolf, even a bear; others were stranger, alien to this place: goat, horse, ram, dog. It was clear they were arranged in a line, maybe in a particular order. But as to their significance, Erlan could only speculate. 'That's the last of them, there.' Einar had stopped some way short of it and merely pointed ahead. 'The ninth.'

Erlan went past him, seeing it was more compact than the others, with a rounder shape to it. A moment later he realised it was a human skull. A small one. Very small. Perhaps even the skull of an infant. One of the eye sockets had been broken, smashed and expanded, so that it looked absurdly large in the skull. The whole face – or the remains of it – dominated by one eye. As he looked at it, he felt an uncanny draw into the well of darkness at its centre, until for a moment it felt like his whole will was being sucked out of him and down into the black heart of it.

He shook himself free of the *urðr* of it and turned away. He was surprised to see Berengar standing there, immediately behind Einar. 'You'll see stranger doings than that if you go on beyond here. Darker things than you'd wish on your enemy in his worst nightmares.'

'We have to go on. We have no choice.'

'Yep. I thought you'd say that.'

'What do they mean?' asked Einar.

'Could be a warning,' said Berengar. 'Though most likely whoever put 'em up there don't give a stoat's turd whether someone enters their domain or not. They hold all the power there. Ain't no one can challenge that. No one who would dare.' Berengar crossed himself, although till then he'd not seemed a superstitious man.

A twig snapped behind them. Erlan turned, and there was

Wyn looking past them all, staring at the human skull. 'What you'll find beyond here is evil. No other word for it,' said Berengar. 'Take it from one who knows these woods. It's surely no place for a monk. No place for a man of God.'

'You're wrong, my friend,' said Wyn. 'The man of God belongs in any place where evil means to prosper.' And after a moment, he clapped his hands. 'Now then, you all must be hungry, and our supper is getting cold.'

CHAPTER TWENTY-NINE

After the sunlit chambers and sweltering heat of Byzantium, the tumbledown hall of Durum seemed damp, dark and cold. It might have reminded Lilla of her homeland halls, but she had done her best to blot those from her mind. It was too painful to think of them. They had been close. *So close...* and now everything she had hoped for, everything she had planned, everything she had hardened herself to, seemed scattered to the winds.

Instead, she was here in this draughty pile of stones, once more at the behest of a foreign lord. Albeit one whose company was not unpleasant, she had to admit.

The room was far too big for the hearth fire the servants had lit, and whatever warmth it had to offer failed even to penetrate her cloak, let alone bring any comfort to her bones. Outside it was raining, a fact all too obvious from the many droplets finding their way through the tiles and rafters to fall to the floor. The place stank of mouldering rushes still lain out when they should have been cleared away days ago.

Were she the mistress of this place, she would have some sharp words for the household stewards.

'Are you quite comfortable?' asked her host.

'Oh, quite,' she lied.

Karil Martel watched her, his luminous eyes making their own judgement for a moment, then he threw back his head and laughed. 'You're right. It is a miserable place. Freezing cold and prey to every gust of wind that blows through here.' He cast his gaze up at the leaking ceiling. 'Durum never was anything but depressing. But at present it is all I have available to me. And my men.' The servants started to bring in the supper on a train of platters. 'Ah, excellent! The food at least is good. And the wine.'

Lilla waited patiently for the servants to furnish the table with assorted cuts of meat and trays of vegetables, dishes that served as another painful reminder that she wasn't far from home. Karil charged her cup.

'To your stay with us.' He raised his own chalice to hers. 'May it be as comfortable as we can make it.'

'To my captivity, you mean.'

'I hope it will not feel as such.'

'However it feels, that's the truth of it.'

'I'll do my best to help you forget the truth and enjoy the more pleasant lie that you are indeed my guest, and I, your host.'

'But you will not be here yourself.'

'No.' He set down his cup. 'Alas, I must face my own realities.'

'Do you have the men for it?'

'Hah! Another painful truth,' he admitted, with a rueful

374

smile. 'No, I do not. I do have the cunning for it, however, and by God I'll need it. As well as all the luck He will grant me.'

'Which of your enemies do you fear the most?'

'I *fear* none of them,' he said, toying with the stem of his chalice. 'The one I respect most, though, is Rathbod.'

'The Frisian king?'

'Indeed. His men are "fearful", if you like.' His eyes flicked up at hers. 'Of the three I face, he is the most dangerous, I think.'

'Why?'

'Plectrude is too protective of her gold, which, to be fair to her, is the sole source of any power she holds.' Lilla was determined to keep pace. Plectrude was his stepmother, to the best of her recollection. 'She believes she can hole herself up in Koln while the rest of us bleed each other white.'

'And the Frankish king? Chilperic, isn't it?'

'His army is strong. Probably the largest in number. But he is not as ruthless as Rathbod – and his mayor, Ragenfrid, has more the malice of a weasel than the cunning of a snake. No, Rathbod is the man you don't turn your back on.'

Lilla nodded carefully. 'My father loved to live by little sayings he devised for himself.' She smiled to herself at the memory. 'Gods, he made so many! He used to say, if it's a man's task for the day to swallow a toad, he'd best do it before breakfast.'

Karil laughed freely at that. 'And if it's to swallow two toads?'

She smiled at him now. 'Then let him eat the uglier first.'

'I see. So you think I should ride north then? To face Rathbod, and afterwards the others.'

'No.' She sipped her wine. 'That's what you think.'

'Mmm.' He scraped thoughtfully at his chin. 'Perhaps you are a queen, after all. Please, for God's sake, eat something! I should hate for your food to go cold. Like everything else in this damned place.'

Obliging him, Lilla took a large mouthful of the roasted fowl which still lay untouched before her, only then realising how famished she was. And truly it was delicious, warm and succulent and tender, nearly drowning in gravy. In her hurry to fill her mouth, some of the sauce spilled inelegantly down her chin. Before she could get to it with her napkin, Karil had reached out and caught it gently on his fingertip, sweeping it away. It was an astonishingly intimate gesture. She should have been affronted. But she said nothing, instead watching the muscles in his jaw work as he ground down his own mouthful of meat. She never would have admitted it, but there was something extraordinarily pleasurable about watching him eat.

'Why do they wish to crush you so completely?' she said, to distract herself from her thoughts. 'Have you done them so wrong?'

'Would you really have me bore you with this?' Amusement danced in his eyes. 'There are far more pleasant subjects for us to pass the time.'

'I insist. I want to know.'

'Very well. It is a sorry tale that reflects well on no one. Perhaps least of all me.' And so, over several cups of wine and the rest of the course, he described the unhappy litany of division and warfare between the petty dominions of his own Austrasia and its rival Neustria, which together made up the kingdom of the Franks; and of the great families that vied for their control. It was his own father, Pepin of Herstal, who had brought some semblance of stability, if only by the force of his will. And by standing on the neck of Rathbod for well over twenty years. But when Pepin died, everything fell apart. 'Rathbod rose up. The Neustrians decided it was time to assert themselves once more now that a woman held power in Austrasia.'

'You mean your stepmother?'

'Yes. Plectrude means to assert her grandchild's claim. And over that, regrettably, we scions of Pepin have fallen out.' He chuckled. 'The old bitch had me locked up, can you believe it? No doubt she meant well. She'd tell you it was all for the good of the family – which really means for the good of herself. That Theudoald, my nephew, was named my father's heir. But what good is honouring my father's wish if it means Austrasia sinks back into submission under Neustria? My father would turn in his grave. Probably snatch up the sword we buried him with and leap right out of it, too!' He sighed. 'No, luckily for all of us, I managed to escape.'

'So that you could seize power for yourself?'

Karil shook his great blond head of hair like a restless lion, his eyes twinkling with mischief. 'It was the other Austrasian nobles who thrust me forward. Someone had to lead them. Some *man*, I mean. They decided it should be me.'

'Of course, you have no ambitions for yourself.'

He held out his palms. 'I lead merely to serve those who would follow me.'

377

She wondered, after all, whether her own ambitions were so selfless and pure. Dear gods, how she had shunned the pretensions of power-hungry men when she was a younger woman! Worse, they had disgusted her. Yet after all this time, had she shown herself any better? Perhaps no lies were so precious – or blinding – as the ones a queen must tell herself.

'So you ride to stop this Rathbod then?'

'In the morning.' With this, he took a deep quaff of his wine.

'Let me come with you,' she said abruptly, all of a sudden overwhelmed by the weariness of feeling so impotent. She thought of how hard she had fought just to get this far. She didn't care to examine the whys of it: she was determined to carry the fight to the Wartooth's son. And she would not sit in this leaky old barn waiting for someone else to determine her fate.

'Come with us, Lady? I don't think you understand—'

'What is there to understand?'

He snorted. 'We ride to war. To battle!' He spoke as if explaining the thing to a child. 'It is no place for a woman. Let alone a lady of your standing.'

'I have stood on the plains of Bravellír when the spear-din roared about my ears. When blood ran like a river across the field.'

'It sounds… unpleasant,' he said mildly.

'It was the greatest battle the north has ever seen. The skalds will long sing of it. I was there. And I assure you, I can stand with you, whatever comes.'

The Frankish warlord slouched back into his great oaken

chair, considering her for a long moment. 'I cannot guarantee your safety. You know this.'

'If you are defeated, can you guarantee my safety here?'

A small frown appeared on Karil's brow. 'I suppose… no. I cannot.'

'Then I see no difference. If you win, I have nothing to fear. If you lose, I am in the same position whether I am with you or here.'

'Yes, but…' He gave a shake of his head, acknowledging the strength of her logic. And then some other idea seemed to enter his head. Something that amused him as he took another draught of his wine. When he lowered its rim, his eyes rested on hers. 'Yes, I think I understand.'

'Understand what exactly?'

'You wish to be near me.'

'Near you?' she exclaimed, astonished at the man's complacency, which was considerable. 'Hah!' And yet, for a man with his back to the wall, he had a swagger that, she could not deny, was potently attractive. But she was wise to that. Wasn't she? This was mere expedience: the way she allowed him to hold her eye; the silence that stretched between them, expressing all that might be said and more; the sudden pushing aside of the thought of Erlan that sprang into her mind. Wasn't she a queen? She was in control. And she meant it to stay that way.

But before she could think of a suitably sparring retort, Karil was pushing back his chair and rising to his feet. 'We leave at dawn then. Now I fear I must take counsel with my men. So I bid you a night of pleasant dreams, Lady Lilla.' He lifted her hand and kissed it. 'One can but humbly hope to feature in them,' he murmured, and left her to her supper.

Later, when Demetrios accompanied her to her chamber, he demanded to know what she thought she was doing.

'Am I to take a chiding from you, my little Greek?'

'Well, I saw it all, my lady. You practically ran the fellow into bed.'

'I did nothing of the sort,' she snapped. 'I merely wanted to convince him to allow me to come.'

'But the danger, my lady—'

'The last thing I intend to do is sit in this place, drinking bad wine and waiting for news that may never come.'

'But what about Erlan and the others?'

'What about them? I cannot change their fate from here. I can only trust in the weaving of the Norns. Or else the hand of your god,' she added, with no little sarcasm, 'whichever truly has the hold of them.'

Demetrios, for once, had no answer, although he couldn't help but raise a cynical eyebrow at all she said.

'We ride in the morning.'

'Ride, my lady?' Demetrios winced. 'In my condition?'

And reminded of his lacerated buttock, Lilla chuckled. 'You had better find yourself a cushion. Hadn't you, my little Greek?'

They rode east most of the next day, following a rain-soaked road to Koln. But when they were still a few leagues short of

380

the town and the great river it nestled against, Karil swung his column north. He explained to Lilla that, while he was no friend of the Lady Plectrude, who currently held the river town, it would serve his cause even less if Rathbod were to get his hands on Koln. Or more specifically on Plectrude's wealth, which, Karil assured Lilla, was quite as large as her own – for the time being misplaced – fortune.

Sending out his swiftest scouts just after noon, the first of them returned shortly before the light began to fail, bearing reports that would have been alarming to a far greater force than theirs. Karil was clearly disturbed by the scale of Rathbod's invasion – the scouts told of five thousand spears – as well as the speed with which it was advancing towards them. He sent word with even greater urgency to his brother, Childebrand, who had taken a force of two hundred riders west towards Bedburg, in case Rathbod should have tried to outflank the Austrasians' smaller force and come into their rear along the Koln road.

But now that Karil knew Rathbod intended to advance like a dagger-thrust straight at Koln, there was nothing for it but to meet him in the field and block his way.

'We need the numbers, though,' he told Lilla. 'Childebrand can be no more than ten miles west of here. If we can recall him to us, we may yet throw Rathbod back into his stinking swamp.'

Lilla had not known defeat. At Bravellír, they had won the day by a whisker. But Ringast's patchwork horde of Danes and Gotars and Wends had maintained good morale even until the last moment, in which all was decided. It was close, but they had never given up.

Yet here, even as an observer, she could feel the creeping, seeping swell of disarray, of disorder among the rebel nobles and their troops. Scouts were unable to answer simple questions, voices barked orders not out of discipline but frustration and anger, carts got stuck in the gloopy mud, fires smouldered and smoked in the drizzle and the damp. And the common troops had a kind of colourless, haunted expression on their faces that had nothing to do with the incessant rain and the miserable cold.

The night passed much the same, or worse. When she and Demetrios had to move among the men, she heard griping and croaking at every campfire. Still there was no word from Childebrand's force, despite that his brother had sent at least half a dozen men now to look for them. And they knew Rathbod's force was camped barely a league north of their position with the little hamlet of Pulla lying in-between.

Karil offered Lilla the shelter of his ox-cart for a bed, with a large waxed-wool covering slung over the top to keep out the worst of the rain. She saw no reason not to accept, especially when Karil himself withdrew to discuss with his captains their stratagems for the morning. She was relieved, not wanting to put herself in any compromising position, but also beginning to wonder whether her captor was the great warrior both he and his entourage seemed to think he was. He was still a young man after all – not yet thirty. And young men were prone to making mistakes.

She spent a restless night lying next to Demetrios, whose sleep was even more fitful than her own, as he wriggled about on his stomach, tutting and hissing and cursing under his breath. Lilla lay listening to the rain, thinking of her servant friend Orīana, and Einar, and Erlan, and the gold... even Marta... and what had befallen them all.

It was a strange, melancholy few hours. In all her days, she had never felt less certain about the future. But come the first greys of morning, she steeled herself for the day. This was her now. This rain. This man. This dreary dawn...

This coming slaughter.

The line of advancing men grew and grew till the horizon was full of them.

Even through the veil of drizzle, the Frisian army looked like a wall of metal. There was no glinting, no sunlight to break and scatter off helms or sword hilts, or razor-honed axe beards and wicked-sharp spear-points. Just a dull, solid mass of steel that had come to the field to kill. To glut on the blood of Karil and his men.

The Frisian king had with him thousands indeed. How many thousands, Lilla could not have said, but there was no comparison with the few hundred that Karil had mustered. From her position they looked a pitiful force. A forlorn hope. Worse, they looked like sheep to the slaughter. And fools to boot.

Gods, what was she about to witness?

Even if these Austrasian rebel lords were brave as the war-god Tyr himself, and the Frisian spear-men nothing but craven dogs, no man would lay so much as a silver ring on their victory. She kept her thoughts to herself, of course – though Demetrios had no such qualms. At least his muttering in Greek could have no worse effect on the men's morale.

'I feel like we should be somewhere else, my lady,' he said, his voice barely audible over the steady rain. 'I mean, I enjoy a good scrap as much as the next man, but this looks to be a bloodbath. And I don't fancy these seats much.'

'You have our horses ready?' she said softly.

He did.

'Then there's nothing to do but watch and observe how they make war in these lands.'

She suddenly wished Erlan was there beside her. Wondered where indeed he was in the world at this very moment. Was he safe? Was he even alive...? Of course, if he were there with her, he would never allow her to stay. He would ask what the Hel she thought she was doing, and why, and...

But he wasn't there. And something compelled her to stay.

At least the ground offered a small advantage to Karil's foot soldiers, she thought. Rathbod would have to advance his shield-wall through the hamlet, thereby breaking up his formation, and then march them up a shallow incline before they came to blows with Karil's line. The difference in height wasn't much, but enough to say the better ground lay with the Franks. But then they had a thick wood at their backs, which would hinder any withdrawal, should it be necessary. Something Lilla judged all too likely.

Karil and his immediate retinue had dismounted, moving ponderously in long mail tunics and leather gauntlets with broad limewood shields, armed with sword, axe and spear. But at least they looked ready to make the Frisians pay dearly for every step closer they wished to come to Koln.

Before he joined his line, Karil came to wish her good fortune for the day. 'God stands with us,' he told her, though maybe he was telling himself, trying to sound optimistic. But she could see the shadow in his face. Even a man of his unmatched complacency would be hard-pressed to buttress the odds he was facing.

'Still no word from your brother, then?'

'None.' He shook his head ruefully. 'I'm bound to say, his two hundred would have been most handy.' Although by Lilla's reckoning, another two thousand would still have been too few.

'Do you fear he betrayed you?'

'Childebrand? Ha!' Karil's face lit up with amusement. 'Not a chance. Between you and me, he hasn't the balls for it. There'll be some explanation. I only pray I'll live to hear it. God keep you, Lady Lilla.'

And with a flash of his pale blue eyes, he drew his long-sword and went with his bannermen to join the centre of his line.

Lilla felt her own heart beat faster as she watched the Frisians advance. Half of her felt curiously detached – as if nothing of hers could be lost or gained in the matter. And yet, she could not deny that half of her – nay, more than half – would have been sorry to see Karil fall. To see his designs all dashed in one morning's bloody harvest. She had not met a man like him for sheer magnetism, and he was still young. Perhaps if he lived, his allure and energy might turn to greatness. And so she willed him to live, to win, even as the sky filled with the beating drums, the wind whipped at the black and gold banners of the Frisian king, and the rain soaked the field of battle. Prelude to the battle-sweat, to the Valkyries' tears, which would flood the turf soon enough.

Neither line drew breath before they met, as they might have in the north. No champions came forward to boast to the gods; no envoys came to parley for terms. From what Karil had said of his father, Pepin had been a hard man, and Rathbod the enemy who had borne the weight of his will, and the keenness of his blade-edge, most of all. There were no words to say. Cold steel would do the Frisian's talking for him.

And so the shield-walls clashed in a rippling thunder of grinding wood and scraping steel. The air at once was riven with the shrieks and cries of the first of the wounded... the first of the dying. The killers and the killed. From where she stood, Karil's line looked perilously thin, whereas Rathbod's was four or five men deep. The Frisian wall was longer, too. And within mere moments, it seemed as if the Austrasian force would be swamped and swallowed up, like some prey of the Midgard Serpent, Loki's kin. Gone in a single gulp.

But the Frankish centre was holding strong, a hard kernel, unyielding as a diamond around Karil's blood-red banner as it flew from a gilded lance. She could not see him, but around him she saw countless blades rise and fall, each time bloodier than the last, if they rose again at all. And where the fray was thickest, there the battle seemed most evenly fought. But the wings of Karil's line were failing. She remembered how her dead husband Ringast had made a point of putting some of his best warriors on his extreme flanks. His brother Thrand was one – the bastard rapist whose throat she would one day cut. The mad berserker cousins, Geir and Grim, and their Danish hirds at the other. They had held and held all day. These Frankish flanks looked like they wouldn't hold even an hour.

'The horses, Lady Lilla,' said Demetrios, breaking into her thoughts.

'What about them?'

'Shall I fetch them?' The note of urgency in his voice was all too plain.

'You think they will break so soon.'

'Don't you, my lady? What you're watching is a rout.' For once, the little Greek's face was serious as death. 'If we don't make ready now, you and I will be caught in it.'

'The centre is holding.'

'I'm no soldier, my lady, but if all you have left is the centre, then what you've got is no more line. No more line, no more army.'

'Where would we run to?'

'Well, "away" is generally the preferred direction,' he replied. 'We can worry about where later.'

But before either could say more, the great yellow banner at the heart of the Frisian line suddenly surged forward. Blazoned on it was an upturned cross and two large ravens. Lilla recognised the birds as the mark of Odin. By the gods, she was close to home all right. Yet she could be closer still to the halls of Hel if Rathbod's war-hounds broke through.

It seemed like the centre was boiling with a new intensity. The distance at which she stood was at once reassuring and frustrating. If only she could fly over the field like an eagle, she might see the truth of what was happening. But even then... the battlefield was already a maelstrom of bodies, some dead, some still living, some about to die.

And then Karil's banner fell.

All at once it seemed like the Frisians were puncturing the Frankish line, like breaches in a sea-wall, prising open the shields and the bodies with their long limbs and still longer spears. Then she saw a flash of sky-blue in all that brown and dirty red and grey. The blood-red banner rose again but it was falling back towards them.

'They're retreating, my lady. You must come now.'

'No. Wait! I want to see what comes of him.'

'He's finished, Lady. We must flee.'

The trickle of Franks falling back would soon become a flood. She knew that. And yet something in her made her want to help him. There was a line of archers near her. They had done nothing yet to help. Just stood there, like useless sacks of grain, waiting for a command that would never come. Meanwhile, the eye of the battle-storm was rolling up the slope towards them.

'What is your wish, my lady? Lady, I'm *begging* you,' the rising panic in Dimo's voice made her glance at him.

But then the line broke in earnest.

Bodies began pouring back towards them. Some stayed to face their enemy; others turned their backs and fled. She saw the flash of blue again. She found she couldn't bear it.

'Wait here,' she said. 'Or run. I don't care which. I must help him.'

Without waiting for an answer, she took off down the slope to the nearest archer, who stood nervously looking at the onrush of men in flight.

'Lady Lilla, what are you doing?' she heard Demetrios calling after her. *'LADY LILLA!'*

But his voice soon blurred with the louder sounds around her, her attention fixed on what was ahead. At the moment the archer cracked, turning to flee, she reached him. 'Give me your bow and your quiver. Quickly now!' The man was stunned, gaping at her as if she had appeared in the madness of his mind, and he was only too glad to divest himself of his weapons. 'Here! Take them!' he blurted, shoving them into her hands and taking off for the trees.

The bow was a simple thing. No embellishments, no exquisite carving. A straightforward length of yew, a sturdy bowstring and a short leather quiver of arrows. She emptied them onto the ground, snatched up six or seven in one hand and ran down the slope.

Men flashed past. They weren't interested in her. The screams and war-cries were louder here, enveloping her like a fog. The smell of slaughter hit her like a wall. Open viscera, sweat and wet waxed leather; piss and vomit and the blood-soaked turf. Still she fixed her eyes only on the splash of sky-blue and ran towards it.

She could see him now. His helm knocked away, the straw-gold hair flailing loose about his face as one of his retainers tried to drag him back, his face a mask of desperate anger. He turned, cut across with his sword, deflecting the fall of a war-hammer in the hands of a big Frisian with black war-braids, then drove the point through the man's neck. He tore it out in a shower of blood, spraying crimson over the sky-blue cloak tied like a girdle around him.

All this Lilla was close enough to see. She had her

first arrow ready; the others clutched in her draw-hand, like her father had taught her. She was determined not to waste them.

Then a shard of reason must have entered Karil's mind, a glimmer of self-preservation. He started moving backwards, his liegemen scuffling with him, protecting him even as the Frisian rage boiled hotter still. Their foemen moved forward, sensing weakness like wolves; a huge man wielding a huge axe ran in from the side. In a single scything blow, he cut the retainer on Karil's right almost in two. The man's head flopped over, barely still attached to his body, gouts of blood turning the rain scarlet. The axe-man didn't wait to admire his work. He raised his axe for a second blow. Karil looked like a child beneath him. Lilla took a knee, drew her string, took aim, loosed, and had another nocked in a heartbeat, then loosed again. *Ziiip, ziiip.* The first took the man under his armpit; the second shattered his jaw. He fell like an oak and Karil ran on.

He was only fifty feet from her now. She should fear for her own life, she knew it. But something in her also knew she had to see him live to fight again. A fleeing Frank came barrelling past, knocking her shoulder and sending her off balance. She cursed and had to catch herself with her bow hand in the mud. Mud was an archer's enemy more than any length of steel. Her hand was sticky with it. Frantically, she wiped the worst of it on her jerkin. Then another Frisian broke through, was running straight for her with a shrieking cry and a baleful look in his eye. He butted her first with his shield, sending her flat on her backside. She felt the wind of an arrow whip overhead, then a searing heat across her crown as the Frisian lifted his hand-axe to finish her. Sluggish from the wind knocked out of her, all she could do was lunge awkwardly upwards with the nest of arrow-points still clamped in her fist. She punched them hard into the man's crotch. He howled as his genitals were impaled four different ways, buckled forward straight onto the end of her bow. It was blunt, to be sure, but his eye was soft, and the wooden tip drove deep through his socket and into his skull. The man collapsed, mercifully to the side of her, shuddering and jerking as the life left him.

She scrambled to her feet. She'd lost more arrows. Still had two in hand, though. Her scalp was on fire. She looked up. The dead were thick around Karil. He was still fighting – two burly Frisians in sheepskin and leather with swirling black tattoos over half their faces. Karil's shield shattered. Splinters burst around him. The tattooed faces gurned and grimaced. They pressed in for the kill.

Lilla's hands worked by instinct, moving faster than thought. *Ziiip, ziiip.*

The first arrow took one in the open mouth; the second straight through the other's neck.

Karil turned, eyes wide with fear and confusion.

'Get clear!' she screamed at him. 'Escape while there's still time!'

He saw her now, his gaze for a moment fixed on her like she was some vision in a nightmare. In a sense she was – a kind of visitation, desperately calling him to live, not throw away his life in this dirty little disaster.

He seemed to come to himself. She saw but not heard him call her name. Then he was running. Running for his life.

Running past her and seizing her arm, spinning her, dragging her, so that she was running too.

Dear gods, he had left it late. It was like racing against an on-rushing tide. But there were still loyal men about him. Men who would throw themselves in the path of his pursuers to buy their lord some precious seconds.

He was bellowing, 'Fall back! Fall back!'

Lilla could feel his iron grip on her arm. The bow was gone. There were trees, and then horses. A rush of bodies and screams and whipping branches. Her little Greek, he was there. Flight, only flight, headlong, with blood-raw lungs crying out for rest, but no chance to appease them. Onward and onward, muscles burning, into the damp and the fear and the gloom, and the sinking shame of defeat.

While behind them, Rathbod and his warriors howled their victory to the skies...

The surprising thing was how many of Karil's men got away.

It was a rout, to be sure. But not a massacre.

'Maybe Rathbod was too surprised at how easy we made it for him to follow it up,' muttered Karil gloomily when they finally stopped for rest.

They felt more like fugitives than an army now, pouring across the Koln road and onwards to the south; there, to re-group. Or at least survive. It wasn't until dusk that Karil called a halt, seeking rest in a beech wood high on a hill overlooking the Rhein valley to the east.

The rain had stopped, and the last of a westering sun tucked under the blanket of cloud, spilling its golden rays through the glistening autumn leaves. A glimmer of beauty before the darkness closed around them.

There was worse news to come. Somehow a rider had broken through from Childebrand. King Chilperic had stolen a march on them. His army was far closer to Koln than Karil had counted on. Childebrand had tried to engage him on the road, but to press home any attack would have been suicide. Afterwards, the king's riders had chased Childebrand some distance to the south, while the rest of his army marched on Koln.

'A fuck-up beyond all fuck-ups,' admitted Karil. 'And now Koln will be under siege. Plectrude had better pray those walls hold.'

'What will you do?' Lilla asked. She was feeling light-headed. She'd lost a fair amount of blood from the arrow wound across her crown, most of it still caked and crusty in the braids of her hair. She felt disgusting, with little sleep, an empty stomach, an aching head. At least the fire they had going was warm.

'Huh,' he grunted without much mirth. 'Drink.' He tossed a flaccid ale-skin to her. 'And eat.' He tore off a piece of soggy bread and threw that to her as well. 'And afterwards, think.'

Lilla gave a rueful smile. 'My father used to say it's better to do one's thinking first. And then act.'

Karil snorted. 'I'm beginning to understand why they called that man a bastard.'

She should have been offended. Instead she found herself laughing. She laughed so long and hard that she realised it must be the nerves coming out of her.

'Are you all right, Lady?' said Karil when the fit was passed, reaching out to touch her hand.

She nodded, smoothing her own hand over her face. 'I will be,' she murmured. 'It has been a strange day.'

'Aye. It has been that.' Karil picked up a stick and gave the embers a stir, staring deep into the fire. 'We lost many good men today... No, I lost them.' His voice was a growl of self-reproach. His eyes suddenly flicked up at her. 'I could have died with them were it not for you.'

'There were many others who were protecting you,' she said modestly.

'No.' He shook his ragged mane of golden hair. 'None who saved me twice.'

'Well then. You can thank my father for that. It was he who taught me how to handle a bow.'

Karil chuckled. 'Perhaps I could warm to the old man after all.' He glanced at the others around the fire. Demetrios was kneeling on his haunches warming his hands. He looked like a man so far from home, it was quite wretched to behold. The others of Karil's retinue were few enough, their faces taut with fatigue and perhaps the memories of the morning re-playing in their minds.

'Come,' he said to Lilla, standing stiffly and holding out his hand. 'There's something I would show you.'

'Something?' She raised an eyebrow.

'The place we've come to.'

She hesitated a moment, then said, 'Very well,' and allowed him to pull her to her feet.

Demetrios's eyes rose with her. '*Kyría mou?*'

'It's all right, Dimo,' she replied softly in Greek. 'Stop and stay warm. We won't be long.'

Karil led her a short distance through the trees. It was not quite dark. She followed, overstepping the undergrowth, Karil pointing out fallen branches and tree roots to beware of. At length they came to a treeline and continued just beyond it, out onto a little shelf of rock from which it seemed the whole world spilled away. A strong, dark line of cloud marked out the skies above them where a weather front was passing through, behind which the air was crystal clear. 'We shall at least be spared rain for the night,' she commented, feeling like someone ought to break the silence, a kind of girlish nervousness coming over her. It was stupid. She was a woman grown, not some naive maiden, like Marta or any other. The sudden thought of the girl tasted sour. There was no comparison between herself and Orīana's daughter worth the making. And yet the consciousness that she and Karil were alone – that his liegemen had let him walk alone with her – was all too acute. She found her heart was beating faster.

'See the river there.' He pointed far away to a broad bold streak of water that stretched from the southern horizon to the north, as far as she could see.

'The Rhein,' she said.

'She is the lifeblood of this land.'

'You mean the commerce she brings?'

'Could bring,' he corrected her. 'She would make us rich. If only we could find our way to peace.'

'Is this where you tell me you fight only for peace?' she said. 'That you long for an end to war so that your people may prosper. Oh, spare me.'

He turned to her, seeming amused at her cynicism. Perhaps amused at himself. 'Huh! Maybe I've told myself the lie so often I've come believe it.' He sighed. 'Or maybe it's my father's lie… Still, I always loved the river. That much is true. There's something about it. Its never-ending flow, always bringing something new around the corner.'

'Something new.' Her lip curled. This, too, seemed painfully transparent. She could feel his unspoken question. 'Am I to be the next new thing?'

He chuckled again. 'By God, you speak bluntly sometimes, don't you?'

'Perhaps it would be simpler if you did, too. What is it you want to say? Did you bring me here to make love to me?'

He looked at her, the lines of his face wavering between that sneer and his smile. He said nothing.

She snorted at him. 'Why, there's a tree. That one's as good as any. In a moment, I can have these breeks off me and you can fuck away to your heart's content.' Dear gods, what was she saying? What was this mood that had come over her?

'Huh.' His face told of his surprise. 'You fight like a man. You speak like a man… If I wanted to fuck a man, I suppose I should not have chosen you to come here.'

'But you do want to fuck?'

To this, he gave no answer. Only moved closer. He was watching her carefully, more like a sparring partner than a lover. She stood her ground proudly, yet something about the situation aroused her. The uncertainty of it. She did not know whether they would part this moment enemies or lovers. Did not know which one she favoured herself.

'Is this you?' he said, tilting his head in curiosity. He was so close he had no need to speak above a whisper. 'Is this the true woman within?'

It was not a question she wanted to examine just then. Nor one to allow him the presumption to ask. 'A true woman,' she sneered. 'What is that? Demure, grateful for all she is given, I suppose. Submissive, servile… a slave.'

'You obviously think ill of me to say that. No, I'm quite sure that whatever desires are in you, whatever you want for yourself, you're more than capable of taking it. But having obtained it,' he murmured, drawing even closer, 'I wonder whether you would find it to your liking.'

She could smell him now. Smell the sweat and the mud on him, and the blood of other men. Smell his desire for her as keenly as she felt it in her own body. He reached out slowly, like a man wishing to stroke a she-wolf. His fingers slid around the nape of her neck, light as gossamer over her skin, though the pads of his fingertips were rough as old leather. It sent a thrill of arousal through her body. Her mind made up, abruptly she stepped into his embrace. Not submitting, but taking – her senses hungry for the smell of him, the taste of him, the sight of him, the feel of him. And for the next moments, they were locked in an ecstasy of movement, pulling at strings and buckles and laces until their naked skin could come together.

All thought was pushed from her mind. She wanted only to feel. She smelled the wet beech leaves, his unwashed body, her own hair across her face; she felt the hardness of him, pressed up against her own softness and then inside of her, heard her own moans and his panting breath.

Dear gods!

The thought was like a burst of light in her head: *he was inside her.* Like the roar of those jets of Greek fire, a blaze of illumination in the black of night. *What was she doing?*

'Stop.' She pushed him away. 'Stop! Please!'

'What?' he gasped. 'What is it?'

'We can't do this... I cannot...'

'Can't do this?' he said, still panting. 'We *are* doing it.'

'I know, I know... I mustn't.'

'Why?'

'I cannot tell you... I mustn't, that's all. I'm sorry.' She got free of his hands and shuffled away from him so she could pull up her breeks, only too aware how clumsy and awkward it all looked.

'By Christ,' Karil sighed. 'What's got into you?'

'That's just it. It's you, you!' She shook her head. 'It's not right. I'm sorry.' She could not tell him suddenly about Erlan, about all that he was to her. How could she even begin?

Karil put himself away and let his tunic fall. 'God forgive me, I'm no saint, Lilla. But I'm also no rapist. I'm not going to force myself on you if you don't want it. But... by all the saints, I really can't fathom you.'

'I'm sorry,' she said again, that bold brazenness sloughing off her like the dead leaves at their feet. 'I'm sorry.'

'You don't need to be sorry,' he said, fastening his belt. 'I obviously put you in a position that did you little honour. Perhaps we've all lost our minds a little this day.' A strange formality had come over him, as if he was trying to salvage what scraps of dignity there were left to either of them. She was hurrying to re-arrange her dress, wanting to get away, hideously embarrassed. But he stopped her, held her arm. 'Forget about this. It was my mistake.' His eyes fixed hers. 'But one thing I'll not forget. I owe you my life. That I won't forget.' He released her. 'Come, I'll take you back.'

She followed him through the darkness now, feeling relieved, but also annoyed, entirely with herself. Feeling everything at once, feeling nothing was resolved inside of her. That night, as she lay under her cloak by the fire, the heat of her desire for Karil took a long while to cool, the sensation of him still inside of her like a ghost. By the gods, she felt a fool. But sometimes even fools make the right decision.

Erlan... Her Erlan. Where was he? They had been through so much together. But if it were only to come to this place, this empty, lonely place... then what was it all for?

Refusing Karil only made sense if Erlan was still alive.

And though she still nursed hope, part of her feared she would never see him, nor any of the others, ever again.

CHAPTER THIRTY

Skírpa. Katāros. Amadeus.

Who was he?

For the first time in his life, he wished he was none of them. That he was no one and nothing. Wished that somehow he could be wiped clean like those slates the teachers of philosophy used in the training schools of the Great City. That he could start again, free of his memories. Free of the mark of other men's sin.

But that was a foolish wish. There was no starting again. No re-birth. The best he could hope for was an ending. A final brutal ending. And then, at least, it would be over.

It was better to think of what he had witnessed that night, under that pitiless moon, as a nightmarish dream. Easier to think of it like that. To tell himself it had not happened. Yet whether a dream or reality, his mind could not let it alone, like a dog licking at a sore.

The mad heat of the fires, the screams of the frightened children, Alvarik's monstrous phallus as he took the maiden

Skuld there on the altar, still slathered with the innocents' blood. And all the while, the leaping ecstasy of those howling beast-men, crying to their one-eyed god, worshipping *Báleygr*, the Flaming Eye.

By Christ, he wished he could wipe it all from his mind.

Worst of all was the memory of what he had done. What he had felt. Fear had become intrigue; intrigue had become excitement. And finally, excitement had become pleasure. The feeling of that dark power within him... *thrilled* him. As intoxicating as anything he had known. He knew he wanted to feel it again. Knew that he would not be able to resist it when he did.

And that was why he must escape.

He had taken some days to make his preparations. Set aside a little food, scrounged another cloak to keep him warm, stolen a firesteel, crafted himself a wooden flask and stopper. He had determined that his best chance was to head south for the river. That way was mostly downhill and he knew he must hit the course of the river in no more than a day or two at most. If Alvarik sent men in pursuit, at worst he could throw himself in the river and float downstream. If not to safety, at least to oblivion and death.

But even death was better than Alvarik's reality. Or worse, the slow transformation into another of his creatures.

At last Skírpa was ready and resolved. He had made his plan, secreting his bundle of provisions in a shallow hole by the southern perimeter wall. That night, he would slip out of the low wooden barracks in which he was shut up each night. There was an outside latch but he had already figured a way to undo it. And none of the other slaves or captives, it seemed, had the heart to try to get out, which meant that the watchmen were seldom put to the test. He guessed they would be drowsy or, if he was lucky, outright asleep.

Dusk came earlier each night now. And this was a placid one. Not a breath of wind in the surrounding trees, a kind of hazy evening melting into a lightless night. A calm, you might say, almost of the grave. Except that there were a good deal too many poor souls around there who had yet to find that sort of lasting rest.

Still, Skírpa did his best to get some rest for himself, if not actual sleep, to give himself the best chance of putting some distance between him and Alvarik's wolves when the time came. Maybe it was the worry of it, or else the weariness of his mind that wore itself out going over the details of his plan, but in fact after some time he did fall asleep, and was deep in that sleep when he was suddenly jolted awake.

'Get up. The One Eyed wants you.'

Skírpa blinked stupidly in the dark, his eyes struggling to focus on the nondescript face looming over him. 'You mean Alvarik?'

'D'you know another? Come on, up.'

And before he could answer, he found himself dragged off his flea-ridden mattress and marched at the end of a spear out of the slaves' quarters and across the compound towards the One Eyed's little hall.

He had grown used to the fact that his first impression of it had been all wrong. He had imagined it a plain sort of a dwelling, hardly better than the house of a freeman of the north. But he now knew it had many intricately carved

details, and its interior was designed to resemble a miniature of some great northern king – with a dais and oak-high
chair. The royal seat of this self-styled king of a hell-hole
kingdom. Alvarik's pretensions were almost as horrifying
as his cruelty. And it was a mystery to Skírpa why these
wolf-warriors, whoever they were, seemed all too willing to
subjugate themselves to the one-eyed demagogue and his
pitiless god.

Moments later he was shoved in through the door
and found himself in the dimly lit 'throne' chamber of this
petty tyrant. To be summoned in the middle of the night
for any reason was disquieting enough. But he was surprised
to see that he was not the only one stood before the One
Eyed. There was a young woman there also. At a glance he
saw she was barely more than a girl. She cut a wretched
figure, her robes torn and dirty, all of one colour, and she
stood stooped over like a much older woman. Her long dark
hair draped from her head like a mourning veil, hiding her
face.

Alvarik, meanwhile, was perched on his enormous high-
back seat, sitting as broad across it as he was tall. The skulls
of wolves and wild goats adorning the wall behind peered
down on them with eery menace. Beside him lay a large grey
wolf on a chain, curled in repose; even in its sleep, it uttered
a soft growl with each guttural breath. He had not noticed the
animal before. But what other pet would a creature like the
One Eyed keep?

'We have need of you, Skírpa,' Alvarik began in his sibilant
rasp, rolling his great block of a head towards him and licking
his lips. 'You speak this girl's tongue.'

'Do I?' he replied hesitantly. It was true that he spoke many tongues, but there was no way that Alvarik could know that. At least, no earthly way.

'She comes from *Grikkland*. A place you know well. Now, speak for me and for her.'

Skírpa thought it wise not to deny he was able to act as translator, still wary of whether this was the only reason he had been summoned. It was only then that he noticed a small fortune of gold coins heaped upon the table. Alvarik reached out, picked up a handful, then let them spill back onto the heap.

'How did you come by this gold?' said the One Eyed to the girl.

Skírpa translated his question.

The girl's head rose very slowly, her filthy hair hanging loose over her face so that even she revealed no more than one eye through the lustreless tresses. 'Does it matter?' Her voice was unnaturally rough for one her age. 'Gold it is. And you will have it wherever it is from, however we came by it... Where is my mother?'

Skírpa had to admire the sullen defiance in the girl's voice, but it was only as he was translating her last words that he made the connection in his head, remembering the Greek which the red-haired woman had uttered...

He felt shame burning hot down his neck but made no sign that he knew the answer to her question. 'Mother?' returned Alvarik with a snigger. 'I know of no mother.' He turned to Skírpa and spoke in their common tongue. 'Do you know what she could mean, boy?' His one eye seemed to prod at Skírpa, as irksome as it was hateful.

'She came here with me,' said the girl. 'I haven't seen her since you separated us.'

Skírpa tried to ignore the clamour of his own guilt, focusing instead on exchanging the meaning of their words.

'Forget anything you knew *before*,' Alvarik told her. 'Mother. Friends. Such things are over for you. There is only one connection, one comforter you need worry about. Wotan. The Flaming Eye. *Báleygr*. He watches over you. Sees right through you.'

'I have only one comforter,' she answered. 'My Lord and Saviour, Christ Jesus. Whatever devils you worship will have no part of me, nor I of them.'

At mention of that name, Alvarik covered his missing eye with his huge hand, as a priest might make the sign of the cross. 'The one you speak of is weak. He has infected the world with his lies. But they will be driven from it soon enough. Blood is the only truth. As all will come to see.'

'The blood of Jesus is stronger than anything of your god. He is the truth. So he said.' She seemed to become stronger with each word she spoke.

Alvarik uttered another snigger once Skírpa had passed the words on. 'You have some fight in you, girl. That is good.' Without warning, he hopped off his huge chair and came forward to stand in front of the maiden. He was no taller than her, and she was hardly statuesque. Yet the massive breadth of him, the great barrel chest, made her seem fragile by comparison. He reached up, turned her face this way and that, till she jerked her head away from his touch. At this, he laughed again. 'Yes... some fight indeed. The One Eye favours a contest. Especially with one so enthralled already to his enemy...

But he has won over many stronger than you.' He left her face alone, and instead stalked around her. Skírpa felt the menace of it.

'Nothing will shake my confidence in my Lord,' said the girl.

'We shall see. Others have thought the same. But the light of the One Eye sees all of you. It shines into the darkest corners. He *knows* you completely. He knows your weakness. And that is why he will win you to him.' And as he spoke those words, something in them made Skírpa shiver to his bones.

'The light of the One Eye?' The girl snorted, full of heart. 'It is written – if your eye is bad, your whole body is full of darkness. If then the light in you is darkness, how great is that darkness.'

'Another of the Great Deceiver's riddles? Oh, you think I didn't know. I told you I know all of you and more. Because of what the One Eye speaks to me. Yes – his light is darkness, but darkness visible. And yes – his darkness will rule all in time.' He raised his unnaturally large hand, pointed a gnarled finger to his own ruined eye. 'Sacrifice. That is what the Flaming One demands. That is the price of his wisdom. The price of his *power*. And for this, he will grant you *all* that you desire.'

'I desire nothing more than the peace of my Lord. And his service. Even to die for him.'

Skírpa looked at her. A slip of a girl. Yet she had more steel in her than him.

'Go on,' snapped Alvarik at him. 'What said she?' So Skírpa told him.

'Hyah!' grunted his master. 'Let us not get ahead of ourselves. No one is asking you to die, girl... But what you speak is a lie also. You do desire more. See, I will show you.' He turned to the guard by the door. 'Hold her.' And then to the girl: 'Kneel.'

Undaunted, she matched his gaze, not eye for eye of course, but with as much resolve as the dwarf had malice. 'He need not hold me. I will kneel.' And so saying, went down to her knees.

Her head was now level with the One Eyed's buckle. Skírpa knew what was coming. But she could not have and he could not warn her. With a sudden jerk, Alvarik clasped her head. He squeezed till his knuckles bulged white and big as shield-studs. But she did not cry out, just squashed her eyes tight shut.

And then it was the same as it had been for him – the weird shamanic ululations and cries into the ether. The devil only knew what the wretch thought he was summoning, but as before, he started to shake all over, his head rocking from side to side like a man with palsy, his great shoulders lurching in their sockets, his arms shuddering. Skírpa watched his mouth open, the obscenely long tongue slavering like a thirsty hound. Then all at once he stopped, his head still, tipping slowly back and back beyond what most men could bear, his one eye staring wide at the shadows above. It was a horrible sight.

'*I will give you the man you desire,*' he said, but in a voice no longer his. A language not even his. For now, to Skírpa's shock, he too spoke in Greek.

The girl gasped – whether from pain or surprise, Skírpa could not tell. Her head was bowed. Skírpa saw a tear drop like a bead of silver to the floor. 'God forgive me,' she murmured.

'*There is nothing to forgive*,' spoke this preternatural voice through Alvarik's ragged mouth. '*What you desire is natural… What is natural is good… Reach out your hand… Reach out and I will fill it.*'

She drew in a deeper breath now, as if steeling herself against physical pain. Or else some other kind of battle. 'Have mercy. Lord, have mercy.'

'*Give in to your desire. Turn from that which holds you back. Be not a slave to some false righteousness. Pay heed to your appetites. Else why would their call be so constant, so strong… so true? They must be sated. Do what thou wilt, child. Follow thy desires. And thou wilt be satisfied.*' The voice was almost a song now, weirdly hypnotic – part spell, part lullaby. Wholly sweet, which seemed all the more grotesque coming from the One Eyed's corrupt and crooked face. '*Follow thy desires*,' he repeated. '*I will give them to you.*' It was a song now, and the tears were falling freely from the girl's eyes.

But then she sniffed, and now she answered, in a language which Skírpa himself did not recognise at first. The words were half-spoken, and then he saw that she too was trying to sing, her throat raw, the melody barely rising beyond a hoarse mumble.

Nevertheless, the sound seemed to enrage Alvarik, or what was in him. There was a sudden snarl deep in his throat. And he started barking back at her in yet another different tongue. But she kept on singing, her voice growing in strength as she went on. And as it grew stronger, Skírpa realised he did know the tongue after all, if not the meaning of the words.

She was singing in Aramaic. And now, as the shaman answered her, Skírpa realised he too was speaking Aramaic.

His broad, squat body became more agitated, shuddering and twitching, and still the girl sung on, till at last the One Eyed's massive head fell forward and, as if coming to himself, he flung the girl away from him in disgust. She fell back onto the floor and for a time lay there panting.

'Take the stupid little cunt away,' he snarled at the guard, who dutifully seized the wretched maiden by the hair and pulled her to her feet. When they reached the door, Alvarik told the guard to stop. Then he turned to Skírpa with a lopsided grin. 'Tell her one more thing.'

And a moment later, Skírpa found himself speaking words in Greek, his voice dispassionate as the cold mosaic faces adorning the palaces of the east. 'Your mother is dead. We gutted her like a sow. Blood is the only truth.' Behind him, Alvarik started laughing, an ugly, snickering laugh.

With a flick of his colossal hand, the One Eyed now dismissed them. The door snapped shut. The girl had not made so much as a whimper.

'Fools. Small-minded fools,' muttered Alvarik, clasping his hands behind his back and stalking over to the little heap of gold. He bent and plucked up a single coin, then turned and went back to his pacing. 'Bah! They don't know what's good for them. They cling to their little lies thinking these will save them. But they know nothing.' Abruptly his pacing stopped and he came right up to Skírpa, laying a heavy hand upon his shoulder. 'But you do, don't you, Skír-*pah*! Heh? You know what's good for you.' His foul breath clouded in Skírpa's face. The eunuch didn't know where to look but he said nothing.

Alvarik was wearing a smile which had no obvious explanation, revealing more than a few teeth missing, and those that were left him were of a sharp and dagger-like nature, giving him the appearance of a panting dog. 'For your trouble.' He took Skírpa's hand and pressed the gold coin into his palm. 'Oh, I have something else of yours too before you go.'

He hobbled over to his tall oaken chair, reached behind it and soon retrieved a shapeless bundle. The light was dim but Skírpa saw the thing was covered in mud. And as Alvarik returned, he recognised with sinking horror his own possessions, the provisions for his escape. The tyrant jammed it into Skírpa's stomach.

'Did I not tell you? The Flaming Eye sees all.'

CHAPTER THIRTY-ONE

Berengar held out his hand, his dirty palm hovering like a lantern in the gloaming.

Erlan signalled the halt to the others who were still further back. Even he could smell the wood-smoke now.

They had been sneaking through the pines like this for the last quarter league. Ever since the wiry tracker had caught the whiff of something on the Immerwald's deathly still air. 'Stay sharp,' he murmured, 'and best arm yourselves.'

That hardly needed saying twice.

It was Einar who had persuaded Berengar to continue on with them. Told him the whole story of it over supper – of him and Oriana. Berengar had listened, nodding, shaking his head, nodding some more. At the end of it, his verdict was a solitary grunt. And then at length a mutter: 'Mebbe I'd go a little ways further with you.'

'Good lad,' Einar had nodded and clapped his shoulder, his thanks no more effusive than that.

Erlan looked now for the others behind him. Caught a

glimpse of Mikkel Crow, stooped and creeping with long, cautious strides through the damp undergrowth, his hand-axe gripped just under its beard, a long-knife in his other hand. There was Bull's hulking shadow, moving with surprising lightness over the forest litter. A little further back, the tall, lean shape of Wyn, whom they all insisted hang back.

'There could be killing done tonight,' Erlan had told him.

'Then God have mercy on those who fall,' he said, and made the sign of the Cross. Who knew what contortions of reason a monk had to make in his head to reconcile himself to the slaughter of other men? But that was no business of Erlan's.

Berengar crouched low against a tall pine, his head tipped as he peered around it. All the trees were tall in this deeper part of the forest, with thick, straight trunks and the branches of them knitting together far above their heads like the vault ceilings of the great basilicas of the empire. The trapper pointed at Erlan and beckoned him forward.

A few moments later, Erlan was beside him, his heart thumping madly in his chest, the wood-smoke now strong enough to sharpen his senses. 'Fifty paces,' Berengar whispered. 'Four – maybe five of 'em. Hard to see. There could be more gathering wood.' He suddenly gripped Erlan's wrist. 'I'm no killer, Aurvandil.'

'Could have fooled me with that bow.'

'I defend myself,' he hissed. 'I don't murder innocent men.'

'No one's innocent,' Erlan returned softly. 'Certainly not these men.' He peered forward. He could see them now: shadows huddled around a small fire. Heads covered by the cowls of their cloaks, those whose heads were visible. Yet they must be the wolf-warriors they were looking for. Who else would be this deep in the forest? He watched for any movement, or for any others moving about their camp, but he saw little. A swig at an ale-skin. A prod at the fire. He could hear at least one murmuring in a low voice, which meant at least two of them were still awake. 'Stay here then,' he whispered to Berengar. 'We'll get this done. Just be ready... in case it all goes to Hel.'

He shuffled back through the thickening shadows to Einar and signalled the others in. As he spoke, Erlan's eyes darted from face to face, nodding encouragement in turn. They were good men – Svali, Ran, and the others. They weren't warriors, but they had the stones for a fight. And that was half the battle won, right there. After a brief counsel, they scattered like a murder of crows. The plan was basic and, with luck, swift.

The six of them split into two, led by Einar and Erlan, each group skirting a wide circle around the fire, keeping the same distance, dropping off a man at even distance until Erlan and Einar came with sight of each other on the far side of the camp. Then, at Erlan's signal – an owl call, what else? – they were to move in at speed and in silence. 'No war-cries,' he said. 'No bellowing to your god. I want these men dead before they know we're even there.'

Erlan crouched, ready. He filled his lungs to make the call and lifted his hands to his mouth at the exact moment he heard footsteps running through the brush. Then his eye caught it, a figure sprinting back to the fire through the trees. '*Sorðinn,*' he muttered under his breath and got to his feet. *Five*

413

of the whoresons then, he thought wearily, as the man's bellow of warning split the quiet of the night.

Erlan drew his unblooded sword in a rasp of steel and unsheathed the seax at his back. 'Now! Go – go!' he cried, all caution thrown to Hel, and praying that his men responded. No stealth now. Only speed.

He ran, his lurching gait shooting shards of pain up his leg as he raced in towards the fire. He could see other shadows running in, thank the gods, but also the huddled figures around the fire throwing off cloaks, springing to their feet. Thirty paces, twenty, fifteen… And the figure he'd marked as his target turned to face the forest, a bearded axe in his hand, a still-burning branch from the fire in the other. The last few strides he roared with full throat, hoping to put the fear of Fenrir in the man – but as he raised his sword arm to strike, his opponent flung the flaming branch in his face. By sheer reflex Erlan jerked his hand across and punched the thing away in a burst of sparks and scorching heat, blinding himself for a second and searing his face. Instinct, finely honed in the chaos of battle, anticipated the other's move. He raised his seax and blocked the killing axe-blow with its foot-long blade. For a moment, they were locked together, the man's gurning face inches from his own, his left hand trying to hold off Erlan's sword, while his right fought to extricate his axe from Erlan's knife and drive the edge of it home. Erlan didn't wait to find out who was the stronger. He shifted his balance onto his right heel then kicked out with his left, buckling the other's knee sideways. The man screamed in pain and went down into the dirt. Erlan's beautiful Frankish blade scythed down after him. He felt the crunch as the edge bit into skull

414

through the milk-white hair. He tore it free in a shower of blood, already looking for the next threat, leaving the man shuddering on the ground.

The little camp had gone from peaceful rest to bloody mayhem in less time than it took a man to sink a horn of ale. Another of the wolf-warriors was felled – *two of five*, he thought – but Black Svali was now writhing on his back near the fire, clutching his arm. Bull stood in front of him, clubbing his axe down on a smaller man who was taking the battering under his shield. Mikki and Ran were in a stand-off with a warrior carrying a long-spear. Before Erlan looked away, Mikki lunged forward, took the spear on his shield and grabbed hold of it, yelling at Ran to 'fucking do some-thing'. Ran duly obliged, jabbing his long-knife up and outwards, taking with it half the man's throat. Einar, meanwhile, was seized by a battle-frenzy that was disturbing to see. His opponent was somehow still standing, but even as Erlan watched, Fat-Belly bludgeoned the other's shield aside and hacked down his axe. The blow cleaved the man's neck wide open. But Einar didn't stop there. He hacked and hacked and hacked again, seeming blind to what he was doing, each blow spraying more blood in all directions. It was butcher's work.

'Einar! He's dead, for Frigg's sake!' yelled Erlan. 'Einar!' But the fat man didn't hear him. Just went on chopping at the warrior's lifeless body. 'He's dead, you maniac!' Erlan didn't mean to shove Einar so hard but he had to snap him out of it. In a flash, Einar spun, his scarred face slathered in blood, a hideous mask of violence, his axe raised ready to strike. For a moment, Erlan thought he would too, the rage in

415

his eyes was so intense. 'It's over,' Erlan gasped. 'Over, d'you hear?'

The words seemed to penetrate the red mist of Einar's frenzy, just for long enough to bring him to his senses. 'Aurvandil?' He looked confused. His axe fell limp at his side. Erlan's shoulders sagged in relief.

'Skipper – look out!' The warning was Mikki's. Erlan sensed the threat at his back. He was still turning when he heard the rustle of steps behind him. He ducked, swept his sword-arm round, but it was already too late for that. A howl of fury filled his ears – then something whipped past his face, a pulse of air, then a stifled choke that silenced the howl in a snap. By the time Erlan was round, a sixth man who'd gone unnoticed came skidding in at his feet. A horrible gargling sounded out of his mouth where an arrow with green fletching had impaled his neck. His writhing death throes soon ebbed to stillness.

Now the glade fell silent, but for the victors' panting.

Erlan bent double, his heart galloping like a war-horse against his ribs. 'Berengar,' he muttered in relief, 'you beautiful son of a bitch.'

Nearby, Black Svali was groaning.

'Well, that went well, didn't it?' said Mikki Crow through heaving gasps. 'So much for your fucking signal, skipper.'

'We did it though, eh?' Bull's massive head was bobbing like a buoy in a storm. Erlan recognised in him the weird nervous energy that battle threw over a man. Meanwhile, Einar was staring down at the wreckage of the warrior he had destroyed. Slowly, he wiped his hand over his face, leaving a stippled smear of blood and gobbets of flesh like war paint.

'Come on, you big sap,' jeered Mikki Crow at Black Svali. 'Ain't that bad. Here, up you get.' And he pulled him to his feet.

'Shut your squawking, Crow.' Blood was welling through Svali's fingers where he clutched his arm. 'Soon give you one to match, if you like.'

Erlan wiped his sword clean on one of the dead men's cloaks, then sheathed it. The man's lifeless eyes stared up into the canopy, the wavering firelight reflected off their surface. And draped across his face, a tangle of pale hair. *Kissed by the moon*, he thought, strange words that slipped unbidden into his head.

A stick snapped nearby. Erlan's eyes jerked up. Wyn was steadying himself against a tree on the edge of the glade, his mouth open in astonishment and disgust at the scene before him. 'There's your silver hair, monk.'

'Same over here,' said Bull, examining another corpse.

'And here,' said Ran over another.

The hair of the man Einar had killed was too drenched in blood to tell its colour.

'Hey, lads, what do you reckon?' said Ran with a chuckle, as he pulled a wolf-pelt off the corpse at his feet, swung it over his shoulders and pulled down the wolf-mask. He looked damned menacing, despite the dopey grin beaming out from under the wolf's long fangs.

'Reckon we've just got started,' said Erlan grimly. 'Now let's clear up this mess.'

*

417

It took them another day to find what they were looking for.

Berengar's mastery of forest lore made it feel straight-forward enough, but Erlan doubted whether they would have got within fifty leagues of the place without him. Looking round at Einar, at the monk and the last of the river-men who formed this unlikely little shield-band, all he could think was that they were a Hel of a long way from any river now.

They had buried all the bodies in a shallow grave. The last thing they needed was another group of *ulfheðnar* discovering their comrades and being put on alert – especially since they still had their horses with them and would be easy to track.

Before they found it, they had seemed to be climbing to higher ground. This was the oldest part of the Immerwald, according to Berengar, where the most ancient trees which had sired all the others still grew. As if to prove it, he had shinned up into the uppermost branches of an oak for a 'look-see' while the others took their rest. He was soon down again, insisting Erlan follow him up there.

It was a strange experience, stirring memories he had long laid to rest. Erlan's childhood had been full of tree-climbing, especially before the accident that had left him a cripple. But even afterwards, he and Inga had often disappeared for hours into the woods above Vendlagard, challenging each other as to whom could climb the highest. And following Berengar up the tree, limb by limb, as far into the canopy as would bear their weight, he thought of Inga. Sweet Inga. And he remembered her laughter and gentle goading. *Come on, sister, you slow pony! Is there nothing I can't beat you at?* Inevitably, she could climb higher because she was lighter and could reach a smaller branch that would buckle under his weight. And then it wasn't Inga he was thinking of, but Marta. The same long dark hair, the same brightness in her eyes. And something insistent and desperate rose up in his chest. That he must save her. He *must*. From whatever fate these weird forest-folk intended for her. He must... because he hadn't saved Inga... Because he couldn't.

He had failed Inga. He would not fail the girl.

'Here's far enough,' said Berengar abruptly. Erlan grunted, wedging himself into the crook of a branch and hooking his arm around the trunk. 'Take a look at that.' Berengar pointed to the south-west.

Erlan did so, and that way saw that the ground continued to rise towards a large, rounded hill. And at the top – you could almost say crowning it – was the mightiest tree he had ever seen. It rose to twice the height of any of the trees surrounding it, for as far as the eye could see. 'What is it?' he murmured in wonder.

'The *Immerbaum*. The Forever-Tree. That there's the oldest tree in the Immerwald. Some have said all the legends of Yggdrasil come from it.'

'What do you mean?'

'Well,' croaked the tracker, 'it's an ash tree. And you never saw a tree so big in all your life.'

'Never.' But now he did, Erlan could imagine it was a thing so remarkable that few men could resist weaving it into a tale. 'Even so,' he said, 'the Tree of Worlds can't stand in the world of men, can it? That doesn't make sense.' He remembered what it was like to ask such questions of Tolla, his old nurse, when he was a boy. He always had questions, but never quite as many as Inga.

419

Berengar chuckled. 'I ain't saying it's true, fella. Just saying, a tree that big gets a man thinking, huh?'

'Why are you showing it to me?'

'Because... don't nobody who knows the woods go up that way anymore. Not after what they used to do there in the dark days before the light of Christ came to these lands.' Here, he crossed himself. He was doing that a lot more the further they went. 'The place is...' He picked at his cheek, trying to think of the right words. 'Well, there's bad airs up there, something like that. Spirits and what not. Don't do to go prying into that place.'

'Yet you're still with us,' said Erlan quietly, not taking his eyes off the great forefather of the forest. Berengar said nothing in reply. Erlan turned to him. 'Why do I get the feeling that's where we're headed?'

Berengar gave a mirthless grunt. 'Same reason I do. That's where the trail's leading.' He blew out a big sigh. 'Are you ready for it, though? I confess I don't know what we'll find up there.'

Erlan snorted. 'I've been in darker places than this.' He was thinking of the oppressive blindness of the Niflagard caverns.

Berengar grimaced. 'Darker, maybe... But none near so evil.'

By the Hanged. Why the Hel does everything have to be done in darkness?

So Erlan thought as he crawled forward on his belly. The others were close by him. Pine needles and the soft earth

420

beneath him smelled sweet and sharp; it was mercifully dry, and free from the thick falls of leaves in the deciduous parts of the forest.

A stroke of luck. It meant they could move about in relative silence. And they needed to since they couldn't yet tell what they were crawling towards. They'd left the horses some way back down the hill in Black Svali's keeping. He'd wanted to come but Erlan wouldn't let him. The wound in his arm wasn't fatal, but bad enough. And he'd be more use covering their retreat than flailing around with a useless limb if things went sour.

Shapes loomed ahead. He saw a long, high impenetrable shadow running across his field of vision. It was a moment before he realised he was looking at a wall. As his eyes grew accustomed and felt out the edges of what he was seeing, he thought it had the look of a stockade. Piles driven into the earth, their tops sharpened to points.

He signalled the others to stop.

Einar crawled up next to him, his face a gargoyle of shadows. 'This is the place,' he gnarred under his breath. 'I feel it... Can feel she's close.'

'I know, my friend,' Erlan whispered. 'Me too.'

Close or not, dead or alive, Orīana and her daughter might as well have been on the moon unless they could figure a plan to get inside. The walls were twenty feet high, and who knew what lay on the other side? Except for the gigantic ash tree at the stronghold's centre, which rose above them into the night like a black storm cloud.

Wanting to get a clearer sense of the place, Erlan sent his two nimblest men, Ran and Berengar, to orbit the fort. To report back whatever they found that could be useful. A few minutes later, the pair returned and described in breathless whispers a gateway they'd seen on the opposite side, flanked by a pair of pitch flares. But the gate itself looked locked and secure. Ran swore blind he'd seen a guard patrolling the top of the wall, which suggested some kind of parapet on the other side, but Berengar said he'd imagined it. He hadn't seen a whisker.

Who to believe?

In any case, a direct assault seemed out of the question. With six men and a monk, there was little hope of success – that is if they even managed to gain entry over the wall. And digging under the piles would be equally bootless. No. Their only way in was straight through the gate; and if that, then by deceit.

They withdrew a little distance to take counsel. A waning crescent moon hung high in the sky, just visible through the heavy canopy, sharp as a sickle. The dark of the night was thick, though not quite complete. Perhaps it could be worked to their advantage.

'We also have the pelts,' he murmured.

'Aye, but that's about all we've got,' countered Einar.

'Could be enough to get us in the gate at least,' suggested Mikki Crow, tapping the haft of his seax. 'After that... cold steel.'

'Cold steel in our own bellies most likely,' said Ran.

'If your liver's too white for this, Gotlander,' snarled Einar, 'go back down and send Black Svali up here. At least he has a pair of stones.'

'Hey, I got me stones,' protested Ran. 'Just reckon running

straight in and breaking a few heads ain't going to get us too far.'

'We're wasting time,' said Erlan. 'We have to think what's most convincing.'

'You need a prisoner,' said Wyn.

'A prisoner?'

'Sure. If they've been abducting children, or your friends, or anyone else, then presumably it's nothing out of the ordinary for a band of them to return with a prisoner in hand.'

'You mean yourself?'

'Well, why not?'

'Because it could be bloody dangerous. We've no notion what they might do to you.'

'It's dangerous for all of us,' Wyn retorted, his voice determined. 'Anyway, it's a risk I'm willing to take. Once inside, we shall have to improvise.'

'Improvise? Gods alive!' snorted Einar. 'You mean make this bollocks up as we go along.'

'Well, do you have a better suggestion, friend?'

'Aye,' growled Einar. 'Matter of fact, I do.'

Erlan rolled his shoulders, adjusting to the weight of the wolf-pelt and Einar's considerable bulk hanging between him and Bull. After the decline of his notoriously large belly during his convalescence in Byzantium, Einar had made solid progress building it back to its former glory. And right now he was playing the role of wounded warrior with great conviction, dragging his feet, and groaning in a manner which suggested the poor bastard hadn't long to live. He had Black Svali's blood-soaked bandage wrapped around his face to gruesome effect, while Erlan and Bull had the hoods of their pelts pulled low as they could.

It was the very heart of night when, they hoped, most of whatever folk dwelled in this place would be sleeping.

The gate stood tall before them. A pair of flares burned steadily in the windless air. On the gable above the gate doors, a goat-skull with huge black horns.

Erlan sucked a breath and thumped hard on the door.

For a few moments, nothing happened. He and Bull exchanged glances but he resisted the urge to look back to the others waiting in the shadows. He raised his fist to knock again but then footsteps and a voice sounded above them. Ran had seen true.

'Who goes there?' the voice called softly.

'Let us in, for fuck's sake,' he called up at the shadow standing behind the parapet above them, praying his accent would not betray him. 'He's been mauled by a bear.'

'A bear? Sigulf – is that you?'

'It's Sigulf been mauled. Open the damn gate quickly! We need to lay him down.'

The shadow hesitated.

'Are you just going to stand up there and gawp? He hasn't much time.'

'Coming down,' called the shadow, quickly followed by a thump of wood as he descended the steps from the walkway.

'Keep your head down,' Erlan whispered to Einar. 'Remember you're supposed to be half dead.'

A few moments later, there was a rattle of chain and a

424

murmur of voices, the clunk of the spar being lifted off its brackets, then one of the doors swung open.

Not waiting for further invitation, they hustled inside, Erlan and Bull dragging Einar's inert corpse, while Erlan kept his head down and muttered curses and half-formed explanations. 'A bear attacked our camp… Three dead… Ripped apart like sacks of meat… Nearly did for four of us… We were lucky to get away…' and so on, talking too fast to give the gate-keepers a chance to properly interrogate them. Always moving, face down in a puddle of shadow.

'Where can we lie him down?' growled Bull.

One of the guards beckoned them forward. 'This way.' He gestured towards a small planked lean-to against the outer wall. 'There's a pallet in there you can put him on.'

'He needs water,' Erlan said to one of them. The man stood there immobile, his white hair shining dully in the brooding dark. 'Quickly, damn it!'

'Fine, fine, I'll go.'

The watchman left, while the other led them into the hut, holding the ragged drape aside. Hurriedly, they bundled Einar in and lay him on the pallet, Erlan kneeling over him as if checking his wound. There was a primitive pine-pitch lamp burning away on a table with a small and smoky flame.

The man stood back. 'How bad is it?'

'Hard to tell. Can you bring the light?'

The watchman obliged, kneeling down with the lamp beside Erlan. Einar's face was grim enough with the scars from his fire-burns, but just then he looked like some Helheim ghoul daubed with Svali's blood. The man peered closer, not noticing the subtle movement of Erlan's empty hand.

Suddenly his whole demeanour changed. 'Hey, who is that?' Then his eyes darted around him at the others. 'Wait a second. Who the fuck are you people?'

Einar sat up. '*Hey-dau*, laddy,' he growled, his Sveär accent thick as gravy. 'They call me Fat-Belly... They call you dead.'

After the first, dealing with the second watchman was simple enough. They waited until he appeared through the door with his bucket, and Bull dealt with him with his bare hands – a simple twist and he was dead without so much as a whisper.

Erlan blew out the lamp. 'Signal the others,' he murmured. 'And quietly.'

Moments later, three more wolf-pelts were slipping through the gate, concealing Ran, Mikki and Berengar. Erlan was about to close the door when another hand slid around the edge of it.

'Wyn? Didn't I tell you to wait with Svali—'

'And I told you, I can be useful.'

Erlan cursed, but if the Anglian wanted to put his neck in the noose, there wasn't time to argue about it.

'What's that horrible stink?' muttered Mikki Crow.

'Best not think about it,' Berengar grimaced.

It was the first chance they'd had to really look at the place. Though from their position, they could see very little. The whole enclosure was dominated by the enormous ash tree, its branches rising like plumes of black smoke at its centre. But there were several other buildings spread around it, all plank-wood, some with turf roofs, others with shingles.

'How do we find the children without kicking over a whole wasp nest of those wolf-men?' asked Wyn.

'Aye, and the gold,' said Mikki, lest anyone forget it.

'The walkway,' said Erlan, looking up. 'There's a better view from up there. Einar, Wyn, come with me.'

A few moments later, they were crouched low and surveying the landscape of shadows below them. From their vantage point, they could at least make out some distinction between the buildings. Some looked to be no more than pit-houses, others like small meet-halls, with a scattering of byre-like stalls among them. There was also a triangular structure visible through the branches on the other side of the *Immerbaum*, for which none of them had an explanation. It was Wyn who spotted the low roofs of the long-houses.

'There.' He pointed to the north-eastern side of the settlement. 'They're being held in those.'

'How can you be sure?' asked Erlan. The things looked perfectly innocuous. They might house animals, or store grain.

'I don't know.' Wyn's eyes slid to his. 'But I am certain.'

'I think he's right,' said Einar, nodding grimly. 'At least we start there.'

Dear gods, thought Erlan. *We hardly have time to go on mere hunches.* But even as he looked at the long, low shadows, something in his gut stirred in agreement with the others. 'All right. Let's move.'

Splitting into two groups, the would-be raiders stalked through the settlement, keeping to the thickest shadows. Not a word passed between them, only signs and gestures, making not a sound but for the soft tread of their boots in the forest earth. Everywhere was the smell of fresh cut wood, which lingered for years around newly constructed buildings. But

427

also that other smell, sickly sweet and cloying, that laced every anxious breath.

The stench of death.

Every one of them knew it; none wanted to acknowledge it. After all, they had come for the living – if they were still to be found.

The whole settlement had a sepulchral stillness to it. Here and there hung an outside torch in a sconce, burnt out earlier in the night. But there was precious little sign of any life. Perhaps these folk felt entirely secure, hidden away so deep in the forest. Or perhaps there were unseen protections that lingered over the place, dark powers that need only be summoned when the need arose.

In any case, they saw no other nightwatchmen at all until they came within half an arrow's flight of the first of the longhouses. It was only there that they saw how low the buildings truly were. They must have been dug down into the earth because the edge of the pitched thatch-roofs nearly touched the ground, and the end wall and gable were so low, any man of normal height would have to go down on his knees to enter. There was no smoke-hole, no windows, each one like a solid chest sunk into the earth. A strongbox in which, Erlan supposed, a man might keep his possessions.

He was about to move forward when Berengar held his arm. The tracker flicked his hawk-eyes to the right and there Erlan saw a silhouette leaning against one corner of the longhouse. The outline was faint against the rest of the darkness. But there was clearly someone standing there.

'Can you take him?' Erlan murmured.

'Do you really have to ask?' The woodsman's teeth flashed

and then, without a sound, he unslung his bow, nocked up, drew a deep breath and held it.

Several heartbeats thudded in Erlan's chest. Then the arrow was away. An instant later came the crumpled sound of a body falling to the ground, and the silhouette was no more.

They found the door to that first long-house chained, secured with a wooden peg that had been hammered into an iron bracket. Erlan tried to prise it open but it was stuck fast. He swore. The last thing he wanted to do was wake everyone up with the sound of his hammering at the thing with the butt of his seax, trying to work it loose.

'Where's Bull?' he hissed.

He could see the others a short distance away, awaiting their next move. Meanwhile, Einar was peering through a crack in the wall-planks. Erlan motioned for the others to cross. Eventually they saw him and came scuttling over into the long-house's shadow.

Even with a combination of Erlan's seax and Bull's brute force, it still took a painfully long time to crack the wood and loosen the peg sufficiently that they could pull it out. Whoever had locked this place meant for it to stay locked until they were good and ready to have it open. In the moments that followed, Erlan might have wished it had stayed that way.

The smells were strong here, too. Not of death, but of something foul enough.

As he put his hand to the latch, he felt a sudden tremor of overwhelming dread. A kind of foreboding – as if this was a door better left unopened.

429

He gave it a shove all the same. Immediately the dead air escaping the darkness within made him gag. He covered his mouth and nostrils.

Inside, everything was silent for a moment. And then he realised it wasn't silence he was hearing, but the suck and sway of breathing. As if the whole building were a lung – diseased, putrid, dying.

'Go on.' Einar impatient behind him, jolting him out of his trance. Truth was, he was fearful of what lay within. Of what they had found. He shuffled forward a couple of steps. Then a couple more. Then his foot touched something solid. Whatever it was retracted from him at once, and he heard a soft scuffling away from him. Slowly, painfully slowly, his eyes were adjusting to the deeper darkness. Trying to draw some sense out of the black abyss into which he was staring. The damn wolf-hood wasn't helping. He pushed it back off his head. Immediately he heard a sound like the sharp intake of a thousand breaths. But before he could make anything of it, Einar broke the eery quiet.

'Orīana?' he demanded of the darkness.

The darkness said nothing. But it was moving now, stirring like the coils of a worm in its underground lair.

'Orīana?' Einar repeated.

'Marta?' said Erlan in turn. He moved further in, his shins knocking against other… *creatures*. Bodies that retreated from him like he carried the plague. The acrid fumes of human urine mingled with faeces were enough to sting his eyes. 'Is anyone there? One of you answer me, damn it.'

For a second, he wished they had some light. A torch, a lamp, a tallow candle – anything that would give him some revelation of what surrounded them. Although he sensed that he may regret it.

'Who are you?' said a voice startlingly close to him. A voice soft and high, though so cracked with infirmity and hardship that he couldn't tell whether it belonged to someone young or old.

'You're not one of them,' said another like it, further away.

'No. Do you know a woman called Orīana? She has red hair… Or a girl called Marta?'

But now his presence had the opposite effect. The more confident the wraiths hiding in the shadows became that he and his comrades were not of the same ilk as their captors, the closer they crept, and suddenly he felt someone – or something – touch his hand. He recoiled. It was cold and damp. Clammy. It took a moment for him to recognise the feel of a human hand. Little fingers gripping his own. Tight as they could, but the grip was feeble.

'Please,' whispered a disembodied voice in the dark, weak and small to match the hand, loud enough for his ears only. 'Take me with you. Please, sir. My name is Fenna. I beg of you – take me from this place.' The little grip tightened in desperation.

And then, without any warning, someone behind him – perhaps Berengar – ignited a piece of charcloth and with that a piece of moss tinder. When the flame caught, for a brief moment – no more than a few seconds – light flared in the close air, shocking as a flash of lightning. In its illumination, Erlan saw a face so gaunt, so grey, with eyes so sunken, so utterly devoid of any hope or joy, lips chapped and chewed, teeth black and broken, that he thought he must have

431

stumbled into the halls of the dead, where Hel ruled over all her minions. He glimpsed other faces, staring faces, young faces, equally sullen and saturated in sorrow and misery and despair, with eyes so wide in sepulchral surprise that for a moment it felt like being hemmed by the souls of the damned.

The sense of engulfing horror was too much. He backed away, wanting to be out of there, to be far away from this place. And far from them. It was an evil response – a recoil of fear and disgust. But it was quite beyond his control. Oriana was not here. Nor was Marta. Just a room full of the dead. Dead children. Dead souls.

But the more he tried to withdraw, the more hands laid hold of him.

'They're not here,' he snarled at Einar. 'Go back. Back, damn you!'

'Is this not why we came?' demanded Wyn, who was nearer the door, beyond Einar. 'To care for these poor souls.'

'Why you came, maybe. Not us. We came for our friends. And for our gold.'

'Have you no pity, Northman? What you have about you is more precious than gold.'

Erlan waded through the pawing hands back towards the dim dark-blue rectangle that marked the doorway outside. 'I've an ocean of pity, monk,' he snarled at Wyn's shadow. 'But there's nothing we can do for these...' He couldn't bring himself to call them children. Couldn't bring himself to call them anything at all. 'They're too many.'

He pushed and shoved his way through his men, a fluttery panic rising in his chest as he pulled free of the hands that tried to keep him there. 'Einar,' he barked. 'We must try another. We haven't much time. These ones won't stay quiet for long.'

When he got outside again, he gulped down the night air – which after the long-house tasted sweet and fresh as mountain meltwater, though not a hundred heartbeats before had smelled rank with the stench of death.

Skírpa had awoken with all the others. Experience and their captors' cruelty had conditioned all of them to become instantly alert as soon as the door to the long-house opened. But at once, he understood something else was happening here, something out of the ordinary. The familiar silhouette of the wolf-garbed men moved differently this time. Whoever it was hobbled into the fester of the room uncertainly. Blindly.

Others had followed him in, as creeping and hesitant as the first.

This was not how the wolf-men behaved normally.

Skírpa had listened and observed, wondering at their confusion, at their sightless fumbling and fear, turning over the golden solidus in his fingers. It had become a habit now. The cold, hard touch of this strange talisman, totemic of another world. A mystery to him, how a solidus stamped with the visage of the Emperor Leo holding a simple cross had journeyed this far in so short a time. Leo had been on the throne less than two years. The coin itself could not have been minted even as long ago as that. Yet here was his image, hundreds, no thousands of miles from the seat of his power, in this dark and damnable forest. Now in his hand. It seemed to herald something. But he knew not what.

And then, in that sudden flare of light, that blaze of illumination which might once have haunted him in his nightmares, the answer was there in front of him, not a dozen feet away. A face illumined. The face of his enemy; no, more than that – of his nemesis. As if those hate-filled prayers he had uttered as he lay languishing at the mercy of the sea had indeed been answered. As if the Author of All Fates had somehow cast their lives back together, entwining his destiny around that of the Northman's once more. *Erlan Aurvandil*. A name as hateful to him as any he'd ever known.

And suddenly it all began to make sense. The red-haired woman's dying prayers; the raven-haired girl and her pious song; the golden coin turning in his hand. All of it somehow came back to that man who had been his undoing. And now this chance lay within his grasp.

He had waited, listened, as the men withdrew, leaving the other captives in a state of agitation. Leaving the door wide open. And yet, it seemed that only he had the mettle to scorn his captors, to break the prison of his mind as well as his body. He slipped his way through the herd of broken children, knowing now for sure whom he must serve. And he felt a thrill of certainty surge through him, lending him strength and speed, felt the delicious anticipation of pleasing his Master.

Alvarik would love him for this.

This thought silencing all others, he slipped out into the darkness and stole like a spirit towards the One Eyed's hall.

*

'Marta?' It was the third long-house they had entered. Their third journey into Hel.

Another guard lay dead outside. Erlan had to admit: Berengar was damned effective, no two ways to that. But still the search was fruitless. And the longer they lingered, the longer for their luck to run out.

'Orīana? *Min elskling?* Are you there? It's me, Einar. *Agápi Mou?*' The fat man's voice became increasingly plaintive. The gruff joker, the violent man blinded by fury, had faded away, leaving only this broken-hearted husk of a man, pleading with the darkness.

Nothing.

Again. Nothing…

Erlan wanted to scream in frustration. To have come this far, to have entered the wolves' lair and still their hands were empty. 'Back,' he said, eager to be away before the children's imploring started up again, which was almost intolerable to him. 'There's one more.'

'And if not there?' said Einar.

'One more,' he repeated. 'There's still hope.'

Aye, but what hope for these wretched creatures?

As he turned to goad the others out through the door, a soft voice spoke out of the shadows behind him. 'Erlan?'

He stopped, looked back. 'Orīana?'

'No. Marta. It's Marta…' And suddenly a shadow was moving through the others, half familiar, yet half unrecognisable from the young girl of their voyage. And before he could scarcely part his arms, she had thrown herself into them, clinging to him with the fervour of a desperate soul. He had to hold his knife away from her, trying not to harm her

435

while at the same time struggling to keep her on her feet as she murmured, 'You came, you came, you came', over and over into his shoulder.

'Where's your mother?' Einar's voice betrayed his urgency. 'Marta – where's Orīana?' Suddenly Einar had hold of her, was turning her towards him.

Erlan felt more than saw her shake her head, felt the sorrow leaching out of her and into the fat man, infecting him with a kind of madness and horror. 'I think she's dead,' she said in a whisper.

'No,' said Einar. '*No.*' The second time was more like a groan.

'They told me... I don't know for sure... I think... I've been praying...' All kinds of half-formed phrases fell out of Marta's lips, none of them giving any reassurance.

'Did you see her die?'

'No, I did not,' replied Marta quickly. 'But...'

'What?'

'I *feel* like she's gone, Einar. I'm sorry.'

Fat-Belly swore softly. 'I won't believe it. Not 'less I see her body with my own eyes. Come on,' he snarled, seizing Erlan and Marta together, shoving them towards the door. 'There's more places she could be.'

But even as they turned back, Berengar, who was watching at the little aperture, said: 'We've got company.'

'Move,' said Erlan. 'Move now!'

And suddenly everything was happening very fast.

It had to. They were running, and yet there were other bodies moving in the shadows now. 'Get the others – we're getting out of here!' said Erlan.

'But Orīana,' protested Einar.

'I know, old friend. I know! But we're no use to her if we're dead. Let's go.'

Berengar was already ahead of them, chasing over to the last of the long-houses to give warning to Mikki and the others. There were shouts of command in the direction of the gate. And then the night began to come alive with howls and yelps and strange bestial noises. Noises that were becoming all too familiar.

'Have we got everyone?' Erlan drew his sword with a *schick* of steel, putting Marta between him and Einar.

'I'm not leaving Orīana in this Hel-hole.'

'What about the gold?' snorted Mikki, breathless.

'Forget the gold. How the fuck do we get out of here?' said Ran. 'Sounds like they already have the gate covered.'

'There's no point fighting our way out the gate if we don't have to. We can go over the wall,' said Erlan. But before he could decide which direction offered their best chance of escape, there was a blood-chilling yell behind them.

'Watch yerself, skipper,' said Berengar, dropping to his knees, and in a couple of heartbeats, he'd nocked an arrow and loosed it into the night. A moment later the yell was cut short. 'More coming,' he said, voice calm as a windless sea.

'That way,' said Erlan. 'Go.' His choice was driven half by blind hope, half by the instinct simply to run away, but it took them through the gap between two of the long-houses, and onwards towards the massive ash tree at the heart of the stronghold. As they ran, Marta stumbled along with them, half-carried, half-sprinting herself, the ragged hem of her robes hitched up in her fists.

They broke out of the cover of the buildings into the open ground in front of the tree, while behind the sounds of their pursuers grew louder. Berengar stopped at the corner of a bigger hall and shot off another two shafts. *Two fewer men to deal with*, Erlan thought, with little doubt that the woodsman had hit his mark.

He led them across the open ground, all pretence of stealth now gone. They just had to get out. Straight and simple. But as he was midway across, his eye snagged on something hanging from the lowest branches of the tree.

He made the mistake of looking.

What he saw made him draw up at once.

'What in the name of all Hel...' muttered Ran.

Dangling from the lowest limbs of the tree were a dozen or more bodies. They were all of them stripped naked, some men – or boys, rather – but most were female. All had been disfigured in horrible ways: their abdomens cut open, their viscera removed, leaving an ugly flap of skin and a dark cavern of nothing. Like an empty eye socket. Indeed, even in that glance, Erlan felt like a grotesque many-eyed monster was staring at them, each eye black and penetrating, peering out at him from the belly of every corpse.

But worst of all by far: the body hanging right in the centre had long red hair.

Einar must have seen her the same moment as Erlan. Because scarcely had Orīana's name formed in Erlan's head than the fat man let out a soul-wrenching cry, full of anguish and despair. If there was any doubt before, there was none now.

'No! No! *NO!*' wailed Einar to the pitiless sliver of moon.

But all the answer he got was a *thump, thump, thump* of axe-hafts banging against linden shields. Erlan turned and saw that way their doom. A line of *ulfheðnar* emerged from the buildings ahead of them. Six, maybe eight of them at a glance. Erlan cursed. He wasn't the only one.

But even as his heart was sinking, he spied their salvation beyond them. The perimeter wall rose like a dark curtain that way, background to the *ulfheðnar's* war-cries and mad posturing. And even in the frail light of the dying moon, he could see steps rising to the parapet walkway.

He sucked a deep breath, summoning what courage and energy he had left for this fight. It had been a long and sickening night. But it was far from over. He rolled his new sword over his wrist. But even before he had shuffled the grip in his hand, Einar had already launched himself at the warriors standing in their way, a terrible cry of vengeance on his lips.

Erlan snarled a command at the others before he lost them to the battle-madness, too. 'Don't stop to kill. Go straight through them and on to the wall!'

That done, all he could do was lead by example. He had no plan. Just blind headlong flight. A human battering ram, dispensing death and mayhem to anyone who stood in his way, puncturing a hole through them like a needle through leather.

The next few moments were a hacking, snarling, whirling storm of blood and oaths and death. He saw hands severed, throats skewered, legs hewn and slashed. Gods only knew where Marta was. The only protection he knew how to give her was to kill, kill, kill again, until there was nothing and no one left.

439

He was dimly aware of a frenzy of steel on his left. Einar's axe rising and falling, again and again, like some baleful blade of judgement, come to drench the world in blood for all its sins.

And then somehow they were running on. The *ulfheðnar* dead or dying, fallen in their wake. He flew, despite that he was a cripple, fleet as Räsvelg, the mighty eagle whose wings beat out the very winds. And he was at the foot of the stairs and chasing up them, only half-conscious that he was dragging someone with him.

At the head of the steps, he flung his companion ahead of him, seeing Marta's long hair whip around her as she stumbled up onto the walkway. Then Mikki was past, his long limbs scooping her up and bundling her to the parapet. Then another and another – Bull and Ran.

Erlan stopped and looked behind them.

Einar was some distance back, but sprinting now, faster than he'd ever seen a fat man run. Yet he was free. He would make it, and even as Erlan had the thought, Einar reached the bottom of the staircase. But then Erlan looked back again. And this time, the sight was not so rosy.

He saw Berengar, his slight figure standing in the open ground. An arrow nocked, his bow stretched. But all around him, *ulfheðnar* encircled him. Closing in, their wolf-pelts and masks pulled over their faces, howling and yipping with all the air in their lungs. He watched as Berengar loosed an arrow. A wolf-pelt fell. But the gap soon closed. Another arrow... his last. Another pelt for his memory. *For his saga-song,* thought Erlan.

By the Hanged, the lad deserved one.

Another body fell. Another gap closed.

And then Berengar's quiver was spent, and the wolves moved in for the kill, and soon the blades were rising and falling, red with his blood.

Aye – Berengar was a saga-hero.

Except what had they really won here? Only more death. But what of life?

It was then that Erlan thought of the monk.

'Wyn,' he exclaimed, turning to the others. 'Where's the monk?'

Mikki Crow was helping Marta over the parapet. 'I didn't see him. Not since the long-houses.'

'It's too late,' said Ran, eyes darting. 'He's lost.'

The Gotlander was right. 'All right,' Erlan said with grim resignation. 'Over! All of you, go!'

'Orīana,' roared Einar to the black sky and the slender moon and the dark and brooding tree at the centre of it all. '*Elskling!*'

'If you want vengeance, brother, first you must live. Now go! That's an order.'

And so the fat man went over the stakes.

Erlan took a last look back, hoping to catch a glimpse of the holy man. But all he saw were the bodies hanging from the tree. Those huge lidless eyes cut into them staring up at him. He shuddered, turned back to the wall, and jumped over into the darkness below.

PART THREE

SKULD

THE WEB OF WHAT IS TO COME

CHAPTER THIRTY-TWO

Fenna rolled over again, still awake.

Her bones ached. Her head ached. It had been days since she had been able to sleep for more than a fitful hour at a time, and the night stretched like a long empty road before her.

Was she supposed to grow accustomed to the fear that gnawed at her? Was she to resign herself to these last hopeless days of her short life, to become deaf to the pitiful pleadings of the other children?

But nothing the wolf-men had done was half so cruel as that brief spark of hope that had shone for one brilliant moment, only to be extinguished in the next. Painful as it was, she relived it again and again through the dead hours of the night, each time willing the memory to a different conclusion. One where the big man with the dark shining eyes took hold of her hand, said it was going to be all right, threw her on his back like her father used to do, and took her away from this place. Far away.

Instead, reality came crashing in like a storm-wave off the ocean. He had prised off her little hand, had receded in disgust. And before any of them had had the courage to follow them out of the door, the wolf-men had returned.

Her mother had told her to be brave. Had said she would have a good life, if only she were a good girl. She had tried. She had meant to. But it had started almost at once. Almost within screaming distance of Dort and her mother's dwelling. If only she could have screamed. If only the fist had not been clamped so hard over her mouth. If only...

Hope was a cruel thing. An empty thing.

God did not see. God did not care. He saw neither her sin, as her mother had often warned, nor anyone else's.

Yet hope was also obstinate. Like a tick that would not die. So maybe she would just let it sit there. She hadn't the energy now to pluck it off her. It could do as it wished.

There was a girl who slept on the far side of the devil's hole they kept them in. At night, at a certain time, she could see the shape of the moon through a crack in the wall. She had watched it wane, watched the dark of the month, and now the birth of a new moon had come. It would not be many days before it would grow to fullness.

Not many more days to endure.

There was only one decision left to her and she was resolved to see it through:

That when the end came, she would welcome it.

Thunarulf ripped the tender rabbit flesh off the bone and didn't bother to wipe away the grease that ran down his beard.

446

He was angry. Seemed like he was always angry these days. But today was worse than others.

It had been their first real test. And far as he saw it, they had failed it miserably.

Fucking Radulf.

What kind of shit-for-brain halfwit would fall for that trick? The silly cunt deserved the knife in the throat that he got. And now Alvarik was pissed because of the girl that was taken. Said he'd had a special purpose for her... the *next time*. Aye, no guessing what that was. But when Alvarik got pissed, it meant life got ugly again. For Thunarulf. For everyone.

It seemed a long time ago now that he was running his own band of thieves, slitting the odd throat along the forest paths some ways north of there for a few coins or trinkets or sacks of grain, then vanishing into the trees. Kept them in bread and ale and coin enough to live on. But even if he was happy to lie to everyone else, there weren't much point in lying to himself: he and his men had been leeches on the arse of life. All right for a time. But there weren't no prospects in it. No future.

Guess that's what Alvarik had offered him. Offered them all. A future. Something open-ended, something which you couldn't tell how it would work out. Kind of gave you hope it might turn out for the good. For you at least, if not for anyone else. But so far it felt a lot like more of the same. But worse.

The whole wolf thing had been exciting at first. It was a lark, dyeing his hair, putting the shits up anyone they cared to. Making a name for themselves. But they weren't proper berserkers. They were scarcely more than the pack of thieves they'd always been, except now they all wore the same clothes. Looked kind of the same. Ate the same. Drank the same. Fucked the same.

By the Fires, it didn't amount to much.

Not until that gold came in. *Aye. That much gold is a pretty thing. Maybe even a way out of here...* Yet even the merest thought of that terrified him. The idea of going against the One Eyed was like a traitor lurking within his own chest.

How did he do it?

The Little Fella, as Thunarulf thought of him – although he would never dare breathe a name like that, not out loud. Not even in his dreams, lest someone heard him and it got back to the vicious prick. But how did the squat brute hold that power over you? Magic? Or like he really had some god in his pocket?

No, the whole One Eyed act was some weird shit. Everyone knew the stories of Wotan. But this was taking it to another level. And Thunarulf was fed up drinking the foul-tasting brews that rotted his head and addled his thinking, just 'cause the Little Fella told them to. One day he was going to lose his reason for good. Didn't matter what the One Eyed gave you then – girls, gold, a chance to split a few heads. None of that were much good if you couldn't think straight no more.

Aye, there were days he reckoned he was as much a captive as the bairns locked up in them stinking human byres.

How did *he* do it?

He'd asked that question enough times now and still come to no answer that made any sense. Only to find himself standing there again come the next full moon, mad as a marten on heat, along with the rest of them. Swept up in it all. Drinking it all down.

Maybe it didn't matter *how* he did it. The fact was, Alvarik did it.

And if anyone's going to challenge him, thought Thunarulf, slipping back into his cowardice like a warm bath... *it sure as Hel ain't going to be me.*

Demetrios's arse was sore.

Of course, there was being saddle sore, and there was what he was experiencing. A kind of epic odyssey into new and fantastical landscapes of pain and discomfort which he wouldn't wish on his worst enemy's rear end.

Well... Maybe he could think of a couple of characters back in Byzantium who might have done with a few hours of it, at least. That taverner in the Strategion for one. The man who'd sold him these sandals for another, which were barely hanging onto his feet.

By Christ, he was a long way from home. Maybe he was ready to admit to himself that he'd got a little carried away. Come to think of it, 'carried away' was exactly what had happened. He'd always been a soft touch for a pretty face and, well... Lady Lilla certainly had that.

Although she had precious little else to her credit just now.

No. The truth of it was, he had jumped, thrown himself all in, only to watch the ground fall away under his feet. And now he seemed to be in freefall.

He was a fugitive in someone else's land, witness to some stilted back and forth between his mistress and her captor.

Karil was a preening cock of a man. Vain, bloated with hubris, and, let's not forget, defeated. In fact, Karil was a man whose future seemed about as bleak as his own.

As for his mistress, he still couldn't quite work her out.

Something had happened between the pair of them that first night after the grubby little skirmish they had called a battle. When they'd snuck off into the wood. If Demetrios were a betting man... Christ's blood, he *was* a betting man, but even so, he couldn't have said where he'd put his money. They did the deed. Or maybe they didn't. In any case, the result seemed to be a kind of cool reserve subsisting between the Sveär queen and this Frankish warlord.

They'd ridden – or rather they'd fled – to the south-west. Into a region they called the Eifel mountains, though in truth they were scarcely more than hills. It seemed Karil had friends all over the landscape, despite that he had been defeated and was now on the run. There was no end of Austrasian folk popping up all over the place only too willing to serve his cause. Too bad they hadn't been with him sooner, or else Demetrios and his much-abused nether parts might have had somewhere reasonable, warm and, above all, dry to recuperate. But that wasn't how it fell out.

Soon after they pitched camp, word had reached them that the Lady Plectrude was under siege in Koln.

'King Chilperic wants her money,' Karil had told Lady Lilla. 'Which by rights is my inheritance,' he'd insisted. Of course, why wouldn't he? This Frankish lord was wronged on every score, the way he told it. But Demetrios had his doubts.

Then there was the Frisian king Rathbod, who was itching for his share of the spoils. But Karil had a plan, so he insisted.

This retreat into the Eifel mountains was not an ignominious defeat, as it plainly looked to Demetrios, but rather prelude to a cunning counter-stroke against his enemies. Although Karil couldn't say when the time was right for that.

Meanwhile Demetrios bravely struggled on, bored and infuriated in roughly equal measure. If only the wound on his arse would start to heal...

But whether the future promised this – or anything else good for him – was a mystery far beyond his fathoming.

CHAPTER THIRTY-THREE

They rode for a day straight without stopping. Heading due north through the forest, best they could tell.

Only after the fall of dusk did Erlan start to feel safe from pursuit. Even so, it was curious. For all their ferocious appearance, the *ulfheðnar* had a surprising lack of initiative. As if they had not the wherewithal to think for themselves, but waited on the will of their leader, like a real pack of wolves. If they had wanted to hunt them down, it would not have been hard to track the horses. But so far, there were no signs of any imminent danger.

This didn't mean they had the luxury of feeling relieved.

Besides, the sense of failure and loss far outweighed any relief they might have felt. And of course, it was worst of all for Einar.

Sometimes nightmares fill a man's head with baseless fears. But sometimes those fears come true. For Einar, he could not have even dreamed the terrible sight of Orīana's ruined body. Erlan had not the words to comfort his friend.

He felt sore enough for the loss of Berengar, not only because his guidance would have been a boon to get them out of the forest, but because he was a good man. A reliable man. Now just another wasted life in the wake of Erlan's wanderings. And Wyn… for all that he didn't understand him, Erlan had liked the man. Had felt there was some profit in his company. But now Wyn was caught in that maw of darkness, either already dead or else destined for a fate that was somehow worse. A kind of living death.

Like those children…

He crushed the thought before it overwhelmed him.

'We've gone far enough,' he declared, now that night had truly fallen. 'We'll camp round that oak.' He pointed out a large old oak tree just off the track they were following, with a trunk of massive girth and knotted and twisting branches that spread in all directions. 'Tie the horses on the other side and we can sleep here.' He marked out the camp and had soon allotted the tasks that would give everyone the food, warmth and rest they needed to continue their journey.

By pure good luck, they had come across a small spring earlier in the day, and all of them had drunk their fill of the brackish water and re-charged their skins and gourds. Black Svali had managed to catch a pair of rabbits while he waited for them, and Ran had brained a wood-pigeon from a lucky shot with a stone and an improvised sling. So they had some victuals to answer the grumbling of their bellies. It wasn't much though, and the scraps of cured venison they had left in their pouches from Karil's stores would not keep them going much longer. They needed to clear the thickest of the Immerwald if they were truly to escape.

'I'm imagining honey-roast chicken,' mumbled Ran, smiling past a mouthful of tough pigeon-meat.

'Apple bacon and warm bread dripping with butter,' countered Bull, closing his eyes and licking his lips.

'I'd settle for a straight-up cut of boiled pork,' said Mikki Crow, considering the miserably small portion that was his lot for the night. 'Or even a hunk of cheese.'

'We'll have decent food soon enough,' said Erlan, trying to sound reassuring, although he had no real certainty of it, even for himself.

'Where are we headed?' asked Einar, who unsurprisingly didn't want to join in the others' attempts to lighten the mood.

'Back to Durum. That's where Lilla will be. And with luck, Karil will be with her.'

'We're coming back.' Einar shot him a dark look. 'Those whoresons don't deserve to live.'

'I know,' he nodded sympathetically. 'I know… But you saw how we fared. We need more men and horses. Properly armed. Now we've found their stronghold, maybe Karil will be willing to help.'

'Sounded like he had his hands full enough when we left him,' observed Ran.

'True,' admitted Erlan. 'But until we know better—'

'What the Hel are we going back for?' blurted Mikki.

'The gold, stupid,' said Bull.

'Vengeance,' said Einar.

'Those… and the children,' said Erlan. 'And Wyn. If he's still alive.'

'You're all of you out o' your fucking skulls,' said Mikki.

'A place like that. You run and you don't stop running till you've put a thousand leagues behind you.'

'What about our gold?' said Bull.

'I didn't see no gold,' barked Mikki. 'Did you? And it ain't worth going back into that Hel-hole just to slit a few more throats. Wyn's dead. Those bairns are dead. Reckon we's damn lucky to be alive ourselves.'

'Maybe we are. But you can't let a place like that go on... existing.' said Erlan. 'It's a boil that needs lancing.'

'Who made you lord of this land, eh?' countered Mikki. 'If folks want to cut each other up, children, monks, whoever, that's their look-out. Ain't no concern of Mikki Crow.'

'The gold *is* there,' said Marta, who till then was curled quietly beside Einar. Her voice was soft and hesitant, feeling its way carefully over each word of Norse which was still a new tongue to her. All eyes shifted to her. 'It came with us. I think their leader means to... to give it to his god.'

'How the Hel d'you give gold to a god?' asked Bull. 'No god's going to walk up and take it off him, is he?'

'She means an offering, I think,' croaked Black Svali. 'You cast it in a river, or a bog, or the sea. Some place you can't never get at it again.'

'Bloody wonderful,' said Mikki. 'And when does he mean to do this?'

'I don't know,' said Marta. 'But... there was another girl... I couldn't understand her tongue exactly. But some words I did understand. Something about the moon. That when it was at its fullest... that would be the end for us. That we would be some sort of... of offering. Maybe the same is true of the gold.'

'When's the next full moon?' asked Bull.

'Twelve days,' returned Black Svali without hesitation.

'You seem pretty damn sure of yourself,' said Ran, turning his gaze up into the treetops.

Black Svali shrugged. 'Some things a man knows.'

Mikki shook his head. '"Maybe the same is true of the gold",' he growled, mimicking Marta in disgust. 'Aye, and maybe it isn't.'

Erlan tossed another stick on their fire. 'There's plenty we don't know. But what we do know is we're no use as we are. That much gold… If it is there, we need the means to transport it. We need more men. A lot more men.' That much seemed plain as the noon-day sun to him. 'But talking about them won't get us any closer to finding them. Durum can't be more than two or three days from here if we keep moving. Everyone get their heads down for a few hours. I'll take first watch.'

The others didn't need any more encouragement than that to get some rest. After the adrenaline of the fight and the long days of travel, a man need only close his eyes for sleep to come over him, heavy as a winter cloak. Even Einar was soon fast asleep.

Erlan sat a little distance off from the others, listening to the night, trying to stay alert to any signs of danger appearing from the direction of the *Immerbaum* and the stronghold of darkness they had left behind.

Different things drifted in and out of his head, images, words, murmurings of the past, blurred visions of the future, but his mind was too weary to latch itself to anything for long. And soon his eyelids began to droop, each blink becoming heavier and heavier, until it wasn't long before he, too, slipped into the gentle arms of sleep...

He was startled awake by the brush of something against his lips.

He lurched onto his elbows, seeing a shadow hovering over him. For a second, neither moved. Then the shadow whispered: 'You came for me. I knew you would.'

'What are you doing here?' Some instinct told him to keep his voice low.

Marta didn't answer. Instead, she bent to him again. Her lips touched his, weightless and warm as sunlight, her fingers slipping through his hair, driving his senses one way while his mind recoiled the other.

'Marta, stop...' He held her away from him. 'Stop.'

'Erlan... *My* Erlan – you came for me.' She slid her body down beside him, laying her head upon his chest. 'Hold me. Please. I need to feel your arms around me.'

'You're not hearing me.' He sat up, put some distance between their faces. 'You're just a child. I came for you *and* for your mother... *We* came for you. All of us.'

'You feel more than that for me, I know it. I've seen it too many times in your face. I've felt the truth of it burning in my heart.'

He shook his head in the darkness. 'I'm sworn to Lilla. You saw that, you were there. Why are you doing this?'

'Oh, sworn to Lilla,' she scoffed, her temper flaring. 'Please! You don't care about her, not truly. You left her behind the moment you knew I was in danger. You came for me. You left her in the keeping of another man.'

'No. It wasn't like that,' he said, trying to order his

thoughts. But the fact was it had been exactly like that. 'I mean, it was, but not because of you. I want to protect you, of course—'

'I've seen it in my prayers.' Her face was hovering under his, those dark sapphire eyes ablaze with intensity. 'God is my witness, I have wrestled with this for so long. But the Lord has shown me that our paths are bound to one another. I saw two strands of rope entwined. Two lives knitted as one.'

'The Lord?' he spat with a withering look. 'Listen, I don't pretend to know what your god tells you. Whether he speaks to you lies or the truth, or else you just hear what you want to hear. But I am bound to Lilla. That's real. D'you understand? Now and for as long as I live.'

'Why would He give you to her?' she said petulantly. 'She's not deserving of you. She cares only for her own power. You're nothing but a means to an end for her... Her own end.'

'That's not true.' Although, by the Hanged, there were moments when... no. No! Lilla was good to him. Lilla was true. Aye, she had changed. Hardened from the wide-eyed innocent, the ethereal mystic he had first met when he had come, a beggar and an exile, to the Uppland halls. But who would not be changed by all she had gone through? 'Go back to the fire, Marta. You've been through some special kind of Hel, I know. You need rest – we all do. Einar needs you now. If you're looking for someone to love, as a daughter... love him.'

'*You...*' The word came out like the snarl of a she-wolf. 'Denying the truth will only lead to evil. You can't hope to run from the will of God.'

'I run from nothing. You're mistaken, that's all.' For a moment, she was silent. Only gazed deeper into his eyes, unsmiling, yet in the gloom a kind of shimmer moved over her face. Was he tempted? Certainly he was confused. There was something about her that was painfully familiar. That passion of first love, raw and undiluted. The same passion that Inga's inner light had shone on him for a time. Burning with intensity, intoxicating, maddening. Dangerous as fire. 'Go back,' he said again. 'We've enough trouble to face as it is. We're still not safe from them. And we don't know what lies ahead.'

'You're afraid.'

'Of you? Don't be ridiculous.'

'Because I'm young. Because you know where it will lead. You're afeared of your own feelings. But some roads must be walked. We have no choice.'

'You don't know what you're talking about.'

'Do I not?'

'You're just a child.'

'I'm old enough to know my own mind. To know what I feel in my own body. What I feel here...' Suddenly she seized his hand and pushed it between her thighs. He snatched it free at once, but not before he had felt the heat of her. By the Hanged, this girl could be his ruin.

'We're done here,' he said, angry now. 'And for the last time, I'll see you safe but there's nothing between us. Now go.' He stood and pulled her to her feet, pushing her back towards the fire.

'Devil! Liar!' she hissed and then went stumbling back towards her place, pausing only to shoot him a resentful glance. He sat back down, feeling relieved but also confounded as to what to make of her. Had she not enough to deal with after the death of her mother, and the ordeal she had gone through? Or maybe she was clinging to the idea of him in desperation as something – *anything* – that might give her security in a world so dark and full of hate.

He pitied her. Yes, above all he pitied her. He knew what it was to lose his heart over someone he could not – or should not – have. But at least now she was safe. He couldn't guarantee that forever, but… she had not been swallowed up in that awful maw of death.

He lay back down, staring again into the darkness that seeped between the trees. And soon the incident was drifting away from him and the sweet oblivion of sleep once more opened its arms and welcomed him in…

He slept. And he dreamed.

At first it was a dream not of sight but of sound. He heard breathing – a soft and mournful sighing all around him. The scrabble and scuff of bare feet on hard-packed earthen floor. Then he felt a little hand slip into his again, fragile and light as a sparrow. But then squeezing and squeezing at his callused fingers, harder and harder like a blacksmith's vice, refusing to let him go, pulling him down. He tried to resist but the little hand was stronger, and suddenly his knees gave way and he sank to the ground. Now he saw. There stood a small figure in his mind's eye. The outline of a little girl, a shadow murmuring: 'My name is Fenna. Come back, Erlan Aurvandil. Come back to us. We need you, Wanderer. We need you, Chosen Son. Come back to us, my child…' The grubby little face came closer, turning ghoulish, one eye shrinking to nothing; the other expanding into a whirling abyss of black. 'Come *back*,' the voice said in a long, sibilant sigh.

The kick in the ribs jerked him awake for the second time.

'Get up, Aurvandil.'

He recognised the voice but not the tone of it. Had never heard it speak that way, not to him.

'Einar?' He blinked up at the looming shadow as it swam slowly into focus.

'I said, get up.' So full of hate.

'What is it? Did you see something?'

'I saw nothing out there,' Fat-Belly growled. 'But I see a *niðing* before me all right. Do you deny it? *Bleyða*.'

Coward? Why would Einar call him a coward? Erlan's mind was a fog of sleep and confusion. 'Deny what? What the Hel's got into you?' he said, annoyed that he felt fear as well.

'Marta told me everything.'

At the mention of her name, Erlan was instantly alert. 'What do you mean, everything?'

'On your feet, *niðing*,' Einar snarled again. This time he drew his seax from the sheath across his thighs, spread his weight on his toes. 'Get up and face me. It's past time.'

Erlan got to his feet. 'What are you going to do, fight me?' From the look on Fat-Belly's face, there was no doubting it. Erlan's mind, meanwhile, was darting like a squirrel among the tangle of half-truths that Marta might have told Einar, trying to land on what could possibly have provoked this.

'She told me what you did to her in Syracusa. What you tried to do again just now.'

'In Syracusa?' By the Hanged, he hadn't expected that. 'What do you mean?'

'You raped her, *niðing*. You gave her those marks. Beat her purple, strangled her. Filled her with your shame.'

Erlan couldn't believe what he was hearing. By the gods, he was no rapist. Wasn't it rape that had forced him into this whole sorry enterprise? For a second, his mind flicked back to what Lilla had told him – of the ogre Thrand holding her face down in the dirt. Now anger properly flared in his heart. 'Of course I didn't fucking rape her. What are you talking about? I never touched her.' And without knowing it, his hand had gone to the seax at his back.

'She says you did. She's no reason to lie.'

Could she be that vindictive? 'I don't know why, but she *is* lying.'

'Is she lying when she says she came to offer you water just now and you tried to have her again? That you touched her... here.' Einar grimaced and gestured at his crotch.

Another lie with just enough of a sprinkling of truth to make it impossible to deny. 'I... didn't touch her like that.'

'Like that?' Einar was quick to catch at his wording. 'But you did touch her.'

'*Sorðinn!*' Erlan threw up his hands. 'The girl's deluded. I don't know what she thinks she's doing. Listen, old friend, I know you're upset—'

'Don't patronise me, *niðing*. Don't you *fucking* dare.'

'For Frigg's sake,' Erlan snarled back, 'you come here, kicking me awake—'

'Should have been awake. You're on fucking watch.'

462

'You're right, you're right. Look, whatever she's been telling you—'

'It all makes sense now,' Einar interjected. 'There's been something unsaid between you and her. And something different between you and Lilla. Since then, now I think of it. And where the Hel were you that day, eh? You went back to the boat early. She was right behind you. Next thing, she turns up beaten black and blue and all shook to the roots, but refusing to give any details… Nah, something happened that day between you two. It were never the same after.'

Again, hard to deny any of this. It hadn't been the same. With her or with Lilla. Had he encouraged her? Had he done something to her and obliterated the memory of it? There had been times when he hadn't known himself, when his mind had gone from him for a time, and he'd come to himself again almost as if out of a dream. But you couldn't forget a thing like that. Could you?

Maybe all of this confusion and doubt was written on his face. Hel, he'd never been a good liar. 'This is horseshit, all of it,' he said suddenly. 'We don't need this between us, you and me. How long have you known me?'

'Does anyone really know you… *cripple*?'

Countless times, all kinds of folk had called him that. But somehow it had never wounded him like it did coming from the mouth of his oldest friend. Hel, his only friend. 'You think I'd do that. To a girl of fifteen?'

'I've seen you do some dark work in my time, Aurvandil,' Einar grimaced. 'You get what you want. And you drag the rest of us after you like the damned whoreson fools that we are. Well, this is one fool that's waking up.' His fire-ravaged face twisted into a look of scorn. He sheathed his seax in disgust. 'Ain't no fighting you. Ain't worth a damn. I'm taking the girl. She's my responsibility now.'

'What are you saying?' Erlan felt a strange leaching away of something between them. Like a tide being sucked out to sea.

'This is where our roads part, you and me.'

'What? Because of what she said?'

'That. And a lot else. I've been doing a lot of thinking these last days. Gave you a chance. You fucked it. Orīana's gone. May heaven keep her if there is such a place. But you... you'll lead us all straight to Hel.'

'Marta's lying to you. And I've done the best I could.'

'Well, your best wasn't good enough.' Einar leaned over and spat his disgust into the dirt. 'The Norns can take you now. And I'll take the girl.'

Erlan watched Einar turn his back, stunned at what he was hearing. He couldn't stop himself reaching out to catch his old comrade's shoulder. But he'd barely touched him before Einar spun and smacked away his hand, his blade at Erlan's throat an instant later. 'You let me go,' he said in a cold whisper. 'Like you should have done a long time ago.'

Suddenly the prick of steel was gone, and Erlan watched his friend stalk back to the fire. Moments later, he heard a jangle of bridles and the soft thud of horses' hooves fading away into the night.

The others were still asleep, exhausted after the hard days that had gone before. Erlan's mind was a swirl of doubt, the only certainty that his most precious friendship was slipping through his fingers like sand.

He lay back down, the quiet rage of injustice pulsing in his head. But even that was no match for the fatigue that overcame him, and it wasn't long before he surrendered to it.

Surrendered to it all.

The last thing he heard before he went under was the words of that little girl he'd left behind.

Come back, Wanderer... come back.

CHAPTER THIRTY-FOUR

Skírpa felt the power increasing in him. Like a seed long dormant that had waited in the darkness for the right conditions, finally it could come forth. Take root, grow in strength.

Maybe he had needed to go through that test – to face his desire to escape, and yet still remain. Maybe Alvarik had known this all along. After all, he could see further into the web of What Must Be. And now even Skírpa's fear of the One Eyed had subsided. In its place had grown a kind of respect, a curiosity – as a student might have for his master.

He could not tell whether this was something that Alvarik had cultivated in him, or whether it arose in the natural course of things. But suddenly the darkness of those first days took on a curious illumination. As if the more he stared into the abyss, the less he felt the impulse to look away; the more he found that there was a kind of light that revealed itself to his mind.

With illumination came responsibility.

Alvarik was pleased with him. Skírpa's warning had prevented greater losses. Thus, although the One Eyed was enraged at the loss of the Greek girl, his ire was directed elsewhere. At those among the wolf-warriors who had failed him so pitifully, at the raiders who had escaped with his most precious prize. And at the monk whom they had snared.

Alvarik had tasked Skírpa to find out all he could from this newest fly to be caught in his master's far-flung web. Apparently fearing that each day might bring a fresh attack, Alvarik wanted to know exactly who these men were and why they had come.

'What's your business?' said the guard over the windowless pit-house where they were keeping their collection of clerics – priests and monks mostly, some of whom had shared the road with Skírpa.

'The One Eyed sent me.'

There was a flicker of doubt on the man's face. Perhaps questioning whether this needed to be verified with their master, but concluding that was likely to cause him more trouble than it was worth, he let Skírpa pass. 'In you go then... sister,' he said with a snigger, and opened the door.

'Sister' was the mildest of the names the wolf-warriors had given him on account of his high voice. 'Skírpa the Cockless' was another, which irked him a good deal more. But he'd decided these puerile slights were not worth challenging. Not yet, anyway. Instead, he ducked inside and the little door closed behind him.

For a moment he stood in the stinking space, his eyes adjusting to the dim light seeping through the walls. There was a scuffle of bodies as the prisoners wriggled away from

467

him, each perhaps presuming that he had come for them. The thought gave him a sudden delicious frisson: here already was power made manifest. These holy men would do more than shrink from him by the time he was through.

'Wynfred of Nursling, come forward.'

So far the man had given nothing but his name. And, unlike the others, nor had he shown the slightest fear, which irritated Skírpa. Did the fool not know the power that Skírpa had over him? Could he not guess at the fate that awaited him?

'I need more answers from you,' he began in the Latin tongue, the language they had already established they held in common.

'I've told you all I have to say.'

'I need more. How did the crippled man come to be here?'

'Why are you so interested in him above all the others?'

'I ask the questions, monk.'

'Skírpa,' murmured another man from a dim corner. 'Why have you sided with them? Can you not see the evil that suffocates this place?' He recognised the voice of one of his fellow travellers on the Via Francorum – the tall companion of Narduin who had ringworm scars in his hair.

'If you wish to avoid another whipping, Brother Medard, I suggest you keep your mouth shut.' The monk slumped back into a brooding silence, doubtless still sore from the previous afternoon.

Skírpa turned back to Wyn. 'Well? The cripple?'

'If I didn't know what I've learned of him, I should start to think you've met before. But if that's true, it could only be by a fantastic coincidence. God alone could contrive such a thing.'

The mention of God made Skírpa instantly uncomfortable. It was a fantastic coincidence, but Wyn need not know that for sure. And the notion that it served some unfathomable purpose of the Divine…? Skírpa found that beyond disturbing. 'A ridiculous notion. Of course I haven't met him,' he scoffed. 'He seems to be your leader, is all. My master wants to know what he will do. Will he bring others here?'

Wyn grimaced. 'The land is at war. All men know this. Alas, when good men are otherwise occupied, cancers like this place are free to grow.'

'So he will not return?'

'I didn't say that.'

'What *do* you say, monk? Come, I've no time for word games.'

'You ask me more than I could possibly know. I don't know the man well. I cannot speak to the counsel of his own mind. And thus what he will do.' From the twitch at the corner of his mouth, Skírpa fancied the monk was mocking him. It was time to knock him off his lofty perch.

'You seem very complacent, Wynfred of Nursling.'

'You would prefer if I were afraid.'

'My preference has nothing to do with it. It's an observation. That's all.'

'What you see is not complacency, but faith and hope in the promises of Our Lord.'

'He is no lord of mine.'

'My Lord, then.'

469

'I have seen this faith, this hope you people peddle, for most of my life. Have lived under its shadow. I've seen it raised to a splendour of which you could only dream. And I've reached the conclusion that it's nothing more than a common conjurer's trick.'

The monk seemed not the least perturbed by this, which only riled Skírpa the more. 'Truly? How so?'

'This faith speaks of humility. Of love. Of caring for those lesser souls than you. But it's only another way of keeping your boot upon the common people's neck. You give them dog's piss to drink and tell them it is wine. You feed their empty bowls with empty promises and tell them their bellies are full. And all the while, you paint your churches with gold and clothe yourselves in silk. The true wonder of it is that the foolish folk still believe you.'

'The truth of God needs no defending. Since the creation of the world, His eternal power and His divine nature have been clearly seen and understood from what He has made. People are without excuse. Yet they forget their Creator and turn away into all kinds of futility and folly. Their hearts become darkened. They give themselves up into all kinds of depravity—'

'I know the scriptures, monk,' Skírpa snorted impatiently. 'You need not patronise me by reciting them. I know you think we exchanged the truth for a lie. But I tell you, power is no lie. The power of what we worship here is pure revelation. Not through some mysterious faith. Not through mere thoughts in our heads. But the actual working out of cause and effect. Blood is the only truth. I see that now. I see why. Blood is the power of life. Take it and power increases. Give it away, and it is lost. The more you take, the more powerful you become.'

'It is simple witchcraft,' Wyn snapped. 'An abomination before God.'

Skírpa scoffed. 'That word, you keep using it, but there is no substance to it. It is as if you try to control me by saying there is a lion behind that door. But if we opened it...' He made a dismissive gesture with his fingers. '... There's nothing there.'

'Then why do you hate Him so, if there is nothing there?'

'I do not hate the nothing, I hate those that try to persuade, that try to control me through a lie.'

'That's not true though, is it?' A thin smile worked its way onto the monk's lips. 'You could destroy all of us. Every one of us. Mock, ridicule, refute. All of it, till no one listens and no one believes. But you would still hate God. Hate the very whisper of an idea of Him in your head. Because His presence is inescapable. And your soul knows the truth of it even if your mind suppresses that truth.'

'Why should I not hate?' Skírpa suddenly snarled. 'If he exists, I hate him for the life he has had me live. If he does not, then I hate him for not existing.'

'Hate cannot sustain you, my friend. Only love can do that. What you need is forgiveness—'

'Oh, spare me your sermon, monk!' Skírpa exclaimed. 'You do not know what life I have lived. It is God who owes *me*. It is God who should crawl before *me* and beg for *my* forgiveness. Then I would laugh in his face. Then I would grind his meek and mild words into the dirt.'

Wyn's face seemed troubled. But not at his own pain,

rather in sympathy. 'You seem an educated man, my friend. Do you not know the futility of warring against God?'

'I am no friend of yours.'

'You will lose. The reason you hate is simple. It is the same for all who hate God. They loved the darkness more than they loved the light because their deeds were evil. Only when we admit that can we hope to come into the light.'

'I want nothing of your light,' retorted Skírpa quickly. 'There is another light. The light of darkness visible. I have begun to see it dimly. A light that once fell but did not lose its brilliance.' Even as he spoke, it seemed like he was confessing his own story. How brightly he had once shone in the emperor's court, and now... He tried to continue, falteringly: 'But I hope...'

'Beware, my young friend. Christ first came as saviour. Next time he comes as judge.'

'Enough of this,' Skírpa snapped, suddenly aware he had exposed more of himself than he had meant to. 'If you will not tell me more, then we shall have to use more persuasive means.'

'Do what you have to. But I tell you no more because I have no more to tell. I am almost as much a stranger to this land as I think you are yourself. I came here for the children. I beg you to have pity on them—'

'Why should I?' Skírpa snorted in reply, glad at last to find a tender place in the man's armour. 'There was no one to pity me when I was a child.' He took a step closer, enjoying how this would make the arrogant monk suffer. 'They will die to honour the light of the One Eye,' he said in a whisper. 'When the moon is full.'

Wyn dropped his voice to a soft entreaty. 'Remember what you already know, my child. If your eye is bad, your whole body will be full of darkness. If then the light in you is darkness, how great is that darkness!'

Skírpa was glad to be able to laugh in the monk's earnest face. 'The darkness is more powerful, fool. *That* is the truth you dare not admit.'

'No. Light will overcome the darkness. Because sacrificial love is stronger than any self-serving power.'

'Only a weak man would say such a thing.'

'Love is stronger than death.'

Skírpa gave a ringing bark of laughter. 'Well then, rejoice, brothers!' he cried, with a final sneer at the tonsured figures strewn about the wretched hovel. 'For we will soon be putting your theory to the test.' He went to the door and knocked. 'Open up. We're done in here.'

CHAPTER THIRTY-FIVE

Under different circumstances, Lilla might have found the Eifel mountains quite beautiful. Mirror-glass lakes surrounded by forest, alive with wildlife. Woodpeckers drumming out their next nest, deer grazing on woodland berries, even eagles circling high over the treetops in search of their scurrying prey.

But as it was, it was all frustration. A fog of unknowing as she waited for any word of her companions. Meanwhile, Karil had sent word about the surrounding lands, drawing men to him.

Each day their encampment was a hive of activity, all of it given to training the growing numbers of his men for war. Karil worked obsessively, determined not to be caught unprepared a second time. But word from the east continued that King Chilperic and his Neustrian army were still investing the walls of Koln, and so the Austrasian warlord was happy to bide his time, perfecting what he was confident would be a decisive blow.

Meanwhile, Lilla was forced to wait.

Patience had never been one of her natural gifts. And her frustration soon became so acute that eventually she persuaded Karil to allow her to school his archers in some of her skills, solely as a means to speed along the passage of each day. But all the while the fate of her companions weighed heavy on her mind.

And yet, for all her eager anticipation of news, it still came as a surprise when, one morning, riders did appear, slowly making their way around the lakeshore towards the tents and campfires of Karil's army.

It was Demetrios who first recognised their comrades. And Demetrios who first realised that Erlan was not among them…

Lilla could not believe this conversation. Everything about it challenged the reality she thought she knew. The reality she was counting on.

She listened as Einar recounted all that they had been through. He spoke in a gruff and distant voice that seemed detached from what he was describing. Watching him, it saddened her as she thought back to the jocular man he had been only the year before, as thirsty for life as he was for his next horn of ale. Her oath-man, the only Sveär warrior loyal to her when she had fled. But the Einar before her was a ruin of that man. No, not a ruin – a kind of inversion. As if somehow he had been turned inside out. Gone was his mirthful nature, gone his jolly face; what was left was a sort of stone man. A hollow statue, hard and brittle on the outside, empty on the inside. *She* had done that to him, she realised. She and Erlan. And the guilt of that troubled her worst of all.

Yet what he told her was bad enough.

In company with him was the girl Marta, and only three of the others: Bull, Ran and Black Svali. When she asked where Erlan and Mikkel Crow were, and Oriana too, Einar scrubbed at his chin wearily and said he would come on to that.

First he explained how they had found Lilla and Karil, and what was left of his army. They'd ridden north out of an ancient forest he called the Immerwald, and were lucky to have crossed paths with a band of warriors led by an Austrasian count, who had heard word of Karil's summons and was riding north to join his growing force in the Eifel mountains. That stroke of luck had saved them what would have been many fruitless days on the road, chasing down the whereabouts of their queen and her little Greek.

But as far as good fortune went, that was the sum of it.

As for the rest of what he had to tell... Certainly the old Lilla's heart would have buckled under it. But as she was now – maybe she had become callused to evil. Maybe she had come to expect it of the world. In any case, she heard him out, watching him carefully as he described the stockade in the forest, the monstrous tree and its gruesome fruit, the wraith-like children, the abandoned monk, their escape, and then their split. He told her what else he had learned from Marta: of the weird one-eyed shaman, that they had their gold. And that at the next full moon, there would be another glut of bloody sacrifice.

476

He spoke dispassionately, even when he described Orīana's brutalised body hanging from that tree. Seeing Einar like that... it crushed her heart with pity. Although in truth, could she have hoped for better news? What in the Nine Worlds had she expected?

And yet, for all that he reported, she knew he was holding something back.

'There's more,' she said when he had finished. 'Something else you're not telling me.'

Einar sniffed, and shifted from foot to foot. 'What else I have to tell you, Lady, is for your ears only.'

'Well then, come, let's walk. The others can find themselves some food. Demetrios, help them get what they need.'

While the rest sidled off towards the cooking-fires, she led Einar a short distance around the lakeshore. For all that this was a land at war, the scene was quite serene. A pigeon, perhaps disturbed by their presence, fluttered away into the trees. The lake was all stillness, the pines on the other shore appearing like an army of green spear-tips in its glassy surface.

Einar gestured at a boulder by the water's edge. 'Have a seat, Lady. Think you're going to need it.'

She did as bid, a quiet dread now mingling with the curiosity she already felt at what he had to say.

'I didn't tell you why we split,' he began.

'No.'

'Something he did.'

He didn't need to say Erlan's name. 'Go on.'

'With the girl.'

She was glad the others weren't there to hear what Einar had to tell her. Although maybe they already knew. She

477

couldn't have said why, but the revelation didn't come as a shock to her either. She felt calm as Einar spoke, thinking back over what had happened in Syracusa. Something about it *had* stuck in her memory, she realised, although she had never truly examined it. Something about the way the girl had looked at her afterwards, and at him. Still... *Could* it have been the way Marta had told Einar? Could Erlan really have assaulted her? Raped her even? Was that in his nature? If it was, it was buried deep.

She forced herself to imagine Erlan raising a hand in violence against a girl like Marta, and found she could not. But then she remembered his evasiveness afterwards, about where he had been. And the haste with which he had wanted to swear himself to her as husband and she as wife... *Dear gods, was it all because of this?*

This man... Erlan. *Or Hakan?* Or whatever was truly his name. This man with two pasts. Did she know him at all?

She remembered his revelations the night before the sea-battle when the Arab fleet was broken. The guilt he carried about his sister. Was that, too, all a lie? Maybe the reasons for his exile were far simpler. Far more prosaic. Maybe he was a simple murderer. Or else a rapist...

No. She could not have misread him so badly.

'I told him I was done with him,' said Einar, concluding. 'Marta is my charge now... now her mother's gone. If she feels unsafe, it's better this way.'

'But where is he? We cannot just – I don't know – *part ways*. Where did he go? And Mikkel Crow with him.'

'He went back. Least that's the way Bull tells it.'

'Back? You mean to that horrible place?'

478

'Bull said he was talking about unfinished business. That they couldn't just leave the children at the mercy of them wolf-pelted bastards.'

'But what chance does he stand alone? What does he imagine he'll do?'

'I don't know. He has Mikki with him. Seems Crow chose to stick.' Einar grunted. 'I wouldn't have called it that way, but sometimes folk surprise you.'

Lilla put her head in her hands. Where did all this leave them? Leave her and Erlan? Leave the prospects of her return to Sveäland? Their ship was stranded, likely broken up by scavengers by now, if not outright stolen. Gods only knew whether the gold they had buried was still there. And the liquid fire... What was there to do?

For a moment, Karil entered her thoughts. Karil, who had no wife yet. Karil, who was still young. Was this whole adventure with Erlan nothing but a sham? Maybe here with Karil was solid ground. Maybe he could be her future. The consort of a true warrior, a true lord – if the subservience of these other men was any indication of his destiny.

But what of her own? Could she lay aside so lightly her promise to her dead husband? Could she deny the oath she had sworn to her living one?

What a mess.

The threads of all that had gone before, finely woven here and there, lives intertwined, forming not a beautiful tapestry of purpose and meaning but rather an unruly muddle, knotted, tangled. An insoluble disaster of a life. What was she to salvage from the wreckage?

'The gold is still there?'

'The girl says so. Though we saw no sign of it.'

'Would you go back?' she asked. 'I mean, if you had to.'

'Me?' Einar gave a disgusted snort. 'Have you not been listening, Lady? I'm through with the Aurvandil.' For a second, he chewed his hairless lip. 'Gods, if you want the truth, I'm but a whisper from being through with you, too.'

She nodded. 'I understand. I grieve your loss too, my friend. Orīana was...' She hesitated, searching for a word that would not sound dull with banality. '... Well, she was yours,' she said at length.

'Aye,' he sighed.

'Oh, let not her death be wasted, dear Einar. We can still—'

'No. I told you, no.'

Lilla fell silent. There was no point pushing a man like Einar when he had made his mind up. Or when he thought it was made up. But something about all this still didn't quite have the ring of truth. 'I want to speak with Marta.'

'I've told you all she told me.'

'Even so, I insist.' She could see the obstinacy hardening in his face. 'Have I not a right to the truth, Einar?'

'I told you the truth.'

'I have to be sure. Bring her to me.'

'She won't want to—'

'Just do it... Please.'

For some moments, Einar glared at her, his hard gaze piercing right through her. Gods, whatever she saw in those eyes was perilously close to hate. She could not afford to lose her most loyal man.

'I only want to know the truth.'

A nerve twitched in his ruined face, and his hard eyes fell away. 'Have it your way, then, Lady... I'll send her to you.'

'Go over it again.'

'I don't see why I should have to,' said Marta, holding her gaze. 'It's distressing enough to remember any of it without recalling every tiny detail.'

'I need to know.'

'You're only torturing yourself.' Marta shook her head. It was astonishing how condescending she could be for one so young. 'I know it must be hard for you to accept, Lady. That the man you love was so beset on having me it drove him to the point of this madness... But sin hides itself well.'

'I'll be obliged if you keep to the point. Tell me again, when and where he approached you.'

'Thank God my mother did not live to see how heartless her mistress truly is,' she murmured, shaking her head. 'I was the victim of that monster's lust. Me!' Tears welled in her large and luminous eyes. 'He wanted me and so he found a way to have me.'

'Then why did you not denounce him at once?'

'He said no one would believe me. Swore he would hurt me again if I so much as whispered—'

'Surely you could have told your mother... in secret?'

'I didn't want to put her in danger. I decided it was safer to keep it to myself. To bear the burden of my shame and his. I thought maybe that way he would leave me alone. That he'd taken what he wanted once, and that would be enough.' A fresh wave of emotion seemed to roll over her and more tears

481

fell. 'But then again… in the forest…' She clasped her hands together and gazed up into the iron-grey skies. 'O Holy Mother, have mercy on me.'

'What happened in the forest?' demanded Lilla, having no patience for this girl's entreaties to the heavens.

Marta's eyes fixed hers, a strange, almost gleeful male-volence dancing in the midst of those blue flames. 'He tried to have me again. He was mad with passion, inflamed with it. This time I fought him off long enough for him to come to his senses. Or at least decide it was not worth the risk. Not with the others sleeping so close.'

'What were you even doing with him if everyone else was sleeping?'

'He was thirsty. I brought him water.'

'You mean to say you put yourself at the mercy of this man of whom you say you were so afraid?'

For a moment, Marta said nothing. Then abruptly the lines of her smooth brow furrowed in anger. 'You saw what he did to me in Syracusa,' she exclaimed. 'You saw the bruises round my neck and my arms. But I did not show you the worst. Here between my thighs…' She gestured at herself as if there could be any doubt what she meant. 'It was your husband that did that.'

'That doesn't answer my question. If you were so afraid of him, why would you allow yourself to be alone with him again?'

'The Lord tells us to forgive our enemies. I wanted to believe in the power of forgiveness. If I gave him the benefit of the doubt, if I gave him another chance… But he threw it back in my face.'

Lilla watched Marta carefully. What was this girl's motive? What did she want? She tried to imagine herself speaking about Thrand in the same way this girl was talking about Erlan and what he had done to her, but found she could not. It had been a kind of agony to confess to Erlan the full extent of her own experience. Each word a labour to drag from inside her. Yet this girl could not divulge enough.

Erlan was not there to defend himself. But did he need to be? Did she not know his character well enough by now? By all the gods, he had sacrificed enough for her. As she had for him. Would it only take a pair of flashing blue eyes to tear all that apart?

'Were you lovers?' she said, feeling naive that the question had not occurred to her before. Though surely that was impossible. Secret liaisons were totally impracticable on a ship full of crewmen. And Lilla had been with him nearly every moment since. Even so... 'He made love to you and then he ended it,' she continued, feeling her way towards something that sounded plausible. 'And now you seek to accuse him out of some kind of revenge. Or vindication, because you feel it was wrong.'

'How dare you?' Marta seethed. 'I was his victim. He attacked me. Twice. And yet you don't believe me. Einar is right. You think you're above us. You believe only what it suits you to believe.' Was that true? It was not much better to think of Erlan being unfaithful with this young girl. But at least that made some sense. Perhaps even a lot of sense, given the undeniable distance that had opened up between she and him.

'Calm down. Please, Marta. It does neither of us any good.'

'Do you believe me?' Marta said, stepping closer, challenging her.

'I... I...' Either she knew absolutely nothing of Erlan's true character, or else this girl was lying. 'I don't know what to believe.'

'I knew it.' Marta's face twisted into a sneer. 'I *knew* it. Well, you don't know him!' she cried. 'You don't know him at all!' And with that, she ran off into the trees.

Lilla watched her go, releasing a long and weary sigh. Aye, this was a mess all right. And nothing she had heard made any of it clearer. She sat for a long time on the rock, looking out over the lake, thinking. Evening was coming on. Night fell quicker in these late days of autumn. And she was hungry.

Where is he...? Who is he...?

But with no clearer answers, she rose and made her way along the shoreline, watching the flames of the cook-fires grow more vivid with the falling of dusk. A short walk later, she struck upon her dwindling band of followers all huddled around their own fire, spooning some kind of stew into wooden bowls and sharing them out.

Einar looked up and gave her a nod. 'Well?'

'Where's Marta?' said Lilla, only now noticing the girl was not among them.

'What do you mean, where's Marta? She was with you.'

'She left me a while ago. She was upset.'

For a long moment, they looked at one another. Then Einar suddenly shoved his bowl aside and got to his feet. 'Where the Hel is she? Ran, check the horses.'

The Gotlander hopped up obligingly and disappeared into the gloom. The others all sat still, spoons hovering, awaiting

Ran's verdict. It wasn't long in coming. He soon came loping back to the fire, short of breath. 'One of the horses is gone. And a pair of saddle-bags…'

'Odin's eye,' muttered Einar, glaring at Lilla. 'What did you say to her?'

CHAPTER THIRTY-SIX

Erlan fastened off the knot and tested that the noose still tightened when he pulled on it. The circle of hemp closed around his fist. 'Ready?'

Mikkel Crow nodded grimly in the dark.

Erlan licked his lips and peered forward to where the southern wall of the stockade rose in front of them, the wooden piles sharp as a row of dragon's teeth.

'Happy this is the same spot?' whispered Mikki.

Erlan glanced to his right. 'Don't know about happy, but... I remember that dwarf beech over there. And the hollow in the ground, those rocks.' If you had the memory for it, there was no end of features in the forest to mark where you were. Erlan was only surprised at how much he did recall, given the fleetness of their escape.

They were concealed on the opposite side of the stockade from the gateway. Night had fallen an hour, maybe two before. The horses were tethered half a league away to the north in another hollow. Erlan hoped they would not become the prey of wolves or even bears this deep into the forest. But that was a risk they had to take.

'You're sure you can make the throw?' he murmured.

'Aye. If we're close enough.' Mikki nodded.

By the gods, Erlan was pleased to have the scowling Estlander with him. Mikki was pretty dismal company when things were going swell in the bright light of day. But he was starting to believe there were few men he'd rather have next to him in a fight than Mikkel Crow. Then he realised, ruefully, that Einar was one of them. But that friendship was done. Somehow Erlan had broken it, despite his best intentions. But maybe Einar was right. They'd been selfish intentions all along.

The wonder of it was that Mikki had come with him. Especially since, of all their crew, he'd seemed the most set on getting as far away from the *Immerbaum* and its grim surroundings as he could. But confronted with the choice of who to follow, he'd stuck with his skipper. For that, Erlan was grateful to the bottom of his boots.

Not that this made their plan any easier.

Plan? Ha! By the Hanged, that was being generous.

It stood on a single notion: bite off the head, a serpent dies. Whether that notion would hold in this case... Well, that was the question. As Mikki had said: 'Big fucking gamble.' Well, they had no choice now but to gamble big.

'Let's go,' Erlan said softly before reason got the better of him, and the pair of them rose like revenants out of the shadows and hustled across the open ground into the lee of the palisade. They looked at each other while Mikki slipped the coil of hemp rope off his shoulder and shuffled it through his long fingers.

Erlan took a moment to listen, but hearing nothing, he nodded. Mikki took half a pace away from the wall and tossed the noose up. There was a faint patter of the rope landing as Mikki peered upwards, mouth agape as if he were staring at the heavens. He gave the rope a tug. It held. Mikki grunted with satisfaction. 'After you, skipper.'

'Aye. That's the way of it.'

Moments later, Erlan had a hold on two points of the palisade stakes. He paused to listen. Still silence. So he went over the top, jabbing himself in the ribs in his haste, but otherwise getting over well enough. He lay tight against the parapet wall, listening in an ecstasy of anticipation to the scraping noises as Mikki scaled the wall in turn. But no alarm was raised.

Then Mikki was over, long limbs sprawling onto the walkway, till he, too, lay flat against the floor.

Erlan took a few shallow breaths, the scent of the pine planks filling his nostrils, his eyes darting from roof to roof below. The presence of the *Immerbaum* was oppressive, though he wouldn't look at it straight. It seemed to push down on him like an unseen hand. But he refused to be cowed. The bets were laid. He was all in. He had come back. To pay his debts? To deal out revenge? Who the Hel knew? But he was here.

He saw the long-houses, the weird triangular structure, a handful of sturdier buildings that looked like the small craft lodges of Uppsala. That must be where the *ulfheðnar* were housed. And then there was another building. Stood a little apart from the others, a little grander in its facade and adorned with a scattering of animal skulls of different kinds, although overall its dimensions were smaller than the lodges.

'There.' And when he whispered it, he was sure. 'I'd bet my head that's where their leader's sleeping.'

'Your head *is* the bet, skipper,' grunted Mikki. 'And mine.'

There was no need for a signal. Just a deep breath and then they were moving. Down the steps, pause a moment, then move again. From shadow to shadow; waiting, listening; move again. Never looking behind, knowing that Mikki had his back covered.

Their blades were out now. Hand-axes, long-knifes. More knives about their person. Erlan's sword – still unnamed – on his hip. They slipped past one of the lodges, then a second...

And there it was.

The leader's dwelling.

They had expected a watchman to deal with. But drawing closer they saw none.

Complacency, thought Erlan. Even after all that had happened. It suggested even more strongly to him that what they were dealing with was not the discipline of the emperor's Sentinels, or even the highly trained hirthmen of the kings of the north. But rather a motley band of thieves, led by a maniac.

They reached the door.

This was the moment, wasn't it?

He glanced back at Mikki, first time he'd done so. Mikki nodded, the sharp lines of his face as menacing as they were reassuring. He would stand watch; Erlan would do the killing.

Bite off the head, a serpent dies.

By the Hanged, Erlan hoped he was right about this.

He bit down on the cold steel of his seax, freeing his hand to raise the latch. It was beautifully smooth, quiet as thought.

He had to stop himself expelling a sigh of relief. Instead, he pushed the door ajar, just wide enough for him to squeeze inside. There, he stopped, letting his eyes adjust, sharpening his ears.

It didn't take the ears of a wolf to catch the soft rattle of sleep from somewhere deeper inside. Erlan drove his consciousness back and back in time, to those games he used to play around his father's steading with the other boys of the yard. With Inga, too. Despite his limp, he was good at stealth. He'd always been good. And there had never been a greater need to summon all his skill than at this moment.

Lightening his gait, feeling pain burn through his calf with his effort to distribute his weight evenly for once, he moved forward. The shapes around him were becoming clearer: a long table, a high-backed chair, a fur slung over it – as if the leader of this pack of rabid dogs was a real earl, or even a king – and beyond them, a doorway to an inner chamber.

Focusing his will, he reached it, gently lifted aside the hide drape. The noise inside sounded louder, but its rhythm rolled on, steady and untroubled. He slipped inside and waited a moment. The air smelled of burnt pine resin. He imagined a low oil lamp had burned out earlier in the night. There was a large bed on the far side – a bed far bigger than the lump of furs heaped at one end.

Here was his first problem.

To bring his victim within range of his blade, Erlan would have to climb on the bed – which threatened to disturb his sleep – or else he must reach over and pull his victim to the edge of it. That risked waking him too, and raising the alarm.

Erlan made his decision.

He slid as smoothly as he could onto the furs, like a considerate lover trying not to wake their bed-fellow. The rattle of the man's breathing continued, guttural as a sleeping hound. Slowly, Erlan spread over him like the dark mantle of death. Then he could see the pale of his face, see the black streaks of hair straying up his cheeks from his beard, smell the sour fetor of his breath.

Gods, he was an ugly bastard, even in sleep. Alvarik, Marta had called him. The One Eyed. He was almost as broad as he was tall; at least it felt that way hovering over him.

Erlan brought up his blade, judged the aim at his jugular, pulsing away under his beard. All of a sudden there was a growl in the corner of the room that chilled his blood. A chain rattled. A wave of visceral panic rushed through his guts: something was wrong. Something he had not accounted for. And before he could drive the point of his blade home, the shaman's eye snapped open, the white of it a rheumy yellow, and his hand seized hold of Erlan's wrist. Shocked but reacting instantly, Erlan drew his head back to butt the ugly face, but then the other hand was round his throat, shoving his head further back, twisting his neck. Both hands were strong as fate.

'I see you, cripple,' this Alvarik sang in a mocking whisper. 'I knew you would come.'

Erlan pulled savagely at the demagogue's right hand, trying in vain to break its hold. And to his horror, a beast in the corner of the room started barking, the walls seemed to come alive, bodies started peeling out of the shadows, hands lay hold of him, dragging him off the bed.

His throat was free, just long enough to utter one long and desperate yell: '*Run, Mikki! RUN!*'

Then he was face down, arms yanked behind his back, the weight of someone's knee on the back of his neck. All the while, the cold realisation that they had walked into a trap snaked in his guts.

The door slammed behind him. He lay on the damp, mud-packed floor, groaning. They had kicked him black and blue, trussed him like a lamb for market. He could feel his eyes already swelling shut.

So much for biting the head off a snake, he thought bitterly. Instead, the snake had bitten him.

He rolled onto his back. It was only then that he became aware that he was not alone in this squalid pit-house. There were other shadows creeping towards him. But these were gentler, more hesitating. Then one of them spoke:

'Wanderer. Is that you?'

He recognised the dry husk of Wyn's voice, the note of astonishment in it unmistakable. 'I think so. Although they kicked Nine Worlds of shit out of me, so who knows?'

Wyn chuckled. 'If you're able to jest, it can't be so bad. Here, let me help you.' He adjusted Erlan's position and bent over him to examine the rope binding his hands.

'You're still alive then,' said Erlan. 'You've more luck than I gave you credit for.'

Wyn gave an indifferent grunt of agreement. 'Nothing to do with luck, I assure you. Hold still.' He began picking at the knot with his fingers. Then he bent even lower to tug at it

492

with his teeth. After a few moments, he gave a yelp of triumph. 'Ha! There! Soon have you free.'

And soon enough he did. Erlan sat up straight, nodding gratefully at the monk and rubbing the soreness out of his wrists.

'We're alive,' said Wyn. 'But may not be for long.'

'The full moon is less than ten days from now.'

'If these devils have their way,' he muttered grimly, 'it will be a savage moon indeed.'

Erlan's heart sank. If the monk's well of hope had run dry, what chance for the rest of them?

'Who are these others?' he asked.

Wyn introduced the miscellany of other holy men. Another monk, a deacon, two priests taken on the road. There were five of them in all, six now with Erlan.

'Were you alone?' asked Wyn.

'No. I came back with Mikki Crow.'

'Where is he?'

'If the Norns are kind, he got away...' Gods, who was he trying to fool? The Norns were never kind.

It was too dark to see Wyn's reaction, but Erlan could guess he was trying to make sense of why Erlan should have returned at all, let alone with only one other man. And why Mikki? But before any question reached the monk's lips, the door snapped open a second time. There was a scuffle of movement, snarled curses, then a shapeless mass was flung down in a heap before them.

'Mikki?'

The river-man could only moan in reply. Seemed he was beaten half-senseless. Erlan crawled forward and rolled him onto his back. He winced when he saw the shimmer on his face. It could be only blood. A lot of it by the looks. Gently, he straightened Mikki's head, eliciting another long groan. He went to lay Mikki's arms alongside him so he would be more comfortable, but when he touched the right one, Mikki gave a wail of pain. Erlan saw why at once. His forearm was drooping off his elbow like a broken barley-stalk. Looked like it had been snapped right back on itself. Erlan's stomach rolled in revulsion. Gods only knew what agony the big fella must be in.

'His arm—'

'I can see,' said Wyn hurriedly, kneeling beside him. 'May I?'

With tender fingers, he took the weight of the arm, but even the slightest movement made Mikki writhe like an eel on a hook. 'Don't touch it.' Erlan pushed away the monk's hands.

'Can't take it,' gasped Mikki, face contorted. 'Can't take the stinking pain. Cut it off.' He suddenly lurched at Erlan, seized him by the collar. 'Please, skipper.'

Erlan was thinking fast. None of the options his mind threw up were pretty. He'd only seen one man in his life with a break this bad, which wasn't in battle. One winter in Vendlagard, a horse had slipped on ice and fallen on its rider. His father had ordered the man's arm amputated there and then. But that was under controlled conditions, with plenty of light and water; fire to cauterise the wound. Here, they didn't even have a blade to cut. Erlan swore again.

'Water,' Mikki pleaded. 'Least give me some water.'

One of the priests came forward with a bucket. Gods only knew how fresh its contents were, but now wasn't the time for niceties. He lifted Mikki's head and tipped the bucket. Much of it went down his face and soaked his chest. But some hit his tongue.

'What can we do?' Erlan looked up at Wyn, feeling helpless.

'I don't know, I don't...' Wyn shook his head. 'We have no implements.'

'Call the guard,' said the other monk, a tall man with a few tufted scraps of hair. 'They will surely have mercy on him.'

'Don't be a fool,' answered the young deacon bitterly. 'Have you not been paying attention, Medard?'

'No... *No*,' said Wyn, with sudden resolve. 'We must pray. That is all. Pray for the Lord to end his pain.'

'The only way this pain is ending, monk,' growled Mikki through gritted teeth, 'is if you finish the job they started, and break my fucking neck.' Erlan had seen men on the field of battle, pleading for the end, driven to the brink of madness by the extremities of their pain. But Wyn seemed not to hear him. Instead, he shuffled closer on his knees, and very gently laid one hand on the shoulder of Mikki's ruined arm.

'Oh Lord, Lord, Lord,' he muttered, his eyes closed, his head swaying from side to side. 'Oh, Lord – not they who have mercy, but you. This is yours, O my Father. All this is yours. I lift my hands to you for this man. Hear me, God... Hear me,' he pleaded, rocking back on his haunches, raising his hands to the rotting thatch above their heads, as if succour might come from there. Erlan was too bewildered at the notion that this could help Mikki in any way to say anything.

He watched Wyn's face in fascination, so intense in his pious fervour that it was as if his face was glowing, even in the gloomy shadow of their prison. 'Bring healing, O God, bring healing to his broken body! For you, nothing is impossible. Yours is the glory, my Lord. In this and all things.'

On and on he went like this. Erlan looked on, not knowing whether to tell him to hold his tongue or else sit back in wonder. Apparently inspired by Wyn's fervour, the other holy men soon fell to their knees too, so that for a while, Erlan felt entirely alone, entirely impotent, entirely on the outside of whatever unseen power had taken hold of these men. He was so fixated on them, he didn't notice Mikki raise his head.

'Woah, woah, woah,' the river-man muttered. 'What the Hel? My arm – it's getting hot... so hot. Gaah!'

'Stop!' Erlan cried. 'Whatever you're doing to him, leave off!'

No one was touching him, but nor did they stop. Mikki was swearing like a Viking on a raiding day, until all at once the angle of his shattered arm began to shift. His hand rolled over, his wrist pulled back into line. Mikki started gasping, but no longer with pain. Erlan stared in disbelief as Mikki sat upright, now gripping his right arm with his left, clasping at himself as if he couldn't believe it either.

The holy men left off their praying. The expressions on their faces suggested they were just as astonished as the Northmen. Then one of them started laughing. And then they were all laughing, even Mikki. And they crowded round him, praising their God and embracing each other and Mikki, far as they were able.

Erlan sat back on his haunches, shaking his head in wonder, convinced his eyes must be lying to him. *They must be.* 'I don't understand,' he muttered. 'What does this mean?'

Wyn turned to him and smiled. 'It means, my friend, that God has not forsaken us yet.'

CHAPTER THIRTY-SEVEN

'You don't know what you're asking.'

'I know exactly what I'm asking. That's why I'm asking it.'

Lilla folded her arms, standing tall in defiance of Karil, son of Pepin, heir to the Mayorship of the Austrasian palace and all of the Frankish realm, who now sat slumped in a field chair inside his tent, observing his guest with a gaze that was half-amusement, half-disdain.

Lilla expelled a small breath, only now concluding that this was maybe not the posture to adopt if she meant to persuade him. After all, she had wounded his pride, embarrassed them both. However sympathetic he had been to her, however well-disposed he might be to her for good reasons and bad, a woman could push a thing too far.

'Put yourself in my position, Lady Lilla,' he said at length. 'I have one chance, and one only. If I don't pull this off, how long do you think these men would stay loyal to my cause? Those still alive, that is.'

'You said yourself you have time enough to gather more forces. Time enough to train them for another fight. A different kind of fight. We both know Koln is still besieged. I'm asking of you only thirty men. And six days at most. Perhaps fewer.'

Karil dragged himself out of his field chair. The camp had now grown into something almost resembling an army. From a band of hungry fugitives, it was indeed a remarkable turn-around. Each day, she saw signs of more discipline and order among Karil's men. And there was no doubting the conviction which burned in every one of them. Loyalty like that was a rare commodity. A precious commodity. Not one to be squandered. Karil went to the little upturned cask that served as his table, snapped up a pair of beakers in one hand, a jug of wine in the other.

'Drink?'

Inside, she screamed with frustration at every second wasted. Now she had made her mind up, all she wanted to do was go. *Go!* But outwardly she gave a courteous tilt of her head. 'Thank you.'

He poured out both at once, spilling wine liberally over the rim and proffering her the brimming cup. Hardly worthy of courtly etiquette in any land. She took it all the same.

He tapped the bottom of his cup against the rim of hers, then threw back the contents in one. He gasped and wiped his lips. 'Were you ever going to tell me what this man is to you?' he said, already re-charging his beaker.

'This man?'

'Must you be so coy?' He sounded rather weary. 'Please. I've no time to drag out of you confessions of the heart like squeezing out a damned splinter. Simply tell me straight. You are married to this man, yes? Erlan Aurvandil.' Karil said the name carefully, like a man trying on a new pair of boots, deciding whether they were a good fit.

She could have demanded to know who told him. But was there any point in denying it now? 'I've been his and he mine for... Well, maybe since the moment my husband died. We were married earlier this year.'

'Hm.' Karil nodded. Lilla couldn't decide whether he looked disappointed or entirely indifferent. 'You could have spared us some... awkwardness if you'd made this clear from the beginning.'

'It was my mistake. I suppose I owe you an apology.'

'Well. I suggest we forget about it.' He sculled off another cup of wine and she took the opportunity to take a gulp of hers. 'Beautiful as you are,' he said, wiping his beard, 'if I'm going to sleep with a married woman, the least I demand is that she enjoy it. A guilty conscience is rather fatal to a man's passions.'

'I'm sorry.'

'Oh, for God's sake, enough apologies. This man is your husband. A lucky man in that regard... Though less lucky, I hear, in others.'

'I need your help. It's that simple. I believe the task is straightforward from what my men tell me. They know the location of this... wolves' lair. They know its strength. I only wait on your acquiescence.'

'My acquiescence. My, what a regal word.' He sighed. 'You are a queen indeed,' he muttered, and not for the first time.

She sensed he was tiring of her. And there was little more unwelcome than someone of whom you had grown weary but to whom you also owed a great debt. 'Shall we make a deal then?' she suggested.

'I'm fully aware of my side of the ledger already, Lady Lilla. I owe you my life. If I were a man of honour, how could I deny you anything?'

'I do not question your honour.'

'Don't you? By God, I do sometimes. Very often, to be frank.'

'Then forget honour. Be the practical man you are. The man of action.'

'Hm! A man of action... I like the sound of that. Although a man of impatience is probably closer to the truth.'

'The result is the same.'

'Perhaps...' He took another thoughtful pull on his third cup of wine. Clearly the strains of his predicament, of what was at stake for him, were playing on his nerves. 'You spoke of a deal.'

'A third of the gold. Without question. Without condition.'

'You seem very confident that we will recover it.'

'With your help, I believe we can.'

'If Childebrand's reports are to be believed, a third of what he recovered is already a fantastic treasure. Why would you give it away so lightly? You are its rightful owner, after all.'

Lilla felt the prick to her conscience. She could hardly lay claim to that. The gold should be safe in the coffers of Khan Tervel in the far away Bulgar lands if the true right of it was to be told. But Karil didn't need to know this. 'It is the price of my freedom.'

'Freedom? I hope you don't think I hold you here under duress.'

'I know you do not. But until I recover the means to go on,' she shrugged, 'I have nowhere else to go. We are stuck with you.'

'Hm. I hope there are worse places you could be.' He flashed a smile at her. And she glimpsed for the first time that his apparently boundless confidence was perhaps not as impenetrable as it seemed. She stepped closer to him so that she was standing over him. He sat back in his chair and looked up at her, relaxed, expectant. She reached down and cupped her hand against his cheek.

'I hope you don't need me to tell you, you are already a great leader. A worthy son of your father. You are still young. You draw men to you. Aye, and women, too.' She gave a soft chuckle. 'If you live, I see a great future for you. Your people will be blessed by your rule.'

'But...' he said, matter-of-factly.

'No but. Only that I, too, am such a leader. I must return to my land and reclaim what is my own. For my sake, but also for the sake of many others.' She bent to him and very gently planted a kiss on his wine-red lips. 'Let us set each other free. Let us seal our friendship and so both our destinies.'

His eyes were fixed on hers, a wry smile twitching around the corners of his mouth. 'I must say, my father's pep talks were not nearly so convincing.'

She withdrew from him and waited for his verdict.

'And the gold will seal our friendship?' he said, gesturing towards his camp bed. 'Not an hour on this rather indifferent mattress?'

'I shall take that as the compliment you no doubt intended,' she replied, with a wry smile of her own. 'But flattering as your attentions have been, the offer remains the same.'

His brow suddenly cleared, as if the games were at an end and he was only now seriously considering her proposition. At length, he stretched out his hand.

'A third, then.'

She accepted his hand. He shook it, then bent forward and planted a kiss on her knuckles so light that she felt the spark of it pass right through her. Gods, the sooner she was out of his tent the better.

'So then, ready your men, Lady,' he said with a nonchalant smile. 'We ride at dawn.'

Lilla had taken a gamble. But there was no other move to make. Whether Erlan had betrayed her or not, she still could not be certain. All she could do was choose to believe the best of him. Even if she was wrong, choosing that would surely forge the better road. A road that would lead, she hoped, to gold; to love again, maybe.

But also – and of this she was certain – to an ocean of blood.

CHAPTER THIRTY-EIGHT

The remarkable thing was that the girl had come back, Skírpa thought to himself, as he regarded his pale naked form in the makeshift mirror. He had fashioned the thing out of an old plough-share, beaten it flat, polished it to a shine, then balanced it on a chest. It was far from perfect, revealing little of the detail he was used to seeing in the ornate pieces he had afforded himself in the emperor's palace. But it served for the purpose. For now.

Yes. Truly remarkable.

They had picked her up wandering near the outer perimeter beyond the stockade, which was apparently as far as the wolf bands would go in the days leading up to a *Máni-Blót*. She had seemed disorientated and confused, as well she might. And yet she was clear about what she wanted. She kept asking for the Wanderer – or 'the Aurvandil' as she called him. Of course, she had been taken to Alvarik straight away. His delight at having her once more in his power was obscene, his yellow eye fairly bulging with lust, the hang-dog tongue slavering with anticipation. He ordered her at once to be locked in isolation, with a special guard of three men to watch her day and night. She would be his precious *Skuld* in the coming *blót*.

Skírpa didn't need to speak with her to guess that she had formed some sort of passion for the cripple, and in her folly had returned the way she knew he had come without the slightest thought of what she would do when she got here.

Well, he thought, *let her fate be upon her own slender shoulders.*

Meanwhile, he must make ready, for the moon was already rising.

He gazed at his outline in the shoddy mirror, standing proud and erect. At the long pale limbs, the lustrous dark hair that once more crowned his head, at his sweetly smooth shoulders pushed back. Only his face was unrecognisable from what he had once been, now a butcher's tapestry of ruined flesh. No matter. He was more than his face. After all, it seemed no matter how low he was cast down, his natural talents always ensured he would rise again. Some had a brilliance that shone from within, a light that could not be concealed. He was one of those. The bearer of an inextinguishable light.

He wound the loin cloth around his waist and looped it between his legs, then round his waist again before fastening it in the Anatolian fashion. He had always enjoyed dressing himself, making ready for whichever ceremony was to follow. He had seen them all – coronations, funerals, weddings, baptisms. Embassy banquets, military triumphs, brothel orgies, imperial audiences of the Golden Hall. This was different, and yet the same. A sequence of formality –

everything in its proper place and for its proper reason. Alvarik had explained it all.

Skírpa had his place, too.

Since his 'act of service' – as the One Eyed called it – the night of the attack, his position in the settlement had improved considerably. He no longer had to sleep among the stinking detritus of the children in their cattle-sheds. He had his own place to sleep, and now his own chamber to make ready. He was a person of significance once again. These last days had proved that beyond doubt. Alvarik spoke to him, not as an equal – he could hardly expect that – but certainly as superior to those howling halfwits who made up most of his following. He had a role. And like all his roles, he intended to hone it to perfection.

On each of these past four days leading up to this last and greatest *Máni-Blót* of the old year – the Great Feast of *Báleygr* – they had dragged out another of the holy men from their pit-house cell and made an offering of him to the One-Eyed God. It had been he, Skírpa, who was given the honour of despatching the man.

He looked down at his hands. Turned them over and back again. There were still dark veins of red infilling the wrinkles in his knuckles, and a seam of crimson lining many of the folds of his nails. Hands stained with holy blood. However much he scrubbed them one day, the night that followed was sure to re-fill the cracks.

On the third day, he had given up trying.

He bunched them into fists. These were his hands, the only ones he would ever possess, and they were unclean. Could not be cleaned.

He looked up at his reflection in the mirror. *Aye, and what of that?* Who would dare claim the right to hold a flame to his conscience?

No one.

No one had authority to judge him because no one had lived his life. No one knew what he had endured. Only he did. Only he understood that all he had endured was justification for anything he did now. For everything. Whatever he wished – to take life or to grant it – *he* had earned that right. The right to play god...

The blade was in his hand now. And he meant for it to stay that way.

The one slight speck of grit in his otherwise deepening satisfaction was the way each of the holy men had faced his end. It was one thing to be stalwart, to put a brave face on a grim fate. To meet death with courage and resolve, like an equal. The north was full of such stories. Brave men, unafraid of death. But these men... They had met their ends, neither with courage nor stony resolution, but simply with joy. There was no other word for it. He could see it on their faces. They were caught in a kind of rapture. As if death were an old and gentle friend, whose coming they anticipated as a sweet and longed-for reunion.

The whole business stank of their faith. It reeked of the lie. Like a great sweltering turd served up on a feast table, it spoiled the rest, no matter how sumptuous the other dishes. And, what was worse, with each sacrifice, Alvarik grew more irascible, until on the penultimate day, when the finger of fate fell upon Brother Medard, the little tyrant had lost his patience entirely. The mange-riddled monk had made a last bleating appeal to Skírpa – not for mercy, but for Skírpa to consider his own salvation – as if they were friends, or brothers even, merely because they had journeyed a few hundred miles together. While he was still bleeding out, rather than hang him with the other corpses on the *Immerbaum*, Alvarik had fed him to his pet wolf. Geri – The Greedy One. By all the gods, the animal lived up to that name.

But now – tonight – was the night of the Great and Living Eye. A lavish moon was rising, bright and lidless in a crisp, clear sky. Pouring its silver light down onto the earth like honeyed semen, there to seed its children. Children of the night, children of the darkness. The clamouring children of death.

Skírpa let the linen tunic fall down over his head, slipping his arms through the sleeves. Then, with care, he lifted the cloak of raven feathers from its peg on the wall and swung it around his shoulders, fastening it with a brooch in the shape of the Midgard Serpent at his chest. It had a strange smell to it, unlike the furs or woollen fibres of other cloaks. He turned a little this way and that, enjoying the play of the lamp's flame off the feathers' jet-stone surface. Then he took the little pot of moistened ashes and with a delicate fingertip applied it around each eye. Then the brilliant white paste of barley-flour mixed with pine resin – he'd had to improvise. Two fingers to smear a pale stripe across each cheek. That done, he reached for the head-dress and fixed it in place.

He stood back and admired the dim shape of himself in the polished iron.

The antlers felt a part of him now. This was who he had become. This was the outworking of all that had gone before.

508

His Skuld. *The debt that must be paid…*

A goat's horn sounded outside. The summoning for all to come. For him to take his place. To stand under the light of the One Eye. To be seen by him.

He pulled the fastening tight under his chin, checked the dagger in his belt one last time.

Then he went out to meet the One-Eyed God.

Erlan stood listening to the beat of the drum.

The same drum Orīana must have heard when she went to her death. He felt a pang for her. For his friend also, wherever he was.

A friend no more.

By the Hanged, he thought, looking out over the mass of people, *Orīana hadn't deserved this seething madness.*

Beneath him was a swaying crowd of men and women in numbers he had never imagined while sneaking about in the shadows, nor languishing with the others in that grubby pit-house.

People. No, it was hard to think of them as such. They were *creatures* – all of them garbed in every kind of wild costume, evoking the spirit of nearly every beast of the forest. The wolves, of course, but also bears and foxes, hawks and badgers; wild-cats, eagles, weasels, deer. Even a figure standing close by on the altar mound clad head to toe in raven feathers, young deer antlers protruding from his head, a fringe of black feathers hanging low over his eyes.

And presiding over them all, the squat block of muscle, this Alvarik, whose twin goat-horns rose so seamlessly off the leather cap covering his oversized head that they appeared a part of him. As if he was some horned monster that had jumped out of one of the Old Time tales.

Amid all that devilry, there were only two figures who gave him any assurance: Wyn and Mikki. Only the three of them were left now, and the gods only knew what fate awaited them. No one had yet told them. Erlan could only assume that they, too, would go the way of their cell-mates, whose bodies he'd seen hanging from the *Immerbaum* as they were led up to the altar mound.

He glanced at Wyn, feeling a shiver of resentment at him. Even betrayal.

The *urðr* of Mikki's healing had given them all hope. Even Erlan had allowed himself to be swept up in it. But then had come the sobering days that led to this one. Seemed like only he could see the truth of it. Believing in their god didn't stop the axe from falling, nor the knife from going in.

There was a jabber and burble of people talking. He noticed skins of ale or maybe something stronger passing among the *ulfheðnar*, now arrayed in all their lupine glory, pelts and masks hiding the men beneath. They were animated, charged with a kind of expectation which, Erlan guessed, presaged nothing good. Everywhere torches were burning, so that in the meeting area below the mound and the great tree, all was quite visible. It was only the shifting shadows over the animal heads, and the painted faces, and the furs and skins in which the revellers were dressed, that created a sense of other-worldly darkness in the place. And the curious structure immediately behind the crowd.

A huge wooden triangle.

Erlan had noticed, when they were marched to the mound, that what had looked like a mere facade had a depth to it; making him wonder whether it was some kind of temple, albeit one constructed in haste, and very poorly at that. Meanwhile, the wavering torchlight below revealed a small window at the apex of the triangle. As he looked harder, he realised it, too, was the shape of an enormous eye.

By the gods – this accursed eye! It was everywhere. He wondered at the meaning of it. Odin's eye, the moon, the great pyramid, the terrible blood-drenched tree. All of these seemed like strands of a web whose centre remained a mystery to him. Who or what was the blood-hungry spider that dwelt in its heart?

A sound distracted him from his thoughts. At first it came so softly that he thought maybe he was imagining it. But it grew a little louder, and louder still. A humming sound rising, he soon realised, from the throats of the crowd below. As it grew, a tremendous dread began seeping into his bones. He watched and waited for the next thing, but it was a long time coming. So that the sound itself became a resonance right through his skull, overwhelming his thoughts and attention.

It was a shock when a woman's voice rose high and sweet above it all – like the rising sun above the dark earth. Or else, he now saw, the rising moon. Her voice was joined by another, and then a third. A beautiful winding harmony pouring deeper into his consciousness with every passing note. He could have listened to it for hours were it not for the sudden screams that shattered everything.

Somewhere further back a door slammed open, and the discordant screaming of young voices joined with the sweet music of the three women. Horror rippled through his veins. The face of that little girl flashed in his mind, gaunt and dirt-stained, too old for its tender years. He could see a procession of them, mere boys and girls, hardly any had reached the years of change to adulthood. Their *ulfheðnar* guards pushed and hustled them through the crowd of onlookers, which parted all the way to the base of the pyramid.

There, two other *ulfheðnar* were already standing, and as the keening procession approached, one of them threw open a hidden door. Erlan could see nothing but darkness within. Two by two, the children were pushed inside. To what purpose, Erlan could not see. But there was something horrible about the way they were shoved in like sacks of meat, almost into an abyss. When the last of them was in, the *ulfheðinn* snapped the door shut, and the wailing inside became muted.

'Mikki,' said Wyn softly beside him. 'Remember what I told you, friend.'

'I do.' Mikki's face was still a welter of bruises and swellings. 'I'm thinking of it now.' Whatever words of hope Wyn had shared in secret with the river-man, Erlan didn't know. But if they had any worth, now was the time to lean on them.

The crowd's attention gradually shifted from the pyramid back towards the altar mound where they stood. The song of the women had reached its end, dwindling to silence. And at length Alvarik, the One Eyed, stepped forward, his hand resting like a crown upon the head of his wolf.

'Blood is the only truth!' he cried, his voice filling the night.

It must have been a saying well known to the crowd for they echoed it right back at him in a thunderclap of voices.

Then silence again.

'We few know, we select few,' the One Eyed declared, 'the true nature of the lord and master of this world.' He spread his feet and lifted up his powerful arms, his hands stretching in appeal to the bright, voluptuous moon. 'We know the sacrifice he made for our sakes. His loss of paradise for this lower world. Nothing we devote back to him can outdo what he has already done for us... This is just as the One Eyed has revealed to me. And I, in turn, have made known to you.'

Erlan listened, trying to make sense of the brutish priest's obscure sayings. It didn't sound much like the kind of goði talk he'd heard in the north when the shamans made their devotions to the High God, Odin. But then nothing about this creature was ordinary.

'The light from above seeds the dark earth here below. We purify ourselves for your coming with the blood of innocents. Light and earth together, bound in forever union. Come, *Forni* – Ancient One! Come, *Foldardrótinn* – Lord of the Earth! Come, *Báleygr* – Flaming Eye!' He was working himself into a fine lather, arms aloft, body shaking, voice filled with passion. He went on crying out other names to the moon, and with each the crowd's excitement rose to a higher pitch, until they too were in a ferment of ecstasy, howling up at the moon, leaping and jumping as if it were almost within their reach.

All at once Alvarik threw apart his massive arms in a signal for silence. Then he turned very slowly to Erlan, Wyn and poor Mikki, who looked singularly uninspired by all that was going on.

'We ripen the earth with the blood of the innocents,' he said, with a look of savoured malice at Wyn. Then he gave a low and grating laugh, raking his broad fingers through the pelt of his pet wolf. 'I know you came here for the children. Did you not, monk?'

'I did,' Wyn replied, undaunted. 'God forgive my failure.'

'So then,' Alvarik sneered. 'Let their blood be upon your hands.'

'You do not have to do this. You can spare them still, I beg of you!'

'Oh, I should be glad to,' replied the One Eyed. 'If you would only disavow your lie.'

'What?' The monk's voice fell to a whisper as he saw the horror of what this fiend in human skin was suggesting.

'You heard me. I put their lives in your hands. If you will repudiate your god then I will spare them. Here and now. Go ahead. Spit on his accursed name! Only deny him, and I will keep my word.' He laughed again, adding, 'Of course, if you refuse… then you leave me no choice.'

He waited. They all waited.

But when Wyn only bowed his head, Alvarik soon lost patience. 'Give me your answer, monk!' he snapped.

Even then, for some time Wyn said nothing. Stood beside him, Erlan could see the anguish on the monk's lined face, his lips moving in torrid prayer. At last he looked up. 'My answer is this. To you, you servant of Satan.' Wyn lifted up his voice. 'To *all* of you who hear me! You must repent of this wickedness! What you do here is whoredom. You whore yourselves to that which is unholy. You bind yourselves to dark powers when your allegiance should be to your Creator. It is He who made you. It is He whom you betray.' His face suddenly lit with an unexpected joy. 'But let heaven be praised – the power in me is greater than the power who enslaves you! The blood of Jesus has already been spilled for your sins and won for you eternal peace. An end to your enmity with God. Ask for forgiveness, even now,' he cried. 'It will not be denied you. But continue on this road and you win yourselves nothing. Nothing! You are deceived! You forge only greater chains for yourselves that will pull you down to hell.'

'You think words will turn our hearts,' the One Eyed barked in scorn.

'Not words,' returned the monk. '*The* Word.'

Alvarik's mouth curved in a dog-like sneer. 'Pathetic.'

Wyn shook his head, seeming for a moment genuinely sorrowful. 'Do what you must then. I cannot deny Him,' he said softly. 'I *will* not.'

'So be it!' bellowed Alvarik, turning to the crowd. 'The choice is made. Bring forth the torches. Ignite the temple!'

Wyn fell to his knees, seeming not to see the laughing visage of his tormentor, nor to hear the baying of the crowd as the torches were borne forward.

'Poor bloody mites,' muttered Mikki Crow. But then Wyn threw back his head and lifted his bound hands to heaven.

'Lord!' he cried, his gruff voice filling the arena. 'This battle is yours, O Lord! Have mercy on your little ones! The battle is yours, El Shaddai! Lord of Hosts, see here! The battle is yours!'

'Silence, you bald-head cunt!' snarled Alvarik with a brutal blow to the side of Wyn's head, sprawling him at the feet of the man robed in raven feathers, who stepped back in disgust. 'You've had your say.'

Erlan knelt down beside Wyn and rolled him onto his back. Wyn was groaning.

'Lie still, my friend,' Erlan murmured, looking back over his shoulder as flames began to lick at the pyramid walls. 'There's nothing you can do.'

Just then something touched his face, making him look up.

High above them, he saw grey wisps of cloud floating across the moon's shining face; and on his cheek, he felt the first flecks of rain.

Lilla looked up at the long roll of thunder.

'Storm's coming through,' said Black Svali, then hawked a wad of phlegm into the dead leaves beside the path.

'Fuck me, Sval,' muttered Bull. 'Who gave you the Far Sight?'

'Piss off, Bullock,' Black Svali grumbled back at him.

Despite the tell-tale rumble, the moon in all its fullness was still visible high above them, hanging there like a giant wain-wheel in the sky. 'We must hurry,' she said. 'Einar?'

'Has to be close now, lassie,' said the voice behind her, anticipating her question. 'Reckon we should leave the horses soon. And put out the torches.'

'Lord Karil? Do you agree?'

'I'm in your hands, Lady.' The Frank looked back into the darkness at the following line of his horsemen. Thirty in all, every man of them hand-picked, and disciplined enough to ride in silence. 'I confess I've never been this deep into the Immerwald.'

Einar gave a cynical grunt and turned away.

'Something to say, Northman?' demanded Karil.

Einar glanced back. 'Cancers grow in unseen places, is all. Let's keep moving.'

Lilla waited until he had ridden on a little distance. 'I suggest you don't rile him,' she said to Karil. 'None of my men has suffered more than him. Yet he's still here.'

'Several of your men are dead. I'd say theirs is the greater loss, wouldn't you?' And he kicked on his mount after Einar and the sorry remnant of her crew.

Lilla grimaced at the sour taste of the truth. Karil was right. Already she had too much blood on her hands. Was she here for the gold? Or for Erlan? Or for those wretched children?

Whichever, she prayed this night could atone for some of it.

The rain was falling harder now.

The torch flames crackled and smoked, fighting against the damp. The fire scaling the temple slowed for a time, held in equilibrium between its own extinction and its engorgement of the flimsy structure. Even so, despite the rain, there seemed little doubt the flames would win out in the end.

'Bring up the girl,' ordered Alvarik to the nearest of his retinue. 'Do it quickly.'

An order radiated out from guard to guard until, some moments later, another smaller party appeared at the back of the gathering. The crowd parted again, and this time there was no screaming. There were no plaintive cries. No voices raised, only the pop and crackle of the flames as the fire crept up the side of the temple, and behind that a solemn, sinister quiet.

The party was still fifty paces from the altar mound when Erlan recognised the figure being led. And his blood ran cold with horror.

Marta.

It hit him like a fist in the gut. What the Hel was she doing back in this pit of evil? The last he'd seen of her was her fleeting shadow melting into the forest. But she and Einar had been heading north, away from this place, surely?

For a horrible moment, he wondered whether Einar, too, was somewhere in Alvarik's clutches. But there was no sign of him.

Instead Marta walked alone. A dignified figure in all the madness, clad in a simple white shift, her long black hair spilling undressed about her shoulders.

Erlan swallowed hard, dreading what malice this blood-mad brute intended for her. Alvarik had moved inside the circle marked around the stone altar. He stood, awaiting the arrival of the procession, his long mouth hanging a little open, the tip of his tongue just visible, flicking from side to side. The *ulfheðnar* marched Marta to the circle's edge. Alvarik beckoned the three women forward, inviting them into the circle with him. Once inside, the oldest of them went to Marta and took her hand, drawing her across the line. The

518

other women closed around her, pushing her forward and then down onto the altar surface.

Marta offered no resistance. Her eyes were bright and calm. But when she was lain out on the stone, Erlan saw her glance in his direction, just once.

Once was enough to break his heart.

'Stop. If it's blood you want, bastard,' he blurted, 'take mine.'

'Blood? Hah! You miserable fool. It's not her blood I'll take – at least not yet. It's her purity... Strip her,' he said to the women.

'I'm warning you,' insisted Erlan, aware his position hardly warranted such threats.

'I suppose you want to take her place, eh?' scoffed the One Eyed. 'I'm afraid you don't make a very appealing alternative.' One of the *ulfheðnar* laughed.

'Don't you fucking touch her. If you must make sacrifice, take me.'

'And who are you? Some bedraggled cripple lost in the woods,' he sneered. 'Some would-be hero caught in a story far beyond your understanding. Shit on that! I suppose you think it noble, this gesture of yours.'

'I don't care a rat's turd what it is. But if you lay a finger—'

'Don't worry, cripple, we shall deal with you in the proper time. The One Eye has a use, even for one as blighted as you.' He turned back to Marta and began unlacing his breeches. 'Hold her down.' At his command, one of the women knelt behind Marta's head and pressed her shoulders flat. The other two each took hold of a leg and pulled her thighs apart. But there was no need to force her. Marta offered

519

no resistance. The odious brute knelt down, his swollen phallus now swaying over her, obscenely menacing, like a cobra about to strike. The crowd stirred in anticipation, animal noises rising off them in a discord of yelps and slavering grunts.

'Marta!' cried Erlan, which only earned him a blow from the guard behind him.

'The devil take him,' hissed Wyn. 'He's already cast his lot with the Evil One.' The rain was drumming down now, a gale blowing up in the trees.

'Doesn't mean he can have her too,' said Erlan. The gods knew he didn't understand the girl, but she didn't deserve this. Maybe there was only one way to stop him now. 'My last warning, Alvarik,' he called, 'you loathsome cunt!'

The One Eyed stopped, turned angrily and got back to his feet. 'I'm getting a little fucking tired of these interruptions.' He signalled to one of the *ulfheðnar* standing by. 'Hang them. All three of them.'

'Master?'

'I said hang those whoresons! *NOW!*'

Skírpa watched the guards seize the three men, their faces alight with the promise of more violence and death. They had ropes, they soon had nooses. They tore off the prisoners' tunics, then looped their ropes around the men's necks and tossed the ends over the thick boughs that stretched above their heads.

'Start with him,' said Alvarik who had now left the circle in his eagerness to despatch the three. He was pointing at

Erlan Aurvandil. The rain was streaming down his leather cap onto his face, making the white paint smeared across his cheeks run. It looked like his face was melting. His ragged mouth gaped wide in anger.

One of his men took hold of the end of the rope and began drawing the slack. The Aurvandil waited calmly, apparently ready to face his death if it meant delaying the defilement of the girl, even for a moment. Skírpa should have felt happy. But something about it seemed so absurd. It was all so bloody futile. What did her virtue matter in a world this rotten? What did the Aurvandil's honour matter? What did anything matter, come to that? Even living itself? Death was as worthy as any life Skírpa had ever stumbled upon.

And yet...

The rope snapped taut. The other men – the monk and the Aurvandil's tall companion – struggled against their bonds but there was nothing they could do. The wolf-warrior pulled and pulled, but he could barely raise the Aurvandil off his toes. Even so, the face of the one man who had so thwarted Skírpa's schemes was turning scarlet. He uttered not a sound; he could not. He swayed on his tiptoes as two men now struggled to hoist him until suddenly the One Eyed lost patience. 'Stand aside,' and he shoved the two men off the rope. The Aurvandil had a moment of respite, gasping down great lungfuls of air while the rope allowed.

'Have faith, my friend,' called the monk. Though the Northman said nothing in reply and Skírpa wondered what was going through his mind. He had professed nothing of the lie in Skírpa's hearing. Yet he was clearly prepared to face his death.

Now Alvarik had hold of the rope and began hauling it down fist over fist until the Wanderer was at last hoisted off his feet, swinging gently in the driving rain. His head tilted grotesquely to the side. Alvarik was gurning away with the effort of pulling him higher – grunting and laughing in equal measure. Even in the wavering torchlight, Skírpa could see the Northman's face turning purple, his tongue protruding, fighting for some lick of air. His hands were bound behind his back, his body flapping rhythmically.

'May God have mercy on your soul, Aurvandil!' cried Wyn.

'Silence, monk,' Alvarik growled through gritted teeth, his face dark as a devil's under the twin goat-horns, arms bulging with the strain of keeping the Aurvandil aloft. 'Ready with the knife, Skírpa!'

Mechanically, obeying without question as he was trained to do, Skírpa stepped forward and drew the dagger from his belt.

'Erlan!' screamed the girl, her stoic resolve finally cracking. 'My Erlan!'

Alvarik was laughing. 'Can you hear me, cripple? I'll fuck your little girl so hard she chokes on it. Then I'll slit her pretty throat!' His laugh pulsed loud and rasping as the croaking of a toad. The Northman could say nothing, his only response the futile bucking of his body as his life drained away. 'Who are you now, eh, cripple? *WHO ARE YOU NOW?*' His one eye flicked to Skírpa. 'Do it. Gut him, you worm!'

Skírpa raised the knife, his ears filled with Alvarik's grating voice, his vision dancing between the Aurvandil's pale belly, so ripe for the gutting, and the gurning, melting face of his master.

That old enemy hanging there, defenceless as a swine trussed for the slaughter. The blade-edge so sharp, its point so wicked-keen.

Who are you?

The question ghosted over Skírpa's lips.

Yes. Who am I?

And something from far, far away came sailing through the air. Or was it from deep within? Some spark in the night. Some light in the darkness that could not be overcome.

Skírpa stepped forward and struck.

CHAPTER THIRTY-NINE

The pressure in Erlan's head suddenly vanished and he fell like a sack of rocks to the ground.

He opened his eyes, vision still blurred and swimming with stars from the lack of air and the fierce panicked thumping of his heart in his chest. He was aware of wild shouting. Screams and curses, and the familiar sound of blades being drawn. He felt himself being rolled onto his belly. There was nothing he could do. But, to his surprise, instead of a knife in his liver he felt his bonds being cut.

Someone shouted his name. It was enough to bring him back to himself.

He sat up and witnessed the chaos around him.

Mikki was on top of one of the wolf-warriors, bent over him like an animal, head-butting the man in the face again and again. Blood splattered with the rain. Then his hands were free, too – and he had hold of a long-knife.

Erlan glanced to his right, clearer vision returning now. The rain was lancing down through the branches. The figure wrapped in raven feathers was wrestling with the One Eyed, apparently locked in a struggle to the death. The haft of a knife was sticking out of Alvarik's side. His twin horns had slipped askew on his head.

At last, Erlan's wits caught up. He made to get up but then a man in a wolf-mask appeared over him, his axe raised. Erlan cursed his own slowness, seeing the hate boiling in the blood-shot eyes above him. Then, out of nowhere, an arrow skewered the man through both cheeks. He fell backwards, clawing at the shaft in vain.

Another arrow whipped past. There were other voices now. Shrieks and war-cries and the thump of axe-hafts against limewood shields. Erlan dragged himself up, still unsteady on his feet.

'Arm yourself, brother.' That was Wyn's voice. Erlan turned and saw the monk grappling to free himself of his bonds, his guards now gone.

'What just happened?' Erlan gasped. But no one answered him. Then he saw warriors pouring into the arena out of the shadows. These wore no wolf-pelts. They had leather byrnies and mailshirts. Long spears, round-helms and oval shields.

Was he dreaming?

Was he already dead, and this was some death-grip hallucination before the final extinction of his mind?

'Aurvandil!' cried a plaintive voice that was high and clear. He realised it had come from the Raven man, though gods only knew why the appeal was for him. But if he was fighting the One Eyed, that made him an ally.

Erlan launched himself at the struggling figures, taking them both with him, driving them off their feet and sending

525

all three of them sprawling against the trunk of the mighty ash tree that rose above them.

His head hit the wood, jarring his neck, but there was no time to feel pain. Alvarik was still very much alive, wriggling and scrabbling beneath him. But the raven-feathered cloak was smothering Erlan's face. He tried to rip it away so he could see again, caught in a tussle of snarls and grunts and flailing fists. Suddenly the feathers whipped away and he found himself face to face with the glaring eye and its empty twin.

'Cripple,' the shaman snarled in a cloud of fetid breath.

The Raven man rolled clear as the One Eyed's enormous hands closed around Erlan's throat. Before they could take a firm hold, Erlan jerked forward, smashing his forehead into the shaman's crooked nose. Blood burst in a shower over his face. He tasted iron on his lips, slipping his hands up between Alvarik's arms and ripping them apart to break the hold on his throat.

'Save the girl!' he managed to yell at the Raven man, who was staggering to his feet, then stumbled backwards, crashing into one hanging corpse before reeling into another, sending them swinging. The stench of decay and death mingled with the bracing tang of fresh rain. Alvarik's legs slipped between his own, then he gave a great lurch of his muscular body and flipped Erlan onto his back. Erlan looked up in horror at the silhouette above him. The two horns at a crazy angle, still menacing as a demon's shadow, that single glimmering eye glaring madly down at him. Erlan writhed in the mud, trying to buck him off, but Alvarik had him gripped between his thighs, like a rat in a trap. Before he knew it, those massive hands closed around his head. He kicked and thrashed, his heels scraping uselessly in the mud, the pain that was crushing his head driving him mad. Then, with a horrible inexorability, he felt two huge thumbs flicking over his face, seeking out his eye sockets like snakes looking for their burrow. He could do nothing to stop them. The brute was too compact, short but heavy as any man, every inch of him hard-packed muscle. Erlan's hands quested for a hold on something, anything, that might turn this fight to his advantage. The world went dark. His eyes bulged like over-ripe berries. Then his hand found something hard. The haft of the dagger, somehow still protruding from Alvarik's iron ribs. How the bastard was still fighting he couldn't fathom, nor was there time to wonder. Instead, he seized the handle and twisted with all the strength in him, feeling the ribs bend and the bone and blade grate. The One Eyed reared up in agony, a great scream tearing from his lips, at the same time as a scalding heat burst through Erlan's left eye.

For an instant he saw only red, tasted fresh blood on his tongue, then a thunder-clap tore the skies asunder, loud as the harbinger of Ragnarok, a flash of searing white light, followed by a deafening crack that seemed to split the world in two...

Lilla had already lost sight of him when the bolt of lightning struck.

For an instant, it lit up the whole mad scene like a terrible vision of the night.

Karil's spear-men had moved in ahead of her few. The *ulfheðnar* had reacted quickly, but there was little order to

527

their defence. They fought in twos and threes with whatever weapons they could scramble together, wild with a kind of berserker frenzy, but without the skill of their cousins in the northern lands.

Then the lightning struck and it was as if a scythe had fallen from the gods on the great tree. A huge portion of it split away and fell like the hand of judgement on the crowd massed below it. For several moments, everyone stopped. Stunned to stillness at the sudden destruction. Dozens must have been crushed beneath the weight of it. The altar stone disappeared in a tangle of twisted branches, together with the women she had seen alongside it.

Then she saw the monk and, beside him, Mikki, armed with axe and long-knife, looking ready to do bloody murder. She yelled his name and he turned and saw her. At once he pointed wildly to the strange wooden temple out of which great plumes of smoke were pouring. Both of them ran to her.

'Them bairns, Lady,' said Mikki. His face was one huge bruise. 'They're in there.'

'Bring an axe,' she said.

'Way ahead of you,' growled Mikki, hefting the weapon in his hand.

'We may be too late,' said Wyn.

'Come on, monk,' returned Mikki. 'Ain't you the one always saying there's still hope?'

'Where's Erlan?' she yelled after them, panic seeping through her. But the two men were already racing towards the temple.

Lilla had also lost sight of Einar, and Bull and the others. All had been swallowed up in the chaos and confusion. With nothing else left to her, she gripped her bow and ran after Mikki.

Fenna was huddled alone in the darkness, choking, dying.

Her tears had long dried up. The falling rafters had already claimed many other lives, and the heat was unbearable. But somehow the rain and the damp had prevented the whole temple going up in a ball of fire. Instead it burned slowly, smokily, smothering them with fumes rather than roasting them in flames. Still, the smoke was deadly enough. Several girls had succumbed. She could see their bodies lying inert on the floor. What she couldn't tell was whether they were dead or only unconscious.

She had little more resistance in her. Why should she resist when she already knew she was lost? She was not even dying among friends. All of them had become wretched and desperate as rats on a sinking ship, jealous of each other and whatever small advantage could be had in their struggle to survive.

The pure darkness was terrifying, the choking fumes, the fear that at any moment the whole edifice might collapse in on itself and crush her tiny body. Her hands were clasped together in prayer, though she knew God could not help her now. His last chance had long passed. So this was all she could do to push back against her fate, expending the last of her failing strength in the grip of her own hands.

No one would come.

She had witnessed the thirst for her death of those horrible beast-folk out there. Better, she thought, to be in here dying, than out there... with *them*.

She curled her body tighter, sucked in another shallow breath, trying not to cough, knowing the end must come soon.

She still had her eyes closed when she realised she could hear something different, faint at first, and then more distinct. A knocking noise on the timber wall. Then a banging. And when at last she dared to look up, she saw now there was a beam of light breaking into the darkness…

Erlan could not see.

His left eye was a well of blood. There was carnage all around him. Darkness and driving rain. He put a hand to the wound and opened the other eye. It was still good, though he could see very little.

Above him, it seemed as though an invisible cudgel had smashed a vast rend in the forest canopy. The naked sky beyond was weeping down on him, weeping with the tears of heaven.

Where was the One Eyed?

Where was anyone?

He pulled himself up on his elbows, tried to look around, tried not to think that he was no better than that half-blind brute now.

The pain was intense. Almost enough to overwhelm him. But the uncertainty of what had happened kept him sharp.

Where was the One Eyed?

There was a mass of branches around him. He grabbed the limb of one and pulled himself to his knees. He was about to get to his feet when he noticed a sudden movement in the tail of his eye.

He turned in time to see a shadow fly at him from another branch. There was a glint of metal. His hand shot up to catch it. The knife-tip stopped bare inches from his face and he was thrown onto his back. Once more Alvarik's mass of muscle was on top of him, writhing and thrashing to get a better grip. Erlan fought desperately to keep the blade at bay, while the One Eyed's other hand closed like a talon around his neck. Squeezing and squeezing.

Erlan felt his vision tunnelling. Felt the strength leaching from his arm. He was losing this fight. It was all over. And he didn't even know why.

What was it all for?

Marta would die. He would die. Wyn would die. Lilla would die. All of them.

So why struggle? If this moon-crazed devil wanted him dead so badly, why not give him what he wanted?

All these and many other mad thoughts flashed through his head. And the final darkness was rising in his mind like a black tide, over-running all else. Only a tiny kernel of light remained. And in it, in that moment before it was snuffed out forever, he saw the curvature of a horn above him, askew on the shaman's head.

As if in a dying dream, he reached up and snapped it off. Turned his hand inward and stabbed with the last of his strength, driving the full length of it straight through Alvarik's thick neck. A hideous guttural grunting came in stuttering fits from the shaman's throat, spraying gouts of thick phlegm into Erlan's ruined eye. His compact body shuddered and shuddered again, the blade fell from his hand and he sank, heavy as a leaden idol, onto Erlan's chest, blood weltering out of the massive wound in his neck, gushing over Erlan's face and into his mouth. Erlan closed his eyes. Closed his mouth. And lay still.

After some moments, the shuddering ceased. Erlan tilted his body and let the dead weight of Alvarik slide off him. He felt blindly for a handhold on the broken tree. Pulled himself upright, then gazed down on his enemy's corpse.

'*Far til Hel*,' he murmured, then pulled himself to his feet.

After all, Hel was the only place this filthy devil belonged.

Skírpa lay wheezing under the weight crushing his chest. Shallow breaths. Doesn't matter how small. In and out. Anything will do.

'Lend a hand here,' said a gruff northern voice. 'This one's alive.'

Alive. Yes. Just stay alive.

There were branches poking into his face. His left arm was numb, couldn't feel it at all. He tasted iron and realised his tongue was bleeding. He moved it gingerly around the cavity of his mouth and felt a deep cut through one side.

'Here, Bull – get your hands on this wi' me.' Something about the voice sounded familiar. But in his daze, he couldn't place it. His face was wet. Through the mesh of branches he saw grey skudding clouds. The colourless streaks of a wet dawn.

'One, two, three – *lift*.'

He heard someone straining, groaning against a weight. Then it felt like the world was lifted off his chest. Something gripped hold of his ankle and he found himself being pulled along the ground. Pulled and pulled till he was clear of the branches and lain out under an open sky.

It was kind of blissful. No one wanted anything from him. Only that he stay alive.

'He was the one,' said a voice he now knew. 'It was he who started it. Without him, we'd all have been hanged.' Wyn. That was it. Wynfred the monk. He remembered now.

'Odin's arse!' exclaimed another voice, a little apart from the others. 'That's Marta under there. Quick now, all of you. Where's that axe, Sval?'

Skírpa lay with his eyes closed, just as he had lain under that deep blue sky, adrift on the Inner Sea. Adrift on the ocean of fate. He heard the hack of iron against wood. Groans and sighs, a weak whimper of pain. Expletives and curses, the crack of branches, the hurried muttering of concerned voices. And all the while he could still smell rotten blood and sodden ashes.

There was movement beside him. Someone else lain next to him. He turned his head and saw the profile of a beautiful young woman.

The girl.

But not as she had been.

Her rib cage was rising and falling, but in short, stifled starts. A trickle of red from the corner of her mouth. That side of her head was matted and sticky with blood. There was a man kneeling over her. No hair. No beard. Just a scalp full of scars. His ear bent low to her mouth.

Skírpa watched her lips, those once ruby lips, pale as marble now, drained of life. But still moving. The corners of his mouth twitched. He'd always been good at reading people's lips. Another skill, another mark of his brilliance, wasted on him. Wasted on his worthless life.

Forgive him, he saw her whisper. *Oh Einar, forgive him... He did no wrong. I loved him... I lied... and I love him... That's all... Can you forgive me?... Can you forgive him?*

Skírpa watched fat tears roll off the bald man's cheek and fall like drops of dew onto her moving lips. He bent lower still, sliding his arm gently under her, scooping her up to hold her closer.

'I'm sorry,' he murmured, his head buried in her neck. 'I'm sorry, kid... For everything... You can rest now. I've got you now, kid. Just rest.'

Her face was tilted to the sky. Her lips seemed to curve in a smile. *Rest*, she echoed in a murmur, as her eyes fell shut.

Rest...

A good word. And the last that she would ever utter.

Karil was toeing the sodden ground, scraping away the ashes and the fragments of old bone. 'I could have done more. Could have saved more. I should have listened.'

'You did all you could,' said Lilla. 'We could not save them all.'

She was surprised how keenly Karil felt the burden of it. Even the resting sneer on his face was softened, his blood-spattered brow furrowed in anguish, his head shaking in self-reproach. 'If we'd ridden harder. If we'd gotten here sooner.'

'I know.' She laid a hand on his arm. 'We did all we could.' Even if she didn't believe it, it was all there was to say.

The children were sitting in a huddle a short distance from the smouldering wreckage of the temple. Fourteen of them had survived. Eleven had come crawling out of the smoke. Mikki and Wyn had found the other three before the flames grew too hot, the smoke too overwhelming, and the structure collapsed in on itself in a great blast of billowing sparks and ash. They sat wide-eyed with blank faces, either looking inward to horrors recalled, or else in uncertainty at these new faces, unable to trust whether they were truly safe now.

Lilla moved among them, sharing water and what little morsels of food she had on her person. Most of the wolf-warriors were dead. They had taken two or three alive. Whether they would live out the day, she doubted. One of them seemed to know something about the gold. Mikki was softening him up, determined to get answers. By all the gods, if anyone deserved a reward at the end of this, it was him.

But even that was almost beyond her caring now.

When she looked upon the children's faces, for a second, she remembered herself. Remembered little Katla and Svein. Remembered the woman she used to be, not the warrior queen she seemed destined to become. Before the words that Saldas had spoken. Before she had laid that curse on her.

Lilla's womb was sealed.

But that did not mean her heart should be.

Wyn was crouched among them, too. One girl seemed especially attached to him. 'D'you think Lord Karil will help return them to their homes?' he asked her.

'Would they even be safe there if we did?' she replied. She did not mean to be cynical. She would have to train her heart to hope for more in the days to come.

'They have a chance at least now,' said Wyn. 'That's all any of us can truly hope for.'

Lilla didn't want to face the ache in her own heart. They still had not found Erlan's body.

'Lady Lilla!' It was Bull. The big lad's face was lit up with something. 'By all the gods!' He was pointing with sudden enthusiasm to the top of the mound beyond where she could see. 'Look there, Lady – it's the skipper!'

Lilla dropped everything and ran to where he was pointing. Ran up the mound, around the massive wreckage of the fallen tree. And there, clawing his way out of the tangle of branches was Erlan Aurvandil. Hakan, son of Haldan. The Wanderer. Her love.

She leaped over the last of the branches that lay between them and threw her arms around his neck. He responded, but only with one arm, murmuring her name again and again into her hair, keeping his hand over one eye.

She leaned back and gently tried to remove it. He resisted. 'Let me...' Insistent, she turned his palm outwards. Beneath was a gaping hollow filled with thick black clots of blood, a cataract of crimson streaked down his cheek. Her gut twisted in nausea. But she refused to look away.

'I'll clean it,' she murmured, pulling him close. 'And dress it.' Just as she had so many of his wounds before. She felt him tense and realised they were not alone.

She turned and saw Karil was standing close by. Shame flushed through her for an ugly second. But when the Frank smiled at them and nodded at her as one who understood, she knew that mistake would be her secret and his to bear. It need not trouble Erlan's heart.

536

Karil still stood there, expectant.

'What is it?' she said.

'I've helped you do your job, Lady. Now you help me do mine.'

CHAPTER FORTY

It was a man named Thunarulf helped them find their gold. Alvarik had had it carried down to the Mosella river, which proved to be only a day's ride to the south of the *Immerbaum*. He had made a great show of dedicating it to the One Eyed God, this Thunarulf said. But those that were there knew it was stored for safe-keeping. Clearly Alvarik had had ambitions in this world, as much as others. The men were given some coin to keep their mouths shut.

Once the gold was loaded and ready for transport, Lilla had expected her men to be buoyant at their success, even if she hardly felt so. But all of them, even Bull, were subdued. Their faces wore haunted expressions, as if they had seen things that ought never to be seen. Like her, they wanted to be done with this land of strange people and stranger gods.

They rode north with Karil and his spear-men to re-join the warlord's gathering forces in the Eifel mountains.

It was the first night in the forest that Lilla suggested Erlan and Einar go for a walk. Alone.

Words were said. Voices were raised, and then... they cooled again. There were tears. An embrace. Memories shared. Lives remembered.

Perhaps it was too exhausting to keep up their defences forever. Better for each of them to see the other's heart.

The friendship would never be the same. There would always be the wound of Orīana. But the wound might one day heal over and eventually scar. And the change in them might make them stronger. Who knew? It was too early to tell. The future alone held the answer.

When the company reached the Eifel camp, they found Karil's brother, Childebrand, in command. He had not been idle. The men who had gathered under Karil's banner had been honed to a razor's edge. They were ready. And their leader had returned not a day too soon.

Word had come from Koln.

Lady Plectrude had at last succumbed. The walls of the city had not been breached; it was Plectrude's resolve which had failed. She had delved deep into the coffers of her late lord husband, Pepin of Herstal, to buy off King Chilperic, plead his forgiveness, and swear her allegiance to the Merovingian line. But Pepin's mountainous treasure was Karil's inheritance by right. So he claimed, anyway. He did not mean to let it leave Austrasia without a fight.

Nor did he mean to miss this chance. He might not get another.

Word went out from the camp – that Lord Karil, the great Austrasian warlord, was a broken blade. That he had fled south to seek allies in Burgundia and beyond. Whether the Merovingian king believed such rumours or not, his army appeared to take no real precautions on their march back to Paris.

Karil's scouts detected an air of complacency about their long column. After all, the Neustrians had won and at little cost, beyond enduring a few weeks camped before Koln in nothing worse than a spell of damp weather.

The report was that Rathbod and his Frisians also marched with Chilperic. A fact which caused Lord Karil no little relish. The chance to add revenge to possible victory was too tantalising to pass up.

Nevertheless, Karil's Austrasian troops were still outnumbered nearly three to one. Surprise was all. And he knew exactly where this was best to be achieved.

There was a section of road to the west of the Eifel mountains, between the town of Malmedy and the Ambleve river. It was a long stretch without springs or streams of any kind. Karil predicted that Chilperic would rest his army once they reached the Ambleve crossing.

'That is where we will strike,' he declared.

And every one of Lilla's men would stand in his line of battle...

Instinctively, Erlan checked the bandage that was wound snug against his head. The empty socket beneath it was a dull throb now. An absence, a memory. The mark that the One Eyed had left on him. How ironic, he thought, that the skalds used to sing that Odin gained wisdom for the price of an eye.

540

His own bargain had not been near so profitable. Was he any the wiser after all that had happened?

Maybe… Just a little.

'Fair few of them buggers,' muttered Einar beside him, gazing out from under the shadow of the trees that hid them all.

'Aye. And still no notion that we're here.'

On the breeze, Erlan could smell the little rushing, winding river, its fresh scent mingled with the stink of an army on the march. Chilperic's troops were strung out nearly half a mile from vanguard to the stragglers in the rear. The royal war banners flapped idly in a light wind, their poles staked in the soft turf of the floodplain. Men were sat down in their order of march in the grass, quenching their thirst, talking, defecating, eating. Taking their rest. Some of the mounted soldiers had led their horses down to the riverbank, patting their necks as the beasts dropped their heads to the water and drank their fill.

'Sheep before a pack of wolves,' growled Einar.

Erlan nodded silently, looking down the line of his own men, and on down the ranks of Austrasian spear-men and mounted troops hidden back from the treeline. The faces of Karil's men were keen, concentrated, their eyes eager as hawks.

'What the Hel are we waiting for?' muttered Mikki on Erlan's left.

'Maybe he wants 'em to pull down their pants and wave us on in?' grinned Bull.

'It'd only be polite,' chuckled Ran.

'Come on, come on,' hissed Black Svali. 'Enough of this horseshit.'

541

'Quiet,' said Erlan. 'The signal will come soon enough.' Still, he was nervous. He tested the hilt of his sword in its scabbard, checking the blade would not stick.

'You come up with a name for that thing yet?' asked Einar, with a casual nod at the emperor's gift.

'Not yet. A sword needs a story 'fore it has a name. Don't know what this one's is yet.'

'There,' exclaimed Bull excitedly, as out of the trees on the far side of the floodplain, a flaming arrow arced high in the autumn sky, then fell to the earth.

That was the signal. All around them, men began unsheathing swords and hefting shields. Low voices called their orders. There was a jangle of buckles and the creak of waxed leather.

Erlan drew his own blade. For a moment, even in the gloom under cover of the trees, it glinted bright as a sun-ray.

'Ah, well, skipper,' croaked Einar. 'I guess you're about to find out.'

EPILOGUE

Lilla watched the seam of land spreading across the horizon. The wind was cold and fresh, even for early spring. *Fasolt*'s prow rose and fell with the swell. Erlan was stood up there, alone, his broad back wrapped under heavy furs. She went forward to join him, slipped her arm through his, leaned her head against his shoulder.

'Do you think he made it to Rome?' she said.

'You mean Wyn?'

'Wasn't that where he was headed?'

Erlan nodded vaguely, his gaze drifting back out to the distant strand, seeing only with one eye now, its ruined twin banded and hidden. She could see he was distracted, his mind racing ahead of them across the waves. 'I hope so.'

'At least we kept our word to him.'

Lilla had seen to it personally that the girl Fenna was returned to her mother. The woman had broken down as soon as she saw her, mother and daughter falling into each other's arms, sobbing uncontrollably. They had stayed like that for an age. Watching them, Lilla had felt a deep pang inside her – that she would never hold her own mother like that again. That she could never have a daughter to hold at all.

'To him,' agreed Erlan. 'And to Karil.'

And for his part, Karil had done everything he said he would.

After his victory, he had been a man on fire. A beacon of hope and resistance, to whose banner more and more of his countrymen had flocked, his cause now buoyed by the great plunder he had taken from the king's army that day. Even if, as he said, the treasure was no more than was his due, the inheritance denied him by his obdurate stepmother.

Whatever the truth of it, with his war-chests newly filled, Karil had no strong designs on their own golden hoard. And he'd been happy to help them recover their ship, repair the damage and make ready for their onward journey. To the north. To their folklands. To their destiny.

The fire of Lilla's impatience had cooled. She had taken Karil's council and agreed to wait out the winter as his guests. It was the least Erlan and her men deserved. The least they needed. Some time to rest.

Lilla looked back at the crew, her glance moving from face to familiar face. They were more than her crew now, she realised. They were her family. Somehow she had come to love them. Though she did not yet presume that the feeling was returned. Perhaps one day they would. Perhaps one day, she would be worthy of it.

Each of them was sitting around, amusing himself. Some were talking in low voices or lost in their own thoughts as the wind bore *Fasolt* northward.

Only one face among them was less familiar to her.

A new face.

He had chosen to stay with them, after the carnage under that savage moon. He said his name was Skírpa. A strange boy. Quiet, but with intelligent and observant eyes. He obviously had some terrible stories in his past. You only had to look at the cruel scars that criss-crossed his face to know that. But he had a kind of gentleness to him as well, a voice so soft it was almost like a woman's. And Lilla felt somehow protective of him.

Protective of them all, if she were honest. And yet...

... she knew what she still required of them. Knew the maw into which she meant to cast them if she were to keep her vow.

As if reading her thoughts, Erlan squeezed her hand. 'Do you still have the dream? The boar... and your father?'

She shook her head. 'Not for many moons now.'

'You're still resolved, though.' It was no question. Gods, if she was not, then what were they doing? What had she put them through?

'It's different. The future is a fog. I see only a road into it. Not through it.'

'Hm,' he grunted. 'The fog of war.' The corner of his mouth twitched in a rueful smile.

'And you?' she said. 'Your father?'

'I see no more than you.' He drew her close, his strong arm tucking her protectively against his ribs.

Maybe that's all you could hope for. A hand to hold tight to as you walked forward into the unknown. She sighed and looked out once more to the land that was closer now. Close enough to make out the pale dunes and the swaying marram grass that carpeted their crests.

'Jutland,' she said softly.

'Home,' was his reply.

HISTORICAL NOTE

According to Theophanes the Confessor, writing in the early ninth century, the siege that historians now call the Second Arab Siege of Constantinople ended on 15 August AD 718. That was the day on which the remnants of the Arab fleet weighed anchor and sailed away, exactly thirteen months to the day after the Arab land forces had arrived at the walls of the City. How much weight we can put on that being the exact day in the year the Arabs left is debatable, given that it conveniently coincided with the Feast of the Dormition of the Theotokos (the Mother of God), to whom the Byzantines attributed their victory. But we can at least assume the siege lasted just over a year, from summer AD 717 to summer 718, the decisive actions that effectively broke the Arabs' chance of success having occurred in the spring of that second year.

Both Theophanes and a later account by Patriarch Nikephoros I of Constantinople record that the retiring Arab fleet's woes did not end with the ignominy of failure. On their return voyage to Syria, they were beset by severe storms in the Sea of Marmara, followed by ashes from the volcano of

Santorini falling from the sky. These natural disasters, in whatever form they took, decimated the returning fleet, Theophanes claiming that only five vessels made it safely home to Syria. Arab sources suggest over 150,000 troops perished during the campaign. Probably an exaggeration, but the figure gives an indication of how great a disaster the siege was viewed in Arab eyes. Katāros was lucky to escape with his life.

One might imagine that such an emphatic victory over the Byzantines' deadly enemy would secure Leo the Isaurian's position as emperor, and his undisputed authority over what remained of the late Roman Empire for a long time to come. But his immediate fears of internal dissent were not unwarranted. Already, in expectation of an Arab victory and the fall of Constantinople, the local governor of far-flung Sicily had declared an emperor of his own, Basil Onomagoulos – a rebellion which Leo now needed to suppress. Meanwhile, closer to home, the crisis of the siege had barely passed before more serious scheming began. In AD 719, Khan Tervel of the Bulgars allied with the deposed Emperor Anastasios II in an attempt to restore the latter to the throne. The plot was uncovered and Anastasios was captured and then executed along with his co-conspirators. One can only speculate what made Khan Tervel switch allegiance from Leo to his rival. Perhaps personal loyalty, since it was with Anastasios that Khan Tervel had signed the Bulgar–Byzantine Treaty of AD 716. But for what it's worth, I prefer to speculate that it was the failure of Leo to satisfy the Khan's prodigious demands for tribute in the form of Byzantine gold. At least that was what formed the conceit for the first part of this novel in my head. By stealing some of his gold, perhaps Erlan did the emperor more of a disservice than he knew.

General Arbasdos is based on a real historical figure: Artabasdos, whose name I shortened for the excellent reason that I couldn't bear to write it repeatedly in full. An Armenian by descent, his real name was Ardavazt. Like many of his peers, he was a man of towering ambition. Appointed *stratēgos* of the Armeniac Theme under Emperor Anastasios II, he survived the fall of his patron by allying himself with Leo the Isaurian in the latter's bid for the throne in early AD 717. The two sealed their personal alliance with Artabasdos's marriage to Leo's daughter Anna soon after Leo ascended the throne in March AD 717. He was further honoured with the office of *kouropalatēs* (master of the palace) and command of the Opsikion Theme (which controlled Constantinople and its environs). However, Artabasdos's loyalty to Leo did not outlast Leo's death in AD 741, upon which the Armenian immediately usurped the throne from Leo's son and successor, Constantine V. Artabasdos reigned briefly as emperor for two years. However, a resourceful man in his early twenties, Constantine was not so easily cast aside. In AD 743, he defeated Artabasdos's forces in the field, took back the throne and eventually captured his rival. By Byzantine standards, Artabasdos got off lightly: he was publicly blinded, along with his sons, and ended his days confined to the Monastery of Chora on the outskirts of Constantinople. The story of all that might itself make a good novel. Perhaps for another time…

By the time Katāros was passing through Rome, the *Urbs Æterna* had only a few short years to run before it would break with imperial Constantinople for good. The reason for the final rupture is something I don't explore in these pages, but it would become a terrible source of division across the late Roman Empire, as well as the burning issue of the age – the question of iconoclasm. Leo III was soon to become the great proponent of this policy, with which Pope Gregory II would have no truck at all. He refused to accept any of the decrees coming out of Constantinople and promptly excommunicated the emperor. There followed a long period of discord and strife between Rome, the Exarchate of Ravenna – still held (just about) by imperial forces – and the opportunistic Lombards to the north. With the succession of crises that followed, Constantinople's control over its Italian territories would not outlive the century. Ravenna fell to the Lombards in AD 750.

Next, they set their sights on Rome. Confronted with a stronger adversary and effectively abandoned by the empire, it was only by appealing to the Franks further north and recruiting their military aid against the Lombard threat that the papal authorities managed to retain their hold over Rome. In AD 756, the Frankish king, having neutralised the Lombards, confirmed the papacy in its dominions and thus the Papal States were born. It's worth noting that it was out of this alliance that the Holy Roman Empire was to emerge; specifically, with Pope Leo III's crowning of Charlemagne as emperor on Christmas Day, AD 800.

However, all this was to come. In the early eighth century, Rome had indeed risen from the ashes of its past imperial glory into a city of saints, a plethora of old temples and municipal buildings having been converted into churches, shrines and basilicas. Even by that early date, it had become a popular destination for pilgrims from the north-west of Europe. The Iter Francorum – or Via Francigena as it would become better known – was one such pilgrimage route, stretching from Rome in the south to Canterbury in the north. By that time, the Christianisation of the Anglo-Saxons was more or less complete, having been seeded originally by a mission from Rome. The late seventh and early eighth centuries saw the reversal of this, with Anglo-Saxon missionaries now setting out from their island shores to spread the gospel on the European mainland.

Winfrid of Nursling (my 'Wyn') was one such missionary. Born in AD 675 in the south of what is now Devon, probably near Exeter, he spent much of his early life as a Benedictine monk, priest and scholar, only venturing on mission to Frisia at the age of forty-one. In so doing, he passed up the opportunity to take over leadership of the monastery at Nursling following the death of his mentor. Truly he abandoned his books to become a man of adventure instead.

And his adventures were many. A number of hagiographic accounts of his life survive. Personally, I owe him a special debt, since without him this series never would have existed. In 2009, I attended a lecture in Oxford in which a theologian called Michael Green described an incident in Winfrid's life which struck a chord with me that's still ringing. This was the story of Winfrid (later known as Saint Boniface) chopping down the sacred oak of Donar (god of thunder) at a place called Fritzlar in the German state of Hesse. Immediately an image was conjured in my head of a great confrontation between the old pagan Europe and the new and fiery Christian faith, set in a dark Germanic forest. At the time, I'd never written a word of fiction in my life. But the image stayed in my head, almost blindingly vivid. My curiosity piqued, this story would prove the catalyst that launched me on a creative journey into writing fiction which, I'm glad to say, has not yet reached its end.

Winfrid received his new name of Boniface from Pope Gregory II when he finally reached Rome, together with a new commission to bring the gospel to the Germanic peoples. He was remarkably successful at this, and is now known as 'Apostle to the Germans'. Towards the end of his life, having established innumerable churches in the Germanic lands, he went on mission to Frisia, a place for which he always had a special affection. But there his journeying ended; he was martyred in AD 756.

An important figure in the formation and establishment of the medieval church across large swathes of Europe, Saint Boniface was also tremendously influential in the secular arena, as chief fomenter of the alliance between the papacy and the Carolingian dynasty, not least through his friendship with Charles Martel. This had huge ramifications for the historical development of Europe.

The character of Karil, son of Pepin, is based on this Frankish nobleman who would become known to history as Charles Martel. He is perhaps best remembered as the victor of the Battle of Tours in AD 732, the high watermark of Islamic encroachment into early medieval Europe from the Moors' power base of El Andalus (the Iberian Peninsula). Historians endlessly dispute the true significance of this battle, whether it turned back a concerted invasion or merely

552

an opportunistic raid. But whatever present-day historians feel able to conclude, certainly the Carolingian propagandists made much of it in the decades and centuries that followed, lauding Charles Martel as the 'Saviour of Europe'. But such controversy aside, he was undoubtedly a figure of tremendous influence in shaping early medieval Europe, not least because he would be grandfather to the Emperor Charlemagne, the historical colossus of early Christendom.

King Chilperic's campaign to destroy the young military leader unfolded more or less as described (at least according to what we know of those events). Charles Martel's career was nearly ended having barely begun. However, having suffered that initial rout at the hands of Chilperic's ally, King Rathbod of Frisia, Charles bounced back pretty hard; he never suffered another military defeat. But it was his son, Pepin, who was to oust the last Merovingian from the Frankish throne, and so inaugurate the new Carolingian Age.

The inspiration for the darker elements of this story may be surprising. They certainly were to me.

The idea of a pagan cult was linked very much to the original story I had heard all those years ago in Oxford. Somehow the notion took hold that my character Wyn's later antipathy to pagan trees and wooden pillars dedicated to the Germanic gods of Woden and Donar stemmed from some horrific earlier experience. And maybe it was with those gods in mind that I was reminded of another source of inspiration for these novels, at least musically so: Wagner's *Ring Cycle*.

Thus, in my 'Alvarik', a nod of homage to Wagner's Alberich (and I couldn't resist throwing in my own variation of the three Rhine-maidens while I was at it).

The wolf-warriors, however, came more directly from the Old Norse world. *Ulfheðnar*, something akin to *berserkir*. The surprise for me was that I was already halfway through the book when I came across a reference which I distantly recalled studying for my archaeology degree. The so-called Torslunda plates: four cast bronze dies found in the parish of Torslunda on the Swedish island of Öland. They date from the Vendel Period (from the sixth to seventh centuries AD), so around the same period as these stories. One of them shows very clearly a dancing shaman with a twin-horned head-dress (sometimes interpreted as the god Odin himself), flanked by a warrior wearing a wolf-head mask. This seemed to fit perfectly with my own narrative and I took it as a sign of its authenticity. In any case, my personal beef with archaeology as a field of study had always been that I could never get close enough to what it had actually felt like to be there. It turns out, writing historical fiction was the answer to my dilemma. (Perhaps it's not too much to hope some professor of archaeology in some obscure faculty might add *A Savage Moon* to their undergraduates' reading list, if only to bring these Torslunda plates to life.)

Another surprise came when researching the idea of child abduction in the medieval period. I came across a list on Wikipedia (which I can't exactly recommend) entitled 'List of Serial Killers before 1900'. I was shocked to discover that there is quite an established historical link connecting child abduction, murder, witchcraft, cannibalism and the occult (including dressing up as wolves in some cases), with the Rhine valley and certain surrounding regions of Germany and France. Mostly the known killers were from later periods (fifteenth and sixteenth centuries) – Pierre Burgot, Michel Verdun, the 'Werewolf of Bedburg' and the 'Werewolf of Dole' to name a few.

One would expect that such grisly connections were mercifully consigned to the past. But, alas, the link between child trafficking, migration, sexual abuse and the ritualised murder of children goes on throughout the so-called civilized countries of the West to this day.

Lastly, I wish to mention the symbol of the One Eye.

Of course, even the slightest brush with Old Norse culture will bring you face to face with some sort of depiction of Odin, or *Óðinn*, the One-Eyed God. *Báleygr* – the 'Flaming Eye' – is indeed one of his many names found in the canon of Scandinavian texts. But I have found this symbol of the One Eye is not confined to the old gods of the north. One can trace it as far back as the Old Kingdom of Egypt on the *benben* stones that cap the obelisks of Heliopolis and other places. The Third Eye, the Evil Eye, the Eye of Providence, the Eye of Horus, the Eye of Ra – all hail from the distant past. And the symbol spans through history to our own day, in which pop stars like Lady Gaga, Katy Perry, Beyoncé and many others make liberal use of it in their music videos and photo shoots. It's traceable in symbols like the 'Just Stop Oil' logo splashed all over our cities and the media; I even saw it tattooed across an actor's chest in a recent blockbuster movie. Once one knows what one is looking for, one sees it everywhere.

Its primary association, at least in more recent centuries, has been with the occult: Luciferianism, Satanism, the darker side of freemasonry, and so on. But who knows how all these things link together? That is, if they do at all.

At the very least, for me anyway, the connotations of a kind of history-spanning One Eye cult with deep roots in the past made Alvarik a worthy opponent for a man of God such as Brother Wyn. And, of course, for Erlan beside him.

Dear Erlan... He has much yet to accomplish. Whether he will have the chance to do so remains an open question. One can but dream...

ACKNOWLEDGEMENTS

Every novel presents its own challenges. For this one, it was an impenetrable brick wall in the plot that fell about a third of the way through the story. It took at least four attempts – and many thousands of wasted words – to overcome this obstacle. And when I say 'overcome', I mean batter the thing down with my head. (At least it felt that way at times.) Eventually the wall succumbed. I'm mighty glad it did because for a long while I wondered whether this fourth book in The Wanderer Chronicles would ever get written. Perhaps some of my readers have been wondering the same.

That particular pile of rubble behind me, I'm happy to report the rest of the novel came remarkably easily by comparison. But I have several people to thank for their patience while I figured all this out.

Not one but *two* editors at Corvus Atlantic – Susannah Hamilton and Emma Coode – who waited and waited and still never saw a word of the manuscript before it was time for them to move on. But more importantly the wonderful Sarah de Souza, who has been the calm voice of reason and encouragement for over a year now, and whose sharp eye and canny insights have made the final version of *A Savage Moon* considerably better than it might have been.

Many thanks as always to Charlie Campbell, literary agent extraordinaire – a man of eminently sensible and sage advice when the mysteries (and vagaries) of the publishing world all become too much.

I would also like to thank the marvellous team at Corvus Atlantic, especially Will Atkinson for his kindness to me over the years. Being part of the Corvus family continues to be a privilege and a pleasure.

Thanks to my wonderful copy-editor, Rachel Malig. Eagle-eyed, indeed.

A note of thanks, too, to my friend Vaughan, who directed me to the YouTube channel of Danish archer Lars Andersen and his extraordinary feats of skill. Well worth a glance, if you're inclined.

Besides all this, my wider gratitude goes out to my readers. Thank you for keeping the faith that a fourth book would indeed one day find its way into your hands. It's a joy to hear from any of you and discover what you made of the next mad vision of my mind.

To my girls – Ella, Talitha and Colette – we've done lockdown, sleepless nights, screaming matches, school runs, and lots and lots of laughing while I've been scribbling away at this book. I love you all to bits.

To Wilmo the dog – not much help with the book, were you? But you keep me humble and you get me outside. For that, I thank you. (And sorry for being a grumpy bastard far too often.)

Finally, to my darling Tash, you are the soul of patience and encouragement. I couldn't have done this without you. In fact, I couldn't do any of it without you. I wouldn't want to.

T.H.R.B.
May 2023

www.theodorebrun.com
Twitter @theodorebrun
Instagram @theobrun